Mature Content Warning

This novel contains sexual content, mild language, and depictions of violence.
It is intended for readers 18+.

For my Matthew,
my ocean-eyed soulmate.

OF SONGS
AND
SALTWATER

HEATHER CARTER

Chapter One

Meryn

I had to get out.

The air in my lungs rushed in and out as I fled through the cool, pre-dawn air toward the docks. I'd been up for hours, crying, pacing, raging in my room. Last night, Anaat and I had argued like we never had before. I could still feel the sting of her slap.

Why didn't she believe me? Why didn't she ever believe me? My own sister. She took the side of that wretched man. He'd said such awful things, but she wouldn't even hear of it.

Anaat didn't understand. No one did. Not even my dear old maid, whom I loved with all my heart. I was alone in that castle with no one on my side.

I was alone in the world.

The salty sea air greeted me as I snuck to the end of the dock. The dinghy was easy to steal. No one was out yet.

I remembered enough from my lessons to get it going. After untying it from the dock, I climbed aboard, the hull of the small boat sinking slightly under my weight. My heart raced as I unfurled the sails and pushed off.

There were no chaperones with me today and no guards. It was just me and the open sea. I sailed across the water—toward my freedom in the distance.

If only for a day...

Sailing from the harbor into the rising sun, I found my breath. The wind slipped through my hair like silk, bringing a smile to my face. It was a weight off my shoulders, being out on my beloved sea. The gentle rocking of the boat soothed me like a mother's lullaby. I'd loved it since I was young—the salty air in my lungs. Everything was blissful for two hours.

And then I felt the first drop of rain.

I raised my eyes to find the beautiful blue sky swallowed up by dark clouds. They spread like a drop of roiling black ink. Terror gripped me as the soothing waves churned, creating angry mountains with the walls of wind that swept over the surface.

Breaking from my terrified stupor, I forced myself to concentrate. Panic threatened to overwhelm me as I tried to recall my sailing lessons. I cursed myself for not being a better student as my hands fumbled with the ropes.

Cold waves broke over the side of the boat, soaking my clothes. I struggled to maintain my footing along the slick wood of the hull. The water came again and again, mixing with the driving rain. My beloved sea was furious.

Choking on another crashing wave, I pulled hard on the rope and the tiller. It was useless trying to steer—the boat was starting to break apart. I thought I did everything right—bow into the flat spots, sails reefed. My old guide's words echoed in my mind, but it was a jumbled mess with my thoughts. Running over and over through the checklist was pointless. I couldn't remember half of it, or even what everything was called.

The storm blew up out of nowhere. Clear blue sky, then sky as dark as night. Just like that.

It was only my third time out by myself. I'd ditched my

guards so no one would know where to look for me. I chastised myself again. This wasn't even my boat. And here I was, about to drown, another sailor at the bottom of the Aslean Sea.

All I had wanted was to feel the sun on my face and maybe a *taste* of freedom. Just a lick. I wanted the pride of knowing I had done something, and that I had done it myself.

That's all I'd wanted when I came out today. Something, anything, to free me from the choking confines of the blonde-wood and stone castle. I wasn't just the duke's daughter, "Fair Lady Meryn." No. I was more than that. I *had* to be more than that.

I peered behind me, hoping to see a shred of something familiar. I strained to see my castle overlooking the sea. There was nothing beyond the squall persistently trying to drown me.

Now, it seemed, I would only be *Dead* Lady Meryn.

Perhaps it was the roaring of the sea, but I swore I could hear a voice mixed in with the crashing thunder. It was deep and resonant, but definitely female. My heart skipped a beat—maybe I could yell to her for help?

As the seconds passed, I realized it was not a voice calling to me. No. It was rhythmic. The cadence rippled over the waves like a poem. She was *chanting*.

The sound mocked my terror with every word. Whoever she was, she commanded the storm with each utterance. Every inhale pulled the waves higher. Every exhale pushed the waves forward. Each wave crashed over my battered dinghy, splitting it apart. Each word was one with the storm. The power of the spell radiated through my chest. I struggled to make out the words against the roar of the waves.

The words don't matter now, anyway.

I gave up trying to steer, crouching down into a ball against the hull. Water rushed over me as a blinding flash lit up my vision. A great crack rang through my ears. Above me, the large mast fell. With barely time to scream, I instinctively leaped from the boat. The mast crashed down, splitting what remained of the boat into pieces.

The icy, swirling water caught me. I flailed my arms and legs, but all control was lost to the power of the current. My body tossed over and under each wave. I grabbed fruitlessly, attempting to reach for large pieces of debris as I struggled to keep my head above water. Terror set in.

But I wanted to live.

Despite my hopes, death was upon me. My lungs struggled to fill with air. I knew I would not survive another wave.

Just like that, my chance evaporated. An enormous tower of water rose above me. The chanting rose above the sound of the waves, filled with urgency. I didn't understand the words, but I knew the spell called for my death.

The wave loomed over me, staring at me like an assassin, grinning at his target. I breathed a quick prayer to Scalae, Goddess of the Sea, before the wave attacked. It crushed me under the surface, and my head exploded with pain as it collided with a piece of debris. Everything stopped. The world went black.

Chapter Two

Meryn

Slowly, consciousness returned. As it did, a blaze of color greeted me. Sky blue faded into lavender, transitioning to gold rings around inky black pupils. They were the most beautiful eyes I had ever seen.

Dark auburn and blond hairs framed these stunning eyes. A pair of thick, masculine brows knit tightly together as the strange man examined me. His hair was the color of a fiery sunset, draping over his shoulders in long, wet waves.

Confused, I studied him in return through the searing pain in my head.

And then he smiled, broad and bright. Relief and awe filled his grin, revealing perfect white teeth. A slight bump on the bridge of the nose moved as his cheeks lifted. As the world righted around me, I focused on the smattering of red freckles spread across his sun-kissed skin.

His breath was warm against my skin as he inspected

the wound on my head. Despite the pain, I found myself watching his full lips lean closer. As he brushed my hair from the wound, I considered how ready his lips looked for kissing.

A man, perhaps a gift from the gods—*something*—was looking down at me.

Why would such a creature be smiling at *me*? Surely, he was some sort of ethereal presentation, here to escort me to whatever eternal fate lay in wait. Warmth and light flooded my heart as it continued to race.

Reluctantly, I tore my eyes from his and swept them downward. He was shirtless. The warmth of his skin warmed my own. He was long and lean, with strong shoulders. A large necklace rested just below his collarbone, made of bleached shells strung from a cord. A menacing tooth rested in the center. He was definitely a gift from the sea. Scalae had heard my prayer.

The beautiful man rested halfway out of the water, perched beside me. The slick surface of a black rock spread out underneath me. The echo of the surf drifted in from an opening to the right of us. We were in some sort of seaside cave.

The sound of the waves knocked me from my stupor as flashes of memory filled me. Water crashing down around me. A voice chanting in the dark. My lungs struggling to fill with air.

I lost all sense of the cave and the strange man before me. Terror gripped me as my hand flew to my chest. I struggled to catch my breath. Panic filled me, tightening around my lungs like a fist. My breath came in short bursts.

I can't breathe! I can't breathe...

A soft, warm hand wrapped around the one now clinging to my throat. "It's okay. It's okay. You're safe now...." His voice pulled me from the dark as he gently squeezed my hand.

His gentle but firm touch brought me out of my panic. The sounds of the cave returned. My clouded mind finally began to understand. Those were calm ocean waves.

Where was the raging storm?

The sea had returned to her blissful state. The water

lapped at my feet calmly. Nothing except the steady drip from the opening at the top of the cave even hinted that there was ever anything amiss.

Returning my attention to those breathtaking and unusual eyes, I found my voice. I asked the question, though I dreaded to hear the answer.

"Am I dead?"

"No," he answered simply.

"Oh..."

"What's your name?" The question came as he gently reached up and brushed a lock of auburn hair from my temple again. I winced as he did. Sharp pain crossed my head.

I'm definitely alive.

"Meryn."

"Meryn..." He let the word roll around on his tongue. I listened as he spoke my name. I'd never heard it sound so beautiful. I found myself wanting him to say it again. "It means '*Of the sea.*' Fitting, I'd say."

"I thought I drowned." I fought the panic off once more. *I am safe. I am safe,* I reminded myself again. "Did you save me?"

Nodding, his eyes traveled once more to my head injury. Again, his expression faltered. "I did. You are badly injured." I didn't argue with his assessment as the pounding in my head continued. "But I think I can help. Will you be all right alone for just a few moments?"

I considered his words, surprised at my response. I didn't want him to leave. His reassuring presence was comforting in the aftermath of what I'd just been through.

His hand reached out slowly to mine again, giving me a reassuring squeeze. I looked at where our hands met and nodded.

Why am I trusting a complete stranger?

"Yes."

Scarcely had the word left my mouth before he was gone, disappearing below the calm surface of the water. As tempting as it was to sit up and watch after him, the pain filled my vision. I slumped back down onto the rock.

I rested against the soft moss growing on the rock,

watching the water ripple. A flash of green briefly caught the corner of my eye under the surface. My mind must've really been playing tricks on me.

Who was this man? How did he save me?

My thoughts were cloudy as I waited. Questions swirled in my mind, but I was also fighting waves of sleepiness. I was grateful to be alive, though I still didn't understand how. More questions about my rescuer swirled around my head. Maybe I was right? Perhaps he was a gift from the gods sent to save me. He must've been something otherworldly to have survived those waves.

As I lay staring at the sky through the opening in the grotto's roof, I focused on my breathing. Time passed and I grit my way through the pain, feeling sore in muscles I didn't even know a person could get sore.

The drips of water from the rock kept the passage of time like the ticks of a clock. It was hard to believe it was already nighttime. I must've been unconscious for quite a while. Every time I closed my eyes now, I saw his gaze again. A small smile tilted my lips, despite my discomfort.

Then it dawned on me how much time had passed. He'd been underwater too long.

Panic overwhelmed me. I could not recall seeing him swim out of the cave.

Surely he did, didn't he? There's no way he's still underwater. He must have gone somewhere for help.

As badly as I felt, I *needed* help. And my one source had just disappeared.

Just when I was giving up hope that the beautiful stranger would return, he did. My heart leaped into my throat when he broke the surface of the water. He had a flower with enormous purple petals clenched between his teeth. He grinned at me as water cascaded around him.

Clutching my chest, I breathed a sigh of relief.

"You frightened me! I was worried you wouldn't come back."

Taking the flower from his mouth, he cast me an apologetic smile. "Forgive me. It takes a while to reach the cave down there." He quickly went to work.

Plucking a stone from the ground nearby, he began

gently grinding the flower.

Curious, I watched him turn the beautiful bloom into a mash.

"You said you dove to a cave?"

"Yes."

"That's a long time to hold your breath."

Pausing, his colorful eyes flicked to mine. Smiling briefly, he resumed his work. "Yes."

Seeing that I wasn't going to get much more of an explanation, I resigned myself to watching him silently.

His hands worked the soft petals, crushing them with the rock and then rolling them along his long, slender fingers and across his large palms. His arms were strong enough to withstand heavy tides. His biceps flexed as he gently pressed his palms together. As he worked, I looked at his hands again. There were no markings or rings of any kind.

Noting my curiosity, he paused. Only then did I realize he was staring at me. Blushing, I averted my eyes to the black rock beneath me. I struggled to fill the silence between us.

"Sorry. I was just wondering, what is your family name?"

"I..." He hesitated. A look of debate pinched his brow before he settled on an answer. "I don't have one."

It was a lie, but one I decided not to press. After all, I was a stranger too.

This time, I settled on a safer question. "Where are we?"

"The Green Grotto."

Furrowing my brows, I looked around and saw nothing but dark rock. "That's an unusual name."

He laughed—a rich laugh that filled the cave and brightened my spirits, comforting me in a way I didn't expect. "It's a bit of a misnomer."

Smiling, I nodded. "I'd say so."

"Where are you from, Meryn?"

Pausing, I thought of how best to answer. He was not giving me straight answers, so perhaps it was best to follow in the same vein for now.

"I'm from Arcadia. West of where I... fell."

He gathered the mashed flower in his palm, bringing it closer to his mouth.

Surely, he's not going to...

He spit several times into the strange concoction before pressing it over my wound. I hissed at both the disgusting action and the pain. Ever the brave one, I bore it as steadily as I could.

To my surprise, it wasn't long before the pain began to melt away. *All* of the pain. He continued to gently work the flower into the wound, and a tingling sensation came over me. A few moments later, it was followed by soothing warmth.

When his fingers finally left my temple, my own fingers replaced them. Gasping, I sat up, feeling my scalp all over, running my fingers over it through my wet curls.

Impossible!

"It's gone! How did you do it?" I exclaimed, trying to fit my exasperation into words.

With a smile, my savior reached up and brushed off bits of the excess paste that were already dried on my skin. "Pilaria Blossom. It has special healing properties."

Again, not the whole truth. I could see it by the slight shifting of his eyes. *Why wasn't he being truthful?* I amended inwardly that if he intended to harm me, he could've done it well before now. He could have just left me to the waves.

"Are you a sorcerer of some kind?"

"Not exactly. Though, perhaps to your people, I am." He shrugged his shoulders, suddenly avoiding my gaze.

"What do you mean?"

Leaning on his elbows, he folded his hands, seeming to search through his mind for the right explanation. I was growing a bit irritated at the subterfuge. I reminded myself again I owed him my patience.

"Where I come from, things are a bit... different. I'm different."

I knew what that felt like.

Straightening, I folded my legs in front of me, thankful I'd worn the short trousers from the hidden stash under my bed. Lifting my eyes to the thin gray clouds beyond the opening above, I sighed. "Do you ever tire of it?"

"Tire of what?"

"Being different."

Out of the corner of my eye, I caught his nod. "All the time. You?"

Frowning, I lowered my gaze back to him. "What makes you think I'm different?"

A shudder ran through me when our eyes met. He studied me, staring at me across the short distance, looking through me. He stared into my soul.

His voice was low, pensive, as he spoke. "Because I know that far-off look. And I have a suspicion you weren't supposed to be out there on that boat today."

Warmth flushed through my cheeks furiously. I wanted to look away and hide. Was I that easily read?

He was reading me, even now, but I couldn't break the contact. Maybe because it was the first time in a long time that anyone had actually *looked* at me.

"That's a very bold thing to say to a stranger." I meant for it to come out as a warning. I pulled back from him for a moment, suddenly reminded that we didn't even know each other. Instead, it came out like a hushed observation.

"I did not realize we were still strangers."

"Of course we are!" I adjusted myself on the rock, pushing myself from him.

"How?"

"Well... I don't even know your name, for starters."

"Fivrial," he answered, shrugging his shoulders as if sharing his name solved everything.

"Fivrial?" My brows knitted together. It was my turn to consider his name. I let the word fill my mouth. "I've never heard of anyone called Fivrial."

Fivrial's smile grew each time I said his name. There was heat in his gaze as he moved closer to me. "Well, now you have."

The tension I felt slowly melted away at the sight of his smile. My thoughts suddenly clouded again as he continued to stare across the short distance.

My manners returned momentarily as I struggled to find the words for what I wanted. "I'm sorry. I'm being a bit rude, aren't I?"

"It's all right. We've only just met."

"I think I'm perhaps a bit worn out. You must be too. I don't mind if you want to come sit by me for a while." The words sounded way too forward the moment they left my lips.

Eyes widening, I rushed to explain myself. "Uh, I mean, you're probably getting cold, being halfway in the water like that. I know the sea is probably not the warmest in this cave..." I gestured toward the water, trying to calm my fumbling mind. "...and I'm babbling, aren't I?" I felt warmth flood my cheeks.

Eyes averting uncomfortably, Fivrial sank lower in the water. Inwardly, I kicked myself. My mouth was continually running away with me. *Then again, how is one supposed to talk to a shirtless man who just saved your life?* The whole situation was beyond believable.

"It's not that. I'm just, well... naked."

If my cheeks were scarlet before, I was blushing from head to toe now. Resisting the urge to slap a hand over my eyes, I forced a passive expression and nodded. "I see. Are your clothes... nearby?" My eyes darted around the small shelf of rock on which I sat. All I could see was shadow.

"No," he answered plainly. "I was swimming without them."

Now, *this* sounded even more unbelievable. I cocked an eyebrow. "Swimming out in rough seas... in the middle of a storm... naked?"

"Well, yes."

Not a hint of amusement pinched his face. I slowly realized he was completely serious. Perhaps he was mad? In any case, he was kind. And naked or not, he'd saved my life.

"Well, I am still in your debt, I suppose. You've saved me and healed me."

A smile slashed his cheeks, and I instantly reciprocated.

"There is no debt, I assure you."

Twisting my brows, I straightened. "No debt? Nonsense! I'd be dead right now if it weren't for you! When we get back, Father will give you whatever you like: money, jewels, a boat—"

"I have no desire for such things."

Staring at him, I tried to read his expression. He was looking at me in that way again that made me feel exposed.

"Then what do you want?" I asked quietly.

There was a heavy pause before he responded softly. "A kiss."

Had I not now been so entranced by his unusual eyes, my propriety would've caused me to recoil. But I also couldn't bring myself to say no as my heart raced, and the breath hitched in my throat. My defenses faltered.

"A kiss?" Trepidation filled me. He was naked, and I was in no state to defend myself if he decided he wanted more. "That's... all?"

"That's all."

Butterflies rose in my stomach. I knew what was about to happen. This man—this stranger—was going to kiss me. I probably looked like a drowned rat. Perhaps I still had blood on my face? Did my breath smell?

"Yes." The word leaped from my lips.

He nodded as a sly smile spread across his lips. "Close your eyes, please."

I did as instructed, my nerves instantly magnifying. There was a small splashing and the sound of dripping as he pulled himself from the water.

Warm breath brushed over my face. Long, slender fingers gently threaded through the hairline behind my ear as his palm lifted my jaw. I felt his hesitation. Our breath mingled together for a moment. Then his lips pressed tenderly against my own.

Warmth flooded me. I no longer felt the chill of the ocean still clinging to my clothes, or the hardness of the rock beneath me. For all I knew, I could've been floating in the clouds.

Is this what it's supposed to feel like?

It lasted longer than I expected, though I never wanted it to end. His lips gently kneaded mine. The salty and sweet taste of him filled my mouth. The smell of his skin hung in the air, something very masculine mingling with the ocean breeze. My hand snaked up of its own accord, tracing down from his hair and resting against his bearded cheek. When he didn't object, I slid my fingers slowly down his jawline.

We paused, and I opened my eyes, nose to nose with him. There was nothing to say. No words were needed. Linking my hands around the back of his head, I pulled him into another kiss, which he gladly sank into. His naked chest pressed closer to me.

My hesitation vanished.

I lost myself in the kiss. I pulled him closer, tighter against me.

Suddenly, a light filled the cave. My eyes flashed open.

A bright turquoise glow spread upward. Moonlight streamed into the cave from above. Gasping, I pulled away. A large fin flapped beneath the surface of the water.

Fivrial's hands clamped around my panicked face and forced me to look at him as he cursed under his breath. His wide eyes were glowing now. "Don't be afraid." He whispered the words as his eyes illuminated in a stunning, jeweled fire. Blood rushed from my head, but I was too shocked to move.

"Fivrial, what's happening?"

Closing his eyes, he quickly uttered a series of words I couldn't understand, still holding my face close and steady so that I couldn't see beyond him.

"I don't understand! What are you saying?" Fear wrapped its icy hand around my heart.

He paused, opening his eyes. His expression melted into a look of heartbreak as the room began to sway.

"It's the Spell of Forgetfulness."

Chapter Three

Meryn

Something tickled the bottom of my feet as I pulled open my heavy eyelids. The bed below me was soft and warm. Perhaps I could just close my eyes and sleep a little longer...

Had it not been for the seabird in the distance, perhaps I would've gone back to sleep. But my attention was captured by the little black bird, hopping about, scavenging the beach. I listened to the sound of the tide as it kissed my feet, only to retreat again.

Slowly, it dawned on me. I gasped, sitting upright. *How did I end up on the beach?* The world settled around me, like waking from a dream. My heart pounded as I blinked hard and tried to determine if this was reality.

Storm... sea... my head against the rudder... It ached. I lifted my head, snaked my arm up, and felt my forehead. No wound. *Was I imagining things?*

I forced my breathing to slow, trying to calm myself. I continued to evaluate my injuries, searching my memories. For the moment, it seemed I was safe.

The tepid morning breeze washed over me. Early morning sunlight turned the sky into an array of golden hues. It was going to be a fair-weather day. Peaceful. There was no sign of the tempest that nearly took my life.

Rolling to my back, I groaned. Every muscle in my body was screaming. This must be what it was like to take a beating. Heaviness pulled at me. Every movement was a chore. Water filled my ears. My skin was sticky with dried saltwater. My body was drained, despite the sense that I'd been in the deepest sleep of my life.

How long was I gone?

"There!" a man's voice shouted from somewhere behind me. He sounded distant, but soon I heard the shuffling footsteps of someone running down the beach, followed by a chorus of shouting. A symphony of voices yelled my name. Moments later, the ground fell away, as arms dove under the sand and wrapped around my exhausted body.

I shifted, leaning my weak body against the hard chest now supporting me. I came face-to-face with Liret Carbor, Captain of the Guard. His gray eyes darkened under his salt and pepper brows as he peered down at me. At once, I felt a measure of comfort. Captain Carbor was a familiar face since I was a child. Even with years gaining on him, he held me without breaking a bead of sweat.

"Lady Meryn." He breathed a sigh of relief. "Can you hear me?"

I winced against the pain of being hoisted into the air. I must've looked worse off than I felt. My throat burned as I fought to reply.

"Water, please," I croaked.

Those heavy brows eased slightly at hearing my reply.

Captain Carbor snapped at a young guard nearby, who quickly handed over a canteen. He lifted the cool metal to my lips. A small, blessed stream of cool water ran down my throat. My arms aching, I tilted it further, taking generous gulps.

The captain eventually took it away. "Slowly, Milady.

You'll make yourself sick. Come, we need to get you back to the castle. You've been missing for an entire day. Your father will be relieved to see you home safe."

My father. Duke Blumley. The man who was hardly a father at all. I barely saw him anymore. His title kept him away at court most of the time. Away from me. Yet, I was expected to believe he was home and overwhelmed with concern for my well-being.

I doubt he even noticed I was gone.

The party of guards whisked me away down the beach to the private entrance that led up to our estate's gardens. Servants were ordered about as we meandered through the halls and stairways up to my bedchamber. Captain Carbor didn't even pause for breath as he carried me high up to the tallest turret.

Guilt wracked me for choosing to live up all those steps. I'd always been of an independent spirit. Father had offered me a whole wing of the castle when I was young. This side was nearly as grand as the one we had reserved for the king, but I chose one of the smallest parts of the house instead.

Up in my sanctuary, views of the endless sea called to me. With the windows open, breezes from every direction could blow through the space. There, I felt most at peace within the confining walls of my home.

We reached the thick wooden door of my room and I was back in captivity once more. I was grateful to be alive, but certainly not looking forward to the tongue-lashing soon to come.

The captain placed me gently on the bed. Servants immediately took over my care. In a flash, Captain Carbor hurried off to inform my father I hadn't drowned.

Nola, my nurse since I was a babe, ordered the maids to quickly fill my bath as she help strip me of my wet, sandy clothing.

Every muscle was aching and drained of energy—as if I'd swam an ocean to get home. When I told her such, Nola said it was from the shock of the experience.

Questions filled my mind again. *How did I get to shore? How did I wash up so close to home?* I was finding more and more questions and fewer answers.

Once in the warm bath, I was scrubbed, rinsed, and scrubbed some more while Nola carefully inspected me for injury. Aside from some bruises, I was otherwise in one piece. I didn't feel in one piece. I felt achy. And somehow... disjointed.

I scarcely had time to think over my strange plight when I was whisked away again, dressed in my nightgown, and tucked into the freshly changed sheets. Exhaustion tugged at me and I waved off the peppering of questions from Nola and the other maids. I needed sleep.

My eyes were already closing of their own accord. I stayed awake long enough to down another glass of water before passing out again.

I don't know how long I slept. Slumber was eventually snatched away again when my bedroom door burst open and a simpering blonde female came rushing in.

"Meryn!"

At once, she was at my side. Her shining blue eyes fixated on mine. Strands of pearls were perfectly woven into the immaculate pile of flaxen braids on the back of her head. They matched the necklace that graced her delicate white neck and plunged down the front of her royal blue gown. Her lips were drawn in a frown. A diametrically opposed picture of regal grace and drama.

"Hello, Anaat." I greeted my older sister groggily.

Her dramatics cooled slightly at hearing my voice. "Meryn! We've been worried sick about you! I'm glad you're all right, but how could you do it? Again?" she scolded, her neatly manicured brows pulling together.

Rolling my eyes toward the headboard, I squared my jaw. This was not the first time I'd received a tongue-lashing from her for breaking the rules.

Rules I never even agreed to in the first place, I thought sourly.

"I'm sorry I worried you. It was not intentional."

"Well, in any case, Father is furious with you. Now that he knows you're alive and well, of course."

"Let me guess, he sent you here to admonish me for my sins?"

A cry leaped from my lips as Anaat pinched me hard on the forearm. Scowling, she lowered her voice to a growl. "Watch your cheek, Meryn! You are in serious trouble. You embarrassed us all and will cost him thousands of silvers in reparation for that boat you stole."

The boat. I hardly recalled sailing it now. It was small. Owned by the rude fisherman who'd said something vulgar to me on one of my morning strolls by the pier. *"I'd love to take you into my boat, bend you over, and make it rock, Ginger Wench..."*

I still shuddered in disgust when I recalled those words. I usually went out in one of my father's boats with vetted guides, but this man got under my skin. A lot of things got under my skin lately.

Mostly, I remembered the beautiful sun and the way it was swallowed up by the horrid swirl of black. I remembered how the breeze that once slipped over my skin and through my unbound hair like silk betrayed me and turned into a violent gale. Instead of peace, there was terror in my chest at the end of what should have been the perfect day.

My heart sank again. *My stolen day.*

"So, I nearly died. The boat is lost. But here I am. What am I to do now?" I replied dryly, awaiting my punishment.

Anaat straightened, ready to hand over the sentence as if she were a sovereign on her throne instead of my nagging sister on an old wooden stool I'd rescued from the beach. "Since you enjoy the ocean so much, you are to work at the docks for one month, three days a week, for the man whose boat you stole."

Shooting up in bed, my eyes were stretched to their limits. "I'm going to *what*?"

Nodding primly, Anaat brushed her skirts as if I'd whipped sand onto her lap. "Father has decided that drastic measures are to be taken this time. Mr. Aurin himself suggested the punishment the moment the boat went missing. Father nearly threw him in the dungeon for his impertinence, but seeing as you have indeed destroyed his

20

craft, he is now inclined to agree."

Every aching muscle in my body tensed up as fury trickled through. Fury and fear. I'd much prefer the dungeon or even the stocks to that. *Anything but that.*

"So, I'm to be sold over to a vulgar man to be a fishwife for a month? Does Father realize what he's done?" I was shouting now, but Anaat barely flinched. I knew she was probably enjoying my demise.

Tilting her head, she laid a placating hand on my knee. "Come now, Meryn. It's not all that bad. You can use a false name if you'd like."

Batting her hand away, I glared at my older sister. "That's not the point and you know it, Anaat."

"I'll see that you are properly chaperoned. Everything will be in order. Besides, a little menial work and humility will do you good." Her nose rose higher. "You always have thought a little too much of yourself, you know."

I thought too much of myself? Was she kidding?

The imperial look on her face told me arguing was pointless. My narrowed eyes shot daggers as I pointed at her across the small space between us. "You're enjoying this, aren't you?"

Pouting, Anaat slumped her shoulders. "Now, how could you say such a thing about your dear sister? Perhaps you are just tired." She rose to leave. "In any case, I'm simply the messenger. If you have an issue with your punishment, you will have to take it up with Father. He will be here for two days."

Steam was practically spouting from my ears. "Oh, believe me, I will."

Bristling, Anaat narrowed her eyes. "Take care, Meryn. Father is in no mood for further insubordination. Do not embarrass our family further with your antics."

My jaw slackened. "You're one to talk! You should've seen yourself the day you petitioned for that dowry increase."

Perhaps I should've shut my mouth sooner. Visible pain etched over her features. Anaat did not like to speak of her marriage. She did not like to speak of anything relating to the monster. His body was resting in the earth now, but the imprint he left on her would haunt her until the day she joined him.

Feeling like the flea on a donkey's ass, I shrank. "I'm sorry. I shouldn't have said that."

Hard, watery eyes glared at me. Though her jaw was tensed with indignation, the bob in her throat told me she was teetering on the edge of tears. She opened her mouth to speak, only to shut it again. She stalked from the room, slamming the door behind her.

We'd never quite gotten along, but this time she'd gone too far. Things were more volatile than usual. We were only three years apart in age, but it might as well have been three hundred.

Sighing in defeat, I slumped back against my pillows. I winced as my muscles protested. *Why am I so sore?* It really did feel as if I'd swam the entire sea. I had sailed farther from shore than I ever had before when the storm hit.

Surely, I didn't—

"I've got some ointment for your muscles." Nola burst into the room, interrupting my thoughts. She shuffled over, bearing a small basket. For the first time, I noticed how flushed her face was. It looked as if she'd been running full speed up and down the stairs. "The doctor will be in to see you shortly. Someone has gone to fetch him."

Smiling apologetically, I thanked Nola for her trouble. I wasn't sure a doctor would be of much help, but I knew there wasn't much point in arguing. Nola's word was as final as my father's. Despite that, I loved her dearly. She was like a surrogate mother to me, having been in my life since I entered the world.

Afternoon sunshine was beaming down over the fair seas as I lay on my stomach and let Nola massage the pungent remedy into my skin. It crinkled my nose to breathe in the sharp smells, but it really did work magic. She gifted me with blessed silence as she worked.

I sighed as the aches were slowly chased away. My mind drifted out of the windows with each soothing, salty breeze.

It was such a curious thing. When I tried to remember anything after hitting my head, my thinking became clouded. As relaxed as I was now, something felt... off. I was

there, and yet I felt miles away.
Something was missing.

Chapter Four

Fivrial

I swam back and forth in my chambers, my fingers resting on my lips as I pinched my brows together. My heart felt as if it would race right out of my chest. I'd done it. *Really* done it. *Why? Why did I do it?*

I sank onto my pallet of sea grasses and pressed my palms over my eyes. All I could see was her—her wide, frightened eyes when she spotted my tail. Such beautiful, beautiful eyes! Like amber jewels.

How many times had I seen her out on her boat, or walking the shoreline, or even standing at her window late at night, searching the sea? How many times had I wanted her to see me, laws be damned?

Years and years of watching and wishing, and I had to go and actually *kiss* her when she didn't know me at all. Something I swore I'd never do. Did that make me awful?

I could've just sung—lured her to me like a fish on a

hook. Pulled her into a cave and had my way with her, or worse—pulled her down into the depths. But I wasn't like *them*. I'd never be like them. I had no interest in her life force. I just wanted... her.

Meryn.

Even now, the phantom feeling of her soft lips against mine filled me with an indescribable feeling. My chest filled with warmth. The memory of her kiss pushed away the chill of the waters of Brinn—our shining city deep under the waves. By Scalae, I'd never felt so alive.

Especially when she pulled me in for another kiss. She felt it too. She *must've* felt it.

And now she doesn't even remember.

But at least she was alive. At least she was safe.

I knew the storm was unnatural the moment the first drops of rain touched the water. Before the song filled the air, I could feel the darkness brimming among the crashing waves.

Clenching my fist at my side, I glared at the rock ceiling. My tail blazed brightly, illuminating the room.

Someone tried to kill her. But who? It was unlike any siren song I'd ever heard. Something ancient, perhaps. Not a siren. The thought shook me. Would they try again?

"You look like hell, Fiv."

I looked over in time to see Renold floating into my chambers. His long, dark braids trailed in the water behind him. His onyx eyes fixed on me, filled with amusement. My best friend often showed up unannounced.

I never minded it, but today was the exception. All I wanted to do was to be left alone to pine and ponder. Still, I could never deny him a visit.

"Hello to you, too, Renold."

He parked his black tail in front of the carved-out shelf where I kept my most precious, scavenged findings and picked up a large oval ring. In the center was a ruby surrounded by diamonds. I often imagined it gracing one of Meryn's delicate fingers, though I would never admit it to anyone. Not even Renold.

"Your collection has grown," he noted, placing the ring back on the shelf. A half-smile played across his face. "I've never understood your affinity for human things—or human women, for that matter."

I rolled my eyes. "Here we go again."

Renold leaned against the wall and crossed his arms. "Fiv, you know I love you, but you've got to give it up already."

"That's rich, coming from you."

He arched a brow. "Nella is a mermaid. And I'm making progress with her."

A laugh came bubbling out. "She finally remembered your name. I don't think that means she's ready to be life-bound to you."

"Well, at least she knows who I am."

My laughter died down. His comment was biting. Even he recognized it and pressed his lips into a tight line. His eyes fell to his fins.

"Sorry. I shouldn't have said that."

I sat up and peered out the hole that served as a window, watching the merfolk swim about their business among the colorful sea life. "It's all right. I know you mean well."

"It's just." Renold circled the room now in frustration. "You've got 'maids throwing themselves at you and you won't even glance at them. You're too busy chasing legs to settle into reality."

His words cut me. It was my turn to be angry. I sat up, scowling. "And what is reality? Settling down with some 'maid who has zero sense of adventure and the personality of a bubble? Or worse, a siren who'll leave our nest cold while she's off getting handsy with human sailors? Sorry, but I think I'll pass."

Renold was unimpressed with my argument. "You know that's not fair."

My gaze fell. I was getting too worked up. He knew better than to bring this topic up. It always led into areas best left undiscussed. Painful areas.

A hand came to rest on my shoulder. I looked up to find

Renold's face close to mine. His eyes were full of regret. "Let's not argue. I'm sorry."

My temper deflated. It was hard to stay mad at him. I was closer to him than I was to anyone else. We goaded each other on, but I knew he had my back.

Nodding, I changed the subject. "So, what are you up to today?"

"I wanted to check on you."

My brows twisted. "Check on me? Why?"

He blinked at me for a moment, surprised by my question. "Because it's the full moon tonight?"

That familiar chill crept over me. I'd completely forgotten. Swimming over to the window, I looked down over the city. Sure enough, groups of sirens congregated to discuss their plans. Their colorful tails and trailing hair looked like a strange, deadly coral formation floating in midwater.

Each was more stunning than the last. It was Scalae's gift to us, but a curse to the humans. It was sickening. They were practically salivating over the thought of luring innocents to their potential demise.

I, myself, would soon feel the familiar pull: the melodic tide. Like an intoxication, it descended upon us and the transformation would begin. We called it the *urge.*

Even then, I could almost hear the music. It built faintly in the back of my mind. As the day went on and the sun sank lower, it would grow until it was near deafening. It would grow until it was released. My hand rose to my throat as my heart pounded in response.

Renold clapped my shoulder, stirring me out of my daze. "Come on, let's go get something to eat."

We swam from my den into the current of merfolk making their way through the city of stone and reef. A colorful school of busy citizens surrounded us. As we made our way through the bustling city, the full moon was the prevailing topic among everyone we passed. Sirens and passive non-sirens alike buzzed with excitement.

As we approached our favorite eating den, I was lost

in thought once more. Beside me, Renold's persistent chatter continued.

Piercing pain shot through me as something hit my shoulder, hard enough to knock me back half a tail-length.

"Watch where you're going, squawker!"

Laughter ensued around us, forcing us to a stop.

I looked back to find Percivan, the biggest scum of a siren under the seas. He floated before me with his usual crew of fellow tormentors.

Across the crowded space, Percivan scowled at me. I glared back at him and it was easy to see why he was a favorite of the 'maids. His long blue tail jutted out from his muscular frame. The long black strands of his hair were braided tight against his head. His dark eyes watched us, full of threats. Percivan was a jerk to any merman he deemed a threat to his ego.

Clenching my fists, I started in his direction. Today was not the day to test me.

Renold's firm hand clapped on to my shoulder, holding me back. "Let it go, Fiv. He's not worth it."

Percivan swam forward with his arms spread wide. His arrogant, amused smile filled his face as he raised his brows, taunting me. "Feeling brave today? Or are you just going to go hide away, as usual?"

My response was quick and biting. "I wasn't aware they let minnow-brains like you out on the full moon."

Kryd, one of Percivan's minions, stifled a laugh—earning a hardened stare from his friend. With a powerful flick of his tail, Percivan was inches from my face. Murder filled his dark eyes.

"Mighty words for a coward who turns his back on his own kind."

Anger burst from me like lightning. Before I could stop myself, my hands connected with his chest. I shoved him, hard.

Percivan sailed through the water until his back smacked into a rough rock-wall several tail-lengths behind him. Against the dark waters around us, my tail lit up and my fins flared.

Percivan was momentarily stunned, but quickly

regained his composure. He shoved against me, pushing me backward again. His thick tail flicked behind him as he barreled toward me.

I dodged him at the last second and he bowled into a group of screaming 'maids. He didn't bother apologizing to them before his fins were flaring again, ready to come tear me apart. Just as he was darting my way, someone blocked his path. He pulled up immediately, his eyes wide with shock.

"That's quite enough."

Grayler, Siren General of the entire Aslean Sea, floated between us. His long silver locks waved in the current as his green eyes drilled into Percivan's. Scars and gouges in his broad, golden tail spoke of the long, war-torn life that led to him becoming one of the most formidable merpeople under the waves.

He also happened to be the grandfather who raised me.

"Yes, sir," conceded Percivan. I could still see his fists clenching, but even he wasn't fool enough to defy Grayler.

I was the next subject of scrutiny as Grayler pivoted. His eyes didn't soften when they caught mine. He never was one to go easy on me. His voice was deep and calm, but still sent chills chasing down my spine, knowing what he was fully capable of.

"You both need to keep your heads on straight and cool your tails. I will not tolerate infighting, especially today. If you want to tear each other apart, do it in the sparring ring. For now, I highly suggest you go your separate ways, unless you want to end up in the brig."

I nodded, avoiding his gaze. "Yes, sir."

Percivan rejoined his friends and reluctantly swam away, but not before throwing a death glare my way. He wasn't finished with me yet. He never was. We'd been fighting since we were children.

Renold waited patiently nearby, wringing his hands and darting nervous glances in our direction. He was terrified of Grayler. Passives like him generally revered the sirens, but everyone with half a brain respected the general. Only Scalae herself was above him.

"Fivrial." I looked up to find Grayler's calm gaze trained on me. "Swim with me a moment, will you?"

Motioning for Renold to go on without me, I nodded. "Of course."

Following his lead, we swam away from the crowds. Light began to reach through the water as we finally arrived at the thick, green kelp fields.

Above us, a large school of small, silver fish darted anxiously through the water. The sunlight glinted off their scales like the jewels on my shelves. I inhaled the cool, refreshing water and felt my adrenaline subside as the glow of my tail faded.

It always flared whenever my emotions got out of hand. Another odd quirk I'd inherited from my mother. Memories floated through my mind as we traveled. I'd loved my mother dearly, but the glow had become another, more painful reminder that I was different from everyone else. It was one more reason for Percivan to torment me. Not to mention, it was a reminder that I was bound to the sea when Meryn walked on dry land.

"So, do you want to explain to me what that was about?" said Grayler, hands grasped casually behind his back.

My hand went to my aching shoulder. "Just old rivalry, I suppose. He said something, and I lost my temper."

"Let me guess, the calling?"

He knew. He *always* knew. My father always said it was impossible to hide anything from him. I suppose it was that insight that made him just as formidable an opponent out of battle as in it.

I nodded, face flushing in shame. "Yes."

Grayler bobbed his head, eyes lifting toward the surface. "It's not easy being in your position, Fivrial. Having your gift."

I resisted the urge to scoff. "It's not a gift."

His eyes found mine. "That's the problem. You don't appreciate what you have. Do you know how many sirens would kill to have your voice?"

As you've told me, many, many times before.

"I know that I'm... different, but I just don't have the

desire to..." *Steal? Kill?* I settled on a term I thought wouldn't offend him. "Use it."

Grayler was quiet for a time. When Grayler was silent, there was no telling what may come next. My heart sped up, but I floated patiently, awaiting his reply. At last, he spoke.

"Fivrial, I'm going to give you some advice, and I hope you'll listen. Figure out who you are, and don't flee from it. I know you want to live as a passive, but you know what can happen to sirens who evade their calling. I don't want to see that happen to you."

His words took me by surprise. It was the first time he'd ever indicated that he cared for me in any capacity. Still, I got the message of his "advice."

"I understand."

"The decision is yours. I will never force you to accept the calling, but I will have to handle consequences if they come. And for right now, try to avoid using your fists. I know full moons are difficult, but the last thing I want is more complaints from Mulrena." He rolled his eyes. We both did.

Mulrena was Percivan's loud-mouthed mother, and it wasn't just her singing that was loud and annoying.

"I will do my best," I assured him.

"Good. Now, I must be off. There's still much to do."

This was my cue to go. Bobbing my head, I turned to leave, but he spoke once more.

"Oh, and Fivrial?" I looked back to find him somber. "Scalae be with you."

With me tonight.

"With you as well."

Chapter Five

Fivrial

The sun seemed to go down faster on these cursed days. After flipping around with Renold for hours, trying to distract myself from the building song, I finally found I could not stand it anymore. The time had come for *the descent*.

Swimming as fast as I could, brows drawn together in agony, I passed the shimmering ball of light that served as the collection point for the life force fealties. The Vitalia Sphere, responsible for housing the portion of life force that every siren must contribute from that which was stolen from humans. Its magic was responsible for life as we know it. Each siren owed his or her strength to the sphere. It powered the lights in our city.

It made me sick every time I saw it. Longevity, fertility, beauty, ocean life itself—all contained in that cursed relic. Every month it waited in a simple alcove, guarded by trident-bearing sentinels, for the time when the sirens would replenish it.

The guards nodded to me as I passed them on my way to my retreat.

My tail and eyes were fully blazing now, lighting the way in the dark waters. I swam deeper into the frigid waters. I silently prayed to Scalae to protect Meryn, just as I did every full moon.

Inwardly, I cursed the fact that I couldn't protect her myself. Being anywhere near the surface on that night would put her in more danger than at any other time. My affections for her would make it all the easier to draw her into my song. I wouldn't be able to fight it. And I'd sooner give up my own life force than take even a grain of hers.

Even now, sirens were spreading all over the sea— around ships, islands, moonlit beaches, seaside towns— *anywhere* humans were nearby. Propping up on rocks, swimming in the shallows... their hypnotic songs were rising into the night, zeroing in on the most prominent life-forces, drawing them from their beds. Whole ships would steer into the rocks, with sailors willingly diving overboard into the waters of their demise.

A caress, an embrace, perhaps a kiss (or more) would slowly draw the golden strands of light from their victims, weakening them like a retreating tide. Not all would die. Many would return to their beds, waking up the next day, weakened and with no memory of the event, and no idea that years had been stolen from their lives. Others, like Percivan and his lot, would take what they wanted and cast the lifeless bodies aside, leaving nothing but an empty shell.

Come dawn, bodies would litter the beaches or float upon the water.

At last, I reached the trench and plunged downward. The cave was waiting for me, as always. No moonlight reached down there. I swam back and forth in the black-rock space, chest heaving, hands pressed on either side of my bursting head.

My throat was tight, and I strained to breathe. *I*

hated this. I hated every single second of it. I hated myself for it. For being a siren. For being a killer of men.

It felt as if a monster was taking over my body, transforming me into something else.

Something *primal.*

Flashes of Meryn continually flipped through my mind. I wanted her. I *needed* her. It was almost too much to bear.

I grasped my hair, a deep growl strangling through me.

Shaking from head to fin, I could no longer contain it, *the song.* It bubbled up from my chest, up my throat, and came pouring out between my lips like a river. Vocalizations in a haunting melody, mixed with an ancient language no one understood. It rose and fell like the tide, my tenor voice filling the space around me. With it came surge after surge of powerful energy. Desire. Release. My light was almost blinding as colors bounced off the dark walls, swirling around.

It went on for hours, but it felt like days. Crescendos, decrescendos, soft vibrato, until at last, my song faded to almost a whisper, and I was spent. My body floated to the sandy bottom of the cave as I curled up on my side, drawing in deep breaths and releasing briny tears.

Another night survived. Another night of shame. I hated this. While I was suffering, passives were off enjoying themselves as if nothing were amiss. Non-targeted humans had been sleeping soundly in their beds and were now getting up to greet the beautiful dawn.

With no life-force taken, I was left weakened. It would take at least a day to recover. Still, I had to check on her. To be sure she was spared. As I was pushing myself up off the ground, I was startled to see a dark figure floating in the cave entrance.

A curvy female with long, violet-colored locs and a matching tail. *Wrenna.* The sorceress of the trench. Her glowing blue eyes pierced the darkness, illuminating her smirk. Her arms were crossed, as if she'd been there for a while, observing me.

"I never tire of hearing your voice."

I floated upright, trying to collect myself. This was not the first time I'd found her in this exact position. "Good morning, Wrenna."

She jerked her head. "Come with me. I want to show you something."

Though I was weary, I followed her—something most merfolk would be too scared to do. Unless, of course, they were desperate. Some merfolk sought her out for amulets and spells. She was known to cure ailments with fertility or a cure for serious illness. Some came to her for help to exact vengeance on someone who did them wrong.

She was powerful, though no one quite knew the limits of her power. Neither siren nor passive, the only thing that made her mer at all was her tail. There was something wild and magnetic about Wrenna that could not be explained. A current of constant energy flowed from her.

Even the oldest of the merpeople couldn't explain why she never aged. No one knew exactly how long she'd been living down in the caves of the trench. I was one of the few that saw her regularly.

Years ago, during the first night I'd felt the pull, she'd found me in the chamber. Despite my fear, she made it clear over the years that I was welcome at any time. A silent, mutual respect existed between us, which is why I dared to follow her now.

Sightless fish with strange glowing eyes floated by as sea slugs inched along the ground over sand, rock, and the bones of predators. It was a place of life and of death.

We came to a long, dark passageway that led to a large cave. I'd been there one other time, and it filled me with awe.

In the center of the cavern, a brine pool glowed with silver-blue light. Small balls of light darted inside of it, rising to the edge of the surface and back down again. They reminded me of tiny, nervous fish, only... they were not fish. They never left the confines of the pool. Even now, my gaze fixated on it as I floated by.

"Slug?"

"Hmm?" My attention snapped to Wrenna, who

held out a shell with several brown slugs.

I smiled and took one, popping the chewy morsel into my mouth.

"Thanks." Not my favorite snack, but I was completely famished after my ordeal.

Wrenna ate one herself and set the shell back on one of her many cluttered shelves. Every surface was brimming with bottles, shells, and strange trinkets. She was a bigger collector than I was. Of course, as I had seen before, everything she collected had some purpose.

"So," she said at last, floating down onto one of her nest-covered rocks with crossed arms. "How is she?"

I took the seat opposite, leaning my head against the wall as I fought off sleep. "Well, I hope. She got caught in a storm yesterday. Out on her boat..." A shudder ran through me at the memory of her motionless form sinking beneath the pounding waves. "I saved her."

Wrenna nodded. "And then what?"

My eyes found the small pool at the center of the floor again as the memory of her soft lips touched mine in a phantom caress. "I kissed her."

"Let me guess, and then you hit her with a Spell of Forgetfulness?"

I nodded. There was no point in being surprised. Wrenna had taught me the spell herself. Still, guilt and longing settled in my chest to hear it confirmed.

"And now your heart is broken."

I shrugged. "I'll survive."

Wrenna studied me curiously. "What if I told you there was a way?"

My eyes flicked to hers. "A way?"

Her lips tipped up in a grin. "I've been working on something I think you'll be very interested in."

She rose and swam across the den, motioning for me to follow. Curiosity thoroughly piqued, I darted after to catch up. We reached the far corner where a large flat object stood propped against the wall. It was a piece of shipwrecked wood, half-covered in algae.

At first, I was confused, but then she grasped the sides of the wood and lifted away, revealing the smooth glass in the frame below.

I found an image of myself staring back. My fingers reached out and grazed the cool, hard surface. Scrolling gold, free of blemish, hugged the large glass in an oval shape. I'd only heard of these and found shards, but never had I seen one fully intact before.

"A mirror..."

"Not just any mirror." She snatched a purple glass bottle from a nearby shelf and uncorked the lid. With a few taps, she produced a small green leaf and passed it to me. "Chew this, but don't swallow."

I eyed it warily. "What is it?"

"Something that will help you see possibility."

After a moment's hesitation, I slipped it into my mouth and began to chew. A bitter taste followed.

"Give it to me."

Wrenna was holding out her hand. Awkwardly, I took the mash from my mouth and placed it in her waiting palm.

Her long tail flicking behind her, she swam over to the pool. From the edge she retrieved a pearl-white conch and with it collected some of the mystical waters. Using her fingertip, I watched in wonder as she mixed the mashed leaf into the waters in her palm. Faintly, she uttered a series of words I could not understand. Her brows furrowed in concentration.

The mixture began to glow brightly. Sparks danced around it. When satisfied, she swam back over to the mirror, gathered a pinch in her fingers, and smeared a line down the center of the glass before quickly backing away again.

"Stand before the mirror."

"Stand? What do you..."

My words trailed off as I looked at my reflection. It was transformed into something nearly unrecognizable. Me, but not me. Gone was the blue-green tail. Instead, legs of flesh rested in its place. Feet... calves... knees... thighs... I knew their names from years of observing humans.

My cheeks colored furiously. Parts normally

concealed under a scaled sheath were now shockingly exposed.

When I went to cover myself with my hands, I felt only scales. Looking down, I found my tail and fins were perfectly present and intact. My eyes darted back to the reflection. Once again, I saw legs.

I was a human.

"How... how is this possible?"

"Because it is." Her hand rested on my shoulder and I found her eyes bright with enthusiasm. "Fivrial, I can help you. I can make your dreams come true. This is what you desire, is it not?"

Her tone bordered on manic. In the dim light of the cave, her eyes began to glow. It both frightened and enchanted me. She spoke the truth. It was the raw, hidden reality that had been screaming at me for years. The longing that no one else could understand.

My heart threatened to burst from my chest. For a moment, I let myself hope. I let myself dream.

"Yes."

A grin spread across her face. "I thought you might say that."

My gaze returned to the reflection as my throat bobbed with emotion. "What do I need to do?"

Wrenna's hand left my shoulder. "All magic comes with a price, as you know. It was very costly to procure this ingredient."

I turned to her. "Name your price."

Her smile faltered. "It's not going to be easy."

"Wrenna. *Name your price.*"

She stared at me, face growing stony. "Grayler's trident."

She may as well have asked for the oceans to be drained.

My jaw slackened. "What?"

"That is my price."

My mind spun. The trident of Grayler was a well-known relic. He had many, but there was one, a very significant piece, that rested in importance above all of his collection. It had been used long ago to defeat an enemy so great that all the Aslean Sea and beyond had been called to battle.

Every warring nation had laid aside their differences to fight her. Every merchild knew the story of the defeat of Rowen, the goliath witch of the deep. It was Grayler's trident that struck the final, deadly blow.

Could I do it? Could I bring myself to steal from my own grandfather? My stomach soured at the thought. To do such a thing would put a target on my back. *A big one.* But only if I got caught.

Just the thought of Meryn being in my arms was enough to fill me with warmth, even in those deep, icy waters. The memory of her kiss, her hair between my fingers... I wanted to sigh.

I had my answer.

"I'll do it."

Wrenna's smile faltered for a moment, but then brightened again. "Good." She turned away and gathered more items off her shelf.

I could hardly take my eyes off my reflection. Something struck me as a bit odd. This was a big change. It was going to take a lot of magic.

"Why are you doing this for me, Wrenna?" I asked, ripping my eyes from the mirror to look at her.

Wrenna stopped what she was doing and slowly turned. Her gaze trained on the glass bottle in her hands. "Because you're my friend, Fivrial." She straightened and looked me in the eye. "I care about your happiness."

My heart warmed at the sentiment. Not many cared about such a thing. "Thank you, Wrenna."

A brief smile lit her face. "You're welcome. Now, about the trident—can you get it?"

I nodded. "I believe so. As Grayler's grandson, the guards won't block my access to his armory. He should be overseeing drills most of the day. I'll go in while he is away."

"Will they let you take it out?"

"I'll tell them he's requested it," I replied, slightly agitated by her persistent questioning. All I wanted was to get the trident and hurry along with the spell.

"Well then," said Wrenna with a smile, "it seems

you have a plan in place."

Getting the trident was easier than I had imagined it would be. The guards were chatting with each other and when they saw it was me, nodded me through without a second thought. I swam into the vast grotto of armor and treasures and headed straight for the golden trident mounted on a piece of coral sticking out from the wall, high above the others.

My nerves rang as I wrapped my hands around the staff. It was precious to Grayler. *More important to him than even me*, I thought bitterly. At the end of the day, it was just another piece of treasure. One of thousands of items clogging his collection.

I removed the trident and looked around for one that most closely resembled it. A shiny brass one lay nearby. It had been a gift from a fae king hundreds of years ago, as legend told. Still not as important as the one I was stealing, but it would have to do for now. Pursing my lips in determination, I mounted the fae trident in the exalted place and made my way to the exit.

The guards were still chatting with each other. Completely inept. And they would pay a heavy price for the misdeed I was about to commit. Guilt ate at my gut, but Meryn's face flashed through my mind. I was doing this for her.

I steeled myself and swam casually from the grotto, nodding to them as I went. They barely glanced at me. I kept my steady pace, the waters flowing swiftly around me. My eyes searched the vast waters for any onlookers. When I was out of sight from the guards, I shot off toward the trench.

Upon reaching Wrenna's cave, I was shaking with fear and anticipation. Fear of what I'd just done and the possible ramifications, and anticipation of holding Meryn in my arms again.

Wrenna was waiting for me. The moment I entered, she snatched the trident from my hands and stood it in the back corner of the cave. Her lips were drawn tight, and her brows furrowed in concentration. It seemed as if she barely noticed my presence. She wrapped her hand around my wrist in an iron grip. She was much stronger than I'd realized.

She yanked me from the cave and up out of the trench, ignoring all my questions. I flipped my fins rapidly, trying to keep up with her quick pace. Wherever we were going, she was determined to get there as quickly as possible.

Water rushed by us as we swam far from the trench—far from Brinn. Sunlight gradually filtered around us. It wasn't until we were out in midwaters, closer to the shore, that Wrenna finally brought us to a stop and released my hand. I immediately snatched it away and rubbed my aching wrist.

"All right, here we are," I said, trying to calm my racing heart. "What do we do now?"

Wrenna floated with her back to me, glancing over her shoulder. "Are you really sure you want to do this, Fivrial?"

Her words were quiet, testing. Almost as if she were hoping I'd say no. It did not help my anxiety about what manner of horrors may lay before me in this process. Still, I nodded. *For Meryn, I would do anything.*

"I'm sure."

She turned and opened her palm. In it were three of the same strange leaves from before. Her eyes met mine once more.

"You need to chew and swallow these. You will gain legs for three moons, but every full moon, you will revert to a siren for the night. Is that clear?"

My brows drew together. "Only for three moons?"

Wrenna lifted her chin, a smile spreading across her face. "If she tells you she loves you, unprompted and genuine, by that third full moon..." A smile stretched her lips. "...you may keep your legs forever."

Hope flooded into me like the tide. "Forever?" An eternity with the woman I loved. It was more than I'd ever dreamed. I immediately popped the leaves in my mouth and began to chew.

"But... if she does not confess her love, you revert to a siren. *Forever.*" Her voice lowered. "This spell only works one time, Fivrial."

My chewing slowed to a stop. *One chance.* That's all I would ever have. What if I failed? What if I somehow drove her away?

Fingertips slid under my chin. I found myself face-to-face with Wrenna. She searched my eyes.

"Chew, Fivrial. Take your chance."

Her words commanded me like a spell on their own. My jaw moved and Wrenna smiled, removing her fingers. She swam backwards several paces before raising her arm above her head and sliding her eyes shut.

The moment I swallowed the bitter herbs, the first syllables left Wrenna's lips. Her words drifted across the water in an unknown language. She repeated several phrases, her voice growing louder.

I felt a shift in the surrounding current. A wavering in my vision. Squeezing my eyes shut, I shook my head, trying to clear it. When I opened my eyes, it was worse. Wrenna was blurry.

"Wrenna? What—what's happening?"

No sooner had the words left my mouth than they were caught up in the rush of water that violently swirled up around me.

That's when everything went black.

Chapter Six

Meryn

I rushed through the halls, my green skirts swishing around my ankles. Father was waiting and did not like to be kept so. His time was the most precious thing above all else, even when it came to his own daughters. Still, my feet worked quickly for other reasons. I had to convince him to reconsider this ridiculous scheme of his.

At last, I reached the doors to his office. Boles, the aged servant who had come to fetch me, caught up with a heaving chest. He glowered at me as he knocked on the door. My father's baritone voice admitted us.

With a tired flourish, Boles opened the doors and entered ahead of me, a tired smile forced on his thin face. He bowed. "Lady Meryn, milord."

No sooner had he stepped aside than I was charging up to my father's large black desk. He sat with his dark eyes still fixated on the paperwork before him, not bothering to greet me. Same as he had not bothered to check on me since I'd washed ashore on the beach.

Fury built inside of me at his obvious apathy.

His red damask robes were lined with gold threads—a typical display of his vast wealth. Father was never dressed in anything less than his absolute best. He was, after all, a favorite of the king, and liked to remind people of that.

"What is it, Meryn?" he asked with a bored sigh.

I slammed my palm on the desk, forcing his attention. "You will rescind this ridiculous punishment, that's what!"

His eyes widened as they raised to meet mine. "Pardon?"

I knew that tone. He wasn't asking me to repeat myself. My father was not one to be crossed. And he wasn't above throwing those loyal to him in the stocks for defiance. However, I'd take the stocks over this punishment any day.

"Aurin is a disgusting pig of a man and I will not work for him." I ground the words out with every bit of resolve I could muster. I'd practiced and practiced my delivery of this line, taking on every bit of my father's imperious tone I could manage.

At last, Father set his papers down and leaned back in his chair to study me. He folded his hands in his lap, looking almost amused at my attempt. "Is that so?"

I nodded as I straightened my posture and smoothed my skirts. "It's insulting and below me as your daughter."

Father laughed. "And stealing a boat and nearly drowning yourself isn't? Meryn, we both know you've little sense of propriety. Nice try, though."

Fire blazed in my bones. "It's not funny! Do you have any idea what might happen if I were to-to—"

"Get your hands dirty?"

"To work for someone like that!" I shot back.

He arched a brow. "So, you're a snob now, are you?"

Crossing my arms, I bristled at the accusation. I had to make him understand. *Why can't he understand?* "It's not about that. Father, do you have any idea what that man said to me? The position you're putting me in? I didn't steal his boat over nothing. He called me a 'ginger wench' and said he wanted to-to- take me into that boat and..." I couldn't finish as bile threatened to come up my throat. It was too disgusting to think about. Too violating. The guard had shut Mr. Aurin up and dragged me away, kicking and cursing.

Father shook his head as his brows drew together. "I'm not justifying his behavior. But nothing justifies what you did either, Meryn. You did the crime, and you must pay the price. I'm sorry, but you're not getting out of this. You'll be guarded, and it will be fine."

"No," I replied sternly, pursing my lips. "I'm telling you that—"

"You're telling me nothing," he snapped, eyes suddenly turning cold. All traces of humor drained from his face.

Rising from his seat, he towered over me. I'd forgotten how oppressive he could be when his mood soured. Immediately, I shrank and lowered my gaze to the floor. My plan to be bold had failed. It was my turn to be quiet.

"You have humiliated me, Meryn," he continued, pointing his finger into the surface of the desk as he glowered. "You've humiliated the entire family. Your actions have not only cost us financially, but our reputation is sullied. *Your* reputation is sullied. All because of your recklessness and pride. Or should I say, lack thereof. Now, you will work for Mr. Aurin, or else I will keep you locked away for the rest of your days until I find a husband for you. Not that any man is going to be jumping to marry you after this."

My mouth fell open. Shame flooded me. He was gambling my safety by putting me with the wretched man, even with a guard. He was willing to risk my life, my reputation, and more just to save face.

There was some truth to what he was saying. Despite father's position, suitors weren't exactly lining the halls. The truth stung, but it was not something that I wanted to hear. My fate was as good as sealed. When he took that tone, there was no more arguing.

With a sigh, he sank back into the chair and pinched the bridge of his nose. "I hope that you'll learn something from all of this, Meryn. It's not my first choice, believe me, but it's the best one."

With a wave of his hand, I was dismissed. Hot tears

filled my eyes as I nodded. Once again, I was nothing but a child in the presence of a father who couldn't understand. I wanted to lash out, run away, protest until the eaves were crashing to the floor, but none of it would do any good.

And so, I turned and forced a steady pace to the door, gaze cast to the floorboards. As soon as the doors were shut behind me, I fled through the halls to the only place I felt remotely at peace.

Waves crashed into the rocks ahead of me as the warm blonde sand squished between my toes. A tepid breeze rustled my hair, the fine curls at my temples matted down with sweat. My long-sleeved gown was too heavy for a day like this. Sand and saltwater were collecting around the hem, despite my best efforts to keep them gathered up. Had I not been so desperate to get out of the castle, I would've dug into my stash of breeches and men's shirts, twisted my long hair under a cap, and snuck out in perfect freedom. Neither Nola nor Captain Cabor would've told on me. They understood me a far cry better than Father.

As it was, Penton, one of many guards assigned to our too-large home, followed me at a broad distance. He was another seasoned guard—a big, hulking man with a dark, piercing gaze that made most men shake in their boots.

Whenever I saw the younger guards cower before him, it always made me smile. They assumed him to be a wild beast, but I happened to know his gentle side. He adored cats, and his thick fingers could play the violin beautifully. Penton also didn't mind following me around if it got him out of sentinel duty. So, he was a perfect choice. I dared not risk Father's wrath any further by leaving unescorted.

I was so wrapped up in my thoughts that I almost missed it.

At first, I thought it was another piece of driftwood. A bulge in the sand was covered in sea grasses. As I drew closer, prepared to step over, I stopped short. Gently, almost indecipherably, the mass moved.

A shrill screech escaped me as a soft moan emanated from somewhere underneath the pile of sand and sea grass.

Surprise filled me as I fell on to my backside and scrambled away.

From the distance, Penton's voice rang in my ears, but I was transfixed. Gathering my wits, I crawled back to the mass.

Brushing away long, slimy pieces of seaweed, I discovered a mass of red hair. As I peeled away more, I revealed a soft forehead, lightly tanned skin, and a gracefully arched nose. My breath caught when I reached the short beard running over a strong jawline...

Quickly, I continued pulling away the debris. Around me, crabs skittered across the hot sand. As the last of it fell away, I discovered that it was indeed a man. An *unclothed* man.

Years of propriety told me I should shield my eyes immediately, but I was too drawn to his beautiful face to notice anything else.

Gingerly, I brushed his high cheekbone with my fingertips. *Please be alive,* I prayed to the gods.

Slowly, his eyes fluttered open, revealing the clear blue sky within them. My brows raised when they found me.

"You're alive," I breathed.

Suddenly, his hand grasped mine. He opened his mouth as if to speak, but his eyes quickly rolled back, and he was unconscious again.

"Penton!" I called over my shoulder.

"Right here, milady!" He reached me a moment later, eyes growing large.

"He's alive. We have to help him," I urged as calmly as I could.

Penton gently grasped my upper arms. "Come, milady, we'll send help—"

"No." My eyes snapped up to his. "We can't leave him. If he wakes up, he might be disoriented and wander off."

Shaking his head, Penton again tried to move me. "I hardly think this is appropriate—"

I shoved him away. "I don't care about what is appropriate, I care about what is right! Now, go get help!" My voice rose with the same authoritative tone my father used.

Growling, Penton rolled his eyes but obeyed. Turning on his heel, he jogged toward the piers. I returned my attention to the castaway.

His hand still rested in mine. The warmth in his touch brought me solace. He was alive for now.

I brushed the wavy copper locks from his temples. His hair was unusually long for a man, and it shimmered in the sunlight. Hints of blond wove throughout. *Perhaps bleached by the sun and sea?* I thought to myself.

My eyes slid to his bare chest. Darker, coarse hair spread across it. I dared not look any lower. My cheeks burned as it was. I'd never been this close to an unclothed man.

Cool ocean water lapped at us, rushing over his legs, soaking my dress. It was refreshing in the heat of the day. A passing thought had me wondering what it would be like to lie at his side, no clothes on, and feel the water running over my bare skin. Nothing but the sun, the sand, and the sea. I'd seen sea creatures all my life. What would it be like to be that free? Part of me envied the non-human creatures that didn't have to suffocate under hot stitched fabrics that trapped one in like a tomb.

Perhaps it was the sun. Such wicked thoughts were not becoming to a "lady". They were certainly inappropriate for the daughter of a duke. All I wanted to do was strip off my clothes and leap into the sea, letting my hair loose in the waves. I wanted to know what secrets were held in the depths. Instead, my life consisted of music, painting, and sending daydreams through the window.

Here, with this strange man, those dreams came rushing back unbidden. For whatever reason, the sea saw fit to deliver him to our shores. And I was to be his savior. If Scalae spared him, there must be a good reason, just as she had spared me.

Enfolding his hand between both of mine, my eyes found the watery horizon and whispered a promise to the goddess.

"I won't let you down."

Chapter Seven

Meryn

It was chaos when the other guards and men from the pier reached us. They quickly brushed me aside as they attended to him. No visible signs of injury could be found, but as they wrapped him in a rough brown blanket and carried him away, I heard him groaning in pain. My heart pinched at the sound.

"Wait!" I followed the men, craning my neck over their shoulders to get glimpses of him. "Where are you taking him?"

Penton barely glanced at me. "We'll take him to the guard barracks. Call the apothecary."

"The what? No, you most certainly won't! Those barracks are draftier than a whore's knickers!"

Horror stole over his features. "Milady!"

The men were equally shocked, but I simply rolled my eyes. Let them think me an ingrate. I was going to get my way.

"You will take him to a guest bedroom in the castle and call for the doctor."

"Your father will never allow it."

"You let me deal with my father. You *will* take him to a guest room. The blue one will do," I insisted, referencing the small blue bedroom near the foot of my tower. Rarely used, it was one of the less opulent rooms, and perfectly out of the way from Father's usual paths.

Penton's jaw feathered. He was unhappy with me, but I had the advantage. And I wasn't going to budge.

"We'll take him through the servants' stairs. Less likely to cause a fuss that way."

I grinned. "Thank you, Penton. Most considerate of you."

Our parade continued, passing curious gazes. I simply smiled and nodded, as if it were an everyday occurrence that we carried groaning, barely conscious men toward the castle.

I followed the men up the long, cliffside stairs and into the servants' entrance. Beads of sweat were on all our brows by the time we were indoors.

I barked at a young guard to go fetch the doctor and Nola. The fewer servants to spread gossip about the castle, the better. I knew she would keep my confidence if asked.

When we reached the door to the blue room, I watched as the man was carried in and carefully laid on the bed. His face twisted in pain. Alarmed, I pushed through the group of men surrounding him, ready to grab his hand again. I was determined to do anything to help. A strong grip latched onto my arm, and I was jerked away before I could reach him. I glared up at Penton, who met me with hardened eyes.

"We've got it from here. I believe it's time for you to retire, milady."

His words held weight this time. I had no excuse to be there any longer. Care was now available in droves. Pursing my lips, I nodded in defeat.

"See that he gets everything he needs. Only Nola and those she appoints are to attend to him. Thank you, Penton."

I turned to leave, but not before casting one last look. My breath hitched to find blue eyes trained on me from across the room. His lids were heavy, and his brows knitted, but there was an unmistakable light of recognition. He *saw* me. And I couldn't look away.

My lips tipped up in a reassuring smile, though I was internally shaken. Especially when his fingers lifted in my direction, as if he were about to reach for me. Color flooded my cheeks when I realized we'd been staring at each other. I whirled around and fled the room, breaking the hypnotic connection.

Chest heaving in panicked bursts, I ran the short distance to the stairs. I took each step as fast as I could manage with my water-logged skirts. The moment I crashed into my room, I slammed the door, pressing my back to it.

By the gods! What just happened?

With a shaky hand, I turned the lock before pressing my palms to my eyes. Perhaps I'd made a mistake? A huge one. What was I thinking, bringing a strange man into the house? Especially one like... *that*. Who was he?

A puff of air escaped me as I shook my head.

Get yourself together, Mer. It's just a man.

Finally, I steadied enough to peel off my wet clothes. The sun was still fairly high in the afternoon sky, but I felt completely drained. I was still not quite recovered from my own experience of being washed up on the beach. All I wanted was to crawl between clean linens and sleep for days.

There was a knock at the door. Quickly, I threw on my dressing gown. Upon opening the door, I found a bright-eyed Nola standing there with three other maids. I smiled wearily and stepped aside as they filed in. Immediately, the maids began to fill my bath as Nola went straight to my wardrobe to find a nightgown.

"How is he?" I searched her face, desperate for answers.

Nola arched a brow. "He sleeps." She laid a long, powder-blue gown across the bed. "Word travels fast around here..."

I laughed, despite the warning tone in her voice. "Incredibly."

She turned to me with worried brows and folded hands. "You've done a noble thing, but—"

"*But* a stranger under our roof, I know."

Sighing, she came to help me out of my dressing gown. "You always have liked rescuing things, haven't you? Birds, cats... I suppose we should add 'men' to the list now."

"I suppose so..."

The bath was filled quickly, and I stepped into the large copper basin to wash away the sand and grit. Part of me mourned the loss of the sea from my skin, but I was glad to ease my tense muscles.

Nola stayed with me, helping me wash my hair, just as she did when I was a child. I poured my heart out to her, relaying the events as they'd occurred. She listened without judgment. It was a balm to my soul to simply talk freely to her.

After I was scrubbed clean, dried, and dressed, I finally slipped into bed. Nola tucked me under the quilts and opened the windows to let the breeze in. She patted my head affectionately and bid me goodnight. I fell asleep almost immediately, swept away by dreams of deep water and a man with sky-blue eyes.

Sometime later, I awoke. Silvery moonlight spilled across my bed. I breathed deeply, staring at the bright orb in the sky, thinking of what lay floors below me.

Was he all right? Was he scared? Confused? In pain?

I'd vowed to Scalae to look after him. Such an odd thing to do. He was neither a bird nor a cat, nor something for me to collect, like a pretty shell. Though there was a uniqueness about him I couldn't quite explain. I felt myself *drawn* to him.

My eyes slid to the door. It would be so easy to throw on a dress, or even my heavy dressing gown, and slip down the stairs.

Would he be guarded? He wasn't a prisoner.

No. I shouldn't. It would be incredibly improper to enter a man's bedroom in the middle of the night. Especially a stranger. It was something a lady would never, *ever* do. My father would have me locked in my room for the rest of my life.

Still, my feet found the cool floor. My arms slipped through the sleeves of my heavy blue damask dressing gown, and I tied it tightly. I forwent slippers, preferring to feel the firm ground against my soles. Quietly, feet stepping as soft as cotton, I stole from my room, down the winding stair.

The hallway was empty when I exited the doorway at the bottom. I looked to my left and saw the door to the blue room was slightly ajar, warm lantern light spilling through the crack onto the hall floor. Steeling myself, I tiptoed down the hall and into the narrow shaft of light.

Lightly, barely a thumping, I knocked on the door. I heard the shuffling of bedclothes and then the unmistakable sound of footsteps. And then the sound of hard thuds on the floor, followed by a hiss of pain. I immediately swung the door open wide enough to slip inside.

He was on the floor, now fully dressed in a billowy white shirt and dark gray breeches. His face was the color of his shirt as he struggled to pull himself up from his knees by way of clinging to the bedpost. Guilt pierced me as I rushed to his side, looping my arm under his.

"Oh! I'm so sorry! Here, let me help you."

Together, we worked to get him off the floor and limping back to bed. He positioned himself to sit back against the headboard, catching his breath in relief. I stood by, hugging my arms awkwardly.

"Are you all right?"

He nodded, his eyes finally resting on mine. "Yes, thank you. Muscle cramps, I think."

I frowned. "That sounds awfully painful. I'm sorry I roused you from bed."

He shook his head. "No, it's all right. I was already awake." A smile tugged his lips. "Hard to sleep under a strange roof."

I couldn't help but reciprocate his smile. It was... kind.

"Where's home, then? We can assist you once you've recovered."

The smile faltered as his brows drew together. Those

lovely eyes left mine. "You know, I'm not sure."

"You mean..." I tread gently. "...you don't have a home?"

He sighed. "I'm afraid I don't remember."

"Oh. Well, what do you remember?"

His eyes were transfixed on the space before him. "I remember the water. The sun..." His gaze slipped to mine. "...and you."

My cheeks burned. I had to tear my eyes away, feeling suddenly exposed. *Does he remember the way I held onto his hand a bit longer than necessary? How I touched his face?*

"Well, I, um, I'm sorry to hear of your... memory loss. I should probably be going though." I forced a smile. "It's late."

He nodded, a shadow of disappointment casting his features. "I understand."

I turned to leave, but then paused, looking over my shoulder. "What's your name, by the way?"

"How about... Finn."

I smiled. "Finn. How fitting."

"Why is that?"

Turning to face him, I found him amused and couldn't help but grin. "Because you're like a fish who came from the water."

Finn's eyes twinkled. "Well, maybe I am?"

I laughed. "I'm Meryn, by the way."

"Meryn..." The name rolled out of his mouth like the tide. "Well, thank you, Meryn. For saving my life. I'm in your debt."

For an awkward moment, I stood there, thinking of what to say next. But I found myself at a loss. So, I simply nodded and slipped from the room, gently closing the door behind me.

I hurried back to my bedroom. The soft sheets around me once more, I succumbed to sweet dreams of magical fish.

Chapter Eight

Fivrial

I couldn't believe my eyes when I awoke on the beach to see her face hovering over me like some sort of gift from fate. It was only a glimpse before everything went dark again, but it was enough to reassure me I was safe. The feel of her hand in mine was an anchor, tethering me to shore, leading me to our future.

How I ended up in the right place at the right time, I'll never understand. Images of the swirling, angry waters of Wrenna's whirlpool flashed in my mind. I remembered flailing through the water toward shore. Without my tail, swimming was nearly impossible to sustain. Somehow, I didn't succumb.

Perhaps Scalae had a hand in this, after all.

I stood at the window. The breeze brought bumps across my new, sensitive skin. I quickly discovered that the soft blue material wrapped around my shoulders kept away the chill. Pink and golden hues tinged the horizon. In the distance I watched the soft waves of the sea I called home.

I took deep long, deep breaths to steady myself. With each breath came dozens of different scents. Although I'd breached the surface thousands of times, I'd never been so enveloped by so many human smells.

Above the smell of the food brought in earlier, and the various odors of the room around me, there was the salty air of the sea. I watched the churning of the waters again. Somewhere out there, they could be searching for me. It was only a matter of time before they discovered the missing trident and realized I was missing as well. Renold would be the only one to notice I was gone, and he would surely sound the alarm. My heart pinched at the thought of leaving behind my only true friend.

My eyes fell to my feet. Such strange floppy things. Like hard, fleshy fins. My body felt so heavy out of the water. The transition from tail to legs was a painful one. Being split apart was... unpleasant. But it only lasted moments. And seeing Meryn's smiling face made it all worth it.

When she'd come to my room in the middle of the night, I thought I might die of happiness. It was so hard to lie to her about my past. But that was the deal. I needed the "I love you" to fall from her sweet lips by the peak of the third full moon or else my chance was lost forever.

Even the thought of the full moon sent a shudder through me. Another stipulation. I would transform back into a siren every time that horrid light hung in the sky. The pull would still occur, and I'd have to leave her. There was no compromise.

A knock sounded at the door. I turned in anticipation but was disappointed when a moment later, a male servant in a stiff blue uniform entered instead. He was a tall, thin, graying man with dark eyes and a kind smile. He looked surprised to find me out of bed.

"Good morning, sir," he greeted with a deep nod. "I've come to see if you need any assistance."

"Assistance?"

"Anything you need. Would you like breakfast?"

I blinked at him. I'd never had anyone serve me before.

If I was hungry, I typically swam off to a feeding den or foraged for my own food. This wasn't the ocean, however, and my stomach was growling at the reminder.

"I... yes?"

He nodded. "Very well. I will be back shortly." The man turned to leave.

"Wait."

Immediately, he ceased and returned his attention to me. "Yes?"

"What's your name?" If I were going to inconvenience someone, I should at least know who to thank.

He paused before answering, "Bernard."

I smiled warmly. "Thank you, Bernard. I appreciate it."

With another nod, he disappeared from the room. I stared at the door for a while. This was going to be a strange experience, indeed.

The rest of the morning was a whirlpool of activity. They fed me strange warm food and liquids that satiated my roaring hunger. Servants filed in and began stretching strips of cloth against my limbs, around my neck, my torso, and my feet. An older woman informed me it was all for the promise of more clothing.

A man showed up with hinged daggers and cut my hair to my shoulders. He wanted to take off more, but I politely declined. It was a weight off my heavy head. *Everything* felt heavy outside the water.

My beard was trimmed, my nails clipped and cleaned. To my dismay everything under the sun was scrubbed once again in the large shiny basin in the small, annexed room. When it was all said and done, a large mirror was brought in and I was forced before it. I hardly recognized myself. The oceanic wilds had been tamed from my reflection, and before me stood a *man*.

I marveled at what I saw. My fingers ran over the deep blue garment that hugged my body over the white shirt. Blue trousers hid my muscular legs, and black shoes covered my new feet. It was a strange concept. I had gained a human body, only to have to cover it all up. The clothes rubbed against my sensitive skin, pinching at tender parts of me. Were they ashamed of their bodies?

At last, most of the servants departed, with only Bernard and another manservant left to clean up any residual mess. Another knock sounded at the door. Bernard answered it before I could take a single step. My heart lifted to hear a female voice.

Bernard started to inform me of my visitor when I pushed past him and flung the door open. Meryn startled, her hand flying to her chest.

Warmth flooded my cheeks. I quickly realized I'd surprised her. Apologies spewed from my mouth as I retreated into the room. "Sorry, I just recognized your voice, and—"

"Oh, it's all right!" She smiled. Hey eyes were bright as they swept over me. "I was just coming to see how you were."

Bernard excused himself and slipped past me out the door, the other servant in tow. I watched them leave, thankful to be alone with her.

"I'm much better, thank you." I rested my hand on my chest and glanced over my new clothes. "I suppose I have you to thank for everything, really."

"Oh, it's nothing. I just knew you needed some things..."

I looked up to find her brows knitted as she studied me. My heart fell to see disappointment.

"Is something wrong?"

"No, not at all, it's just... they cut all of your lovely hair."

My hand self-consciously ran over my shortened tresses as I nodded. "They did... is that all right?"

Her cheeks reddened as she stumbled over her words. "Oh! Of course! It's very becoming on you! I mean—it looks nice. I just wasn't expecting it, that's all."

I leaned my shoulder against the door frame and crossed my arms with a smile. "It's a change, that's certain."

My eyes briefly wandered up and down, subtly drinking in the sight of her. A light purple dress gently hugged her curves before flowing like waves, skimming the top of her matching shoes. Her beautiful curls framed her face in long strands while the rest of her hair was gathered in a thick braid that hung down to her waist. Memories of my fingers intertwining with those long, silken strands came rushing back. Those smiling lips on my own...

I had to look away as a rush of heat hit me. It was too soon to dwell on such things. I had to be patient with her. She didn't remember our moments.

"Would you like to walk with me?" She smiled. "If you're feeling up to it, of course."

Truthfully, I was exhausted, and my muscles were still sore, but I nodded. "Sure."

Meryn beamed like the sun as I stepped into the hallway with her. "We can stay in the castle, of course. I can show you around town when you're more recovered."

"That sounds wonderful. I don't want to impose on you, though."

She rolled her eyes. "Trust me, it's no imposition at all. This house is too big and boring. My father is away most of the time, so we don't have many guests. Lots of breathing room."

Breathing room, indeed, I thought as we strolled through the vast passages of her home. Wood and stone married together to form the biggest, most complex den I'd ever seen.

I'd never dreamed it was this beautiful inside. It felt unnatural, to be cut off from the outside by so many doors and locks, but it was breathtaking. Creations of images hung on the walls. Colors and minerals were fashioned to create things that had little practicality beyond pleasing the eye. It was hard to restrain myself from brushing my fingers over every piece.

We saw so many rooms, each having some sort of purpose. A room for eating, a room for reading, a room of old weapons, even a room for music. It was there that I found myself most uneasy.

A large, black, curvy object fashioned from wood sat in the center of the music room. Its flat surface glistened like lava rocks. The rounded legs held it upright nearest the tall windows. Flat white sticks were laid out in a row on an outcropping. Meryn grinned as she sat on a bench and pressed on some of the sticks. The first notes of music reached my ears, and I found myself swallowing hard.

I'd heard the same sounds before, winding through the

open windows when I'd been near enough, hiding under the pier. My natural instincts were to vocalize, mixing my tones with the sweet melodies filling the air. It would be harmless now—to open up and release my voice. I was neither siren nor under a full moon. Still, I was shaken. I detested the thought of getting my songs anywhere near Meryn.

Then, something unexpected happened. Her lips parted and sweet notes slipped forth. Not just vocalizations, or the strange, ancient language of the sirens, but real words. I found myself wrapped up in the sound like a warm embrace, completely enchanted.

Come to me, my love
Come o'er raging sea
By land, o'er the mountain
Come, my love to me

My heart is full
Of tender longing
For the warmth of your hand
Your face I long to see

I'm sinking in the deep
Drowning in the sea
Encased by the waves
Come, my love to me

Do not delay, my love
Not a moment to spare
Come o'er the raging sea
Come, my love, so fair

When she was finished, she sat back, hands folded in her lap, and sighed. When she met my wide eyes, her cheeks blazed. Her gaze immediately fell to the floor.

"My sister says my songs are scandalous. We've got lots and lots of 'proper' music, but I've played them all so much that I grew bored." The corner of her lips tugged up in a half-grin. "I suppose I still enjoy it more than embroidering and poking my fingers to death with a needle."

My heart was thumping in my chest. "You... your voice is beautiful." *More beautiful than a siren...* "Your song is lovely as well."

"You aren't shocked by my impropriety?"

I laughed. "Not in a bad way."

Meryn met my eyes with a toothy grin. "Thank you, Finn." She rose from the bench and motioned for me to sit down. "Would you like to try?"

I blanched. "I'm afraid I don't know how. I've never touched one of... those."

"A piano."

"Piano. Anyway, I might break it."

She was already at my side, tugging my elbow over to the bench. "Nonsense! It'll be fun! I'll show you how to play something simple."

Relenting at last, I smiled and nodded. My stomach was doing flips at the sudden closeness of being pressed together on the small seat. The moment she bent down and gently took my hands, I nearly stopped breathing. She was closer than I expected her to be.

"Now, you place your fingers on certain keys to make it easier to reach..."

Carefully, she maneuvered each finger to a corresponding "key", until my hands were splayed in a way that satisfied her. Then she did something entirely unexpected. Her fingers laid on top of mine, her arms stretched in front of me.

"Okay, now, we'll play a simple tune, and you'll see how everything is laid out in a scale, from lowest to high. Once you figure out where the notes are, it's just a matter of putting them in order. Sort of like arithmetic."

She was enthusiastic, but just detached enough to be a dutiful teacher. I did my best to concentrate on the lesson, and not on the lovely way her hair smelled, or the warmth of her hands on mine.

Pressing with just the right amount of firmness, she sank one of the keys into the wooden base and a note emanated from the box portion. Immediately, I felt the music clang through my bones at the contact. Another note, another rush. It was a simple series of notes using my right hand. She patiently pressed and lifted my fingers to create the song.

The pull was nearly unbearable. Music intoxicated me quickly, threatening to sweep me away. My throat was tight with the urge to sing along. I hated it. If she kept on, I would have to find somewhere to let it out. Siren or not, my voice frightened me, especially around her.

At last, she pulled her hands from mine, bringing a mixture of relief and disappointment.

"Now, you try."

I snatched my hands from the keys. "I... I don't know if I should."

Meryn laughed. "Nonsense! You're not going to break it. Just give it a try."

A thought occurred to me; she may very well think I'm a coward if I don't. Inwardly, I cursed. I wanted to please her. *Needed* to please her. And so, with shaking fingers, I placed them on the piano keys and slowly played the tune she showed me.

After only a few missed notes, she smiled brightly and clapped her hands together. "Wonderful job! I knew you could—"

Suddenly, a surge overtook me. My fingers continued to move over the piano. It came as naturally as the tide, rushing through my bones. The music filled me to overflowing, bursting from my fingertips. My skin felt alive. Notes, rising and falling rapidly in a voracious, all-consuming melody poured from the instrument. It was alive, just as powerful as the songs from my throat, which I found I was miraculously able to tame.

Time slipped away as I overtook the piano, body rocking in time with the rhythm. Surge after surge of music flowed through me until I was in a different place entirely. Meryn faded away.

I scarcely felt the bench beneath me. I was floating in a space that was neither on land nor in the sea. Closing my eyes, I gave in to it and let it sweep me away. I was lightning. I was air. The euphoria was all-consuming.

At last, I floated back down. The melodic tide receded, and the notes slipped from my bones. I was left exhausted, beads of sweat on my brow. Just like the full moon nights in Wrenna's cave, when I let the music burst forth from my lips, only to end up curled up on the sandy seafloor, I felt as if I could sleep for days.

Upon opening my eyes, I found Meryn standing next to the piano, hugging her arms, tears streaming down her cheeks. There was nothing I could say. No explanations to offer. I couldn't even explain it to myself.

She sniffled and smiled, wiping her eyes. "I think you may have touched a piano before, Finn."

I nodded. "Perhaps you're right." It was a lie, but I let her assume my clouded past and faulty memory was to blame.

We stood there, staring at each other in awe for a moment. Awe at what just occurred. I wanted to pull her into my arms, thank her for this gift of release. Music without harm. But I caught myself and broke eye contact, rising from the bench.

"Shall we continue with the tour?"

Meryn took a deep breath. She then shook her head, as if she too were coming from some stupor. "Oh! Of course. Though there isn't a lot left to see. We can always—"

"Meryn."

Our attention was drawn to the source of the stern voice. A fair-haired woman in a deep azure dress stood, glowering, in the doorway.

Color seeped from Meryn's features. "Anaat! I didn't realize you were at home today."

Anaat strolled into the room, light eyes dancing between the two of us. "Are you going to introduce me to our... *guest*?"

"Of course," said Meryn with a nervous smile as she glanced at me. "Anaat, this is Finn. Finn, this is my sister, Anaat."

I was the subject of scrutiny as Anaat stepped over to us, her eyes sweeping over me like I was a piece of algae-covered debris which had washed upon the shore and dirtied her slippers. She was intimidating for a woman, and I found myself wanting to hide.

"Where do you hail from, Finn?" she interrogated, eyes

burning into me.

I held her gaze as steadily as I could. "I don't know, I'm afraid. I have no memory."

Her brow arched. "No memory whatsoever?"

Nodding, I grasped my hands behind my back. Meryn stepped between me and her sister.

"He washed up on the beach. He's had an accident." Her chin raised in the air as she squared her shoulders.

Anaat stared at me. "He looks perfectly well."

Meryn marched up to her sister and pointed toward the door. "I need to have a word with you. In the hall. *Now.*"

"Fine by me," Anaat spat back.

Turning back to me, Meryn flashed a brief smile. "Excuse us for a moment, will you?"

I nodded, my anxiety rising. The two young women stormed off through the open door and promptly slammed it shut behind them. Muffled arguing ensued. Unsure of what to do, I sat on the piano bench, steepling my fingers under my chin.

Chapter Nine

Meryn

"Are you insane? Bringing a strange man into the house?"

Anaat paced the floor in front of me, gesturing wildly toward the music room door. She wore that same look so many times before. Every time I disappointed her in some way, shape, or form. Every time I broke the rules and got caught. I *hated* that look.

I tried to keep my voice low, but it came out speared in my anger. "What was I supposed to do? Leave him on the beach?"

"Someone else could've taken him in! Or we could've put him up in the barn at least!"

Narrowing my eyes, I seethed. "The barn? Seriously? He would've died! And it would make no sense to force someone else to spend precious resources when you know we've got it in droves. Anaat! Where's your sense of compassion?"

She pointed a finger in my face. "Do *not* preach to me about 'compassion,' Meryn. You know this is far more complicated than hospitality." She lowered her voice to a sharp whisper, glancing at the door. "He could be a criminal! Ready to murder us in our beds. Or worse!"

Crossing my arms, I looked at her dryly. "Or worse? Really?"

Anaat pursed her lips. "You have *no* sense of propriety, Meryn. You are clueless about the ways of men. Think of your reputation."

I laughed. "My reputation? I have no reputation. And I don't give a damn about it, quite frankly. Father doesn't either, or else he wouldn't have agreed to make me work the docks with that pig of a man."

"Mr. Aurin," she corrected primly.

"I don't care what his name is. All I know is I'm going to smell like fish guts and sweat starting tomorrow."

Anaat sighed. "Well, it's the punishment you will have to bear for your crimes. Perhaps you'll finally learn something this time. And as far as that—" she pointed once again to the music room door, "—goes, Father will not tolerate him for long."

She was right. I hated it, but she was. Father's generosity only went so far, even as rich as he was. The family's reputation was everything to him, with the exception of my upcoming punishment at the docks.

"Especially since Lord Trevion will be here the month after next."

My eyes snapped to hers. "What?"

"Yes, and you are expected to entertain him."

"Me? Why me?"

"You know why."

Her tone chilled me. Lord Trevion. Eligible bachelor. Another one of Father's schemes, no doubt. Not the first one, and probably not the last, unless he had his way. Father had been trying to marry me off for the last three years, ever since my eighteenth birthday. I was flaunted around like a show pony the moment I turned sixteen. The thought of doing it again made me sick.

I didn't want any of the suitors he deemed worthy. Each was just another preening, snobbish aristocrat who cared more about their fine carriages than walks on the beach. Most were old enough to be my grandfather, let alone a husband.

Lord Sebastian Trevion was introduced to me last year at a ball. Surprisingly young for my father's taste, he was no less prudish. Father dangled me in front of him like bait on a fishhook. A very *reluctant* bait.

I was made to wear a red dress with a much lower neckline than was comfortable. The tight-laced cinch around my waist nearly caused me to pass out. Throughout the night, I was constantly reassured by Anaat that I was the 'most beautiful creature in attendance', but I didn't want to be that sort of creature at all. That kind of beauty wasn't real. It was a kind of beauty that was cracked and curled around the edges, hiding the char beneath.

No, I had no interest in doing that again. We shared three dances that night. Trevion wanted more. I turned him down flat and hid the rest of the evening, much to the insult of his mother and father, who were equally invested in the potential match. Now, it would seem, all was forgiven and forgotten. A new scheme had taken its place.

Anaat stared at me, daring me to voice my opposition. She was my older sister, but had the authority of a mother. We didn't spend much time together, but she still seemed keen on running my life.

I sighed. "Will you at least be home this time?"

She nodded. "Of course. Someone must entertain his mother. Father and Viscount Trevion will be away on a hunting expedition, so it'll just be the two of them here."

"You mean, they're going off hunting without Lord Trevion? That's odd."

Anaat's brows raised knowingly. "It's arranged this way for a reason."

The reason being me. I should've known Father would try a desperate tactic. Clasping my hands together in front of me, I gritted my teeth. I wanted to march down to Father's office and make more demands. However, it had not gone so very well the last time.

"Is Father home?" I asked.

"No. He just left."

Once again, not bothering to say goodbye...

Anaat continued, interrupting my thoughts. "He won't be home until he has the Trevions with him."

Two months without his oppressive presence. Some of the tension left my shoulders. "I see."

"Now, about that man in there—"

"Finn. His name is Finn."

Anaat scoffed. "All right then. *Finn.* I hope you know it was a mistake to bring him here the way you did."

My eyes fell to my shoes. Logically, I could see the sense in what she was trying to say. But his haunting piano melodies still floated in my mind. The desperate way he grasped my hand on the beach, as if I were the only one in the entire world who could save him... Surely that wasn't happenstance?

"I don't think it was. And that's that. I won't apologize for it either." I found her gaze and softened a bit. "It's what Mother would've done."

Her hardened stare melted. We rarely talked about Mother. Gone for nine years, the memory of her demise was painful. But I was right. It was exactly what she would've done. I could see in her face Anaat knew it too.

At last, she nodded. "All right. I'll allow him to stay for a while, but he must be gone before Father returns with the Trevions, or we'll both be in the stocks."

My eyes widened. "Then... you won't tell Father?"

A half-smile spread across her cheeks. "He doesn't need to know about every single houseguest, now does he?"

With a happy cry, I threw my arms around her neck. "Thank you! Thank you! Thank you!"

She chuckled as she untangled me from her. "You act as if I've let you keep a stray dog."

I grinned proudly. "I've rescued a stray fish."

"Oh, please don't tell me you've been subjecting the poor man to your dreadful sense of humor."

"At least I have one, you old codger."

Anaat pinched my shoulder with a twinkle in her eye. "All right, then. I've got household matters to attend to."

Then her finger was pointed at my nose again. "Behave, Meryn. And I mean it. If you leave the house with him, bring a guard. I will not have you seen around town with a strange man, unchaperoned. Gods know we don't need another scandal."

She finally strolled away, leaving me feeling relieved. Well, almost. Tomorrow would be the start of my awful punishment for taking that blasted boat.

I looked at the music room door with a sigh. This would be the last day I wouldn't reek of fish around Finn. Perhaps he wouldn't end up sticking around very long after all.

When I re-entered the music room, I found Finn sitting on the piano bench, eyes fixated on the space in front of him. It took a moment for him to register my presence, and when he did, he leaped to his feet with a nervous smile.

"Forgive me, I was just... lost in thought."

I smiled. "That's all right."

His eyes continually flitted over my shoulder. "Is everything all right?"

"Yes, quite. Just had to have a little chat with Lady Anaat, but everything is settled."

That lovely smile of his broadened. "Good. Well, what should we do now?"

Shrugging, I strolled lazily over to the broad white shelves built into the wall. Several instruments sat propped up on custom displays. I wondered if I could trigger more of his memories with different music. Perhaps there was more to discover?

I caressed the curved edge of the rich brown violin before carefully removing it from its stand. Tucking it under my chin, I picked up the bow and caught his curious stare. I couldn't help but smile at his confusion.

When I drew the first long note, his pleasant demeanor became intent, focused once more. I played another note, a third, followed by a sweeping trill. As I continued to play, he stared at the instrument, completely transfixed. His throat bobbed as if something were caught in it. Curious at his reaction, I swayed. Subtly, his body followed suit.

I then did something I only ever did when I was alone: I began to dance around the room as I played. Twirling, swishing, leaping to and fro... Every time I looked, Finn was following me around, hypnotized by the melody. I rushed to one side of the room; he was quickly at my side. I was no longer smiling, but just as glued to his expression as he was to the violin. When I stopped moving, my breath hitched when his eyes suddenly jumped to mine.

The music ground to a halt. His stare burned into me. I clutched the violin to my chest, wanting to shrink away. His eyes were filled with fire, and I wondered if he wanted to strike me... or kiss me. Either notion scared me for very different reasons.

At last, he spoke. His voice was barely above a whisper. "Are you a siren?"

My brows rose to my hairline. "A what?"

After holding my gaze a few moments longer, he cracked a smile and shook his head. "Never mind."

As he stepped away, my tension loosened a bit. Still bewildered by everything that occurred, I chose the wiser course of action and returned the violin to its resting place. Out of the corner of my eye, I caught sight of Finn looking over the other instruments. Flutes, a harpsichord, our large cello in the corner... he was completely enamored.

"So, do you know how to use more of these..."

"Instruments."

His cheeks reddened. "Instruments."

I stood back with my arms crossed and sighed as I took in our sizable collection. "I play them all." Catching his wide eyes, I smiled. "It's the only indoor activity I enjoy, I suppose." My smile faded a bit. "That, and my father wanted to ensure I was very accomplished."

"It's a lovely thing to accomplish. You're very good at it."

His compliment was weighted with sincerity. Judging by his odd reactions to the music, I trusted his opinion. When I turned, I found his face alight with a smile, but pale. Concern flooded me.

"Finn, are you feeling all right?"

He rubbed the back of his neck. "Yes, just very tired, that's all."

Guilt lanced me. "I'm so sorry. We've been walking around all morning. I'm sure you need your rest."

"Maybe I should lie down for a little while." He winced. "I'm sorry."

"Sorry? Why should you be sorry? After your ordeal, it's no wonder you're exhausted! Here—" I looped my arm around his elbow and tugged him toward the door. "I'll take you back to your room."

Finn allowed me to lead him from the room without protest. I purposely kept our pace slow. He really did look worn to within an inch of his life. There were dark shadows under his eyes and a small limp in his step.

As we turned the last corridor, I was keenly aware of how it felt to have his strong arm connected with mine.

Chapter Ten

Fivrial

Her arm was warm. I was surprised when she slipped it around mine. And yet, it felt so... natural. As if it belonged there all along. As we strolled through the halls, I relished in the feel of it. I only hoped that perhaps part of her felt the same.

Patience, Fiv.

The moment we reached my bedroom, I realized how tired I was. Just the thought of lying down and closing my eyes was enough to make my lids heavy. Still, I chided myself for being weak.

Meryn released my arm, much to my disappointment. "All right, I'll leave you to rest now, but should you need anything, pull the cord on the wall and a servant will be up to attend to you. And feel free to wander around if you get bored. Oh! And if you get hungry—"

"Meryn."

"Yes?"

"Thank you."

She melted into an embarrassed smile. "You're most welcome."

Crossing my arms, I leaned against the doorframe and peered at her. "And what if I should need you?"

Her smile faded. "Me? Why? Why would you need me?"

I shrugged. "You're the hostess, are you not?"

Twisting her fingers nervously, Meryn averted her gaze to the floor. She was squirming, and I found myself strangely amused.

"I, um, I need some fresh air, I think. So, I'll be... out." Her eyes leaped back to mine with a too-bright smile. "Pleasant dreams, Finn."

With that, she turned on her heel and quickly retreated. I watched her with a grin until she turned a corner and disappeared.

Retreating into my room, I found that I welcomed the soft bed. It was such an odd thing—to feel such a heavy pull on one's body. It was exhausting just to walk from one point to the other. Crawling beneath the warm materials was paradise.

As I lay there, however, sleep only came fleetingly. My mind was still swirling with the phantom music notes. Visions of Meryn dancing gracefully through the room still enchanted me. I don't know what came over me, or how it happened, but I felt as if I'd lost control.

From the moment that first sweet note was drawn over the smaller instrument, I was a captive. I craved it more than fresh, clear water. I craved *her*. The melody and Meryn intertwined into something so strong, so intoxicating, it was almost... seductive. It seeped into my bones and I found myself moving not of my volition.

Powerful magic. It must've been. But how? How could a human possess such a thing? She was lovely, to be sure. Different, perhaps. But magical? Whether she knew it or not, in those moments, she had me spellbound. There was no fear, unlike with Wrenna's spells. There was only exhilaration and a sense of longing...

I shuddered. The only time I felt such powerful feelings

was on the night of the full moon when my songs burst forth, and I thought of her. When I felt the pull. *Could it be that all this time, somehow, someway, it was her calling to me?* I'd never heard of a human siren. All I knew was that I was drawn to her like a riptide, and I had no desire to escape it.

I didn't see Meryn the rest of the day, to my disappointment. Granted, I slept through the afternoon and the early evening. Aches permeated my muscles, and I felt as if I hadn't rested in weeks. Those blasted legs looked strong, but that was part of the illusion. Wrenna did excellent work. I was grateful. But unnatural limbs could not quite behave as *naturally* as I expected.

Several times throughout the day, I woke up in a panic when I couldn't sense my fins. My sore legs would flail against the mattress in a panic. I only breathed a sigh of relief when I finally recalled I now had feet. It did not help that they continued to cramp now and then.

The next day, I woke up to raindrops tapping on the window. Rested, at last, I rose and looked out over the sea. Dark, roiling clouds were gathering in the distance, competing with the blanket of gray already stretched overhead. Days like those were typically spent far below the surface, away from the large choppy waves above.

It was only a few days prior that weather like that had almost claimed Meryn to the depths. Memories of the chanting on the breeze came floating back. My mood darkened like the sky. I had to get to the bottom of this somehow.

Meryn was curiously absent. I walked the halls and then walked them again, searching for her. When I couldn't find her, I started to wonder if I'd offended her the day before. Perhaps she was hiding from me? I kicked myself. Somehow, I'd have to find a way to control my instincts. It wouldn't do to scare her off when I'd scarcely begun to get to know her.

At some point, I wandered into the music room again. I

was hesitant to do so, but one look at the piano had my fingers flexing at my side. It too called to me.

After ensuring that the room was indeed vacant, I crept in and sat on the bench. The white keys were pristine and seemed to wait for me. I loved the cool feel of them beneath my fingertips. When I pressed down on a note, it sang through me. My eyes slid shut, and I breathed deeply. A dark, soulful tune slipped out, matching the dreariness of the day. It wasn't the same fevered rush as the previous day, but it consumed me, nonetheless.

I was so caught up in the melody that I failed to notice the music room door opening. It wasn't until I finally finished the tune and caught a figure out of the corner of my eye that I was aware I was being watched. My attention leaped to the doorway. The intruder gasped and ran off.

"Wait!"

Abandoning the piano, I hurried from the room in time to see a man rapidly retreating down the hall. Guilt twisted me. Judging by the pace, he was either frightened or angry.

"Wait!" I called again, taking off down the hall after him.

He slowed to a stop and cursed, burying his face in his palm. As I got closer, I saw he was soaked to the bone, with deep red stains on his blue shirt and light brown pants. At once, I was alarmed.

"Are you hurt?"

Then it hit me: the smell. I would know it anywhere. *Fish.*

"No, I'm all right."

My eyes widened. Auburn curls clung to the nape of a slender neck from underneath a cap. This was no man.

"Meryn?"

She turned to me with a smile and tears in her eyes. "Hi, Finn."

I gaped at her. "What happened?"

Wiping her eyes with soiled hands, she couldn't meet my gaze. "It's complicated." Continuously, she looked down the hall, angling her body away from me.

"Are you sure you're not injured? You appear to be... bloody."

She looked down at her shirt with reddening cheeks. "It's not mine. Well, mostly not, I believe." Cursing again, she took several steps back. "Let me get cleaned up, and I'll explain in a little while."

Before I could respond, she turned and fled down the hall, disappearing around the corner. I stared after her in shock. Not knowing what else to do, I returned to my room.

I waited for far too long, all the while anxiously worrying. *Is she hurt? In trouble?* I paced the floor, gripping my chin, running a hand through my hair.

At last, there was a knock on the door. I flew across the room and flung it open, startling Meryn. She was now clean and wearing a simple green dress that complimented her eyes. Her long braid was still wet. My eyes scanned her carefully, searching for any visible sign of injury. Long sleeves hid her arms, with lace cuffs hanging over her knuckles.

Without thinking, I grabbed her hands and inspected them. I found emerging blisters and a few small cuts on her fingers. My nose curled in distaste. Her wide-eyed gaze watched me examine her. My heart thumped wildly in my chest as questions continued to flood my mind.

"Meryn, what happened to you?"

"I was working." Gently, she extracted her hands from mine.

"Working?"

She nodded and motioned for me to follow her into the hall. We made our way over to a blonde-wood bench and sat. Her shoulders slouched forward as she launched into her tale of woe. "The other day I stole a boat."

Raising my brows, I thought back to that awful day. I thought it was strange that she was out without her escorts, but it hadn't occurred to me that it wasn't one of her boats.

"You did?"

With a groan, she buried her forehead in her palm. "I did. Mr. Aurin's boat. He angered me recently. And then Anaat made me really, *really* angry. I... had to get away. The boat was just sitting there, unattended. So... I just... took it. I'm not even sure why."

I waited patiently for her to continue. She glanced at

me, probably looking for some expression of horror. When she found me steadfast, she launched back into her story.

"Anyway, a storm blew up. The boat was wrecked. I almost died, but Father was much more concerned about Mr. Aurin's boat and our 'tainted reputation', of course. So, he agreed with Mr. Aurin that I should work for him at the docks—three days a week for the next month. Today was the first day." Tears flooded her eyes again. She laughed and wiped them away. "Sorry, you must think me terribly wicked now."

Grayler's trident flashed through my mind. If only she knew what I'd stolen from my own grandfather just to be with her, perhaps she would think me the wicked one. Perhaps freedom and love made wicked things of us all.

"Not at all. I am sorry for your situation." I resisted the urge to lay a hand on her shoulder and let her wipe those tears on my shirt. I'd dealt with flirty 'maids before, but never a crying one. It was imperative now that I use caution.

She rolled her eyes. "I have to go back to that chum bucket pig of a man the day after tomorrow. Do you know what I did today?"

I shook my head, afraid to answer.

A visible shudder ran through her. "I wound heavy ropes, and then I actually cleaned those damn chum buckets! He wanted them to 'shine'! Can you believe it? When he's just going to fill them up with a vile concoction the next day! Ugh. I spilled one. All over me." She pouted as her eyes slid to mine. "Sorry for the smell."

My lips twitched into a half-grin. "You don't have to apologize, I assure you. In any case, you smell just fine now."

Meryn slowly cracked a smile. "Thank you. I'm sure that's not entirely true, but thanks all the same."

By Scalae, I love it when she smiles…

I wanted to ask more about her day, but I didn't want to see the return of those tears. So, I clapped my hands together and smiled. "Well, it's a dreary day all around, I'd say. What can we do to make it better?"

She tapped her chin as her brows knitted. "Well, I suppose we could play music. Although…" Her face lit up like the sun and she hopped to her feet. "We'll paint!"

"Paint?"

No sooner had the word left my mouth than she grabbed my hand and yanked me to my feet. We took off down the hall at a clipped pace.

"Let's see if you're an artist, fish-man!" Her laugh echoed off the walls.

I couldn't help but beam back at her. The feel of her hand around mine made me feel lighter than I had since I'd been plucked from the sea. To see her joy returned was a relief that was hard to describe.

Chapter Eleven

Meryn

Giggling, I dragged him through the halls, up the winding servants' stairs, to the little room in the attic we'd designated as an art studio. Rain still tapped on the panes of the tiny window tucked up in the eaves. The lighting wasn't the best, but we lit lanterns and donned smocks, ready to make the best of it.

We promptly set two white canvases up on easels. Finn watched patiently as I prepared paints with powders and oils and pulled from my ready-made stash. He didn't complain when I jabbered on and on about my old art teacher and the dreadful paintings I'd made as a child.

"So, you painted dead things?"

I shrugged. "More like... *undead* things. Specters. Corpses come back from the grave. Things like that."

His brows were nearly reaching his hairline.

I smeared black paint onto a pallet, avoiding his stare.

"Perfectly scandalous, right?"

Finn laughed. "I wouldn't know. Perhaps."

The yellow came next. "At any rate, the teacher was horrified. I thought the old man's heart would give out when I proudly showed him my painting of a fanged sea creature with red eyes and tentacles. One of my best pieces, if you ask me."

"Tell me," Finn mused, leaning an elbow on the worktable behind him. "Have you ever seen such a creature?"

I should've known he'd ask. I paused, finally meeting his gaze. Trepidation filled me. "Well... not exactly. At least, I don't think I have."

His brows lowered. "What do you mean?"

Our eyes locked as images of a foregone dream danced across my mind. "I... dream of things... sometimes. Since I was a little girl."

He held my gaze, unflinching. "What sort of things?"

A lump formed in my throat. "Dark things. So vivid that at times I've wondered if they were dreams at all."

Finn didn't shy away at my confession. I hadn't spoken of the dreams in years. Only Mother had known, and she was long gone. Why I'd just told a strange man I'd only known a couple of days was beyond me. But "stranger" didn't quite fit his description anymore. I couldn't put my finger on why.

At last, I smiled and turned back to preparing the palettes. "Anyhow, it makes for good art subjects, I suppose. Even if they'll never be hung on the walls."

We took our seats before the prepped canvases, and I began the lesson, showing him how to hold his palette, and walking him through the brushes. Starting simple, I painted a daisy. Finn did his best to replicate.

"Did I do it right?" he asked, tilting his head with squinted eyes.

I peered at the yellow and brown blobs on the canvas. "Well... I think you'll get there. In any case, it's art. We'll just say that's your interpretation of a daisy."

Finn cocked an eyebrow. "I think you're being generous."

"I prefer 'gracious'."

His face was full of doubt. With a huff, he cleaned his brush and started again. "I'll keep trying."

We continued painting daisies all over the canvas until we ran out of room. Mine looked like a carpet of cheery flowers while his looked like... paint. Lots of paint.

Sighing, Finn rinsed his brush and set it in the cup. "I'm sorry I wasted your paint."

"Wasted? What? I think it's perfectly lovely!" I declared as I gathered the supplies to wash up.

He scrutinized his work. "Lovely to who? It doesn't even look like anything."

Pulling off my smock, I tossed it at his head with a laugh. "Lovely to me, silly!"

With a shy smile, he folded my smock before tugging his own off over his head. As he did so, part of his shirt came untucked, revealing a line of his toned torso.

I paused, staring at his abdomen long after he'd righted his shirt. Visions of him lying on the beach unclothed danced through my memory. My throat suddenly felt a bit like cotton. Tearing my eyes away, at last, I set the supplies down and tapped the counter with my finger.

"Is something wrong?" he asked.

Feeling unusually bold, I met his confused stare. "May I draw you?"

"Draw?"

Nodding, I abandoned the paint supplies and found a sketchbook and the box of charcoals. My hands were shaking. I pointed to the stool in the corner.

"Bring that to the center of the room and sit on it. The light is best there."

To his credit, Finn did so without question. After he sat down, I picked out a charcoal stick and pulled up a chair opposite him. I plopped down, readying myself to draw.

Something was off.

The light just wasn't doing justice to his thick, fiery hair or the way his eyes captured the light. I need to capture how his sharp, angular facial features framed those eyes perfectly. The gentle bump of his nose flowed to a graceful tip above full lips that lit up the room when he smiled.

Even if it was only a black and white sketch, I had to capture it somehow. Pursing my lips, I stared at him.

He looked confused. "What is it?"

I rose and set the book and charcoal on the chair before crossing the room. He sat patiently while I stood over him, studying closely. "The angle's wrong." Hesitantly, I reached out and hovered my hands over his cheeks. "May I reposition you?"

His cheeks colored a bit, but he nodded. "Whatever you need to do."

Gently, I rested my hands on his cheeks, his beard brushing against my palms. The contact sent an unexpected flood of warmth through me. I nearly let go but reminded myself to be professional. Slowly, I brought his face to look slightly toward his left shoulder. Quietly, I issued more instructions.

"Now, stay like this, hands folded in front of you, and keep your eyes on me."

Our gazes linked. Crystal pools of blue were staring back at me. For a moment, I couldn't move. I couldn't think. *What were we doing again?*

His voice was hushed. "Is this all right?"

I smiled softly. "Yes. Perfect."

My hands were still on his cheeks. Reluctantly, I forced myself to remove them and back away, only tearing my eyes from his to gather my book and charcoal.

I hardly felt the chair below me as my hand moved around the page. It was only a black and white drawing. It did not do justice to the brilliant hues that made up the man before me. I longed to bring color to those piercing blue eyes. Every time I looked up, his eyes were trained faithfully on mine again.

Could he sense my straying thoughts?

It took a lot of willpower to keep a stoic face. I was unaccustomed to spending time alone with a man, much less one like... him. There was no denying he was a beautiful subject. I wanted to draw and paint him from every angle.

Unaware of how much time had passed, but completely aware of the heat growing inside me from staring at him for so long at last, my hand left the page. I couldn't help but smile.

"Finished."

Finn relaxed at last. "How is it?"

"Come see for yourself."

He came and hovered over my shoulder, studying my work. I was vaguely aware of his radiating warmth. I tried desperately not to think about how he smelled like a fresh ocean breeze. My pulse quickened a bit as his warm breath caressed the skin of my neck. Briefly, my eyes slid shut as I tried to focus on the artwork and not on the warm shivers running through me.

"Well, what do you think?"

His fingertips gently caressed the edges of the paper as he stared in awe. A smile split his cheeks.

"I think it's amazing. I can't believe you can create things like this."

A sense of pride filled me as I sat a little taller. "Thank you." I dared to turn my head again and look at him. "I would say I had a good subject as well."

His gaze shifted to mine, and I thought I would melt right through the chair. We shared a wordless moment. If my pulse was fast before, it positively raced now. Beautiful, endless blue oceans stared back at me. If I wasn't careful, I would dive into them and drown.

Somehow, it all felt strangely familiar—as if we'd been in this position before. A strong tingling sensation shot through my head, and I blinked hard.

The intense moment was broken, and embarrassment flooded me, burning scarlet into my cheeks. I rose from the chair and returned to the worktable to resume clean up duties. I dipped my hands into the water barrel and scrubbed with a nail brush.

"Are you hungry, Finn?" I asked, trying to appear nonchalant and calm my rapid breathing.

He stood with his palms resting on the back of the chair. It took him a moment to answer over his shoulder. "A bit, yes."

Turning on my usual cheery demeanor, I grabbed a nearby towel to dry my arms. "Me, too. I think it's close enough to dinner time that we can have something sent to the dining room. Unless, of course, you'd rather eat in your room again..." I shifted uncomfortably, allowing myself to hope I knew the answer.

"I'd rather eat with you," he chuckled as he returned the stool to the corner.

Pulling my sleeves back down, I gathered up my sketchbook and practically skipped toward the door.

"Good! Because Anaat eats impossibly late at night, and I usually end up having a boring meal by myself. Unless, of course, Father's home, which he rarely is."

He laughed again and joined me as we made our way down the stairs.

"Well, I can't promise I won't be boring."

"Nonsense! You are *not* boring! Now, Anaat, *she's* boring. Don't tell her I told you that, of course. All she wants to talk about is 'society and gossip'," I explained, doing my best high-nosed impression of my sister. We exited into the hallway.

"And I suppose you'd rather talk specters and sea monsters?" he teased.

Whirling around with a grin, I walked backward a few steps. "Exactly!" My eyes swept over the expansive hall with a dreamy sigh. "This house is hundreds of years old. It's got its own share of ghosts, I suspect."

Finn craned his neck as he took in the ancient construction. "Have you ever seen any?"

I shrugged. "I've got a few stories."

"Well, I'd love to hear them."

He was genuinely smiling, brows raised in fascination. I laughed and looped my arm through his.

"Then I'll tell them to you... *over dinner*."

His bicep flexed against my forearm, sending a curious thrill chasing down my spine. Whatever life he led before he washed up on that beach, it was not one of slothfulness, that's for sure. What would it be like to be in those arms? To feel them wrapped around me as we...

I blinked hard and shoved such thoughts back into the recesses of my mind. After all, I barely knew him. My only task was to be a good hostess and see that he was recovered.

Although, there was nothing that said I couldn't enjoy

his company in the process...

We spent the rest of the evening chatting and laughing over dinner until our half-eaten food grew cold. He didn't mind my fantastical stories of spooks. I didn't mind his theories on the sea monsters I dreamed of. For someone with no memories of their life, he proved to be highly intelligent and an engaging listener.

Sunlight brought a warm, pleasant breeze the following day. It was far too beautiful to stay indoors, so we went for a walk along the pier. The salty air filled our lungs as we strolled among the busy stalls. Merchants called to us, trying desperately to hock their wares.

I pointed out all our smaller boats along the docks. Finally, we reached the end of the pier and watched The Endeavor, our enormous galleon, docked in the distance. It was a large, black beauty of a ship—the pride of Arcadia.

Though he nodded and smiled, Finn didn't seem to be as impressed with the ship as I would've hoped. I was expecting more admiration, but there was only polite amusement. I hid my disappointment and searched for something else to do as we strolled the boardwalk.

"Would you like to see the town?"

Finn followed my pointed finger toward the road that led past our estate into the village. I could see the weariness in his eyes.

"Perhaps another day. I'm afraid I'm starting to wear out a bit." He frowned. "I'm sorry."

I smiled, pinched with guilt. "No need to apologize. I'm probably pushing you too hard. We can head back and find something else to do that doesn't involve walking."

Finn offered a grateful smile. "Thank you. That sounds great."

We turned and strolled back in the other direction, nodding to Penton, who appeared relieved to turn back toward the castle at last. He was ahead of us now, keeping a quick stride. I was in no hurry, however. The last thing I wanted to do was wear Finn out so much that he had to crawl back into bed the rest of the day.

The space between us disappeared as we walked with our shoulders gently bumping. I caught his smile out of the corner of my eye. Perhaps he enjoyed it as much as I did. There were people everywhere on the pier and the docks. They nodded to us as we passed, perhaps curious at the new face out with the duke's daughter.

We were out for everyone to see. Still, I couldn't help the urge to slip my arm around his once more. And so... I did. It was perfectly acceptable for a gentleman to escort a lady out in public, of course.

Once again, I felt his arm briefly flex around mine like an embrace. I looked out across the water, pretending not to notice. The warmth his touch brought across my skin rivaled the summer sun.

I continually caught him studying me out of the corner of my eye. It was entirely amusing and nerve-racking at the same time. Just a quick look and I could've caught him in the act, but I pretended to be oblivious, though I couldn't wipe the silly smile from my face.

"Well, if it isn't Lady Chum Bucket!"

My skin crawled. Freezing in my tracks, I looked to the source of the crude cackling and found a young, dark-haired deckhand just stepping up from a small dinghy. I recognized him instantly. Peter Tungley, one of Mr. Aurin's employees. He'd harassed me the entire day previous, bringing me to tears as I completed my tasks.

I felt Finn's arm tense up as Peter strolled up to us with a grin, adjusting his black cap.

"And who have we here? Sir Seaweed?"

Narrowing my eyes, I resisted the urge to shove him. He was too close and smelled of sweat, rum, and dead fish. "His name is Finn. Now, go away."

Peter's brows raised. His smile was full of malice as he crossed the dock, though his eyes had a familiar drunken haze. I watched him stumble as he neared us. He had certainly been drinking. "I believe I was speaking to *him*, not you. Can he not talk?"

"I can speak and hear just fine," Finn responded, voice edged like a knife. "Now, if you'll excuse us, we'll be on our way." He started to walk on, removing his arm from my own and placing his broad hand firmly against the small of my back.

Peter's greasy hand grabbed roughly at my arm, wrenching me from Finn.

"I wasn't finished—"

I struggled to pull my arm free, turning in place to see Finn's eyes flash with a strange fire. Peter's hand instantly released my arm as Finn grabbed him by the shirt collar. In seconds, Finn had Peter pinned against one of the long wooden posts lining the dock. The sound of cracking wood filled the air as Peter's body made contact.

"You dare lay a hand on her?" he ground out through gritted teeth. His eyes seared into the wide-eyed deckhand, only inches away from the other man's face.

Peter started to stammer a reply, but Finn pulled him forward and shoved him back with even more force than before.

"Consider this your one and only warning, *sir*. If you ever lay a finger on her again, I will rip your throat out and feed you to the sharks. Is that understood?"

Terror seeped into Peter's features as his face turned a pale white. He nodded, raising his palms in surrender.

"All right! All right! It won't happen again."

After glowering a moment longer, Finn finally released him with a violent push. Shocked at what I'd just witnessed, I slowly took Finn's arm, pulling him toward the castle. Beneath my palm, I could feel the tension radiate from him.

"Come on, Finn. Let's head back now."

Taking steadying breaths, he nodded and rejoined me. His other hand enclosed mine as it rested on his arm. It was shaking.

Once we were far enough away that I was certain Finn would not turn back again, I slowed to a stop. Finn's breath was still coming in short, quick bursts as I pulled him around the side of a small storage house, away from prying eyes.

"Are you all right?"

Breathing deeply, he nodded. "Of course." My breath caught in my throat as he reached out and took my forearm between his large palms, as if inspecting it for signs of injury. "I should be asking the same of you."

"I'm all right." I tried my best to reassure him, but my nerves were unsettled, and my words tumbled out quick and high.

His eyes darted in the direction from which we'd come. "Who was that man?"

I wiped the sweat from my brow and grimaced. "Peter Tungley. He's a lowlife cad who works for Mr. Aurin."

Finn tensed up again. "You mean you have to be around him on your workdays?"

I nodded. "Unfortunately. Mr. Aurin and Tungley are the worst men on the docks. They spent all day yesterday making perverse remarks and tormenting me."

His brows lowered. His voice was low, full of unreleased fury. "And your father thinks it's acceptable to put his daughter in such a situation?"

"I..." Words evaded me. A lump formed in my throat. I simply shrugged, averting my gaze to the ground in shame.

Finn exhaled sharply. "Well, while I'm here, you're not going to be left to their mercy."

I laughed cynically. "Well, I'm afraid you have no say in the matter. Going against my father is akin to going against a god around here."

Embarrassment and fear washed over me. I knew that tomorrow I would pay for what Finn had done. I felt my arm drop from his, pushing past him toward the pier. My shoulders shook as the reality of the situation settled on me.

Within seconds, Finn's warm hand was on mine, pulling me back toward the side of the shack. I looked back to find his eyes trained on me.

"Your father is not a god, and for your safety, I would take on Scalae herself."

My eyes grew wide. "Finn..."

He shook his head. "You saved my life. I'll be damned if I leave you to the mercy of men who mistreat you."

His passion and dedication surprised me. But he was steadfast in his determination. His hand squeezed mine tighter. His thumb began to draw small, comforting circles across my skin. My heart lifted a little.

"I appreciate your enthusiasm, but I'm afraid there really is no way for me to get out of this."

Gaze holding mine, I could see the debate swirling behind his eyes. His thumb brushed the back of my hand again. When he spoke, it was with conviction.

"Then I will work with you. Side by side."

Chapter Twelve

Fivrial

When that filth dared to touch a lady—*my* lady—I could have killed him on the spot. The possibility that any man would be foolish enough to threaten her filled me with a fury I'd never experienced before.

Her hand in mine was soft and warm. Perhaps I'd cursed myself by speaking against Scalae, but it was the truth. *I'd take on the entire world for her and all the gods.*

"Finn, you don't have to do that. You need your rest."

"I'll be fine. I promise." It was probably a lie, but I wasn't about to let on how tired I was just from our walk.

She studied me for a moment. Her scrutinizing gaze drew me in. "Can I ask you something?"

I watched her lips move, wishing again to feel the sweet taste of her kiss in my mouth again. It took me a moment to realize she had asked me a question.

"What? Ask me a question? Yes, of course."

Brows lowered in thought, she stepped closer until we were toe-to-toe.

"Are you sure we haven't met before?"

My nerves were suddenly standing on end. *How could I lie to her?* Her amber eyes were locked on mine, and even the hint of untruth would probably betray itself. I never wanted to lie to her, but our time together was being built atop a large one.

The guilt twisted like a knife in my gut the more I thought about it. '*Hello, I'm really a merman who rescued and kissed you before eradicating your memory,*' didn't sound like a believable response. She'd think me mad and turn me out of her house.

"It feels as though we have, doesn't it?" A non-lie. It would have to do for now.

With a nod, her eyes slid down to our joined hands. "Yes, I suppose it does..." Slowly, she raised my hand and pressed a soft kiss on the back of my palm before breaking into a beaming grin. I thought my heart would leap right out of my chest.

"What's that for?"

She squeezed my hand once more before releasing it. My hand responded to the absence of her warmth immediately. My heart sank a little.

"It's a 'thank you'. For what you just did for me. No one... no one has ever stood up for me like that before."

She shrugged her shoulders, but I could see the painful truth behind her eyes. Anger rolled in me again that not even her family had protected her.

I opened my mouth to respond, but she had already turned to head back toward the open pier. It took me a moment of standing there, eyes glued to her retreating form, before I forced my feet to move.

Despite my fatigue, I caught up to her quickly, promptly taking her hand again and tucking her arm around mine. She made no objections. My heart soared, even as guilt sat once again in my gut.

She did not deserve to be deceived.

When we reached the castle, we spent the rest of the day making music together. It was draining and exhilarating at the same time. I found that if I played the piano while she played her violin concurrently, our music intertwined in a new sort of phenomenon.

The notes and melodies took me to another plane of existence altogether. The music flowed out of my fingertips and through the piano, infusing with music from her violin.

We were making love with melodies.

Perhaps she didn't experience it quite the same way, but I never wanted it to end. The euphoria it brought was otherworldly. I could feel... her. Her soul, her heart, flowed through me like a current. I could swim in it for eternity.

Meryn played every instrument in the music room with ease. I found I could easily pick up the wind instruments as I did the piano, but the violin and cello were a bit more challenging. The large golden harp was a dream to play. My fingers danced over the strings. The echoing notes were like something straight from the gods.

As I played the harp, Meryn vocalized harmonies. Her intuition was remarkable, following along with perfect pitch. I watched her closely. As we made our way into each melody, her eyes would close, only to open again focused on something unseen in the distance. Each note poured from her perfect pink lips.

She, too, was entranced by our harmonies. The sound of her voice stirred something within me I couldn't explain. I'd seen her from the water many, many times, but this new side of her was... magical. Even the most skilled siren couldn't compare to the woman before me.

By the time dinner rolled around again, it was late in the evening. We abandoned the music room at last and strolled down to the empty kitchen to see what we could pick from the day's leftovers. We found mostly cold meat, bread, and cheeses. I didn't complain. Being alone with her was far more agreeable to fetching a servant or dining with her sister.

After we ate, Meryn heated something called a "kettle" to make tea. I'd never had tea before. She assured me it was good for the digestion and relaxation. I decided to take her word on it.

As we sat at the thick wooden table in the old stone

kitchen, I watched her pour the tea in the warm glow of the lantern light. White porcelain cups with dainty, looped handles sat before us, now steaming with liquid the color of Meryn's eyes. She spooned white sand into them.

I wrinkled my nose in disgust, prompting a laugh from her.

"Do they not have sugar where you come from?"

"Apparently not..." I watched her stir the strange concoction as she assured me again it would taste good. It was certainly one of the strangest human customs I'd witnessed, but I kept my mouth closed in a smile.

At last, when everything was prepared, she grinned proudly and lifted her teacup in the air before bringing it to her lips and sipping. I followed suit.

A pool of sweet lava hit my tongue as a few small drops made their way down the wrong part of my throat. I had seen her work on the water and watched the steam release from the cup like warm waters from a lava stack, but I was unprepared for the sudden scorching of my mouth.

Out of instinct, I spewed the liquid back out, all over the table. Meryn leaped up, rushed to my side, and firmly patted my back as I coughed.

"Oh! Finn, I'm so sorry! I should've mentioned that you're supposed to take small sips! Are you all right?"

She snatched a towel and tucked it into my hands. I nodded my thanks and mopped up my dripping beard in embarrassment. Heat flushed across my face as I went to work on the mess spreading across the table.

"I'm sorry! I should've been more careful."

Meryn grabbed another towel and took over the cleaning, mouth wrenched to the side. "So much for introducing you to tea."

Our gazes snagged as she leaned close, wiping the front of my shirt again. All was quiet for a moment before we burst into laughter.

Meryn threw down the towels and sank back into her chair. Her face turned a crimson color as she giggled, each attempt to catch her breath making her begin anew. "What a proper pair we are!"

I gripped my side and tried to contain myself, but one

look at her had me laughing harder. She was nearly as red as her hair, and she snorted. It was the most perfectly endearing sound I had ever heard.

We didn't try tea again that night, but I vowed to look for more opportunities to make her laugh. Her joy was completely infectious. I had never enjoyed myself so much.

The next day, I stared at the ceiling as the rising sunlight filtered through the windows. I'd been so happy with her. Her music filled me even when it wasn't in my ears. Even when I'd acted strangely, or bumbled around like a fool, she was patient with me.

What am I doing? She is the sun... and I am just a fish in disguise. I closed my eyes, sighing deeply. *Pull yourself together, Fiv.*

I dragged myself from my thoughts and forced myself to get ready for our long day ahead. Meryn needed me, and I would be there for her. The idea of her working around those scoundrels alone made me ill and hot-tempered. I was ready to use my fists if one of them so much as looked at her disrespectfully.

When Meryn knocked on my bedroom door, I hardly recognized her. Dressed as a man, her beautiful hair was secured under a black cap. Her eyes were shadowed by the hat's brim. The womanly figure I had spent so many hours secretly admiring was hidden away under a dingy, billowing white shirt and loose-fitting, black fisher's overalls. The large boots she wore looked much too big for her small feet.

What was most uncharacteristic, however, was that her lips were drawn into a frown. No light shone in her eyes, and there was no laughter. I sighed and leaned my shoulder against the doorframe, peering down at her with pity.

"Meryn..."

"I'll be all right. But you don't have to do this, Finn. You can stay here and do whatever you like. I'm telling you."

Shaking my head, I stepped out of the room and shut the door behind me. "Nope. I'm coming with you, and that's that."

"Finn."

"*Meryn*. There is no force on earth that will convince me to leave you alone with those men. Not even you. Now, let's go."

She grabbed my hand as I pushed past her. Grinding to a halt, I looked back to see tears in her eyes. My brows knitted.

"What's wrong?"

With a quivering lip, she stared at me for a moment before doing something entirely unexpected: she threw her arms around my neck and buried her face in my shoulder. I stood there in shock for a moment before my arms were snaking around and pulling her into a full embrace. She melted into me as she sobbed.

We stood there, just letting time cease for a while. I could feel her sorrow pulsing through me as if it were my own. Her shaking limbs would not still regardless of how tightly I held her body close to mine. She felt so much smaller and vulnerable in my arms. *My fierce, beautiful, wild Meryn...*

My anger was stoked, somewhere down beneath the surface. Anger at her father for putting her in this position. Anger at the Aurin fellow and his sea-scum men who would torment an innocent woman. If I had my tail, it would've been blazing at that moment.

At last, she muttered into my shoulder. "Thank you."

Gently, my thumb caressed the base of the back of her neck as I squeezed her a little tighter. I wanted so badly to knock the cap off and feel her hair in between my fingers again, relishing in the thought of what it felt like when it was dry and soft. It smelled nice, even through the fabric—like wildflowers growing by the shore.

I dragged my thoughts back from the memories of the grotto. My voice struggled above a whisper. "You're welcome."

Meryn pulled back enough to look up at me, our arms still around each other. She smiled. "You need a hat, you know. You might get sunburned."

Shaking my head, I couldn't tear my eyes from hers. "I'll be all right."

Her smile slipped away. Dainty fingers gently twirled the back of my hair, sending rivers of heat coursing through me.

She brought her palm to my face, fingers dancing along my jawline, studying me. "I must've met you before. I don't know where or when, but I know you, Finn."

My heart was racing now. Could she feel it pounding against her own chest? The urge to confess threatened to overwhelm me. But it would make the spell all for naught. She was too precious to risk. Her opinion of me mattered more than my carnal satisfaction.

Still, I found my eyes flicking down to her lips again. I remembered the way she had returned my kiss in the grotto. The feel of her skin against mine. It would be so easy to pull her a little closer. I longed to taste her again.

Meryn's pupils were large and her breathing deep. I could feel her heart pounding more the longer we looked at each other. This wasn't my imagination, or merely my own longing. It was too soon for her to love me. Far too soon. But right then—at that moment—she wanted me. Her body was warm against mine, but that was nothing compared to the heat in her gaze. A warm pink color was flooding her cheeks, her lips... I found myself wanting to explore all parts of her, to see where else I might spread that delicate blush.

There was a gentle pull against the back of my neck as her other hand lingered against my jaw. Her chest pressed against mine as she lifted her chin. With a sigh, her eyes slid shut, and she pressed her soft lips to mine. *Finally...* the word spread across my mind.

Her hand bloomed into my hair, bringing pleasant tingles.

I returned the kiss tenderly. It was a struggle to restrain myself from devouring her the way I wanted to. I reminded myself that, for her, this was our first kiss. Still, it rivaled the lightning of our first kiss.

She tasted like nothing I'd ever experienced. She was all sweetness and fire wrapped up in a swirling eddy. The way we savored each other—lips kneading gently, her tongue teasing... it was pulling me down into the depths and I was quickly losing resolve.

A whimpering hum resonated deep within her throat as her hands began to move—running down my jawline, my shoulders, massaging my hair. The soft curve of her breasts pressed into my chest. Molten lava pumped through my blood. When she pressed me gently against the door to my room, something snapped within me.

Unable to stand it any longer, I reached up and whipped the cap from her head, releasing a cascade of curls. At long last, I laced my fingers through them again. This time they weren't damp and tangled from sea water, but soft and warm. I spun her around until it was her back now pinned against the hard wood of the door.

With tangling tongues and roaming hands, passion crashed down around us in that early morning light. Without breaking the kiss, I trailed the back of my fingers lightly down her arm. I nearly broke into pieces at the sound of her soft moan in my mouth. I loved every single inch of her, every plane, and every curve. I *needed* every single inch. I craved her like fresh water after a storm. With every soft noise she made, I knew the feeling was entirely mutual.

Just when my hand was running over the gentle slope of her breast, Meryn broke the kiss. Her hands left my hair, pressing firmly against my chest. As I stepped back, she stared up at me, panting. Fire danced in her eyes.

"We... we can't do this." She bit her lower lip and looked at mine. "Shouldn't... do this..." A deep sigh escaped her as she leaned her forehead on my chest. "I'm sorry, Finn."

I gently lifted her chin, and once again found her eyes filled with tears. "There's no need to be sorry." Catching the stream on her cheek with my thumb, I smiled. The words 'I love you' nearly leaped from my lips, but I caught them in time.

"I'm a terrible excuse for a lady, I'm afraid. I think I'm just a bit stressed and something just came over me. And..." She swallowed hard and averted her gaze before extracting herself from my arms. "It won't happen again. We'd better get going or we'll be late."

The sudden coldness was like a punch to the gut. She was already twisting her hair up and pulling on the cap. The air between us changed, and it was like all light had left the room.

I watched her walk away. My human body felt a new kind of heaviness. My thoughts were still spinning. Her warmth seeped away from me and it was like losing a piece of myself the further down the hallway she walked. This was going to be harder than I thought.

Patience, Fiv...

"Are you coming, Finn?"

I looked up to see her standing down the hall, flashing me her usual cheery grin, though her eyes were rimmed red. At least she didn't hate me. Yet. New terror filled me, rivaling the familiar guilt. I was playing a dangerous game. What would she do if she ever found out I'd taken her memories?

With a nod and a smile, I jogged to catch up. She didn't loop her arm through mine, but we walked close enough that I could feel that blessed warmth when her shoulder gently bumped against mine.

Chapter Thirteen

Meryn

I was glad to work at the docks again, even though I hated it. Mr. Aurin was worse than a barnacle, but I needed the air and distractions after this morning.

With Finn helping me, I was getting things done in half the time. Mr. Aurin nearly refused him, especially after hearing what he did to Peter, but I put my foot down and the deal was sealed. *No Finn, no Meryn.* And so, together, we mopped bloody decks, scrubbed buckets, and mended sails.

My mind kept drifting back to those heated moments with Finn. He was so strong... so hungry. I'd never kissed a man before. Not a real man. When I was young, I'd kissed a young aristocrat who came to our castle for a ball. His breath smelled of onions, but I was fifteen and entirely too curious to care.

Finn's kiss made that boy's look like a slobbery peck.

The boy hadn't made me weak in the knees or filled me with coursing fire. Even as I scrubbed bloody fish guts from a bucket, the fire still lingered.

I caught sight of Finn again, despite my best efforts not to look. His sleeves were rolled up to his shoulders as he hauled huge barrels across the dock. His sun-kissed skin glistened in the heat of the day. Those fiery locks of his were gathered back, but a couple of stray tendrils teased around his temples and down his neck.

He really did look like a gift from the gods. Perhaps it was wicked of me to think such things. Anaat always said my imagination was far too wild and needed taming. But now that I'd had a taste of him, the things I was imagining were not simply wicked. Images of his lean, muscular body pressed against mine raged beyond control.

Growling, I turned back to my task. *Fish guts...* Finn's lips... *blood...* Finn's hand in my hair... *sweat...* Finn's warmth when he was—

"You'd better pick up the pace! Another boat just pulled in and there's more to be cleaned."

I glowered up at Mr. Aurin as the older brawny man walked across the boat. His salt and pepper hair gathered at the nape of his neck, and the crazed thick brows furrowed over his dark, beady eyes. He was gaining in years, but was still a formidable force, though a disgusting excuse for a man. The day he'd called me a 'ginger wench' and said he wanted to take me into his boat, bend me over, and "make it rock" was the day he lost any possibility of respect from me. Now he just seemed hellbent on tormenting me because I'd had the audacity to spurn him. A thought crossed my mind that perhaps other women had not been so lucky as to be allowed to spurn his advances. My stomach heaved. I wondered how many women he had forced himself upon.

"I thought you said this was the last one?"

He narrowed his eyes. "I said no such thing. You need to clean the wax out of your ears."

I looked at the fishing boat that was just unloading their overflowing barrels of fish and my heart dropped. It was large and would take ages to scrub down. My hands and back already ached.

"What's the problem?"

Finn stepped up behind me, hands on his hips as he squinted in the sunlight. I pointed to the boat.

"More to do."

Mr. Aurin crossed his arms and a vulpine grin spread across his face. "What's the matter? Getting tired?"

Though not an entirely pleasant one, Finn flashed a smile. "Of course not."

Aurin's eyes sharpened. He'd been trying to wear Finn down all day, giving him the most brutal tasks. He had grown smug over the free labor but seemed keen on revenge for the loss of the opportunity to hound me with inappropriate remarks.

Today he had kept his vulgar mouth closed, though the previous workday had been wrought with indiscreet comments on my figure. Terror filled me each time he got too close. Despite my father's assurances about my safety being a priority, he'd sent a young, inexperienced guard who was now sleeping in a chair on the dock.

I wanted to punch Aurin in his face. If it would not have doubled my punishment, I would have.

It was a hot, grueling day. By the time we finished, the sun was low in the sky. My skin was red and sore, even through my shirt. Finn fared better, but I could tell he was exhausted.

At last, we were heading down the nearly empty pier. I'd sent the guard back to the castle the moment we were released. The young man was red as a tomato and looked as if he would fall over at any moment. I tried to feel sorry for him, but part of me thought it might be an apt punishment for sleeping the day away. Finn reassured him he'd see me safely back home. I was grateful that the man finally agreed.

"I think I'll have a cold bath tonight," I confessed as I trudged along. "And Nola's muscle ointment. I'll have her send some for you, too. Smells bloody awful, but it works miracles."

Finn breathed deeply. "I could go for a refreshing swim right now."

A thought occurred to me, and I brightened. "You know what?" With a grin, I snatched his lunch pail and bundled it with mine before grabbing his hand. "Then you shall have one!"

He cocked an eyebrow. "Now? But it's sunset? And aren't you exhausted?"

I rolled my eyes at his excuses and dragged him down toward the end of the pier, where the stairs met the sand. "I'm not a stranger to evening swims, Mr. Finn Fishman!"

Laughing, he kept up my anxious pace. "Finn Fishman?"

I nodded. "I've decided that's your surname for now. Until we finally learn your real one, of course."

He grew quiet. When I looked back, he was staring across the water as we trudged across the sand. We slowed to a stop. I squeezed his hand.

"Is everything all right?"

His attention snapped back to me with a broad smile. "Hmm? Yes, fine." He returned the squeeze on my hand and butterflies fluttered in my stomach.

I tugged him along. "Come on. We've got a little bit of a walk."

"Where are we going?"

"There's a more private stretch of beach I like to go to," I confessed.

His brows flicked up. "Private?"

Color would've filled my cheeks had they not already been beet-red from the sun. Perhaps that came out wrong. I wasn't about to correct myself, though. So, I just smiled and pulled him along.

It was a hike through the sand, up a grassy hill, and down a stony incline, but we finally reached the beach as the horizon burst with beautiful colors. Pinks, reds, and golds kissed the rapidly retreating blue.

"I've been coming here since I was a little girl. Most people go to the stretch by the pier, but the water is calmer here, and in my opinion, clearer. You can see some beautiful fish if you swim toward those rocks over there..."

The sight of the familiar beach washed away the pains of the day. When we found a stopping point, I rushed to pull off my boots and socks. I groaned in relief to feel the sand between my toes after a long, hard day. I whipped off my cap and tossed it in the small pile, letting my flattened curls tumble down my back. My body was slick with sweat and fish guts. Just the thought of the cool seawater on my skin had me ripping the disgusting clothes off.

I looked back at Finn to see him frozen in place, eyes glued to my body. I looked down and realized I'd stripped down to my lacy, white chemise and thin, worn breeches without even thinking. My first instinct was to snatch my clothes and run off, but it was far too late for that. I straightened my shoulders and smiled with false confidence.

"Finn? Are you going to swim in your boots?"

His gaze snapped back up to mine. "What? Oh! No. Of course not." With an embarrassed smile, he pulled off his socks and boots. I turned my attention toward the sea, listening to the soft sounds of him undressing. A voice, which sounded very much like Anaat's, reminded me of how inappropriate this was. I could not bring myself to care.

The moment his movements ceased, I looked over to find him shirtless in his cropped day breeches. My eyes grew wide, and I averted them. I wasn't sure what I was expecting, but it wasn't... that.

I cleared my throat at the sight of his rigid body. He pushed the red locks from his face, and I thought my heart might literally stop. A familiar heat, which had nothing to do with the warmth from the sun, spread across me again.

Taking a deep breath, I reminded myself that it was a long day, we were hot, and we were there to cool off. At the moment, however, I felt anything but cool. I needed to get into the water. *Quickly.*

Flashing a bright grin, I looked Finn in the eye. "Race you!"

A mischievous twinkle sparked in his eye, but I was already laughing and taking off across the sand, into the surf. No sooner was the water up to my knees than I was swept off my feet and swung around. I clung to Finn's bare shoulders as he grinned and tossed me like a sack of potatoes. I screeched, hitting the water with a splash.

The cool water enclosed me like a soothing blanket, bringing with it instant joy and relief. When I found my feet again and stood, I ran my hands down the back of my wet tresses and laughed. Upon opening my eyes, I didn't see Finn.

"Finn?"

With my hand shielding my eyes from the glare, I searched the gentle surface of the water. No bubbles appeared. No currents or ripples floated by. Pursing my lips, I took a few steps deeper and called his name again.

Suddenly, something grabbed my ankles. I screamed, scrambling back toward shore. Seconds later, Finn popped out of the water, laughing.

Narrowing my eyes, I pushed hard, sending a huge splash right in his face. He sputtered and wiped his face. When his eyes locked onto mine and narrowed, I knew I was in trouble.

"Oh, no you don't!"

A volley of splashes came rushing at me. I turned my back as it hit me like a tidal wave.

"What's the matter, *Lady Meryn*? Can't take a little sea water?" he teased as I stood there, laughing. I wiped the water from my face.

I immediately retaliated with splashing of my own, working my way in his direction. When I reached him, I leaped up, grabbed his shoulders, and shoved him down under the water. He grabbed my legs behind my knees and quickly stood, flipping me backward. I hit the water with a screech.

We played in the water like children until the sun disappeared from the sky. Much too soon, the moon and stars took their place in the sky. The cool evening breeze soothed my sunburnt skin as we lay in the shallows like beached fish, letting the wakes wash over us. It was much the same way I'd found him on the beach, when I had the wicked thoughts of lying next to him, unclothed. I wasn't unclothed now, but much closer than I was that day.

Our hands were tucked behind our heads as we watched for shooting stars. I pointed out the constellations and other facts I'd learned from my governess growing up. Finn listened with fascination.

"It sounds like you had an excellent teacher. You know so much."

"Ms. Grady was cross half the time, but she was a good teacher, I suppose. Well, in a way. Father says she was terrible because I didn't grow up to be 'ladylike' enough." Sadness tugged at my heart. "Anaat says it's because Mother died too young."

I felt Finn's gaze on my cheek. I couldn't bear to meet it.

"What happened?" he asked quietly.

I pressed my lips into a line and swallowed hard before answering. "She went to visit relatives across the sea. Her ship wrecked. I was only twelve."

He watched me for a while. I stared up at the stars, biting back tears. Part of me wanted to snatch the words back—to keep that ugliness out of our perfect evening. But there it was. The words left me open and raw, like an old wound.

"I'm sorry, Meryn," he said at last.

Rolling my head to the side, I met his misty eyes. They nearly glowed in the waning moonlight. Like luminescent crystals, they were precious. And sad.

"What are you thinking?"

The corner of his lips twitched up in a sad smile. "How hard it must've been to lose someone so young."

I nodded. "It was one of the hardest things I've ever had to go through. She..." I hesitated. "She was the only one who understood me. She never questioned my paintings or my dancing." A small laugh bubbled up. "Though she might question me swimming at night, improperly dressed, with a half-naked man."

Finn laughed and buried his face in his hand. "Sorry, I guess I don't know what's considered 'appropriate' here."

I smiled. "That's why you're my friend, though. I like that about you."

His hand slipped down to his chin as the laughter died down. "Am I really your friend?"

Nodding, I sighed. "Yes, Finn. I daresay you are."

He beamed. "Well, then. I'm honored."

"I will admit though, you're also kind of my *only* friend."

"What? How come?"

I groaned. "All the women think I'm far too shocking,

and men only want to marry me for my title."

"I see... and I suppose you don't want to marry?"

Shrugging, I crossed my ankles and stared at the stars. "Someday. Just not to any of the dreadful suitors my father likes to throw at me." I paused, remembering the impending visit from the Trevions. "I suppose..." I chewed my lip in thought. "I suppose I just don't want to be *chained*. I want to be free to make my own choices, sail a boat, wear what I want. Anaat says I sound like a man. Or a witch."

Finn laughed. "A witch?"

I rolled over on my side and propped myself up on my elbow. "I know. *Perfectly wicked*, right?"

He rolled to face me with a smile. "I don't know. If you were a witch, I don't think you'd be a wicked one."

Now my interest was piqued. "Do you think there is such a thing as a good witch? Someone with magical powers and a wild nature, but they only use it for good?"

He nodded. "I believe that anything is possible. If there ever were such a thing as a good witch..." He paused, as if considering his words carefully. "Someone who was kind, generous, magical, and beautiful..."

My brows rose.

He smiled. "It could just as easily be you."

He leaned toward me again, leaning his weight on one arm above me. I watched his lips for a moment, remembering the feel of them against mine. The urge to kiss him again threatened to overwhelm me, but I fought to rein it back in. Trying to stabilize my rapid heart, I took a deep breath before continuing. "Why, thank you, Finn."

He reached out and brushed the sand off my cheek with his thumb. "You're most welcome."

We talked for far too long. The moon was high in the sky before we realized we needed to return.

We dressed hastily, and I fought the urge to watch Finn's lithe body move across the moonlight. After successfully sneaking in, we grabbed a bite to eat in the kitchen before bidding each other goodnight at Finn's door.

I decided it was safe to give him a chaste kiss on the cheek before I left him for the night. When I did so, his eyes blazed, but he gave me only a polite smile in return.

"Goodnight, Finn."

"Goodnight, Meryn."

As I walked off down the hallway, I didn't hear his door close until I was disappearing up the stairwell.

Chapter Fourteen

Fivrial

The next two weeks were absolute bliss. Even the days on the docks were bearable, as long as I could break up the monotony with Meryn's laughter in my ears. We spent every waking moment together.

Too many of my days under the sea were spent alone, scavenging for human artifacts, hunting, or exploring caves. Renold was a good friend, but he didn't quite understand me. None of the merfolk did. A siren who hated to sing was unheard of. I was a gifted coward. The strange grandson of the great Grayler.

Mermaids still eyed me with flirtatious grins and flicking fins, but I was nothing more than a bit of fun for them. I was a hot-blooded male, and I'd be lying if I said I wasn't tempted to tangle tails with a few, but for the most part, I had little interest. Renold was right. I *was* chasing legs. *Meryn's.*

Every time I thought about them, my blood boiled hotter than the sun. I had to be careful. My body's reaction to such thoughts wasn't so easily hidden in my human form.

One day, I waited in the hallway for two hours, sitting on the bench, staring out the narrow window, tucked into an alcove between rooms. It was another cloudy, drizzling day. Meryn was supposed to teach me how to play something called "chess". It sounded confusing, but she was excited, so I couldn't say no. As more days passed, I found that saying "no" to anything Meryn wanted to do was difficult. I would do anything for her to smile and bat those long lashes of hers at me. And I had the feeling she knew it, too.

At last, a maid found me and informed me that Meryn was "indisposed for the day". I received no further explanation. *Had I done something wrong? Was she ill?*

With no Meryn, I anxiously wandered the hallways, trying to keep myself occupied. I strolled the music room, the library, and the art room in the attic. The day waned, and I walked every single room I could remember. With no Meryn, they just weren't the same. I scrounged up food in the kitchen, and sat for a while, keeping out of the cook's way, hoping perhaps Meryn might show up.

A young maid with a flirtatious grin offered me tea. I politely declined.

At last, the sun went down, and the house grew quiet. I paced around my room, pinching my chin in thought. Something was wrong. I could feel it. I should've found Anaat and just asked her how she was, but Anaat still scared me a bit.

Staring out over the dark sea, the reflection of my room cast as a ghost upon the pane in the lantern light, and I drew my courage.

There was only one place I'd yet to go.

Grabbing the lantern handle, I exited the room, shutting the door behind me as quietly as I could manage. Eyes darting up and down the hall, I found it deserted. *Perfect.*

Just a short jaunt away was the arched doorway to the tower stairwell. I crept up the stone steps quietly. Fear trickled over me. I expected every squeak to bring a raging Anaat upon me, ready to filet me for dinner. At the top was a small landing and a white wooden door with an iron doorknob. Warm, glowing light filtered through the cracks at the bottom.

Bracing myself, I raised my knuckles and rapped softly. I heard the rustling of bedclothes within, followed by a groan.

"Who is it?" asked an exhausted female.

My concern was multiplied. She didn't sound like herself. Something was definitely wrong.

"It's me... Finn."

Another groan and more shifting. I slowly turned the knob and pushed the door open a crack.

"Meryn, are you all right?"

She exhaled sharply. "I'll be fine."

Pursing my lips, I opened the door all the way and slipped into the dim room, shutting it softly behind me. When I turned around, I found her curled up in the bed under a colorful, heavy quilt with frayed edges. Her weary gaze peeped out of her cocoon. Dark circles shadowed the soft amber of her eyes, as if she hadn't slept a wink for days.

I quickly set my lantern on a tall piece of furniture before kneeling at her bedside. Brows drawn with worry, I reached out and smoothed the frizzy red tendrils from her forehead. Her eyes closed at the contact.

"What's wrong, Meryn?"

She shook her head. "I'm okay. You shouldn't be in here, Finn."

Arching a brow, I tilted my head. "You are *not* okay. Don't try to lie to me."

Meryn started to roll her eyes but ended up wincing in pain instead. Her arm moved under the quilt, and I could see that she was hugging her lower abdomen. I blanched.

"You're injured, aren't you? Here, let me see—"

I went to peel back the quilt, but she snatched it back over herself with fire in her eyes.

"Leave it alone!"

Taken aback, I raised my hands in surrender, but my frustration was growing. "Meryn, what in the hell is wrong with you?"

She immediately barrel-rolled, turning her back to me

and cocooning herself even further.

"It's none of your business, Finn."

"None of my—are you joking? I don't see you all day, and then I find you injured, and you won't even give me an explanation?"

Meryn growled. "I don't owe you an explanation. You're not my husband and you're most *certainly* not my father!"

Narrowing my eyes, I stood and snatched my lantern. "You know what? Fine. Just stay here and suffer then. I'm going to bed."

This side of her was leaving me with a sour taste in my mouth. It was a mistake to come to her room. Just when I thought I was getting to know her better, she had to go and—

"Finn?"

I whirled around and snapped, "What?"

She sat up in bed, the blanket slipping down from her shoulders, revealing the sleeveless, white nightgown. Pouting, she ran her hand over the back of her neck.

"I'm sorry. Don't go."

Part of me still wanted to storm down the stairs and let her stew in her foul mood. My own wasn't the best now. But she looked at me with those big, pitiful eyes, and I found myself setting the lantern down again and returning to her bedside with crossed arms.

"Are you going to explain to me what's going on? Because I'm not going to stay if you're going to be a crab."

Wrenching her mouth to the side, Meryn's gaze fell to her lap. "Well... see it's..." She groaned and buried her face in her hands. I caught mumbled words.

"I'm sorry?"

Again, mumbled words, a bit louder this time.

"Meryn." I placed my palms on the edge of the bed and stared at her. "You need to speak up."

She slapped her hands down in her lap in frustration and her gaze shot to the ceiling. "I'm on my monthly!"

I blinked at her. "Your... monthly? Monthly what?"

Her eyes found mine. "Finn. I'm *menstruating.*" Scarlet filled her cheeks as she grabbed the pillow behind her back and buried her face in it with a moan.

Confused, I hesitantly reached out and laid a hand on her back. "I'm afraid I don't know what... *that* is. But if it's something I can help with, please, let me know."

Suddenly, her shoulders shook with laughter. She sat back up and looked at me with an embarrassed smile. "I suppose you don't know much about women, do you?"

It was a bit of a barb, but she was right. I didn't. I was certainly more confused now than ever.

"I suppose I don't. But please enlighten me?"

Straightening her shoulders, she eyed me thoughtfully. "You really want to know?"

"Of course."

"You might not like what you hear. I'm warning you."

I shot her a dry look. "I hardly think you could shock me at this point, Meryn."

She shrugged and took a deep breath. "All right, then..." Biting her lip, she hugged the pillow to her chest. "You see, when a woman of child-bearing age isn't... *with child*... she bleeds. Once a month... for days on end."

"She bleeds? Is she injured?" My eyes swept over her concealed form, concern rising. A firm hand laid on my shoulder. I met her stare.

"Finn. No, she is not. We bleed from our womb... it comes out from in between our legs."

It took a moment for her words to register. She held my gaze, nodding in encouragement. My eyes grew wide.

"Oh! I see."

Meryn smiled and her hand slipped from my shoulder. "Yes."

Now, I was fascinated. "So, you bleed for days, and you do not die?"

A laugh burst out of her. "Finn, come on! Don't you think I'd be dead by now?"

I elbowed her with a wink. "I don't know—perhaps you're a specter? You rather look like one now..."

The pillow came flying at my face. I grabbed it and whacked her back as her laughter filled the air. The sound of it brought me back from my sour mood. *I missed her so much today.*

"So. You're not dying," I said, once my laughter died

down. "But you are in pain?"

Her shoulders slumped. "Yes. I'm sorry for not meeting you today. I've always had it harder than most, and the first day is always the worst for me. It feels like someone's driving a knife up my..." She caught my raised brows and blushed furiously. "Never mind."

I tried not to think of the strange visuals brought on by this conversation. Mermaids weren't exactly forthcoming with this information either, so I settled into the fact that I was entirely ignorant. I wasn't about to ask Meryn for an anatomy lesson amid all of this either, so I decided the best thing to do was offer support without further question.

"Well, do you need anything?" I knew damn well I couldn't get her anything to help. The pilaria blossoms were the only thing I could think of for pain, and I couldn't dive that far down in my human form, especially at night. Still, it seemed like the right thing to say.

She tapped her chin. "Well, Nola just brought up a hot water bladder and yarrow root, so I'm pretty set, I suppose. Of course, neither one of those help entirely." A long, whimpering sigh escaped her. "I'm just doomed to be a damn mess, I suppose. I could go for something sweet, though."

Her eyes grew bright, and she grasped my hand. "You know, Nola brought me a lovely slice of lemon cake earlier! Do you think you could go down to the kitchen and see if there's more? Oh, please?"

There was no way I could say no. With a grin, I rose and snatched my lantern again.

"I shall return soon, milady," I announced with an obnoxious bow I'd seen the servants use before exiting the room.

The trip down to the kitchen was a swift one. I located the cake on a stand atop the marble counter, underneath the glass cloche. After finding a blade, I sliced off a triangular hunk and plopped it on a cloth napkin. I was about to walk out of the kitchen when I whirled around and fetched a slice for myself. Eating together seemed to be a romantic activity, even if she was having her 'monthly'.

When I returned, I knocked softly before entering,

bundles of cake balanced in my splayed fingers as I grasped the lantern with my other hand. Meryn was still in a sitting position, a pillow stuffed behind her back. She was just opening her eyes again when I shut the door behind me. Instantly, she beamed as her eyes trained on the bundles.

"Oh, you're the best, Finn!" She clapped her hands together as I handed one to her, resting on the edge of her bed.

Quickly, she unwrapped it and held it near her nose, taking in a deep breath.

"Cook makes the best lemon cake in Arcadia. Nola always has her make some especially for me when I'm... well, you know."

"*Menstruating*. It's okay to say it, Meryn."

She eyed me thoughtfully. "So, you're not repulsed?"

I furrowed my brows. "No. Why should I be? It's natural, isn't it?"

"You know what, Finn Fishman?"

I took a large bite of the sweet, soft cake. "What?"

A smile split her cheeks. "I think you're possibly the best man I've ever met."

My heart swelled, and I wanted to kiss her. Instead, I simply smiled. She had no idea the compliment she'd just paid me. I wasn't sure I was worthy of it, but it warmed me, nonetheless.

When the cake was consumed, we spent a little while talking, but I could see Meryn was wearing down quickly. Her brows continually flinched in pain. I wanted nothing more than to take it away, but I was powerless to do so.

At last, I rose. "It's very late. I should be heading to bed now."

Meryn's face fell. "I wish you could stay."

I froze midway across the floor. "I will if you want me to," I offered quietly over my shoulder.

Thick silence filled the room. Then I heard the rustling of bedclothes.

"Then stay."

I slowly turned to find her lying on the far side of the bed, curled up with her back to me. Her bare arm rested atop the quilt, draped lazily over the curve of her hip. Her beautiful, messy hair splayed over the pillow behind her, beckoning me to come bury my face in it.

My heart was pounding. I knew I couldn't have her yet, but I wanted her. *Badly.* Flexing my fists at my sides, I debated.

"Finn?" Her voice was soft, my name from her lips almost a plea.

Exhaling slowly, I nodded. "All right. Just for a while, I suppose."

I quickly removed my shoes and crossed the cold floorboards to the bed. In debate, I stood at the edge, staring at her blanketed form, before I gently crawled onto the mattress and lay atop the quilt beside her. I tucked my hands behind my head to stare at the ceiling.

Meryn whimpered beside me. I looked over to find her hunched up in pain. My heart pinched at the sight. I felt helpless, watching her in agony. The only thing I could provide was comfort in the way I knew how.

I carefully rolled to my side and slipped my arm under hers, around the dip of her waist. Instantly, I warmed. Her hair lay under my cheek atop the pillow. I breathed it in, letting my eyes slide shut. Even through the blankets, I felt the curve of her body... her warmth... Only inches above where my arm was, the upward slope of her breasts started.

As if reading my mind, Meryn grabbed my hand and tugged me in even closer to her, folding the lower half of my arm upward across her upper body, in between those breasts. I thought I'd die of desire right then and there. She was turning me to flame. I fantasized pulling up the blankets and pressing myself closer to her, touching her bare skin...

Meryn's breathing deepened. But it was slower, steady. She was fast asleep.

With a sigh, I blinked away my heavy thoughts. Such thoughts would have to be reined in until another day. For now, my role was to watch over her.

"Goodnight, Meryn," I whispered into her hair, tucking her into me.

Goodnight, my love...

Chapter Fifteen

Meryn

That night in my room, something shifted between us. Finn was still my best friend, but I suddenly found it harder to use that label. Friend seemed too shallow, and brother repulsive. Yet, he wasn't my lover. He was just my... Finn.

Of course, I'd found him wildly attractive from the moment I met him. I wasn't blind. And that kiss we'd shared was still burned into my mind. I felt like mush every time I thought about it. But now there was something different that I couldn't put my finger on. I found myself wanting to be a bit more reserved around him.

In the mornings when we didn't have to work, I took the time to fix my hair nicer. I wore my nicer dresses.

At night, when I was alone, I pulled out the sketchbook I'd taken to hiding under my bed and flipped through the drawings. Almost all of them were of Finn. His face from every angle, his hands, his strength as he worked at the docks... I'd even drawn the both of us, lying on the sand that night when we looked at the stars. So many memories were piling up.

He'd been with me for close to a month, but it felt like longer. Every day with him, whether toiling under the hot sun or making music together, was a gift. I was growing physically stronger with the hard labor and found that I enjoyed completing tasks with him. Finn said my work ethic made him proud. If only he knew how much his compliments buoyed my spirits.

One morning, he wasn't waiting for me on the hall bench as usual. We'd fallen into the habit of eating breakfast together to start the day. The dock work was finally complete, and our mornings were finally free.

Filtering in from a distance, piano music filled the air. I knew exactly where he was.

When I reached the music room, I found it full of angry, swelling notes. Finn didn't even look up when I came in. His concentration homed in on his fingers pounding against the keys. Beads of sweat had formed on his brow. Cautiously, I approached the piano.

"Finn?"

No response.

I pulled up a chair and sat nearby, angled toward him. His black shirtsleeves were rolled up past his elbows and his collar unbuttoned. His strength poured out of him like pulsing waves as he rocked with the rhythm.

"Are you all right?"

His eyes briefly snapped to mine, and there was a strange wildness to them. I startled. Even the color looked altered. Before I could study them closer, they averted, and his lips pressed into a tight line.

"Fine."

It didn't sound like my Finn. His voice was rough, almost pained. Confusion and worry swept over me as I watched his furious fingers work. Still, I had the distinct feeling that to interrupt him now would be incredibly unwise. His obsessive playing was not to be trifled with.

The violin sat across the room. I rose and took three steps toward it before turning back and looking at Finn's flying fingers on the keys. There was no way I could keep up with him now. *And with the mood he's in...*

I didn't want to abandon him either. A thought floated to the surface. Hitching up my skirts, I fled the music room, down the hall, and up the stairs to the art room. I gathered up as many supplies as I could and began hauling them down to the music room. It took me multiple trips, but Finn didn't even notice. He was completely lost to me.

After getting things set up and donning my smock, I went to work making a preliminary sketch on the canvas. A man, hunched over a large piano, wavy hair hanging partially over his face. His expression was fierce, wild.

I soon uncapped my paints and quickly prepared the palette. The black of his shirt contrasted sharply with the fire of his hair and beard, caught in the golden morning light pouring in through the bay windows. I caught glimpses of the brilliant blue of his eyes, though he seemed keen on avoiding my gaze. Sunkissed skin stretched over the strained muscles on his long arms.

In a frantic attempt to capture the brilliance that sat before me, I blended the colors constantly. No matter how hard I tried, I could never do him true justice. When one painting was complete, I moved my setup to a different angle and started a new one.

I captured his long legs as they worked the pedals. His black trousers fitted tight over his muscular calves. His god-like profile peeked out from the curtain of hair that had fallen over his face. The slope of his nose, the fullness of his lips... I painted it in the greatest detail I could.

Canvas after canvas, followed by sketch after sketch... I never wanted to stop re-creating the beautiful man before me. Hours and hours, he went on playing—like a man gone mad. He never slowed, never hit a sour note. It was just a never-ending river of music pouring out of him. I wasn't even in the room as far as he was concerned. He hadn't spoken a single word beyond the solitary one that morning.

The afternoon sun was sliding low in the sky. Neither of us had taken a break, much less eaten. My fingers and wrists ached. Yawning, I set my sketchbook down on the shelf and stood to stretch.

Finn was still playing, just as voraciously as before. His back was heaving with strained breathing. Alarmed, I slowly approached him from behind.

"Finn?"

No response. When I got close enough, I stretched my hands toward his shoulders.

"Finn, I think you should stop so we can eat dinner—"

The moment my hands came in contact with his shoulders, he slammed his hands down on the piano keys with a growl and stood so fast I stumbled backward, tripping over my skirt and landing hard on the floor.

"Don't touch me, Meryn!" he shouted, voice serrated and raw. "Don't you dare touch me!"

Shocked, I crawled back until my back hit the corner. Tears leaped to my eyes.

"Finn, you're frightening me."

He braced his palms on the window and grimaced, as if in great pain. I wanted to leap up and help him, but heeded his words. A strained groan tore from his throat before he suddenly turned on his heel and fled the room.

"Finn!"

Despite my fear, I jumped to my feet and took off after him, calling his name. Once in the hall, I found it empty, but heard rapidly retreating footsteps pounding against the floorboards in an adjacent corridor. I followed them, only to find that hall empty, too. Again and again, I tried to track him, skirts hitched almost to my waist as my legs pumped as fast as they would go.

I chased him through the house until I couldn't hear the footsteps any longer. I found the back door through the kitchen standing wide open. Spooked servants pointed the way. Their eyes were full of confusion and fear.

Bursting into the humid air, I ran through the back garden and the open gate, sure I'd see him fleeing down the stairs, or over the grassy hill that led down toward the pier. But he was nowhere to be seen.

I made my way down the stairs and stood at the top of the hill, calling for him.

"Finn! Where are you?" I choked on a sob. "Come back!"

Sinking to my knees, I sat on my heels and buried my face in my hands as the tears unleashed themselves in uncontrollable torrents. Something was terribly, terribly wrong.

A hand laid on my shoulder and I gasped. When I looked up, however, I only found Anaat standing over me, catching her breath. My heart fell.

"What is going on, Meryn?" she barked.

With a quivering lip, I rose to my feet and attempted to wipe my eyes.

"It's Finn. He's run off."

Anaat crossed her arms. "Meryn. He's a grown man, not a pet. If he wants to leave, he's free to do so."

"You don't understand! Something's wrong with him! You should've seen him before he left. He wasn't acting like himself, he shouted at me, and h-he was in pain—"

"And none of that is your concern if he didn't want to make it so. Honestly, Meryn! Will you listen to yourself? He's our guest, not our prisoner."

My burning gaze snapped to hers. "This is his *home*, Anaat. He's as much a part of this household as you and me now. As much as the eaves themselves. I won't have you talk like he doesn't matter."

She scoffed, "He *doesn't* matter, Meryn."

My hand connected with her cheek so fast, even I was surprised. Still, I glowered at her with a squared jaw.

"He matters *to me*."

Her hand rested on her cheek as she gaped at me. She seethed between clenched teeth.

"Listen to me, Meryn, whatever infatuation you have with that man ends *now*. Father will be home with the Trevions in three weeks and your attentions will be needed elsewhere. Scalae help you if you fail at this!"

Trepidation crawled like spiders up my spine. "What do you mean, 'fail'?"

Her eyes darted around before boring into mine. "This is your last chance, Meryn. Father says that if Lord Trevion won't have you, then no one will. He'll..." She briefly pressed her lips into a tight line. "He'll send you away. To the priestesses."

It felt as if the ground had been ripped from under my feet. The convent—where I'd be devoted to the service of Scalae, forsaking all others, until the end of my days. No more family... and no Finn.

Too numb to cry, I slumped to the ground and stared off into the horizon. "He means to be rid of me one way or the other, doesn't he?"

Anaat sighed and tugged my upper arm. "It's not set in stone yet. You still have a chance with Trevion, of course. But you *must try*, Meryn. Promise me you'll try?"

Her pleading tone was shallow. Anaat never truly cared for me as deeply as she professed in times like these. At least, I never felt it. Still, it was useless arguing with her. So, I nodded and let her help me to my feet and back into the house.

Finn didn't come back, even after the sun went down and the full moon bathed everything in silvery light. For a long while, I paced my room in front of the windows, looking out across the landscape and the sea. I clasped my hands together, wringing my fingers until I thought they'd form blisters. When I couldn't settle, I threw on my dressing gown and retreated to the music room, where I sorted through the various paintings and sketches strewn about on shelves and surfaces. My heart nearly snapped in two with each one, tears smearing the paint in a few places.

My violin sat on the shelf, staring at me. I hadn't touched it today like I usually did. I still didn't feel like playing. It didn't hold the same magic when Finn wasn't there.

The piano was quiet, bathed in the moonlight. I stared at it for a long while before stepping over to it with a sigh. I ran my fingers over the polished edges before dipping them down onto the keys. A single note rang out softly.

Memories of Finn's music hung in the air. The painful memory of his anger lingered in my mind. He was out there somewhere, possibly hurt or lost. Just the thought brought a lump to my throat. *Would he be able to find his way home?*

I couldn't stand the idea.

Straightening my spine, I went to work opening all the

bay windows, letting the cool night breeze tousle the gauzy white curtains. Taking a seat at the piano, I drew a deep breath before I began to play.

Words drifted out as a song grew from somewhere deep inside of me. Part of me hoped and prayed that the music would carry out across the land and sea. I needed him to hear it, wherever he may be.

Come to me, my love
Come o'er raging sea
By land, o'er the mountain
Come, my love to me

My heart is full
Of tender longing
For the warmth of your hand
Your face I long to see

I'm sinking in the deep
Drowning in the sea
Encased by the waves
Come, my love to me

Do not delay, my love
Not a moment to spare
Come o'er the raging sea
Come, my love, so fair

I sang it over and over until I was sobbing over the piano keys. My eyes stung, and a pain grew across my temples. With a discordant slump, I rested my forearm on the piano and poured out my sorrows.

Chapter Sixteen

Fivrial

It was utter hell. All day. My head was so full of music, I thought it would burst. It hurt. The only thing that brought any kind of relief was throwing myself into the piano with abandon. Even that didn't stop the gradual pull of the melodic tide. Or the growing ache in my legs.

I sensed Meryn's presence throughout the day. She should not have been there to see me like that. Yet, she stayed. Some small part of me, under all the mess I was in, craved her gentle touch. It craved the soothing sounds of her violin. Craved her laugh, the sight of her lips curled up into a smile...

But the longing for her was buried deep beneath primal urges that demanded more. I'd never experienced a full moon day like it. While other sirens would be happily making plans to drain their victims that night, I was fighting the hunger right then and there. *The seduction.* All day I fought to ignore it, unable to do a damn thing about it until the sun went down, when I could transform and hide myself away in the deep.

The sound of her voice grated against my ears as she tried to ask me what was wrong. It clashed with the music and assaulted my ears, as if she were shouting. The carnal part of me wanted to feel her hands all over me—to throw her atop the piano and have my way with her.

I fought the urge all afternoon. Not simply because it would be improper to take her like an animal and in a public place, but lingering behind my desire to taste her again was the intoxicating need to capture her life force like a sweet elixir.

If I stopped, even for a moment, I would not be able to hold back from harming her. The last thing I ever wanted to do, even in that monstrous state, was to hurt her.

So I let my rage stay at the forefront of my mind. It was better to be angry than to succumb. I raged at what I was. I wanted to rip my own throat out. It was tight with the swelling melodies the lower as the sun dipped in the sky. *To be a siren was to be cursed.*

It was getting close to the time for me to leave. I could feel it in my bones. The overwhelming ache spread from the soles of my feet across my entire body. The skin on my legs burned with the scales forming just under the surface. Soon they would erupt, and my legs would lock together. I dreaded the thought, longing for the pain to be over.

I heard her voice again. This time, it came from behind me. My ears were keenly attuned to the sound. I sensed her drawing near, and it filled me with a nearly uncontrollable blaze. Her scent reached my nose, and it was intoxicating. I was close to losing control and giving in. She was in danger.

When her hands touched my shoulders, I snapped. I had to get away from them. From *her*. Like a small fish taunting a shark, she had no idea the gravity of what she'd done.

I shouted at her. I'd frightened her. *Good.* Let her be frightened. Better frightened and safe.

Looking out the window, I saw the sun was lower in the sky than I'd anticipated. Waves of pain rolled through me.

Music, pain, desire... it was time for me to get out of there. *Fast.*

Ignoring Meryn's pleas, I fled the house as fast as my pained legs would carry me. I had to get to the beach as soon as humanly possible. Faster and faster, I ran. People looked at me strangely. I shoved past a few on the more crowded shores.

When I finally reached the private beach where Meryn and I had swum under the stars, barely a sliver of the sun was visible over the horizon. I ripped free from my clothes, tossing them in a pile before charging across the sand. The moment I hit the water, the scales erupted from the skin on my legs. I cried in relief and pain.

My ankles drew together, and I tripped, plunging below the water's surface. I rapidly inhaled the cool water as I watched in horror at my legs snapping together. Excruciating pain erupted over me as the bones cracked and morphed. Scales burst from my skin and settled over me like a blanket. Fins shot out of the bottom. My tail instantly blazed.

The physical pain of the transformation finally ended, and I shot off through the water, trying to recall my bearings. Soon, I recognized boulders and corals. I had to steer clear of Brinn. *I must stay on the outskirts.* Too many questions were likely floating around.

It was a long detour to make it to the trench without being seen. I had to come in from the opposite end I usually did and swim the length of it. It felt like forever. By the time I finally located the cave, I was in overwhelming pain again. The moon was rising higher in the sky.

I nearly toppled over Wrenna as I shot toward the cave opening. She darted out of the way at the last moment. To her credit, she didn't attempt to stop or question me.

Once in the cave, the song burst from deep in my core. Like a rushing tidal wave, it crashed forth against the walls so hard I was sure they'd collapse. Water wavered all around me. Light and color shot out like lightning. Every muscle in my body tensed like stone. It was worse than the cramps I had when my legs were new.

It went on for ages. One long, never-ending torment of

release. I was a prisoner of my own nature. My body, my blood, was taking over.

Hours later, the pain finally subsided. Unable to handle the exhaustion, I slumped over and drifted to the bottom of the cave. The sand displaced in a puff as I hit the ground. My eyes could barely stay open.

In my daze, I saw Wrenna swimming toward me, arms outstretched. She scooped me up under my shoulders from behind and, with surprising strength, dragged me from the cave. Up, up, up toward the surface.

When my head broke into the air, the night sky was already fading into the pre-dawn light. With powerful flicks of her tail, we rushed through the water. Soon, I felt sand brushing against my arm. She released me on the shoreline.

As I lay there, exhausted and panting, Wrenna sat nearby, watching from the shallows. My eyes dragged to her stoic face.

"Thank you."

She shook her head. "Don't thank me yet. You won't be feeling too well when the sun rises."

I managed to laugh. "Can't be much worse than what I just went through."

"Are you sure you want to go on with this, Fivrial?"

"What do you mean?"

Wrenna sighed. "I mean, is she worth it?"

Thoughts of Meryn floated by. Her smiling face... the feel of her in my arms... anything and everything she was. I nodded, even as the pain was growing in my blue-green tail.

"Yes. She's worth it."

Her next question caught me off guard.

"And how does she feel about you?"

Pausing, I gazed down at the sand. *How does she feel about me?*

She'd kissed me, but then told me I was her friend. We were... close. But what did that mean?

Before I could respond, Wrenna issued a warning.

"Before high moonrise, two full moons from now, Fivrial. That's all you have. If you want a life with her, then you know what must happen."

A sick feeling washed over me. Just the thought of not

being successful was enough to send chills down my spine. I nodded.

"I know."

"And the words from her lips must be *true*."

"Wrenna, *I know*."

She eyed me across the water. "You're an interesting one. I'll give you that Fiv."

A smile tugged at my lips. "You're one to talk, *sorceress*."

For a moment, her gaze softened. A shadow of a grin looked like it would make its appearance, but then she looked at the sky. "We're out of time. I should be going." She shuddered. "I can't stand the surface."

The pain was growing. I could feel my bones creaking again and the scales shifting.

"Can you do me a favor?" My words came out strained.

"Depends on what it is."

I forced a deep breath and looked her in the eye. "Please tell Renold that I'm okay? He might be worried."

Probably the only one who's worried...

For a moment, she simply stared at me. Finally, she gave a terse nod.

"I will tell him if I see him."

"Thank you."

Wrenna nodded again. "Goodbye until the next moon, Fivrial. Scalae be with you."

With that, she disappeared below the surface, her fins briefly splashing upward.

Seconds later, the sun broke the horizon. My tail lit up in a glowing blaze and I cried out. My bones separated in a painful crack, scales sloughed away, revealing new skin stretched over new muscle. My fins retracted into fleshy feet. My body was simultaneously being ripped apart and put back together.

Finally, it was over. I lay panting, half in the cool water. I felt wholly relieved... and wholly exposed without my scales. With a groan, I dragged myself to my feet and trudged across the beach until I reached my clothes, still on the rock. It took some effort to dress myself, but the moment I did, I set off for the castle.

Guilt wrapped around me like a wet blanket. I'd been awful to Meryn. Probably frightened the life out of her. Then I'd just left her. It was not a side of me I was proud of. I only hoped that she would take me back.

It seemed like an eternity before I was finally stepping through the kitchen door. The kitchen staff all avoided my gaze. I'm sure I'd frightened the life out of them as well, barreling through there as I did. I passed polite smiles and ducked my head, feeling guilty for the sand I was tracking in.

Through the halls, up the flights of stairs. I, at last, reached the familiar, sunlit corridor with a sigh of relief. The thought of a soft bed was enough to make my eyelids heavier.

My relief was short-lived. There, curled up on the floor in front of my door, was Meryn. She was fast asleep in her nightclothes. *Perfectly scandalous*, as she would put it.

My heart leaped at the sight of her. Head resting on her folded arm, with her knees tucked into her chest, curls splayed across her bare shoulder... *my Meryn*. She'd waited for me, despite my wickedness. And here I was, coming home like a guilty minnow.

I crouched down and gently brushed the hair from her cheek. Her eyes opened slowly, blinking back sleep. When she looked up, those eyes widened and filled with rage.

My Meryn was not happy.

"You!"

I rose and took a step back as she uncurled herself and leaped to her feet, lips pursed in fury. She stormed over and shoved me in the chest as hard as she could. I flinched.

"Ow! Meryn, I—"

"Where were you, Finn?" she shouted. "Where in the blazing hell did you go? I've been worried sick!"

I opened my mouth to respond when she shoved me again, nearly knocking me to the ground. Then I made a mistake.

"Meryn, will you please calm down?"

If I thought she was angry before, I was sorely mistaken. Her face became a deep scarlet. Fire blazed in her eyes. She *smiled*. It wasn't a happy smile.

"Calm down? *Calm down?* I will *not* calm down, Finn! You act strangely all day yesterday, you shout at me, and then you disappear! How am I supposed to be 'calm' after all of that? I thought you thought more of me than that! I thought we were friends!"

I was growing frustrated. "We are!"

Her eyes grew glassy as she came at me again. I caught her by the wrists as she shouted in my face.

"Friends don't abandon each other, Finn! They don't do that! They don't..."

She stopped fighting me and broke down into sobs. Immediately, I pulled her into my arms and crushed her to me, despite our fiery tension. She clung to my shirt and melted into me.

"I thought I'd lost you. I was so scared something was wrong with you, and I couldn't help."

I tucked her head under my chin and sighed into her hair. "I'm sorry, Meryn. I'm here now. I'm right here."

She sniffled. "I know I have no claim over you Finn, but please, don't leave me like that again."

Little did she know just how much of a claim she did have on me. She had all of me and more. There we stood, in rays of early morning light pouring in through the window.

I was both exhausted and revived. If there were a way to confess all my sins and feelings to her—to make her understand—I would have done it at that moment. I knew I was hurting her by keeping secrets, but it would hurt her now to tell her the truth. Hurting her was akin to hurting myself.

"I'm sorry I've let you down. I..." I swallowed down the paralyzing guilt. "I wasn't myself yesterday."

I was completely myself...

Extracting herself from my arms, Meryn glanced up at me with a nod.

"I understand. Perhaps I've been selfish to not consider your... condition in all this."

I pressed my lips into a sad smile. "I guess I'm a bit more complicated than we thought."

Her gaze fell to the floor. "Perhaps."

It killed me to see the disappointment in her eyes. I'd

really mucked things up. But it was out of my power. The chances of her loving me had just gotten infinitesimally smaller.

Resigning myself to her need for space, I stepped toward my bedroom door.

"I'm going to lie down for a while if you'll excuse me."

"Pleasant dreams," she muttered over her shoulder.

Without further word, I stepped into my room and leaned against the back of the door. I wanted to dash back into that hallway and beg her forgiveness over and over. There was no point. I had no excuses to offer her.

I stripped down to my breeches and climbed into bed, relishing the soft comfort. One thing I had to hand to the humans was their sleeping arrangements. The feel of a thick, warm blanket draped over...

My door softly opened and clicked shut behind me. Light footsteps tread across the floor, and there was a depression on the bed. Just as I was turning to investigate, the blankets lifted and a slender, warm body pressed up behind mine.

Meryn slipped her arm under my own, around my chest. My cheeks blazed the instant I realized she was with me. *Everything* blazed. Without a word, my arm folded atop of hers, our fingers lacing together.

The feel of her curves and legs pressed up against me, only the thin clothing separating us, made it difficult to sleep. Her warm breath at the base of my neck was driving me wild. I wanted to roll over and take her—explore those curves in great detail. Still, I controlled myself with a shuddering breath and forced my eyes closed.

This woman is going to be the death of me.

Chapter Seventeen

Meryn

I don't know what I was thinking when I crept into his room. All I knew was that I needed to feel him a little longer. I needed to know that he was *there*. I needed to know he wouldn't fade away.

It was probably one of the most brazen things I'd ever done—slipping under the blankets with him. I wasn't even properly dressed. We'd seen each other in various stages of undress, but somehow, this felt different.

We were teetering on the edge of something. One push in either direction would send us crashing down like a waterfall. My thoughts whirled as my body melded to his. I closed my eyes. I relished in the feel of his bare skin against my arms and the exposed patch above the collar of my nightgown, and his strong arm as it enfolded mine over his firm chest.

We just... fit. Perfectly.

I imagined what it would be like to be in that position every night and every morning. *What it would be like if he were truly my Finn? What if he were mine, in every sense of the word?*

I listened to the rise and fall of his breathing. *If he were my husband, would I be happy? Could I tame my wildness just enough to devote myself to him and see that his needs were met? Would he meet my own?*

So many strange, new thoughts were swirling around in my mind. One thing was for certain, I wanted him to roll over and kiss me. I'd been so angry with him, but I'd also been afraid. More afraid than I'd ever been before. And now, here he was, cuddled up in my arms as if he would never leave.

Without thinking, I pressed a soft kiss at the base of his neck. I felt his breathing pause. His fingers flexed between mine. It was a curious reaction.

Slowly, I kissed him again. His skin was warm beneath my lips, the dampness of his hair brushing my cheek against the pillow. He released a deep breath and shifted slightly as his thumb brushed the top of mine. The action sent a flood of warmth surging through me.

I was just contemplating kissing him again when he released my hand and rolled over. Fire blazed in his eyes as they drilled into mine, nearly taking my breath away.

"What are you doing to me, Meryn?" he asked. His voice was a husky whisper.

I couldn't look away, no matter how much I wanted to. The way he was looking at me was so intense, I thought I'd melt right through the mattress. His hair was aflame in the morning light, contrasting with those piercing blue eyes that held me captive.

Propped up on his elbow, he drew his face close to mine as his fingers traced my jawline. His lips hovered close to my own, taunting me in circles as his warm breath caressed my skin.

"What is it you want?"

Heat shot through my core. I reached my hand up to grasp his, but he grabbed my wrist and pushed it down onto my bed next to my head, rolling me to my back. In a slow slide, he positioned himself on top of me, legs straddling my own.

With hands pinning my wrist, Finn's face was next to mine. The rough hairs of his beard touched my tender skin as he whispered in my ear.

"Tell me, Meryn. Why did you come to my bed this morning?" Each word sent warm shivers down my spine.

I half-heartedly wriggled below him, but I was a willing captive. My mouth was dry as cotton. His lips grazed my ear and nipped at the lobe. I swallowed hard.

"I... I... wanted t-to."

"Wanted to... what?"

His lips were then dragging on my neck. I arched into him with a gasp, pressing my chest into his. A hum of pleasure resonated from deep in his throat.

"Kiss..." His damn lips were on my neck again. "Kiss you." The confession leaped from my lips.

Finn pulled back to look me in the eye. Fire lit his heavy gaze. I felt it in his blazing warmth. My breath caught in my throat at an unfamiliar firmness pressing between us near my waist. I should've been shocked and embarrassed like a proper lady, but I wasn't.

"Would you like me to kiss you now, Meryn?"

I peered into his beautiful, endless eyes and nodded. "I would."

He lowered his lips to hover over mine. "Well then..."

My eyes slid shut as his lips softly connected with mine at last. I was expecting him to devour me, but it was a pillowy embrace. With heartbreaking gentleness, he continued to seek my lips.

Finn's hands slipped from my wrists upward to interlace our fingers. His body flattened out on top of mine, covering me with the full weight of his warmth. I relished the feeling.

Slowly, our kiss began to deepen. His tongue slipped into my mouth, teasing and dancing with mine. I welcomed it with a soft moan.

The sound seemed to spur him on. He released my hands. His warm hand gripped the back of my neck. The other hand began traveling the length of my body, hitching my knee up around his hip before running it up and down my thigh.

The first roll of his hips against mine brought out a whimpering moan. He pressed into the most sensitive area of my body. Even through my nightwear, it left me breathless. Again, he repeated the action, kissing me deeper.

My hands were tangled in his hair, sliding down his shoulders... running along his back... With every repeated motion of his hips, I felt myself growing hotter. I wanted to burst out of my skin. When his lips left mine and traveled down my throat, I sucked in air. My hips arched into him again.

His hand slipped under the top of my nightgown and gently palmed my breasts before tugging at the fabric. My fingers leaped to the buttons in the center. When the top of my nightgown was loosened, he wasted no time in pulling it down, exposing me to the open air.

There was no hesitation as he worshipped me with hungry lips, all the while rolling into me down below.

My moans grew louder. Finn's hand clamped over my mouth, but he didn't cease his sweet torment. His own groans were only muffled by his mouth against my skin. Motions between us were growing more urgent.

"Meryn..." he pleaded in a whispering moan.

"Mm-hmm..." I whimpered behind his hand.

His free hand dove between my legs, yanking up my nightgown. They found the waistband of my undergarments and crept downward. I was flaming with anticipation of what he was about to do to me.

Just when he was discovering me in a new way that stole my breath, there was a knock at the door.

We froze as our attention snapped toward it. Finn's hand quickly retracted, and he rolled off me. I sat up and quietly slipped from the bed before laying on the ground and crawling underneath.

Finn scrambled for his shirt.

"Just a moment!"

Heart pounding like thunder, I quickly redid my buttons and curled up in a fetal position. Anything to make myself less noticeable.

Finally, Finn answered the door, head poking out of the

crack.

"Oh, good morning, Bernard! How can I help you?" he greeted cheerfully, as if we hadn't just been doing... what we'd been doing.

"Good morning, sir. I was coming to ask you if you'd like breakfast sent up to your room."

Finn yawned. "No, but thank you. I'll be sleeping in today. I'll ring if I need anything, though."

"Very good, sir. Pleasant dreams."

The door was closed, and footsteps retreated beyond. Finn and I exhaled sharply. A moment later, he was on his knees, bending down to peer at me.

"Are you all right?" he asked, offering me his hand.

Cheeks aflame, I nodded with a brief smile. "Yes."

I accepted his hand and moved out from beneath the bed. When I was on my feet again, we stood there awkwardly. With my gaze trained on the floor, I searched for the right words to say. What was there to say after an experience like that? We'd come so close to...

Gentle fingers lifted my chin. Finn's eyes were soft with admiration. I couldn't help but blush even harder. His hand cupped my cheek.

"You are so beautiful in the morning light."

My smile broadened. "You've stolen the words from my lips, Finn Fishman."

Finn laughed as he drew me to him and slowly kissed those lips. Another kiss followed. He pulled me into his arms as we continued to seek each other. I wanted him. *Badly.* But a thought crossed my mind. I broke the kiss and leaned my forehead against his.

"I should probably go. Nola will be missing me. And if I'm caught in here..."

Finn grasped the back of my nightgown and took a deep breath. "I understand."

"And you need your sleep," I noted further, gently tapping the tip of his nose.

He half-laughed, half-whined. "You think I could sleep right now?"

I smirked. "I think you *need* to sleep right now. You look exhausted."

"Thanks."

"I'm serious, Finn. You need to sleep."

Nodding, his eyes drifted downward toward my chest before dragging back up again. The action sent fire through me. His gaze grew heavier.

"Can we perhaps pick up where we left off later?"

"How about..." I unfolded his arms from me and backed toward the door. "We *talk* about it later?"

Relenting at last, Finn ran his hands through his hair with a nod. "All right."

I reached for the doorknob, but he grabbed me by the other hand, yanking me to his chest. I thought for sure he would kiss me, but he only grinned playfully.

"Better let me check the hallway first."

I shoved him away with a laugh as Finn stuck his head out the door. When all was confirmed to be clear, he motioned for me to sneak past him. When I reached the stairwell doorway, I turned back and found him still watching out his door.

He raised his hand in a small wave. I waved back with a smile before disappearing up the stairs, feeling lighter than air.

When I reached the top of the stairs, my door was ajar. I paused on the landing. I didn't remember leaving it open. Steeling my nerves, I stepped into the room.

Nola stood near the window, a basket of clean laundry sitting on the floor nearby. She was staring out across the sea. When I stepped on a squeaky floorboard, she turned. A smile was on my face, expecting her usual cheery greeting. I found only a look of disappointment.

My stomach immediately twisted in knots. This would not be a pleasant conversation. I closed the door behind me, leaning my back against the ancient wood.

She sighed. "Have a seat, my dear."

I nodded and crossed the room to sit on the edge of the bed. Ever since childhood, this was the routine whenever I'd made a grave mistake. Father ranted and raved, Anaat scolded, Nola *talked*. It was Nola's disappointment I dreaded above all.

The old maid folded her hands in front of her and eyed

me sharply.

"You know you shouldn't, Meryn."

My eyes danced away. "Shouldn't what?"

"You know exactly what I mean."

Shrinking beneath her stern gaze, I stared at my dangling feet. "Nola, I'm a grown woman now. I think I can make my own decisions."

"And what of propriety? What of your reputation? Hmm? Have you considered that?" Her voice was not raised, but it scolded all the same.

I pursed my lips. "I think you know by now that I have no reputation to speak of, Nola."

"And I say that you do. You're not as lost as you think, Meryn."

Tears stung my eyes. "Father seems to think so."

"Well, I don't. And I daresay I know you a bit better than he does, now, don't I?"

Nodding, I wiped my eyes. "You do."

"Meryn, you know I love you as if you were my own. And I wouldn't be saying any of this if I didn't. But I want you to stop and consider what you are doing."

Frustrated, I rose to my feet and crossed my arms. "I know, Nola."

"And what of Finn? Do you know him?"

I whirled around. "Know him? Of course, I know him! He's my best friend!"

She calmly held my burning gaze. "He doesn't even know himself. How can you know him?"

"I... I... well, I know that he's kind and funny, a-and intelligent—"

"Is he married?"

Her challenge brought me to a screeching halt. My heart froze as I gaped at her.

"What?"

Nola crossed the room to stand before me. "Meryn, if he has no memory of his past, there's no telling if he has a family out there somewhere. While you're building a new life for him here, there may be people out there missing him terribly. You should be doing everything in your power to help him regain what he's lost."

Slowly, her words seeped in like thick, black tar. *A family. What if she was right? What if he does have a family? Is there a wife who loves him?*

My gut wrenched. *Could there be children out there waiting for their loving father to return?*

Nola was right. I was being inconsiderate. I'd almost made love to a man who was trusted to my care by Scalae herself.

He was vulnerable, the previous day being evidence of that above all. *How could I have done such a thing?* My reputation be damned, but his... no. His life *mattered*. Finn was everything good and sweet in the world. He deserved better. Certainly better than my behavior.

I sighed and slipped my arms around Nola's neck, nestling my cheek upon her soft shoulder. Like a grandmother, she wrapped her old arms around me without question. "I do feel lost, Nola," I confessed.

She stroked the back of my hair. "I know you do, dear. Love will do that to the best of us. But you're a good woman. And I trust you will make the right decisions in the right time."

I stood back and nodded. With a smile, Nola patted my shoulder.

"Now, how about I bring up a nice cup of tea for you before you head back to bed and get some rest?"

Though I smiled and agreed, my heart felt cracked. "All right."

The moment Nola left the room, I was fighting off tears again. I had to pull myself together. For Finn's benefit and for the difficult conversation I knew I had to have with him. But at that moment, all I wanted to do was fall apart. And so... I did.

Curling up on the bed, I mourned the beginnings of what had just begun to bud between us. The man in the bedroom below me still firmly held my heart—forbidden or not. Somehow, someway, I would have to rip out those roots until the day I knew for sure he was free to be loved. But for now, I cradled the memories we'd just made, tucking them into the recesses of my soul. I cried myself to sleep, knowing what was to come.

Chapter Eighteen

Fivrial

I lay awake for a long time after Meryn left. The shift of events left me breathless. Could it be? After only a month, could she be falling in love with me?

She didn't say it, of course. But I could *feel* something. The way she cuddled up to me and kissed the back of my neck was so... intimate.

The feel of her body against mine still lingered. Her softness, her warmth, her scent, the taste of her skin... It was all haunting me. When I rolled over and caught the heated look in her eyes, I knew she wanted the same thing I did. And I couldn't stop myself this time. *We* couldn't stop it. No more than someone could stop rushing water with splayed fingers.

I wanted to strike Bernard for interrupting. Had he not come to the door... We would've finally crossed that precious threshold.

I'd seen it once before, a couple on a beach where they thought no one could see. I didn't mean to spy, but it was the first glimpse I had of human love. The way they held each other afterward, they looked so... happy. Perhaps if things hadn't been cut short, Meryn and I would be cuddled up at that very moment, basking in the afterglow of our love.

I rolled to my side and rested my palm on the place where she'd been. *What would it be like to have her every morning? Would we wake up with the sun and make love under the golden light?*

She was ethereal. Her large amber eyes and hair the color of the sunset on a warm summer's evening. Her breasts fit perfectly in my hands, like they were made for them. I loved the gentle slope of her side as it bloomed into her hips...

I loved every single part of her. Even the parts I couldn't see. Her laugh echoed through me. Her voice brought me peace. Even the way she called me "Finn Fishman". Last night, I learned to love the way she shouted at me when she was angry. Even our music fused together perfectly.

It was clear, in all my pining and pain, I'd found my match. I hoped she was finally seeing it, too.

With a smile on my face, I drifted off to sleep, dreaming of our future.

When I finally rose, it was late afternoon. After ringing Bernard for a bath and a light meal, I wandered from my room to find Meryn. I checked our usual places first, only to find them void of her presence.

I was thinking perhaps she was still in bed when I heard a woman cursing loudly from behind the library door.

Debating, I stood before the green door, knuckles raising and lowering. It sounded like Meryn, but it could've been Anaat. We typically avoided her throughout the day, as she preferred to spend it out socializing with friends and shopping. The thought of being cornered by that woman unnerved me to no end.

I was constantly waiting for her to interrogate me and

throw me out of the house. Pushing aside my anxiety, I finally knocked on the door. An irritated voice responded.

"Come in!"

Definitely Meryn.

I slipped into the room with a smile, expecting her to instantly perk up at my presence. Instead, she glanced up at me from the large, dark-wood desk by the window and sighed.

"Hi, Finn."

Books were cluttered all over the surface of the desk. Thick ones, thin ones, some that looked as if they'd disintegrate at any moment. Large chunks were bare on the shelves that ran floor to ceiling around the perimeter of the room. The library was a giant mess.

Meryn was a mess herself. Her hair was bundled into an unkempt mass atop her head, with frizzy spirals poking out at every angle. She was wearing a wrinkled, dark gray dress with a stain under the collar. Dark circles sat under her eyes. I still thought she was the most beautiful thing I'd ever seen.

As I approached the desk, hands in my pockets, she didn't even look up. Her brows were drawn together in concentration as she pored over the volumes before her, a small pencil and sheet of paper poised at her right hand. I stood opposite, a smile on my face as I watched her.

"What are you doing?" I finally asked.

Frowning, she wrote something on the paper and scratched her scalp with her other hand.

"Studying."

My enthusiasm dimmed a bit. She didn't seem happy to see me. Something was off.

"Studying what?"

She rolled her eyes and slumped back in the chair as she rubbed the back of her neck. "Well, nothing if you keep interrupting me."

Her biting tone made her slightly less appealing. Perhaps she hadn't slept enough? Either way, I wasn't keen to be the target of her sour mood.

"Very well. I'll leave you alone. Sorry to have disturbed you." My own response came out a bit more edged than intended, but I turned and stalked toward the door.

Her groan reached my ears. "Finn, wait!"

I paused, my hand on the doorknob. "Yes?"

"I'm sorry. You can stay."

Turning, I found her massaging her temples. Pain etched her features.

My instincts tugged at me. I crossed the room to stand behind her. Gently, my hands found her shoulders and began kneading away the tension. Meryn exhaled, eyes sliding shut.

"Thank you. I've been at this damn desk all day."

I continued to work her muscles, pressing and dragging my thumbs into the exposed skin of her upper back and behind her shoulder blades. She wasn't the only one who was enjoying it.

"And why have you been at this 'damn desk' all day?"

Her head lolled back against the chair and she looked up at me.

"To help you, actually. Well, to try anyway."

My hands ceased. "Me? What do you mean?"

Meryn sat up, abandoning my hold on her. Her hand swept through the air over the massive pile of books before her.

"Memory loss, dreams, injuries to the head, sailor's mythology... anything I could think of that might possibly relate to your situation." She pressed her palms to her face and groaned. "But it's like a needle in a haystack. I keep trying to find anything useful. I've only got two pages of notes, and I'm not sure any of it is helpful."

I swallowed hard. She was throwing herself in a direction I hoped things would not go. The pressure of the lie lay in the back of my mind at all times, and it was something I fought furiously to bury. I had to find a way to redirect her.

"Meryn." I kneeled at her side, placing a gentle hand on her knee. "You don't have to do all of this."

Crossing her arms, she bit her bottom lip and stared across the room.

"I *should* be, though." A cynical laugh escaped her. "I've been parading around with violins and paints instead."

I gently caressed the outside of her knee. "I happen to

like your violins and paints."

Her eyes fell to my hand, and she froze. I could see her delicate throat bob as she swallowed hard. Her eyes met mine. They flashed with what looked like desire, but then she rose from the chair and quickly crossed the room.

Confused, I followed her. "Meryn?"

She scanned a shelf before grabbing a seemingly random book. I stood behind her as she flipped it open and began reading the contents.

"Hmm?"

She meant to ignore me, but I wasn't to be ignored. With a sly smirk, I closed the space between us and slipped my arms around her waist from behind. My lips pressed into the base of her neck in a slow, sensual kiss.

"Meryn..."

Straightening, she shrugged out of my arms and crossed the room again to stand in front of the desk.

"I'm trying to read, Finn."

I was not to be deterred. I pursued her, standing toe-to-toe.

"I think you're avoiding me," I challenged with a grin.

Her wide eyes snapped up to mine. "I-I'm not avoiding you! Don't be silly. I'm just busy—hey!"

I'd snatched the book from her hands and set it on the desk, pressing myself into her as I did. She flashed with irritation, but then caught my drilling stare and froze. My hands snaked around her waist and bottom and in one swift motion, I sat her up on the edge of the desk.

"I think you need a little break."

"I... don't..." Her words were wholly unconvincing as her eyes flicked to my lips.

My tactic was working. I watched her breath catch in her throat. She was pliant in my arms as I leaned into her. There was a brief pause before our lips crashed together.

Meryn's hands found my hair, and I growled at the sensation. I grasped her knees and parted them, yanking her into me. She gasped behind our kiss.

Just when my hands were running under her skirts, up her thighs, Meryn broke the kiss and shoved me away, nearly dropping to the floor as she grasped the edge of the desk.

"No!"

I regained my footing and stared at her with furrowed brows. "Meryn, what's wrong?"

Catching her breath, she clutched her chest. "We... can't." Briefly, her eyes danced to mine. They were full of guilt. "We can't, Finn."

"Why not?"

Her hands hugged her upper arms tightly as if trying to make herself small. The sight twisted my insides. My heart was pounding, but not from desire. Something was terribly wrong. I took a step toward her, but she shied away, staring at the floor.

"Meryn, I... Have I done something wrong?"

She shook her head. "No. I have." Biting her lip, she squeezed her eyes shut. "Finn, I think we should maybe stop doing... *what we were doing.*"

I froze. It felt as if cold water had been dumped over my head. The abrupt change in her demeanor left me grasping for solid ground.

"Why? Do you regret it?" My question was quiet, despite my growing anxiety.

Meryn was quiet for a long while. The clock on the wall ticked away, counting the moments we stood there. I waited for her to reply, holding on for dear life to the edge of a precipice. At last, she spoke.

"Finn, when I found you, I vowed to Scalae to *help* you. Whatever life you had before was stolen from you—someway, somehow. And we don't know what kind of life that was or who might've been in it. And I..." She shook her head with tears filling her eyes. "Have been a bloody awful excuse for a friend by taking advantage of that instead of helping you regain what's been lost."

"Meryn... is that what you think?" I crossed the room to reassure her in my arms, but she stopped me with a raised palm and a firm look.

"Finn, please listen. This is not easy for me to say, believe me. But you must listen."

My heart was already cracking. I could see the resolve in her eyes.

"All right. I'm listening," I replied numbly.

She straightened her shoulders. "You're my best friend, and that doesn't have to change. I like you. But that's all it can be right now. We have to slow down until we can figure out what happened to you."

The words were like daggers in my chest. All the progress I'd made with her crumbled away like sand in the wind. I stared at her across the room, resisting the urge to fall at her feet and beg her to reconsider. But it would do no good. Her heart was too pure for the likes of me and my lies.

At last, I nodded. "I understand. I..." the room suddenly felt too small. Too warm. "I won't touch you like that again. I'm sorry."

Before she could see the emotion trying to twist my features, I turned and stalked from the room. Guilt ravaged me as I made my way across each corridor. I did not make it to my room before the tears fell.

Chapter Nineteen

Meryn

After watching Finn leave the library, I was a mess. I knew I'd done the right thing, but it was more difficult than I'd anticipated. The look of hurt and betrayal on his face killed me.

The rest of the day was spent in the library, attempting to study, and staying far away from Finn. My concentration was just about nonexistent, but I forced myself to trudge through it. Anaat stopped in to check on me, and when I told her what I was doing, praised me for my efforts. It was rare that she did so, and it cheered me up a bit. Still, when the sun went down and it was time for bed, sleep came fleetingly, despite my exhaustion.

When I awoke the next morning, I was still dragging from the previous day, but it was with renewed determination. If Finn was depending on me, then I would not let him down.

After a refreshing bath and donning my favorite lilac dress, I marched downstairs. Distant piano music filtered through the halls. It was slow and somber. When I reached the music room, my heart fell. He looked so despondent, staring at the keys as he played. Not my usual Finn at all.

I took a deep breath and steeled my resolve before crossing the room to sit on the outer edge of the bench next to him. He barely glanced at me but did not object when my hands laid on the piano beside his and began to intertwine a melody with the upper registers. We'd never done this before, but it created a new song—a happier one.

Before long, I caught his smile out of the corner of my eye. My heart warmed. I bumped into Finn's shoulder, and he chuckled, not missing a note. When he bumped me back, however, my finger slipped and hit a sour one. I laughed and tried to find my place again, to no avail.

"All right, you're better than me." I grinned as I rose.

Finn continued to play, but his eyes followed me across the room. "What are you up to?"

I reached for my violin and bow. Without another word, I began to play a jaunty tune and dance around. Finn laughed and followed along. It felt good to see him jovial again.

When at last we concluded our little song, I returned the violin to its resting place and marched back to the piano. Finn looked up and stopped playing. He narrowed his eyes.

"I know that look. You're up to something."

I shrugged. "Perhaps."

"And?"

"And..." I stepped around the side of the piano and grabbed him by the elbow, hauling him to his feet. "We are going to town today."

His brows lowered. "Town? Why?"

I cast him a dry look. "Finn. You've been here for over a month, and I still haven't taken you into town. Aren't you getting bored?"

He shook his head. "Not really."

"Well, we're going regardless. I think it will do you good to have a change of scenery."

I looped my arm through his and tugged him toward the

door. Finn followed without gusto.

"Do we have to?"

I laughed. "Yes, we do! If we're ever going to jog your memory, you've got to see things, Finn. Obviously, we know that you're musically gifted. Artistically, not so much..."

"Oh, thanks."

"I don't mean it like that, silly. I'm just trying to lay out what we know about you so far."

"All right then." He side-eyed me as we walked down the hall.

I continued. "We know that you're a good swimmer and you're, well, *strong*. So, you probably had an occupation that kept you active."

As if on cue, Finn flexed his arm against mine and grinned. "Why, thank you."

Giggling, I extracted my arm and elbowed him. "Don't go getting a big head now!"

He knitted his brows. "Big head?"

"It means don't become a pompous ass."

Pretend horror stole his features. I nearly collapsed with laughter as he slapped his hands to his face. "Why, Lady Meryn!"

"Oh, come on. We both know I'm no lady."

I said it jokingly, but this time he didn't laugh with me.

"I wish you wouldn't disparage yourself like that, Meryn. That's not true."

His eyes were trained on me, but I stared ahead. He was being generous. A lady wouldn't have thrown herself at him the way I had. Still, I shook off my misgivings and grinned mischievously.

"Well, maybe I'd rather be a witch?"

His gentle hand slipped around mine as he looped my arm over his again, sending a flood of warmth.

"Who says you can't be both?"

I looked over to find him still staring at me. His eyes were as beautiful as ever and steadily held mine. I tried to keep things light between us, but it was hard. Perhaps it would always be this hard to be close to him, knowing he couldn't be mine.

"A lady witch? Interesting concept, I suppose."

Finn's lips tipped up into a half-smile. "Anything is possible."

I clung to those words as we found a guard. The morning light greeted us as we made our way out of the castle and through the gates toward town.

The walk was not a long one, and the day was cooler than it had been. The breeze swept through the streets, coming in from the sea. Of course, the air was never quite as fresh in town as it was on the beach. Smells from shops and other, less pleasant things always lingered.

The cobblestone streets were teeming with life that morning. People moved about the streets. Some townspeople shopped, while local fishermen hustled their wares. I was never terribly comfortable here. It just felt so... crowded.

With every step, I felt eyes on me. Those eyes weren't always kind. Anaat was the beloved daughter of Duke Blumley. I was wild and untamable Meryn. I was simply... *the other one.*

I noticed, however, that many more curious eyes rested on Finn. He was a new face, and I was on his arm. Surely the gossip wheels were already spinning. Not that I cared what anyone thought of me, but Finn was a different matter.

Discreetly, I slipped my arm from his and took a step to the side, widening the gap between us. Finn was so caught up in the sights around him, he didn't seem to notice. A bit of disappointment stung my heart. I was secretly hoping he'd scoop my hand up like usual. Still, we weren't here for that.

The first place we stopped was the hat shop. I wanted to get a new hat to wear on our beach walks. Though I was used to being outdoors, my fairer skin did not always appreciate the gesture. Finn never burned. I was supremely jealous.

As I perused the selection of wide-brimmed straw hats, Finn walked around the shop with a curious expression on his face. I kept my eye on him, waiting to see if anything clicked. I waited to see if there was anything he'd seen before. Part of me prayed it wouldn't be a woman's hat.

After wandering around, running his fingers over the

brims of a few selections, Finn made his way back to my side. I smiled and held up a broad straw hat with a purple ribbon and bow at its base.

"What do you think of this one?" I smiled.

He cocked an eyebrow. "I don't think it would look nice on me at all, if I'm honest."

Laughing, I jammed my elbow into his arm. "For me, you codfish!"

Finn grinned and swept the hat from my hands. He inspected it for a moment before carefully positioning it on my head. Taking a step back, he studied me, pinching his chin.

I blinked at him impatiently. "Well?"

A soft smile spread his cheeks. "Perfect."

Beaming, I straightened my shoulders. "Why, thank you. I think this one was my favorite."

"Indeed."

There was a weight to that word. The way he was staring at me, I knew what he meant. It still made my heart flutter. But I knew I had to be careful. He wasn't mine to have.

After removing the hat, I handed it off to a shop assistant and went back to browsing. This time, I pulled Finn over to the men's section. I searched through the selection of top hats, determined to find something for him.

"Really, Meryn. You don't have to get anything for me," he insisted. I ignored him and kept looking. "My head is just fine with nothing on it, and you shouldn't waste your silver."

"It's not a waste, Finn. You're getting a hat."

"I've never worn one before. I don't know why I should start now."

My hand stilled. I popped up and stared at him. "What did you say?"

He rolled his eyes. "I said I don't need a hat—"

"Not that. You said you've never worn one before."

Finn blanched. I came around the hat stand with a smile on my face.

"How would you know you've never worn a hat before, unless..." Grasping his hand, my smile widened even more. "Finn, I think perhaps you've just remembered something!"

"I... I-um, I don't know. Maybe I was just..." His throat

bobbed, a pained expression on his face. "I think I need some air, Meryn."

Before I could speak, he quickly turned and left the shop.

"Finn?" I hurried after him, instructing the guard to stay behind.

Outside, it took me a moment to locate him. He stood in a small, grassy area between buildings not far away, his hands hanging behind his neck. I rushed to his side.

"Finn, are you all right?"

He blew a lungful of air and nodded. "Yes, sorry. Just feeling a bit ill for a moment, I suppose."

"Ill?" My palm immediately went to his forehead. Cold and clammy. "Oh, I'm sorry. We can head back if you'd like?"

"No, no, it's all right." He smiled, somewhat unconvincingly. "You've got a day planned for us and I wouldn't want to spoil it."

I crossed my arms. "Finn, we can come to town any day. It's not an inconvenience to go home."

"No!" he shouted, startling me. Then a look of guilt passed over his features. He took note of a few passersby giving us strange looks and sighed. "I'm sorry. It's just that... I don't need to be coddled like a minnow."

My own irritation was rising. I crossed my arms and glared, keeping my voice low. "Well, I wasn't aware I was 'coddling you like a minnow', whatever the hell that means. I only want to make sure you're all right. Because that's what friends do, Finn."

He stared at me. "Yes. Friends."

The word 'friends' dripped from his lips like venom. I could see the pain in his eyes. Our carefree morning was a façade to the hurt beneath the surface. A lovely smear of yellow paint over a charred canvas. I wanted to leap into his arms and take it all away, but the potential inferno it could bring us both would leave us in ashes.

I could only nod. "All right, then. Let me finish up in the hat shop and we'll move on."

Finn's gaze fell to the ground. "I'll wait here."

I stood for a moment in silence, staring at the back of

his head, waiting for him to say something. When it was clear he was not going to turn around and offer more explanation to his sour mood, I trudged back to the shop.

After the hat shop, we attempted to lighten our moods again as we moved on to various other places to look at trinkets and clothing. Finn was most fascinated by the jewelers. With some convincing, the attendant allowed him to handle various items. He held them up to the light in awe, inspecting every cut and prism with complete fascination.

One such item was a ruby ring on a delicate gold band. He smiled as he held it out to me.

"I think you should try it on."

I glanced at the grinning jeweler, who nodded in encouragement.

Color rising in my cheeks, I laughed. "Oh, no, it's all right. It's a beautiful ring, but I—"

Finn took my left hand in his and gently slipped the ring on my middle finger. It wasn't the right finger for... *that*, but my face fell all the same.

A chill spread down my spine. Finn had picked it out expertly and slipped it on without a second thought. My stomach heaved as I realized... it was like he'd done it before. Had he once slipped such a ring on another woman's hand?

It fit perfectly, catching the light in a dazzling sparkle. My eyes widened as my heart sank.

"Oh, my..."

"It looks lovely on you, milady," declared the jeweler, a twinkle in his eye.

I shrugged, speechless.

"It compliments your hair," said Finn.

"Thank you, but I think we should be going." The faces of both Finn and the shopkeeper filled with shock at my words. I quickly returned the ring.

My shoulders shook as I walked swiftly out the door. The ding of the bell resounded in my ears as I tried to still my breathing. Every time Finn smiled, every time I let him get close, I forgot what we were really in town for. I forgot I was supposed to be helping him discover himself again. Eventually, he would remember. Eventually, he would leave.

A warm hand laid on my shoulder. I turned to find blue eyes staring back at me. The way the sunlight caught them, turning them more beautiful than any jewel, always took my breath away. I should have looked away, but I couldn't. Butterflies filled my stomach.

"Are you ready?" he asked, breaking the morose spell that had fallen upon me.

I blinked. "Oh, yes. Sorry."

I made no move to grab his arm this time. I had to stop forgetting.

He was not mine to keep.

Chapter Twenty

Fivrial

The ring was nearly identical to the one in my collection. I knew from the moment I saw it that it had to go on her finger. For a moment, I thought she would take it. I knew the human custom of rings and what it would mean.

I saw our future together as I slid the ring on her finger. I wanted that future more than anything and I would do anything to get it. Together, we were just... right. I could only hope that she felt it, too.

So why had she looked so scared?

At the end of the road, just before we turned on the path toward the castle gates, a graying woman with a frayed black wrap stood on the porch of an old house off to the left. Her steely blue eyes bore right into mine. A curious sensation washed over me, and I came to a halt.

"What is it?" asked Meryn.

I tore my eyes away from the old woman long enough to glance at Meryn. "Who is that?"

She leaned closer and whispered in my ear. "That's Mrs. Rigby. Used to be the town's apothecary and midwife. Also known to tell fortunes."

"A witch?"

Meryn laughed. "I suppose."

Just then, Mrs. Rigby crooked her finger and bid us to come over. For the first time since we left the shop, Meryn smiled. She tugged me eagerly toward the worn clapboard house. I did not share in her enthusiasm though, eyeing the woman warily.

"Meryn, are you sure this is a good idea?"

She bumped her elbow into my side. "Of course! She's perfectly harmless and serves lovely tea."

The thought of boiling tea wasn't exactly appealing, but I decided to trust Meryn's guidance and put on a smile. We came up the stone sidewalk with weeds poking through and stepped up onto the creaky covered porch.

Mrs. Rigby offered a brief smile before turning toward the open door. "Come in."

"I shall wait outside if that's all right," said the guard behind us. We turned to find him still standing midway across the yard, looking nervous.

Meryn frowned but nodded before turning back to Mrs. Rigby, who didn't seem to notice the guard's unease.

We followed her into the small front room of the house. My nose immediately filled with strange fragrances I couldn't describe. Dried plants hung from the beam that separated the front room from the small kitchen, near the rear of the house. To the right of us was a cozy, mismatched seating area. Several chairs had been arranged around a low table. In the center of the table sat a vase of red roses. I watched the dust dance across the sun's beams as Mrs. Rigby pushed open a set of lace curtains.

"You're looking well, Lady Meryn." Mrs. Rigby motioned toward the chairs as she stood in the soft glow of the window.

Meryn bobbed her head politely. "Thank you. You as well." She threw me a smile. "Mrs. Rigby, this is Finn."

The old woman's eyes rested on mine. She was studying me carefully, the corners of her eyes crinkling. "Yes, I see…" After a strange, arresting moment, Mrs. Rigby's cheeks twitched up in a smile. "Do have a seat and I'll make some tea." She stepped away into the kitchen and left us to seat ourselves.

I took the green armchair opposite the window and Meryn chose the sandy-colored rocking chair to my left. She slumped back into the chair and began to rock, sliding her eyes shut. She seemed to slip away, lost in thought.

Of course, Meryn would be at home in a strange place like this, I thought to myself. She showed no concern for the old woman's strange air or the guard's unrest.

I watched as Meryn rubbed the spot where the ring had been only a few minutes before. A sadness rested in her features.

After a short while, Mrs. Rigby entered the room with a tray of tea things. "Finn, be a dear and move those flowers?"

I hopped up and gently took the vase, relocating it to a small side-table across the room. When I took my seat again, Mrs. Rigby was pouring the tea. A small plate of tarts accompanied it, and we all settled. I took several cautious sips and miraculously drank without burning myself. Meryn beamed at me proudly.

"So," began Mrs. Rigby, her teacup clinking as she set it on the saucer, "tell me about yourself, Finn." Again, her eyes pierced mine from across the room.

I shifted uncomfortably in my chair. "Well, I suppose there isn't much to tell."

Meryn sat up in her seat. "You see, recently he—"

"I want to hear it from Finn, if that's all right, dear." Mrs. Rigby was gentle but firm in her words. Meryn nodded, retreating into her teacup.

My nerves wound as those steely eyes trained on mine again, awaiting a response. I wanted to join the guard outside. An interrogation was not something I was expecting. And that's exactly what this felt like.

"I washed up on the beach with no memory recently. Meryn found me. I've been living with her ever since."

There. Short and simple.

Mrs. Rigby continued to scrutinize me. "No memory, you say? Interesting…"

I nodded and sipped my tea, tearing my gaze away from hers. We sat and took tea wordlessly for another minute, with Mrs. Rigby watching me the entire time. Even Meryn looked uncomfortable. At last, Mrs. Rigby spoke.

"Lady Meryn, would you mind taking some of these tarts out to your guard and waiting there for a few minutes? I want to have a chat with Finn."

Meryn's brows drew together, but she nodded, gathering two tarts on a small plate. She looked at me as I inwardly begged her to stay. Our eyes met for a moment. Her words were hushed as she spoke. "Finn. She might be able to help you. Perhaps give us answers."

She said the word *us,* but in my gut, I knew it was her who needed answers. It was her questions that remained. It was only I who could give her the truth.

I nodded. Now my nerves were really standing on end. I wanted to beg Meryn to stay. I had the distinct impression that what was coming was no small matter. But she obediently stepped from the house, the door clicking shut behind her.

It was just me and Mrs. Rigby, alone in the small sitting room. Tension filled the air. I shifted uncomfortably in my seat.

At last, she spoke. "Why are you lying to her?"

My eyes snapped to hers, and I nearly dropped my teacup. "I'm sorry?"

Mrs. Rigby folded her hands in front of her. "You are not what you seem."

We stared at each other across the room as a clock ticked nearby. With every tick, I felt my future with Meryn slip away. My heart was trying desperately to free itself from my chest now. I considered running. *Maybe I could make some excuse?* The look in her eyes told me there was no hiding. I set my cup on the table and ran my hand over my beard.

"How do you know?" I asked with a sigh.

"I see the sea in you. You cannot erase the mark of your kind. Not completely."

Leaning forward, I braced my forehead on my palm as a wave of dizziness washed over me. I was wholly unprepared for this scenario. I was *exposed*. My life with Meryn seemed more precarious than ever.

As my thoughts were beginning to tailspin, Mrs. Rigby continued. "It's strong magic you've got on you. Care to tell me how this came about?"

I took a deep breath. "First, I need to know. Are you going to tell her?"

Mrs. Rigby shook her head. "I've no intention of divulging anything." I sighed in relief, but then she added, "Because it should come from you."

A pit formed in my stomach. The tea felt unsettled. I looked at her with watering eyes and my confession spilled forth. "I've loved Meryn for years. Protected her without her knowing. A sea sorceress offered to help me, and I accepted. I've got until the full moon after next. If Meryn doesn't tell me she loves me by then, I'll never have legs again and we'll be parted forever."

A small weight lifted off my shoulders. It was the first time I'd confessed my secret to anyone. I was astonished at how easily she'd drawn it from me.

"I see." Mrs. Rigby frowned. "Have you not considered the consequences of what you've done?"

"Yes, every full moon I—"

"Not that, you fool," she snapped. "The price of the magic!"

Grayler's trident flashed through my mind. I swallowed hard. My betrayal was easy to forget when I was with Meryn. I'd all but banished it from my thoughts.

"I know."

"I don't think you do. What you have on you is dark magic, siren. One cannot partake of such a thing without paying the price in the end. And believe me, the price is worse than a trinket," she admonished sharply.

I froze. "*Dark* magic? But the one who helped me is good—"

"Even a good witch can be seduced by darkness, Finn. There has been great deception. And now you and Meryn both are in danger."

Her dire warning rang through me like a clanging bell. I leaped to my feet, my heart pounding. "What have I done..." My gaze met Mrs. Rigby's stern stare. "What can I do? How do I protect her?"

"You must tell her the truth."

The blood drained from my head and once again I felt faint. "What?"

Mrs. Rigby tilted her head and peered at me. "Tell me, siren, how long do you think you can go on lying to her? How long until it becomes unbearable? Deception only opens you up for darkness. And love that is selfish is a heavy weight that will drown anyone. I'm telling you this because there are forces at play here that are far beyond what you see."

"Selfish? *Selfish?*" I glared at the old woman. "Perhaps I was hasty, but my love for her is not *selfish*. I gave up everything to be with her, to-to—"

"Someone is coming for that young woman and you are merely a pawn in their game," she retorted, making no move to rise from her seat.

Ceasing my rant, I stared. "What do you mean? Who is coming for her?"

Mrs. Rigby leaned forward and took her tea in hand once more. "I do not know. But you would do well to use caution and consider your actions. Love can blind us to many things. Don't let it distract you. Or her."

I ran my hands through my hair and flicked my eyes to the ceiling. The room began to shrink around me. "I will protect her. No matter what. But I'm not about to give up on her, either. I will not allow someone to threaten our love."

"Then take care that you do not meet your doom by way of your own folly, siren. A tragedy is imminent otherwise," she responded, sadness tingeing her words.

Through the window, I caught sight of Meryn chatting with the guard. She was smiling as the sun hit her face. So bright, so full of life... My heart felt like it was melting right out of my chest. Just the thought of something happening to her broke something inside of me.

"You may fetch her now," instructed Mrs. Rigby in a cheery tone, as if we hadn't just been discussing darkness and doom.

Numbly, I nodded and walked out the door. Meryn turned to me when I stepped off the porch. Her smile faded when she saw me.

"Is everything all right, Finn?"

I forced a smile and nodded. "Yes, fine. I think we've imposed on Mrs. Rigby enough, though."

Drawing her brows together, Meryn nodded, fiddling with the now-empty plate in her hands. "I suppose so. I'll return this to her, and we'll be on our way then." She stepped past me into the house. I wanted to grab her and pull her away, to forbid her from stepping foot in it again, but I merely joined the guard and waited patiently.

"Old woman gives me the willies," grumbled the guard as he looked off into the sunset.

I stared at the ground. "I suppose so."

"Are you all right, then?"

Crossing my arms against the sudden chill, I nodded. "Yes."

He laughed. "You look as if you've seen a ghost."

I regarded him somberly just as Meryn reappeared. She seemed to be filled with hope, though she did not take my arm again.

"We'll have to visit her again soon. Are we ready?"

"Lead the way."

The knot of worry in my stomach tightened as we walked back to the castle. I would not allow anyone to harm her.

I'll be by your side, no matter what.

Chapter Twenty-One

Meryn

Finn acted strangely in the days following our visit to town. He was adamant about spending every waking moment together. Not that I minded, but he clung to my side like a barnacle. Though his smile never faltered, I got the sense that something was worrying him.

I could hardly blame him, as heavy things weighed on my mind as well. The last few nights I had hardly slept. I dreamed of beautiful, red-haired children playing in the sea. A little boy and girl frolicked in the sand. The girl with crystal-blue eyes would yell "Mama," but when I tried to answer, someone else's voice replied. I watched for three nights as Finn lay on the beach with another woman. I woke every morning to tear-stained pillows. Her voice rang in my mind like a song, "I was waiting for you..." she whispered to him again and again.

The reminder that my father was going to return home

soon was another burden in the back of my mind. My father and... *him*. Lord Sebastian Trevion. There were so many times I opened my mouth to tell Finn the news of the impending visit, but then I saw his far-off gaze and stuffed it away for another day. Those days were flying by far too quickly.

It was only a week away, and we were sitting in the art studio when I finally gathered my courage. With a sigh, I placed my sketchbook down on the small table beside me. Finn noticed immediately, closing the book he was pretending to read. Our eyes met across the room.

"Did the light shift again?"

I twiddled my thumbs and stared at my lap. "No, it's not that. It's just that there is something I've been meaning to talk to you about."

"All right, then." His voice shook as he spoke. It was no wonder. We'd barely said anything to each other since leaving town, though we'd barely been apart. "What is it?"

The tremble in my hands grew. I gripped my sides to keep them still.

"Next week, my father is returning."

Silence fell around us like a companion lurking in the corners. I looked up to see Finn watching me. His face was a mask of confusion and concern.

"Are you nervous about his return?"

I nodded. "I am, but it's more than that. You see, he's bringing guests with him. The Trevions. He'll be leaving again shortly thereafter with Viscount Trevion to go on a hunting trip, but Lady Trevion and their son, Lord Trevion, will be staying here."

Finn nodded, his face falling. "And I suppose I've overstayed my welcome."

My eyes widened. "Overstayed? No, of course not. This is your home, Finn. For as long as you need it."

He relaxed a bit, eased by my words. "Thank you. I appreciate that... but, what has you so nervous then? Are the woman and child ill-behaved?"

I stared at him, my heart already crumbling before the words left my lips. "Finn, Lord Trevion is not a child."

The light slipped away the longer he met my gaze. He

sat wordlessly for a long while, absorbing my words. I didn't want to continue. But I knew he deserved to hear it from me.

"My father..." I choked on the words for a moment. I could not stand to look Finn in the eyes and see his betrayal. "He wants me to marry Lord Trevion. And if I should somehow fail, I will be sent away."

Stone-faced, Finn stared at me. I wanted to take the words back somehow—to go on with another carefree day. Walk on the beach, go for a swim, shop for another ring... anything but see the look on his face at that moment.

At last, Finn rose, releasing a slew of curse words as the book tumbled to the floor. He crossed the room, wiping a stack of papers off the drawing table with one hand. He dragged a hand down his face and laughed cynically. "And you have waited all this time to tell me?"

His words stung. I felt myself recoil like I'd been slapped. "Excuse me?"

"It seems most convenient that you've waited so long to tell me. I've got hardly any choice but to stay here, while you gallivant with this *man*."

Fury filled me, my blood boiling. I stood to face him, knocking the stool behind me. "Convenient? Nothing about this is convenient for me. It is not convenient for me to have no choice over my own life. It is not convenient for me to be servant to the whims of men."

"Oh, and you have no say in this, do you? I guess neither of us has a say." He was shouting now, pacing around the room.

"Not really, no. I don't have a say. I don't have a say in what happens in my own life. I don't have a say in where I go, who I see, not even who I marry, apparently. I don't even have a say in whether or not my best friend remembers enough to know if he has a whole separate life out there!" I shocked myself now. The words continued to spew out.

"You want to know what's *really* inconvenient? I worry every minute of every hour that you'll wake up and remember that you belong to another, but I have no say in that either!"

I watched my words hit home as Finn paused in his

incessant pacing.

"I love you, Meryn, I am yours."

My attention snapped to his face, his words still echoing in my head. Hot tears threatened to spill, but this time I refused. "But are you, though?" I asked him, my heart breaking because we could never be sure of the answer.

His eyes only met mine fleetingly, filled with pain as he seethed. "I could throttle your father." Finn stalked toward the door, pausing with his hand on the knob. "I'll try to stay out of the way."

I couldn't take it anymore. I leaped to my feet and crossed the room in a rush. Before he could walk out the door, I wrapped my arms around him, holding him in place and resting my head against the warmth of his back.

Finn stopped and sighed.

"Don't walk away from me," I begged. "Not yet."

He closed the door and wrapped his arms over mine. We stood in the silence for a few moments, neither one of us willing to be the first to break away. I absorbed his warmth and the feel of his body in my arms. I wanted to remember, to savor, every bit of him. Every second of our time together was precious, even as it quickly ticked away.

At last, he lifted my arms enough to turn and pull me into a proper embrace, tucking my head to his chest. I listened to the rapid beats of his heart. His pulse matched the fervid beat of my own. It had been far too long since I'd been held by him like this. I didn't realize how much I missed it.

"I don't know how to let you go, Meryn."

"Then don't."

His hand stroked the back of my hair. "I want you in ways I can't have you."

I lifted my head and looked into his eyes. They were so incredibly beautiful... and sad. I wanted to wash away the sadness—to reassure him that everything was going to be okay. That *we* were going to be okay. But things were far from okay, and we both knew it. We were beyond lies.

My fingertips traced his jawline, running gently over his deep red beard. Finn's eyes briefly slid shut at the contact. "Meryn..." It was a cautionary plea.

As I slid my palm up to cradle his cheek, Finn leaned into it, eyes meeting mine again. Longing, sadness, desire, heartbreak—I had never known so much could be transmitted by a simple look.

I felt it. I felt his love. It tore a hole in my heart and filled it up again. He might have had another life before his accident, but in this life, he truly loved me. We would have to part soon, but I found that just for that moment, I didn't want to let go of him. Not yet.

Pressing myself into him, I guided his face toward mine. Our lips connected. Finn's arms wrapped around me tighter. A slow smolder began to build the more we tasted each other. I wanted him. *Needed* him. Perhaps it was wicked of me to want him.

We weren't supposed to have this. But we were bruised and empty without each other. To deny it was to deny the tide. Perhaps he did have a past that should've kept me from him, but there, in the present... nothing else mattered.

As our kisses grew deeper, the smolder sparked into a flame. I felt a familiar ache—one that only he could satisfy. I craved his touch. Finn's hands traveled, tracing down over my shoulders... slowly embracing my curves... He was driving me mad.

My hands were no longer under my control. They roamed his back and shoulders, feeling every muscled inch of him, desperate for more.

I could feel his firm arousal growing between my hips, and it set me aflame. Gathering my courage, I slipped my hand between us. I stroked him with my palm as he released a deep groan. The feel of him, even through the fabric of his trousers, was intoxicating. I felt like a different kind of Meryn—one with no caution or care.

Suddenly, his hands gripped the back of my thighs and he lifted me, carrying me across the room to the worktable. With a sweep of his hand, he knocked away the remainder of the sketch supplies, sending them clattering to the floor. The cool hardwood surface of the table greeted me.

Eyes dripping with desire, he crawled over me and hungrily found my lips again. His deft hands slipped my dress above my hips, lowering himself to lie between my legs.

He gently removed my hand from his trousers, placing it above my head. I moaned softly behind our kiss as he pressed against my center. I wanted to tear away the fabric in between and finally connect, but he was tortuously patient.

Finn's lips trailed down to my throat, where he left open-mouth kisses over my collarbone. I sucked in air, my free hand tangled in his hair. He feverishly worked at the ribbons on my dress, loosening the front enough to expose my breasts. He eagerly worshiped each one, licking and teasing. I felt as if I might turn into a puddle and slide right off the table.

I couldn't stop the gasps and whimpers coming out of my mouth. When he moved lower, my eyes grew wide with both fear and anticipation. His lips jumped to my inner right thigh, kissing up the length of it. He started at the sensitive spot on the inside of my knee, working his way slowly, torturously toward my pelvis. Gentle tugs pulled my short undergarments aside, his fingers lightly grazing new territory. Part of me wanted to slam my knees shut from embarrassment, but I settled into the experience. *I might perish if he stopped now.*

Finn took the other thigh next, taking his time and leaving sweet, sensual kisses behind. He paused right before he reached his destination. When he looked up at me, fire was in his eyes.

"May I taste you?" His voice was low and thick.

I nodded. Keeping his smoldering eyes on mine, his fingers found my waistband and gently pulled them, sliding them down over my hips. He dragged the motion on, enjoying the torture he was inflicting on me. An eternity later, he whisked them over my feet.

My heart pounded in my chest as his warm hands returned to my knees and slowly parted them before sliding reverently down my inner thighs. I was fully exposed to the cool air, but I felt anything but cold. My body was on fire with need.

Finn's gaze lowered to my sex, and his brows flicked. First, his fingers grazed me. Then, with a bit more pressure, parted me. He seemed entirely drunk on the sight. When he lowered his mouth to me, I inhaled sharply, grasping his hair. He gripped the outside of my thighs, worshipping me in a way I never dreamed possible.

I had to bite my sleeve in a futile attempt to drown my moans. We were up at the top of the house—away from most everyone. Still, I wished it was storming outside—anything to muffle the sounds we were making. I was losing control.

Soon, all I could focus on was Finn and my driving need for him. Overwhelming waves of pleasure increased inside of me. I felt like I was about to burst. Heat and tension collected at my core.

I writhed under his touch. "Finn..." I moaned breathlessly.

He hummed in response and continued to take me with a voracious appetite.

There was a tidal wave building, looming in the background. All control was lost as my hips moved with the gentle rhythm of his tongue. Suddenly, the wave crashed down on me. My entire body went taut and the moan that escaped me disappeared into the eaves. It was the most intense pleasure I'd ever felt in my life, rushing through my veins. Finn continued to work his magic, sending me deeper over the edge.

Just when I thought I would die from it, Finn crawled over me again, wiping his mouth on his sleeve before finding my lips again. He paused, our panting breaths mingling. His eyes pierced mine.

His hard cock throbbed against my leg as he leaned closer. The question lingered in the air between us. *Did I want more? Did I want all of him?*

My answer was another long, sultry kiss. "Yes..."

There was a quick rustle of clothing as Finn removed his clothes. Soon he pressed in on me again. I broke our kiss long enough to look down. For the first time, I wasn't afraid to see all of him. Heat surged through me again. I'd never seen him like that. Anaat had explained the basics of how it worked, but it failed to prepare me for this moment. Failed to prepare me for...

I gasped as he began to slide inside of me. I grasped at

his shoulders.

Finn paused immediately.

"Am I hurting you—" His voice was thick with longing as he paused.

"Don't stop. Please."

Resuming course, he pressed in further. It hurt, but the pain mingled with pleasure. Soon, I was filled with *him*. Finn released a sigh, groaning. He stayed there for a moment. His eyes slid shut. I ran my fingers through his hair and pulled him to my lips again.

Finn began to move. At first, he was slow and gentle, giving us time to adjust to the feel of each other. Our passion built. His motions grew more urgent. His lips trailed all over me as he delivered powerful thrusts. He tugged at the tender skin of my neck, his hand kneading my breast. My hands roamed fearlessly, tracing over every toned bit of him.

"You feel so good, Mer..." He kissed the spot below my ear as he whispered. The sound of his voice drove me wild. I raked my nails down his back without giving it a second thought.

Finn's motions grew more frantic; faster and harder. I was building up again. With every move of his hips against mine, I wanted to cry out.

Before long, I was. Finn's kiss covered my mouth and absorbed the sound as I descended into madness. Soon, he stilled on top of me and moaned. I felt a flood of pulsing warmth.

We lay there, chest to chest, panting. Sweat covered us. Finn posted his elbows on either side of my head as we watched each other. There were no words to say. We couldn't go back now. Quite frankly, I never wanted to. But the future was bleak. Still, if there was one thing I knew for certain, it was that the man before me was unlike any other.

And I wanted him forever.

Chapter Twenty-Two

Fivrial

From the moment our lips collided in the art studio, I knew it was hopeless. I couldn't stay away from her. When we made love, everything else just... stopped. All the doubt, all the turmoil. It didn't matter in those precious moments I spent with her. At the first taste of her, I was addicted.

It was six days later, and we lay in my bed, moonlight streaming through the window. Only four days before I would have to leave her again. Only *hours* until the Trevions arrived with her father. I detested the thought of either of those situations, so I stuffed them down into the back of my mind for now and cradled her to my chest.

We'd been making love for what felt like hours until we were exhausted and sore. She'd snuck down well after the servants had retired and we leaped on each other like we were starving, even though it was only a matter of hours before that when we'd hidden ourselves away in the art studio again. When we weren't making love, we were discreetly flirting and laughing. I'd finally convinced her to stop looking to the past and enjoy our time together. And enjoy it, we did.

There we lay, in bliss once more. Meryn had yet to say the words to me, but I was confident it was coming. I felt her love like I felt the sun. The way she looked at me, the way she cared... it was there. She just had to say it.

Meryn's fingers played with my chest hair as she stared off into the distance. I caressed her bare arm, exposed on top of the blue blanket we were under.

"What are you thinking?" I asked, kissing the top of her head.

"A lot of things." She sighed. "Too many things."

I knew what those things were likely to be. I was afraid to ask, but wanted to know her mind. "Do you want to tell me?"

Meryn slid her arm across my middle and squeezed me. "I guess I'm a little scared."

I was quiet for a while, choosing my words wisely. Tomorrow would mark the turning point. *The arrival.*

"Scared about tomorrow?"

She nodded. "I just... I don't want things to change. Between us."

"Maybe they don't have to."

Raising her head to look at me, Meryn's brows knitted. "What do you mean?"

Taking a stabilizing breath, I finally spoke what had been on my mind for days. "I want you to come away with me."

She stared at me, wide-eyed. At first, I wasn't entirely sure she heard me. "What?"

"Meryn," I began, nerves ramping up, "we could leave this place. Go anywhere. I'd find work to take care of you and we could start over somewhere." My heart was racing as I brushed her cheek with my knuckles. "We can be together."

I was expecting her to be overjoyed—to throw her arms around my neck and say yes. Instead, she released me and sat up, the blanket sliding to her waist as she pressed her palms to the side of her head. I sat up next to her and rested my hand on her back in concern. She immediately tensed up.

"Meryn, what's wrong?"

She shook her head. "I... Finn, I don't think you know what you're asking."

My brows lowered. "I believe I'm asking you to marry me."

The color drained from her face. "Marry..." Meryn's breathing became fast and shallow. Her eyes glazed over in panic. I immediately crawled forward to face her and placed my hands on her cheeks.

"Meryn, just breathe, okay? You don't have to answer me right now." It hurt to say those words. I wanted her to jump for joy at the prospect, but her reaction was frightening me.

She grasped my wrists and shook her head as she removed my hands. "No, no, no..." Meryn slipped from the bed, retrieved her nightgown, and began dressing.

"What are you doing?" I asked, hopping from the bed and rushing to her side. When she didn't respond, I grabbed her shoulders and forced her to look at me. "Answer me, Meryn," I demanded.

Meryn finally looked me in the eye, full of fear. "Finn, I can't marry you."

My heart froze in my chest. "What? Why not?"

"Because you may already be married. And I..." Tears fell from her eyes. "I don't know if I want to be a wife. To anyone."

It felt as if an anchor had slammed into me. I stared at her, a cold feeling seeping through my skin. Had I misread her completely? *No... no, there's no way, unless...*

My hands dropped from her shoulders. "Meryn, have you been using me?"

Hurt flashed across her face. "Using you? *Using you?* Finn, why the hell would I use you? Not when I..." she sighed and grasped her forehead. "No, I'm not using you."

My own hurt was choking me. "Then tell me, Meryn."

"Tell you what?" she snapped.

I grasped her chin and lifted her eyes to mine. "Tell me how you feel about me."

Our gazes remained locked. I wasn't letting her go until I got an answer. *Enough games.*

"I..." She smiled through her tears. "I don't know. You're just... *my Finn.* I don't know any other way to describe it. When I'm with you, I feel like I'm lighter than air sometimes. Other times, I'm on fire. Sometimes you make me sad. And..." Her smile faded. "I don't want things to change. Not yet."

We both knew they had to. It was unspoken that with the arrival of Trevion, her obligations would shift. Our time was running out like a fistful of sand. Still, I nodded and pulled her into my arms.

"Okay." I sighed into her hair and held her tight. "Just stay until sunrise?"

She nodded and left my arms to return to the bed. I crawled in after and cuddled up behind her, where I remained for the rest of the night.

Meryn left me in the early hours of the morning. I awoke to an empty bed. It was cold without her.

I reluctantly dressed, dragging myself from my room hours later, not looking forward to the meeting that was to inevitably come. My plan was to hole myself up in the music room and stay out of the way as long as possible. However, when I made my way there, I heard someone playing the piano, a melody floating through the halls. It was a strange song I'd yet to hear.

Upon reaching the music room, I found it full of strangers. A young man with dark features and a dashing smile sat at the piano, sheets of music propped up before him as he played the tune. He wore a crisp black suit with a high-collared white shirt beneath. I instantly knew who he was. My jaw tensed.

Meryn stood next to him, back turned to me. I hardly recognized her—long hair gathered up at the back of her head in several neat braids. All its wildness had been tamed.

She wore a green dress with tiny white flowers that I'd never seen before, and her waist looked stiff and smaller than usual.

On the other side of the piano, Anaat stood in a crisp blue dress next to an older woman in a purple gown dripping with lace and jewels. They watched Lord Trevion on the piano with bright smiles.

Two men stood across the room, conversing in their stiff-looking jackets. One of them caught sight of me in the doorway and elbowed the other, speaking quietly. The other man, a bit taller than the first, turned and peered at me, his dark mustache drawn into a frown.

Just then, the song concluded, and there was light applause from the ladies. Lord Trevion stood and smiled, focusing his charm on Meryn. He finally noticed me, stepping away from the piano.

"Oh! Perfect timing! Fetch us some brandy, please, thank you," he instructed me.

Meryn whirled around, her smile fading instantly. She stepped up alongside Lord Trevion and nodded toward me. "Actually, Mr. Fishman isn't a servant. He's in residence here for the time being." She waved toward me. My eyes swept over the looks of curiosity, and I reluctantly entered the room and went to her side.

I got the distinct impression that I was being scrutinized. *Carefully.* Still, there was a polite smile and Lord Trevion extended his hand.

"My apologies. Sebastian Trevion."

With a firm grip, I accepted his hand. "Finn Fishman."

He chuckled as he released me. "That's quite an interesting name you have there."

I caught sight of other amused grins; Meryn excluded. They meant to humiliate me right away. I would not give them the satisfaction. I nodded and smiled. "I suppose."

"Apparently, my daughters have been most charitable while I was away," explained the taller man, an edge of disdain in his voice. When I dared to look at him, he offered a smile that didn't quite reach his eyes. I got the message loud and clear: he was not pleased with my presence.

"I see," said the viscount. His eyes trailed over me as if I were something pulled from a mud pit. He had a long, hooked nose that reminded me of a squid's beak. Something about him oozed falsehood. His attention jumped back to the duke with a cordial smile. "Your daughters are most gracious, of course."

I found Meryn staring into the distance out of the corner of my eye. When I turned, I saw her face was blank. She looked devoid of the usual life she held in abundance. A chill ran down my spine. *Have they broken her so quickly?*

"Lady Meryn, I hear you play the violin quite well," said Sebastian, turning on his oozing charm. "Would you care to show us your lovely talents?"

Her lips twitched in a smile, and she nodded before crossing the room to her violin. I had to get out of there. Without being at the piano, the violin affected me too strongly.

"If you'll excuse me, I..." All eyes turned to me. I suddenly felt nervous. "I have things to do. Nice meeting you all." I started to turn, but a hand clapped my shoulder.

"Oh, come now!" said Sebastian, "You can surely stay to hear a song?" He was jovial but insistent.

I could not think of another excuse to refuse without insulting Meryn. Forcing a smile, I nodded. "Very well."

We stood watching as Meryn tucked the violin between her chin and shoulder. She positioned her bow and glanced at me. I wanted to run.

The first long note drew across the strings. I felt my nerves come alive with a tingling rush. Meryn continued to play, standing still as stone. No dancing, no smiles. It was a subdued piece I'd never heard before. Still, it affected me. I felt her music pouring through my veins, echoing in my head. It called to me like a siren. My feet wanted to move. They yearned to take me to her side. I shifted where I stood, resisting the urge to give in. It was a beautiful torment.

Everyone was enraptured by her skilled playing. I hoped they wouldn't notice my discomfort as I was being pulled to a different plane entirely. The room was fading away as I zeroed in on the sound... and her. My throat ached with the urge to sing, and it wasn't even the full moon. Without an outlet, I was on the verge of losing control of my melodic instincts.

Just when I couldn't stand it any longer, the song ended.

Everyone clapped. Meryn nodded and smiled before quickly returning the violin and bow to its resting place. I took a deep breath and thanked Scalae I'd survived without drawing attention to myself.

Meryn met my eyes and for a moment, I could see her own relief. We both knew the strange spell her music put me under. She was powerless to speak out on my behalf. Or her own, for that matter.

While everyone else chatted amongst themselves, I gave a subtle nod to Meryn and slipped from the room. Once in the hallway, I released a lungful of air and retreated to an empty part of the house, *away* from the call of her music.

Late that night, I paced my room. At last, the doorknob turned, and Meryn quickly slipped in. She was still fully dressed but her hair was loose at last. My heart dropped at the sight of her careworn face and red-rimmed eyes. She barely looked at me before trudging over and slipping her arms around my neck.

As I wrapped my arms around her, I was surprised to find her waist completely encased in stiff material. My brows lowered. "Meryn, what are you wearing?"

She groaned into my shoulder. "The 'latest fashion' according to Anaat. It's meant to make me slim and proper. And torture the hell out of me."

I scoffed. "Slim? Why would you need to be slimmer? You're fine the way you are."

Meryn stepped from my arms and flopped back on the bed, holding her stomach. "Not 'fine enough' apparently."

Stretching myself out beside her, we both stared at the ceiling. It was a long, difficult day for the both of us. More so for her, I imagined. We weren't used to being apart, much less under those circumstances. My hand found Meryn's and brought it to my lips.

"I'm sorry, Meryn. You don't deserve to be treated that

way."

She laughed. "Father seems to think so. He's the one that ordered Anaat to 'straighten me up and make me presentable.'"

"Well, if it's any consolation," I rolled over and propped myself up on my elbow, "I think you're perfect just the way you are—soft waist and all." I stroked the hair from her temple and planted a gentle kiss there.

Meryn smiled, her weariness lifting a little. "Thank you."

I knew there was a bigger issue hanging in the air that we'd yet to speak of. *Him.* Just the thought of another man pursuing her brought bile to my throat. What was worse, Sebastian Trevion looked like an ideal man to snag her. Before I could bring up the subject, Meryn beat me to it.

"I don't like him, Finn. I didn't like him last year and I don't like him now. Slimy charm and a nice face, but I still don't care for his spirit." Her weary eyes found mine. "He's not like you."

I crooked a smile. "I should hope he isn't."

She rolled her eyes. "I'm serious, Finn. All day long, they've practically thrown us at each other. It's exhausting."

"I'm sorry they're doing this to you," I said, wrapping my arm around her waist and pulling myself closer to her side. There was nothing else I could think of to say. All I wanted was to be in each other's arms, hidden away from the rest of the world.

Meryn looked at me and sighed. I could see her sadness swirling. "I miss you already, Finn."

I wrapped my hand around her cheek. "I miss you, too." I leaned into her and placed a slow kiss on her lips. "Now," my gaze met hers as I grew warmer, "how about we get you out of this torturous piece of clothing?"

Meryn half-laughed, half-whined. "*Please.* It's been poking my ribs all day."

I laughed. "Tell me how to help."

After a lot of maneuvering and giggles, Meryn was finally free of her dress and 'stays.' She lay on the bed again in her thin, white shift and took deep breaths with a smile on her face. "Thank you. This is the best I've felt all day."

I grinned and crawled on top of her. "How about I make you feel even better?" Her body was soft and warm, instantly setting my blood to boil.

She accepted my sultry kiss, but then placed her palms on my chest with a guilty look in her eye. "I really am exhausted."

Exhaling sharply, I re-gathered my wits and nodded. "All right."

Meryn pulled me into an embrace. "I'm sorry, Finn."

"There's no need to be sorry. We'll just rest." Rest for her. I didn't know how I could sleep a wink. Still, I rolled off her and tucked us under the blankets.

Meryn immediately cuddled up to me, tucking her head to my chest with a yawn. "Just for a while."

I stroked the hair from her face and watched her fall fast asleep. Her words echoed in my head. We only had a short time with each other.

If only she knew how short that time really was.

Chapter Twenty-Three

Meryn

I hated every second of it. Annat woke me up early the morning of their arrival, stuffed me into that contraption, and practically smothered me with the new dress. Her hands were rough as she pulled my hair back so tight it brought tears to my eyes. After leaving Finn, I'd only barely fallen asleep in my own bed before she'd arrived, and I was immediately cross with her. She let me nibble a bit of brown bread and tea for breakfast, but nothing short of sleeping half the day and ignoring the Trevions would have improved my mood.

The first moment Sebastian Trevion laid eyes on me in the sitting room, I knew this wasn't going to be easy. His eyes swept over me with approval, as if I were some sort of prized mare to be bought. Anaat must've done a good job even though I felt like a strange, dowdy doll.

Father was pleased to see me as well. Or at least he

acted as if he were. He embraced me and placed a wet kiss atop my head—as if I were his most beloved daughter.

"My Meryn!" he said jovially.

He'd never once referred to me that way. Mother had. I was always the thorn under his heel, constantly getting into trouble with my adventurous ways. Perhaps now he assumed I'd finally 'grown up' after my latest incident with the boat. Little did he know, it was merely a breaking of my heart.

The day was full of chatter about the upcoming tour of the castle. It was Sebastian's first time visiting our home, and Father insisted I lead the way like a good little hostess. My ribs pinched with every movement; all I wanted to do was grab the nearest blade and slice up the seam of my dress.

Sebastian's parents were overly cordial and obnoxiously proper. His mother sidled up to me often, taking my arm and offering lovely compliments about my hair or some other mention of my appearance. We both knew my reputation was in question, so she had little else to say about me. I tried to remember how to reciprocate pleasantries, but internally I screamed at her to take her awful son and get out of my house.

It wasn't until we finally made it to the music room and I showed off my accomplishment on the violin that there was any genuine praise. I chose the most boring, formal piece I could think of and still they applauded.

My mind was on Finn the entire time. I knew his strange, unexplainable reactions to my music. And I wanted to land my fist in Sebastian's face for insisting that he stay. Poor Finn struggled through the whole song.

I could see his expression out of the corner of my eye, as much as he tried to hide it. Had it not been viewed as too forward, I would have insisted that he accompany me on the piano. But Father would've been furious. Anaat told me he was already unhappy when she had to write to him days before his arrival and inform him of Finn's presence. Still, to his credit, he did not turn Finn out.

The next morning, Anaat again woke me early. My mood had not much improved from the day before. In fact, it was much worse. Finn had been cautious not to let me sleep too long in his room. My heart ached as I left the warmth of his bed.

The servants scrubbed me until my skin felt raw. My hair was pulled into a tight bun while still wet, making it heavy as it pulled against my scalp. I teared up as Anaat jammed me with hairpins.

Today's dress was a deep-blue, long-sleeved ensemble. It dripped with lace, especially around the collar. The front scooped much lower than I was comfortable with. A black bow settled at the midpoint. The corners of the bow lined with the crevice of my breasts, which had been nearly lifted to my chin. The skirts were extremely full, gathering around my hips to make them look much larger.

If the goal of the uncomfortable undergarments was to make my hips slender, why did I also have to wear skirts to make them look full?

Style would never be a passion of mine. I stared at myself in the full-length mirror and frowned, while Annat stood by and beamed proudly at her work.

"Do you like it?" she asked, ignoring the scowl permanently etched across my face.

"I don't even look like myself."

Grasping my upper arms, she rested her chin on my shoulder, smiling at my reflection. "Meryn, you look beautiful. Lord Trevion will be absolutely enchanted."

I looked at her in the mirror. "Well, I don't care if he's 'enchanted.' I'm uncomfortable. Why can't I just wear one of my other dresses? I'm certainly not going to dress like this for the rest of my life, so he might as well get used to it now."

The smile slipped from Annat's face. She straightened, hands planted on her hips. "Meryn, we've talked about this. You must look your best if you're to bait a man."

I turned to her and crossed my arms. "Is he a man or a fish?"

Her lips curled into a tight smile. "It doesn't matter what he is. He's wealthy, and he's eligible."

With an exasperated sigh, I stalked to my wardrobe, flinging it open. "Then why don't you marry him, then?"

"Ha, very funny. What are you doing?"

I continued digging through the bottom drawer. "Looking for a shawl. I don't want to walk out there on display like this."

A vice grip closed around my arm and dragged me away. Anaat glared at me. "You most certainly will. You have nice..." her face twisted in embarrassment, "*assets*. There's nothing wrong with showing them off just a little. You're still in keeping with a lady."

I glanced down at my 'assets'. "Well, I certainly don't feel like one." With pursed lips, I turned back to the wardrobe. "And I'm not comfortable, Anaat."

She yanked me away again, this time bracing her hands on my shoulders with an intense glare. "Listen to me, Meryn," she said firmly. "This isn't a game. As I told you before, this is your *last chance*. I know we have our differences, but I do not want to see you shipped away to that temple. You and I both know it would kill you."

For the first time, I saw genuine terror in her. A shudder ran through me. "Anaat, I—"

Anaat shook my shoulders roughly. "*Everything* I'm doing right now, I'm doing for you, Meryn. You must understand that. It's the only thing I *can* do. When Mother died, I..." tears brimmed, threatening to spill, "I promised Father I would help you. Be a good example. I've failed up until now, but I can't fail this. I can't fail you again."

She flung her arms around me and dissolved into tears. Still absorbing her words, I slipped my arms around her and held her close. We rarely hugged each other. Anaat rarely cried anything more than crocodile tears. This time, it was genuine.

My heart felt as if it were being pulled in two different directions. I longed to be free—to spurn the pressure and be myself. But underneath our animosity, I still dearly loved my sister. And the memory of our mother was something sacred to us both. *Was I disparaging that memory by putting our family's reputation at risk?* Just the thought was enough to fill me with dread.

"You haven't failed me, Anaat... and I'll try. For you."

The promise felt like a promise of poison. It seeped

through my veins. She was right—going into the priestesses would kill me. To be the wife of a man I didn't love might very well kill me as well. But at least I wouldn't break my family's heart in the process.

I could bear to break my own heart, but could I break Finn's?

I didn't see Finn almost the entire day. His bedroom door stood open as I passed, revealing an empty room. Father and Viscount Trevion left for their hunting trip, much to my relief and sorrow. Lady Trevion clung to Anaat's side, and they made their way into town, leaving me to entertain Lord Trevion *alone*.

When I was alone with Finn, I never once felt nervous. Not in a bad sort of way. He was a bosom friend from the moment we were together. But with Lord Trevion... it was different.

As we walked the halls, he went on and on about his recent accomplishments, sharing funny anecdotes about his time with 'Lord So-and-so.' He loved to talk about himself, and I was content to let him do so—even though it gave me a royal headache.

We ended up in the music room again. He sat down and played a tune that again required me to turn the music for him. I think he liked the fact that I had to lean in front of him. I silently cursed Anaat for making me wear that cursed dress. Of course, she thoroughly knew what she was doing. I caught his eyes on my body more than once throughout the day.

Done playing the piano, he stood and motioned toward the bench. "Would you care to play something?"

I shook my head with a shy smile. "No, that's quite all right. You're much better than I am."

"No, surely not. Come, I insist." With a guiding hand on my back, he led me to the bench. I sat down and shifted uncomfortably.

"Now, what would you like to play?" he asked, flipping through our selection of music.

"Actually, Lord Trevion, I play by ear."

He paused and looked at me with a curious look in his eye. "Really now? That's remarkable."

I smiled and placed my fingers on the keys, ready to throw myself into a traditional tune, when he leaned an elbow on the piano and stared at me.

"I want you to call me Sebastian, by the way."

My smile faded as I met his stare. "Why?"

He laughed. "Because we're friends, are we not? 'Lord Trevion' is so formal."

We were not. I did not venture to correct him. "All right then. Sebastian."

Pleased with my response, he nodded. "Thank you, Meryn."

I had not permitted him to call me that, but again, I bit back the cold response that I wanted to give. "What would you like to hear?"

Sebastian drummed his fingers on the polished wood. "Something you can sing to."

I blanched. "You want me to sing as well?"

He held my gaze. "I would love to hear you sing."

Swallowing hard, I looked down at the piano keys and racked my brain for a song that I could play and sing. I settled on a short tune about gnomes in the garden. It was one I'd learned as a girl and used to sing for Mother. It was a jaunty little melody, but one I could perform without a second thought.

Once the piece was over, he smiled a humoring sort of smile, as if doting on a child. "You play and sing beautifully."

"Thank you," I replied politely. "Would you—"

"Play a love song."

My eyes widened. "I'm sorry?"

Sebastian's lips twitched with a hint of a smile. "A love song. Surely you must know some?"

I shifted uncomfortably. The only love songs I knew by heart were my own. And the only person I played them for anymore was Finn.

Sebastian glanced toward the music room door, which stood open for propriety's sake. To my horror, he walked over and peeked out into the hall before closing it. When he returned, he pulled up a chair next to the piano, angled toward me.

"There, now no one can hear if that's what you're nervous about."

"Lord Trevion—"

"Sebastian," he corrected.

I sighed. "Sebastian, I'm not sure this is entirely... proper."

He leaned his temple against his fingers and peered at me. "I want to get to know you, Meryn. Without pretense. Please sing for me?"

My eyes continually darted toward the door. My ears piqued to any approaching sounds. I nodded at last, though my stomach was turning in knots. This felt wrong. *Beyond* wrong.

When my fingers found the keys, they were shaking. I settled on a song I'd written years ago. It took me a moment to remember how to play it. It was in a minor key, and I hoped dreary enough not to give him the wrong idea.

The day we met
The day we danced
My heart, it nearly died
You've gone away
You've gone astray
My tears, I've all but cried

We cannot stop the tide
No matter how we try
The world goes on and on
My heart has all but died

The day we held
Each other's hand
I thought that I would fly
But you left me cold
My love, you stole
Now years are passing by

Of Songs and Saltwater

We cannot stop the tide
No matter how we try
The world goes on and on
My heart has all but died

I concluded on the chorus. When I looked up, I found Sebastian staring at me in surprise. I shied away and folded my hands in my lap.

"Now, that is much better than gnomes. I don't believe I've heard such a beautiful song before. Where did you learn it?" He seemed truly fascinated.

I twiddled my thumbs and blushed. "I wrote it."

"You wrote it? Really? How splendid!" He laughed.

My brows raised. "You really think so?"

Sebastian nodded. "I think you have a gift, Meryn."

I studied his face for any sign of jest but found sincerity. Narrowing my eyes, I crooked my mouth to the side. "You're sure you're not scandalized?"

He leaned closer, conspiratorially. "I'm not opposed to a good scandal now and then."

Eyes widening, I felt the color flood my cheeks. He was flirting with me. I rose from the piano. "Um, you know what? I think it's about noon now. We should probably head to the dining room. I'm sure your mother and my sister are already there."

The slyness slipped from Sebastian's face. A polite smile arose in his place as he stood from his chair. "Of course."

I made a quick exit from the room. He hurried to my side and offered his arm. I stared at it for a moment in debate, heart thrashing in my chest. I wanted to slap it away and run ahead. But Anaat's words echoed in my head. *'This is your last chance, Meryn.'* And so, much to my self-loathing, I accepted it.

Chapter Twenty-Four

Fivrial

I spent the day at the private beach, collecting shells and swimming. Though it was hard to be away from Meryn, I desperately needed a break from the castle. It felt far too crowded.

The water was refreshing as I waded up to my waist and dove in. I couldn't breathe under the surface in this form, but I found I could hold my breath for a fairly long time. As a result, I could easily reach the seafloor in depths well over my head.

As I swam, I found more and more that I'd missed it terribly. I couldn't swim as well with legs as I could with a tail, but simply being clothed by the sea brought a smile to my face. Colorful fish and coral were as dazzling to the eye as rubies.

Could I be happy again under the sea? Without Meryn? Could I be happy living my days among the merfolk, possibly settle down with a 'maid, and give up my collection of trinkets? The thought brought a sense of dread with it. Still, it was a reality I may have to face soon.

I grabbed a large oyster and pushed off the sandy bottom, shooting for the surface. My stomach was roaring. I shoved the oyster in my pocket with the other and swam for shore. The sun was centered in the sky.

Once on dry land, I plopped the oysters in a bucket with the others and headed for a shady spot under a palm tree. I dug out the knife from the bucket and went to work shucking them. Under the sea, I was used to using a sharpened rock. The knife was far more convenient.

Before I ate the meat, I collected the pearls. I'd hoped to collect enough to have some sort of jewelry made for Meryn. Perhaps something for her wrist. I'd seen pearl items at the jewelers, so I hoped it meant he could help me.

As I sat eating my lunch, something caught my eye. At first, I dismissed it as a trick of the light, but instinct told me to look again. I froze, dropping my knife in the sand. There, not far offshore, was a woman. Not just any woman. *A siren.*

I recognized her instantly. Druscella. I knew her for her dark hair and emerald tail. She'd pursued me over the years, but I never felt for her as she did for me. Now, here she was, staring at me with wide eyes. Her face paled, as if she'd seen a ghost.

Druscella swam closer until she was nearly beached on the sand. "Fivrial?"

The name was a shock to my ears. It felt like forever since I'd heard it. I'd grown into the role of "Finn" so easily.

Rising to my feet, my eyes darted around to ensure we were alone before I jogged through the sand and into the shallows. I stood near, crossing my arms over my bare chest.

I kept my gaze averted, keenly aware of her own exposed chest, as was the custom for merfolk. I'd never given it a second thought before Meryn. Now it felt as if it would've been... *unfaithful* to look.

"Druscella, what are you doing here? If Grayler catches you, it's the pit."

She scoffed. "*Me?* Fivrial! Look at you! H-how did this

happen?"

I pinched the bridge of my nose and sighed in frustration. "Druscella, it's none of your concern. Go back to Brinn and forget you ever saw me."

I caught her hard stare out of the corner of her eye. "Fivrial. Out with it. Now."

"Druscella—"

Her tail slapped the surface of the water.

"I'm not leaving here without answers."

Finally, I met her stare. "It's a spell, okay? It turned me into a human. Now, leave."

She pursed her lips. "Why would you want to be human? Sirens aren't good enough for you?"

I sneered at her. "You don't know the first thing about me. Or humans, for that matter."

"Oh, I don't? I think I've handled far more humans than you ever will."

A sick feeling twisted my stomach. "You mean *killed*?"

Druscella eyed me with suspicion. "Why are you so keen on defending them?"

"That's none of your concern," I spat, turning my back to her. "Now leave."

"You're in love with one, aren't you?"

I froze in my tracks, water sloshing at my calves. "What?"

Druscella's tone went from biting to amused. "You know, I'd always heard rumors about you. I never believed they were true. But honestly, it all makes sense now."

My nerves wound as my heart pounded in my chest. "You don't know what you're talking about."

"It's okay, Fivrial. You can admit it," she coaxed. I felt a soft hand brush my calf. "I won't tell."

I turned to her with a burning glare. "I wouldn't trust you if my life depended on it."

"And what if it did?"

I clenched my fists, my tension rising. Druscella boldly held my stare. She knew she had the upper hand. All she had to do was open her mouth and sing, and I would be under her spell. A human was no match for a siren, even when the moon wasn't full.

"Is that a threat?"

Druscella shrugged. "That depends."

My reply was sharp. "On what?"

I felt the brush of her fins across my ankle as she smiled. "Are you going to tell me what I want to know?"

Taking several steps back, I shook my head. "Don't do this, Druscella. You're better than that."

My feet pulled out from under me. My back smacked against the water. I gasped for air as my head briefly went under. A pair of strong arms wrapped around my neck and upper back, pulling my head above the surface.

Druscella's emerald eyes drilled into mine. I watched, helpless, as soft high notes slipped from her lips. The music instantly took hold.

I couldn't move. Couldn't think. The undulating notes filled my head. My body felt weightless as she held me in her arms.

Druscella swam us even further into the shallows until my back hit sand. She continued to sing, coaxing me further into the trance. Her slick body rested against mine. Her hands eagerly, painfully, ran through my hair. She scraped her long fingernails down my face. She didn't hesitate to continue downward as her hungry hands explored my chest. The music rendered me an immobile shell.

The words she sang echoed through my head. "Tell me the name of your love..."

My mouth opened of its own accord, my thoughts spilling out in a pained whisper. "Meryn."

Druscella smiled in satisfaction. She continued to sing. "Is she human?"

Something sprang up within me. The will to fight. Some part of me knew I had to protect Meryn at all costs. I strained, pressing my lips together, turning my head away.

Druscella's steel grip grabbed my face and pulled it back to hers, planting a soft kiss on my lips before increasing the volume of her song.

"Does she have legs?"

"Yes."

I felt defeated. The answer slipped out despite my best efforts. It was futile to resist the call of a siren. Druscella seemed keen on getting what she wanted from me.

"Where does she reside?" she sang in a sweet soprano trill.

Again, the answer was extracted. "In the castle on top of the hill."

Druscella kissed me again as if rewarding me for my efforts. Under the spell, it was sweet and luscious. Beneath the haze, a part of me was still repulsed.

Those were not the lips I longed for.

"Tell me, dear Fivrial," she sang, "do you miss the feel of a mermaid?" Her hand drifted lazily up and down my side.

This was one answer I didn't feel guilty about. "No."

Druscella ceased her song as her brows furrowed. "What?" Her voice was full of fury.

The haze quickly cleared. I responded through gritted teeth as I violently shoved her off me. "Go to hell, Druscella."

I rose quickly, running onto the beach, putting as much distance between us as possible.

"You'll be sorry, Fivrial," she warned.

Whirling around, I shoved a finger in her direction. "May Scalae curse you for what you've done, Druscella. If you even think of trying that again, or if anything happens to Meryn, you won't live long enough for Scalae to do the honors."

Druscella's eyes narrowed. She sank into deeper waters before disappearing beneath the waves with a dramatic splash of her fins. I watched the surface of the water for a long time to ensure she was gone.

Enraged, I kicked the bucket of oysters, sending shells flying over the sand and grass. Sinking to the ground, I grasped my head in my hands and tried to catch my breath. My mind was spinning faster than a whirlpool.

What have I done? How could I have been so weak? Furiously, I rubbed my lips. I didn't want any remnants of Druscella's taste on me. I felt... violated.

The rest of the afternoon was torment. I mostly stayed

on shore, afraid of another encounter. All I thought about was Meryn and my own vulnerability. If she told me she loved me, and if I could convince her, we'd move far inland. We'd find a house somewhere away from the sea and all the dangers within. I had to protect her at all costs, and time was not on our side. Somehow, someway, I had to make this work.

When I finally dragged myself back to the castle, I was exhausted from the sun. It was twilight, and I hoped everyone would be dining. My path would circumvent the dining room and I could make it back to my room without incident. Bernard would be more than happy to bring a meal to my room and aid me with filling my bath. I needed to wash off every trace of that demon siren.

I was nearly to the stairs that led up to my floor when I stopped in my tracks. There, coming toward me, was Meryn... on the arm of Sebastian. She was a strange vision in a shimmering, red gown. Her breasts were half-exposed beneath a glittering diamond necklace and long, glossy strands of curls. Something had been applied to darken her lashes and redden her cheeks and lips. When she saw me, her eyes briefly widened.

They did not stop. I received polite nods in passing, but I may as well have been a statue. In the brief moment that I met Meryn's gaze, I got the sense that she was full of shame.

If she only knew my own.

After my lonely dinner and bath, I got into my long nightshirt and lay on the bed, staring at the ceiling. Everything that occurred that day was a swirling eddy in my mind. A weighted pit sat in my stomach, setting my nerves on end. Things were not going to plan. Just the memory of Meryn on his arm brought a sick feeling I couldn't describe.

It was late into the night when my door finally opened, and Meryn slipped in. She was in her nightgown. Her waist-length hair had been tamed and re-curled in an artificial fashion. It was beautiful, but odd. The markings on her face appeared to have been scrubbed clean, but her eyes were puffy and red again. Still, I breathed a sigh of relief to see her.

Holding my arms out to her, I welcomed her into the

bed. Meryn crawled in beside me and tucked herself under the covers. She clung to me wordlessly, shaking from head to toe.

Furrowing my brows, I held her head to my chest. "Meryn, are you all right?"

Her answer was clipped. "Yes."

I shifted and looked down at her. "You're lying."

Meryn drew a shuddered breath. "I don't want to talk about it tonight."

"All right." I was entirely concerned, but decided not to press it. "What do you want to talk about, then?"

Groaning in frustration, Meryn flopped on her back. "Why do we have to 'talk' about anything? Can't we just... just..." she buried her face in her palms. "I don't know."

I tread carefully. "Do you just want to rest?"

She dropped her hands to her sides and stared at the ceiling. "I don't know."

Now I was extremely confused. "All right, then. I'm just going to lie here. We don't have to do anything." Truthfully, I didn't mind it either. I was exhausted and on edge, having had a brutal day—

Suddenly, she was on me—kissing me hungrily, hitching up her nightgown. Meryn straddled my hips, rolling into me. Stunned by the abrupt shift in her behavior, I grasped her by her shoulders and broke the kiss.

"Whoa! Meryn, slow down for a moment."

She arched her brow and whipped off her nightgown. I was both surprised and heated to find she wasn't wearing anything underneath. "Maybe I don't want to slow down?" Grasping my nightshirt, she tugged it upward.

I gently wrapped my hands around her wrists and stopped her, holding her gaze. "Meryn. I want you, *trust me.* But something is wrong."

Meryn stared at me for a moment longer before tears filled her eyes. She buried her face in her hands, and sobs burst from her as lowered herself to my chest. I wrapped my arms around her and sighed.

She stayed there for a long time, her tears creating a river along my torso. Eventually, her sobs dissolved into sniffles. We lay there in the silence, a chasm stretched between us. I patiently waited for her to cross it.

At last, she spoke, cheek still pressed to my shoulder. "He tried to kiss me tonight."

My breathing ceased as the blood rushed from my head. "He... what?"

Meryn clung tighter. "After dinner. He escorted me to the bottom of the stairs, bid me goodnight, and then leaned in. I offered my hand instead."

Fire filled my blood, coursing through my veins. I wanted to hunt the man down and turn him into chum. The audacity of trying to kiss her. *My* Meryn. Just the thought of another man's lips on her incensed me. Still, I tried to rein in my tension.

"I'm sorry," was all I could think to say, though I wanted to scream curses at the top of my lungs.

Meryn sat up enough to look me in the eye. She studied me closely. "You're angry, aren't you?"

All I could do was meet her stare with hardened features. I tried to soften, to deny my emotions, but it was hard to hide anything from her. Not when I felt like connecting my fist with Sebastian's face.

"Your face is red," she observed.

I rolled my eyes and sat up. Meryn rolled off me and watched me hop out of bed and stalk across the room. Trying to control the shaking that flitted through my body, I folded my hands behind my head. A deep, angry laughter escaped from my chest.

I was not angry. I was *furious*.

"Perhaps."

She pulled the blanket up over her chest and frowned. "Angry at me?"

My brows raised as guilt flashed through me. "You? Of course not. You've done nothing wrong."

Meryn nodded, her eyes fixating on her lap. "Still. Maybe I shouldn't have told you. I didn't mean to upset you."

"Upset?" I quickly crossed the room and pressed my palms into the mattress, staring her down. "Yes, Meryn, I'm upset. How can I not be? I mean, this man is trying to take you away from me! And now, on top of everything, he has made you cry! I just..." I dropped my head, taking a deep breath. "You've done nothing wrong by telling me. I want you to trust me. But, yes, I would be lying if I said this was easy."

Meryn snapped. "Easy? Of course, it isn't easy, Finn! How do you think I feel? I'm going to be sold off to the highest bidder while you're free to live your life however you choose. Don't talk to me about *easy*."

My jaw dropped. "I never said that I thought this was easy for you."

She was already throwing the blankets off. She leaped from the bed to face me. Poking a finger into my chest, she glared up at me.

"Listen here, Finn Fishman, you have no clue what it's like to be in my shoes right now. To be a woman. Men are the ones who have it easy. I'm bound with invisible chains while you get to make whatever choice you see fit, with little consequence. It's either the marriage bed or the temple for me. I'm not free, and I never will be. And I hate that. Sometimes I hate *you* for that. I hate everyone. And I can't," she swallowed as her eyes filled with tears, "I can't figure out how to go on living like this."

An icy spear pierced my heart to hear that last sentence. That she was even thinking like that frightened me. I stared at her with wide eyes, my chest rising and falling like ocean waves in a storm. "Meryn... don't say that."

"Why not? It's the truth."

I slipped my hands around her cheeks and glared at her. "Meryn, don't *ever* think like that. You can't let this get to you like that. You can't..." I squeezed my eyes shut and took a deep breath. "Hate if you want, but fight. Don't ever stop. *Do not give up*."

"Why not?"

"Because your life is worth living, Meryn. You are worthy of everything good in this world, whether you realize it or not. Whether they realize it or not." My throat bobbed. "I realize it."

Meryn's face crumpled as she slipped her arms around my neck. "I don't deserve you, Finn."

I buried my hand in her hair and held her close,

breathing in her scent. "You deserve far better than me."

She planted a soft kiss on the side of my neck. "It's you I want." Her lips traveled higher up, just below my ear. My blood heated.

"Ask me again." Her voice was a whisper in the night. I felt my heart skip in response to her words. "Ask me to leave with you again."

Disappointment filled me. *She isn't ready to be married,* I reminded myself. Hope filled my chest, though, as her words sank in.

"Leave with me. Leave them all behind. Don't marry him. Don't go to the Priesthood. Go with me."

"I need you, Finn," she whispered. "I know I'm not supposed to. Maybe it's playing with fire, but I need you. I can't stay here anymore and pretend to be something I'm not."

She pulled back, and I knew she was praying for understanding. She wasn't promising to marry me, but she would let me help her. She would let me save her. Maybe, for now, that was enough.

As I nodded, her eyes grew heavy with longing and hope.

"When should we leave?" I would leave it to her, but in the back of my mind, I knew we couldn't wait long.

"I need time. I want to be prepared. We'll need supplies. We must be far away before Father notices." I watched a twinge of pain flash behind her eyes, and I knew she was thinking, *If he notices.*

"A few weeks?" The question hung in the air between us.

"Two weeks. Before Father comes back." New determination filled her features as she took a deep breath, as if a great burden had finally lifted from her.

I kissed the top of her head again, aware of everything she was risking. Everything she was leaving behind. Her hands raked gently down my back as she kissed me again.

Her lips were soft, but her touch was full of need. "Please?"

There was no way I could deny her. I responded with a slow, deep kiss. "All right, then."

We made wild love that night, eager to wash away all

traces of another. I took her against the wall, driving into her until we both dissolved into cries of passion. She was warm and alive, our bodies working in perfect sync. I loved the feel of her around me.

After we met our release together, Meryn collapsed against my chest, sucking in air. All the tension fled her body as I held her close, still connected. I carried her to the bed and carefully laid down on my back, completely exhausted and happy.

"Finn... that was..." Meryn laughed before she raised her head and met my lips with a deep kiss. She then rolled off me and cuddled up to my chest with a smile on her face. "Thank you."

I kissed the top of her head and laid my cheek on her hair. Words couldn't express how much I loved her at that moment.

She had yet to tell me how she felt, and time was running out.

Chapter Twenty-Five

Meryn

The Trevions had been with us for three days and would likely be there for many, many more. Father's 'hunting expedition' was a far-off one that would keep him away for weeks. I knew his scheme. I knew my role in it.

I also knew my own plans to escape it.

Every time I thought of running away with Finn, my stomach twisted with both trepidation and excitement. I would abandon everything I knew, but it would come with a freedom I'd craved my entire life. Finn and I would start over somewhere together. Perhaps a little cottage with a garden. Something cozy and modest. I was through with drafty castles and tapestries. I was through with being told what to do and how to act. As long as Finn was at my side, I could change my life for the better.

All these thoughts and more trailed through me as I stared at the ceiling above my bed.

It was another tiring morning of preparations. I took my bath before Anaat arrived, conscious of the state I was in after my encounter with Finn the night before. His scent was on my skin and my hair was a mess. Nola helped me comb it out after it was cleaned. I saw her disapproving glances in the mirror as she did so.

Today's dress was a deep purple gown with shorter sleeves. Anaat pinned an amethyst brooch in the center of my neckline, highlighting my bust. She was determined to draw attention to my 'best features,' as she referred to it. I was disgusted and let her know several times. Again, she refused to let me cover up with a shawl.

Once I was finally cinched and my hair wrapped up in an intricate mass of braids, Anaat dragged me from my room, parading me toward the dining room. We were to have breakfast with the intruders. They waited patiently in the sitting room adjacent, and Sebastian rose from his chair when we entered. His smile was bright as he unabashedly looked us over.

"Good morning, ladies. I see you are looking well."

He looked dapper in his form-fitting blue suit, but it did not change the feeling of repulsion in my stomach. Despite the way my stomach churned in his presence, I forced a polite smile.

"Thank you. Good morning."

Anaat took over the pleasantries from there, exchanging compliments with Lady Trevion before we headed to the dining room. Sunlight poured in through the tall windows as we sat around the long oak table.

Painstakingly slower than I wished for, servants brought us our meals. My portion was noticeably smaller than usual—two poached eggs in cups and a bit of plain toast. I knew this was all Anaat's doing. No doubt she told the servants to take their time, and she probably hand-selected the meal I finished well before everyone else. I resisted the urge to sneer at her across the table.

Throughout breakfast, I noted Sebastian's eyes on me out of my peripheral vision. Of course, he'd sat next to me. It was much better for intimate conversation. Anaat and his mother proceeded to pay attention only to each other, leaving us to either ignore each other or speak and fall madly in love. I only thought of stabbing him with a fork if he dared to lean my way.

He soon tested my resolve by doing exactly that.

"Your cook is most excellent."

She was, but I saw little of that excellence in my meager fare. I nodded politely as I dug into my egg with the dainty spoon. "I'll pass on the compliment."

Sebastian cut into his sausage. "So, tell me, Meryn. Do you enjoy a lot of fresh foods from the sea?"

"I suppose. It's easily sourced, after all."

He glanced at the other women before his lips tipped up in a grin. "Well, I happen to enjoy fishing. Something tells me perhaps you do as well."

I froze with my spoon in mid-air. The sounds of the fateful storm floated through my memory. "Is that supposed to be a joke?" I whispered indignantly.

Sebastian blinked in confusion. "Joke? No, why would it be?"

Turning to him with my jaw dropped, I nearly delivered a biting remark. Was it possible that he had not heard of my accident? I was sure that news of it had spread far and wide—especially to someone with an interest in me. Still, he showed no signs of teasing. Closing my mouth again, I took a stabilizing breath.

"Actually, I do enjoy fishing. It's just... been a while."

Sebastian smiled. "Well, I think it's high time we fixed that. Why don't we take a boat today and catch something delicious for dinner?"

Truth be told, I missed the feeling of being out on the water. I longed to feel the wind in my hair and the gentle rocking of the boat. I'd yet to go out on a boat with Finn or anyone else, for that matter. Not since my accident. The thought filled me with both apprehension and excitement. Sebastian seemed genuinely enthused by the prospect.

"I suppose we could take a short trip."

His smile broadened, and he clapped his hands together. "Excellent! We'll prepare straight away," he declared as if he were lord of the household.

"What's this about?" asked Lady Trevion with a curious

smile.

Before Sebastian could respond, I leaned past him to grin at her. "We've decided that we're all taking a fishing excursion today."

I caught Sebastian's falling expression out of the corner of my eye. His own lack of clarity had thwarted his hope of alone time with me. I silently relished the victory.

"Fishing? Oh, nonsense!" Lady Trevion giggled. "I've no interest in such things. Anaat and I have other plans."

Anaat met my eyes with a look that said volumes. "Yes, we will be busy today. The two of you are welcome to take a boat out and enjoy yourselves. Just be sure to wear a hat, Meryn."

Sebastian beamed. I did not. It seemed my victory would be short-lived.

After breakfast, Anaat brought me the most ridiculous outfit I've ever worn. It was a bathing costume that looked like white and green striped fabric vomited all over me. The short, puffy sleeves squeezed at my muscled arms. The only thing even remarkably tolerable was the high collar. A split skirt gathered at the ankles, making my legs look like strange puffed pastries. The swollen fabric swished between my legs as I walked to the wardrobe to get my hat.

"Anaat, I look absolutely ridiculous!" I whined, fingering the lace ruffles at my shoulders. "Why can't I just wear normal trousers? Or the overalls?"

She rolled her eyes. "You're not dressing like a man, Meryn, and that's *final*. You look perfectly lovely. It's the latest fashion."

I silently mocked her as I pulled the wide-brimmed straw hat on over my low, simple braid. At least I rid myself of all the hairpins. This thick, stuffy fabric would be nearly unbearable in the blistering sun, though. Still, it was not a battle I would win.

At last, I met Sebastian in the kitchen. It was then I realized another benefit to this ridiculous ensemble. I hoped he thought me as atrocious as I felt. To my disappointment, his face lit up with a broad smile. He was wearing cropped tan breeches and a blue vest over a billowing white shirt. It was the most casual I'd ever seen him. I half-expected him to show up in formal dinner attire.

"Ready to go?" I asked with a small smile as I accepted the lunch basket offered by the cook.

Sebastian took the basket and nodded as his eyes swept over me. "I am."

My cheeks heated, and I pushed past him. "All right then. Right this way."

A hand gently grasped my elbow and brought me to a halt. I stopped and whipped my head around to find him offering his arm to me with a smile. The thought of refusing was tempting, but I saw the kitchen staff watching with eager interest. Anaat would find out if I refused, and I'd never hear the end of it. Biting back a sigh in frustration, I slipped my arm around his and we set off toward the pier.

We gathered supplies and a small dinghy as Sebastian continued to boast of his sailing abilities. I was content to let him take over. My heart raced the moment we left the dock. Despite his bravado about his sailing accomplishments, I could not help but notice the way he stood out among the true sailors at the dock. Sebastian's clothes were pristine, his hands neatly manicured. It took him several minutes to untangle the mooring line of our boat—something I learned in a few minutes on Mr. Aurin's vessel.

The only pleasant part of the afternoon would be no guards and no guides. It would be just the two of us, sailing out into the open waters. I cast a long look back at the castle as we pulled away, and it could've been my imagination, but I thought I saw Finn standing at the back gate watching us. My heart lurched with guilt.

After we were far from shore, Sebastian set up the fishing poles. Once more, he blathered on about his successful fishing trips and all the leviathans he'd conquered. I did not bother to feign interest, as he didn't bother to allow me to respond. The man loved to talk, talk, talk.

"And then there was the time..." he began again, but I was well beyond listening.

I wonder what might happen if he were to fall out of the boat? I thought to myself wickedly. *Am I lady enough to pull him back into the boat or would he have to swim to shore?*

"So," he began after a blessed stretch of silence. He squinted at me through the glare of the sun. "Tell me more about *Meryn*."

Genuine shock filled me. "I'm afraid I don't know what you mean?"

"Well, I know that you're quite accomplished in art and music. You're well read. But I still don't feel as if I *know* you. What kinds of things do you like? What do you dream of? That sort of thing."

Surprised that he actually took any sort of interest, I was speechless for a moment. Why was he asking such things? Did Anaat put him up to it? The only person I ever really talked about such things with was Finn. Not that any other man had ever cared to know before.

"I..." I raked through my brain for a coherent response. "I suppose I like the sea."

Sebastian nodded, his gaze drifting toward the horizon. "The sea." His lips tipped up in an amused grin. "I see."

My attention turned back to my pole, hoping that would be the end of that line of questioning. I tried not to groan as he pressed on.

"What is it about the sea that you love? Don't you get bored with it, living by it day in and day out?" His eyes watched me again. I shifted uncomfortably against the hard wood of the hull.

"I don't know. I think perhaps it's the way it smells."

His brows rose. "The way it *smells*?"

I nodded. "When the breeze comes through. Over the water. It's like nothing else in the world." I braced the pole between my knees and angled toward him. "And swimming in it—it's like entering a whole *new* world." A smile lit my face the more I thought about it. "You know, sometimes I imagine there's an entire world somewhere under the sea. One with a society of creatures we've never seen before. Ever since I was a little girl, I've wondered what it would be like to live there. I wanted to dive deep into the cool water instead of trudging around on land under the hot sun. To be wild and free of..." *Clothing. Forced marriages. Fathers who didn't care about their daughter's happiness.* I nearly said it all.

Sebastian was staring at me strangely. Almost as if he thought me entirely mad. Perhaps he did. If that were so, maybe he would give up his scheme of marriage. I returned to my pole with a sigh.

"Anyway, that's Meryn. Take her or leave her."

"Perhaps I'll take her," Sebastian responded quietly.

Just as I was turning to respond, Sebastian wrapped his hand around my fishing pole and took it from me, placing it in the holding ring on the side of the boat. He kneeled at my side and took my hand in his. I froze in place with nowhere to run.

"Sebastian, what are you doing?"

His blue eyes pierced mine. "Meryn, you must know that I've loved you since the ball last year."

My brows raised as high as they would go. "I'm sorry, come again?" I squeaked out. This was not going the direction I thought it would go. Not so soon. My panic built.

"I know I've given a different impression, but I was a coward, to be honest."

I gulped. "A coward?"

"Yes, a coward." He laughed, finding my eyes again. "I'm not so cowardly anymore, though. And I think perhaps you can sense the connection between us now." As if to emphasize his point, he brought his large, sweaty palm to rest on the thin fabric covering my knee.

The word 'connection' made me want to vomit over the side of the boat. My stomach roiled. Pressing my free hand over my abdomen, I swallowed the excess saliva suddenly collecting in my mouth.

"Sebastian, I don't feel so well."

He chuckled. "I'm a bit nervous myself, I confess."

"Nervous about what?"

A warm hand slipped around my cheek as Sebastian leaned into me, his eyes flicking to my lips. "About this." He tilted his head to get under the brim of my hat and pulled me into him, capturing my lips with his own.

It was a heated kiss. I could sense his urgency—as if his desire had been building up for a long time, only to be released upon me in that moment. Too stunned to move, I sat there rigidly. The acrid feeling in my stomach was building.

New fear filled me. A confrontation with him out in a boat could end very poorly. I had nowhere to run. I was prey caught in a trap.

"Lord Trevion, I hardly think this—" I began to express how improper his actions were, my hand gently pressing against his broad chest.

A boom of thunder shook the air. Sebastian startled, falling backward. The moment he turned to see the dark clouds rushing upon us, I vomited forcefully over the side of the boat. He cursed, briefly laying a sympathetic hand on my back before turning to the sails.

When I sat up and wiped my mouth on the back of my short sleeve, horror filled me to find the blue sky was rapidly being eaten up by a rolling mass of black. Sharp, painful raindrops pounded against my skin.

"I'm sure it will be over quickly." Sebastian's voice boomed above the wind as the boat rocked.

It wouldn't. I'd seen this happen once before.

"No..." I whimpered, clinging to my seat. "Not again."

"Get the rods!" Sebastian barked, breaking me out of my terrified stupor.

I quickly collected them and reeled them in before tossing them in the bottom of the boat. Lightning flashed in the sky.

The waves kicked up with the incoming winds. Sebastian threw me a rope. "Tie this around your waist!"

I did so with shaking hands. My stomach was tumbling again.

This has to be a nightmare. There's no way this is happening again!

As we rode the rolling sea, the rain drove into us and lightning struck all around. Sebastian fought to steer us toward the flattest waters, but I could see he was tiring quickly. He seemed to make things worse, turning the boat away from shore instead. Every time I offered to help, he shouted at me to huddle back down in the hull.

The storm only grew in magnitude. Hailstones the size of large grapes crashed against my skull. I clung to the bench next to me and ducked, having long since lost my hat.

Then I heard it. Above the sound of the wind and the thunder, the chanting echoed around me. Like a familiar song, it called the waves. Chills ran down my spine and it had nothing to do with the cold water. This was no ordinary storm.

Something *wanted* me. Wanted to drag me down to the depths. I felt it in my bones.

The chanting grew in volume, mingling with every roll of thunder like a melody. It echoed through the air, setting my hairs on end. Everywhere I turned seemed to be the source. It surrounded us in a maddening cacophony I couldn't decipher.

I slammed my hands over my ears. Sebastian appeared wholly unaffected. His attention was consumed by steering the boat. I wanted to shake him. How couldn't he hear it?

Deep inside, I already knew the answer.

My heart thumped wildly. Something was telling me to stand. A coaxing pull deep inside me wanted me to rise to my feet at that very moment. I fought it as hard as I could. It wasn't safe. I should stay where I was.

Still, I rose, like a woman possessed. I vaguely heard Sebastian's shouts over the din and the pulse in my ears. I climbed to the top of the bench, my tears mixing with the rain.

A moment later, the main sheet snapped. The boom swung through the air, connected with my back, and knocked me into the churning waves. The rope around my waist broke.

It was like hitting stone. My body tossed violently in the water before I sank into the cold, roiling tomb that encased me. It was impossible to get my bearings. All the while, the chanting reverberated in my chest.

I couldn't find the surface. I couldn't breathe. Up was down, and down was sideways. My body was tossed about like a rag doll.

This was how I was going to die.

Thoughts of Mother filled me. Memories of her smile and the warmth of her arms around me. I thought of Anaat. I even thought of Father... but mostly I thought of Finn.

I wasn't ready to let him go yet. *No.* This couldn't be the end. We hadn't had enough time together. Not enough time to express how much he meant to me. Not enough time in his arms.

Scalae, help me.

Two arms wrapped under my shoulders. I opened my eyes and found myself face-to-face with a strange, dark-eyed man. He smiled, long dark braids framing his face. Out of the corner of my eye, I saw a swish of black. We shot toward the surface.

We broke into the air, where I gasped and choked. The chanting had ceased. Above us, the storm was already dissipating. Sebastian was desperately calling my name.

We'd ended up far on the opposite side of the boat. My savior spoke into my ear, "Don't answer yet, please. I can't be seen."

Through my daze, I looked over his bare shoulders and saw the unmistakable hints of fins breaking the surface. My eyes widened.

"You're a—"

"Shh," he whispered, voice clear and calm in my ear. "It's all right. I'm a friend. I'll swim you to the boat now."

I nodded, clinging to him like a buoy. Swiftly, we made it through the choppy water to the dinghy, where a despondent Sebastian was still calling for me.

With a great push, the stranger lifted me out of the water enough so I could cling to the edge of the boat. When I looked back at him, he put his finger to his lips. A sly grin spread across his face before he sunk beneath the waves.

I bit back my astonishment and called for Sebastian. He rushed over to me, flailing around the boat as it continued to rock. He hauled me over the side of the craft and into his arms.

"Oh, thank the gods! Your rope snapped, and I thought you were dead!"

Sebastian planted kisses on my head and held me to his chest as if I were a child. I stared off into the calming waters.

"So did I."

If not for Scalae... and a merman.

Chapter Twenty-Six

Fivrial

I waited on the docks with the guards, my heart thrashing against my ribcage. From the moment the first roll of thunder echoed across the sky, I knew something was wrong. A sick feeling crept into my stomach.

Meryn was out there.

The morning was clear when I watched the two of them sail off on the small craft. It wasn't long before darkness swept over the sky. *It's just a little summer storm*, I told myself again.

The sea filled with fury, each wave growing higher and higher. Fishermen scrambled to moor their boats, but some wouldn't be as lucky. Panicked voices filled the air.

There were many ships and smaller vessels still out in the bay. My stomach retched as enormous hunks of debris floated in on the waves. From the size of the debris, some of the duke's larger ships must not have survived.

If the larger ships couldn't withstand the storm...

Then, I heard it. An angry female voice drifted across the water. Someone was chanting—urging the storm on.

No one else could hear it. Around me, townspeople had gathered to aid the boats along the docks. Wives waited anxiously to see if their husbands were still on the sea. Their faces filled with horror at the sudden onslaught, but they couldn't feel the darkness. Their ears were not attuned to the voice that called the waves in an insidious tongue. Words called forth the gales that could be taking the life of the woman I loved, and I was trapped onshore with useless legs. All I could do was silently appeal to Scalae to spare her life.

Just when I thought I would go mad, the chanting ceased and the storm swiftly dissipated. Guards leaped into boats and took off across the water to locate the missing lady and lord. I tried to join them but was told in no uncertain terms that I would only be in the way.

I paced along the pier. Anaat and Lady Trevion were waiting anxiously back at the castle, deemed too delicate to be out in the weather. Lady Trevion's antics before I left were positively ear-splitting.

An eternity passed as my impatience grew. At that moment, I would have given up everything to don fins once more to seek Meryn out among the wreckage. I thought my heart was going to crack in two every time I considered the idea of the guards coming back empty-handed. If Wrenna were there, I'd beg her to end the spell early and give me a tail so I could find Meryn myself. To hell with consequences.

Mrs. Rigby's warning played in my mind continuously: *"A tragedy is imminent..."*

Did I bring this on myself? Was I the one to put Meryn's life in danger?

The mere thought was sickening. I'd sooner throw my human self into the sea than cause harm to the woman I loved.

With each passing moment, my legs grew weaker. I found I could not pace the dock anymore. Instead, I perched in the center of the longest dock. One way or another, I would wait for her return.

She had to come home. Somehow. Someway.

I lifted my eyes to the skies, which were turning blue again.

Please, Scalae...

A commotion rose around me. People pushed past me, flooding to the end of the dock. A pair of boats limped into the harbor. The sails of the largest vessel were torn. Sailors, looking worn and weary, struggled to keep the ship on track. Towing behind the ship, a battered dinghy limped along. My heart snapped back together at last.

It took what felt like an eternity for them to finally reach the docks. When my eyes laid on Meryn, a deep, shattered breath escaped my chest. I ran my shaking hands through my hair.

I watched as they made their way across the gangplank. Her untamed locks fell limply along her back. Her eyes held a horrified, dazed look. Sebastian guided her with an arm around her shoulders. I didn't even care at that moment. She was *alive*.

When her feet hit the dock, a deep need took over. I had to touch her. I needed to hold her and feel she was okay.

I pushed through the crowd of spectators, anxious to reach her. Meryn's slender shoulders were dwarfed by a large, gray blanket. When I broke through the crowd, her eyes found mine and filled with relief. My feet carried me through the crowd in a daze, pushing through the people who had gathered. I finally reached the edge as she gave the most subtle shake of her head. It stopped me in my tracks.

It stung. All I wanted was to feel her in my arms—to feel the rise and fall of her chest with every breath she took. I wanted to put my ear to her breast and hear her heartbeat. But it was forbidden.

They escorted her past me as if I were nothing more than another gawking citizen. Sebastian's arm was still planted around her, and she didn't object. There was no crying or shoving him away. I watched them walk back toward the castle, looking like a pair of lovers. The gossiping whispers of townsfolk rose with every step.

Downtrodden, I followed behind at a distance, keeping my gaze trained to the ground. I couldn't bear to see it. I tried to focus on the fact that she was alive and well. Scalae had spared her. Tragedy was not the order of the day after all. I should have been more grateful.

Anaat's cries echoed through the entire castle the moment Meryn reached the garden gate. Deep, fearful wails spewed from Anaat as she squeezed Meryn's shoulders. Lady Trevion gently sobbed against Sebastian's broad chest. He patted his mother's back gently, but his eyes never left Meryn.

Through it all, Meryn was unusually quiet. When they peppered her and Sebastian with questions, I scarcely heard more than one-word answers from her.

"Thank the stars you are both all right," said Lady Trevion, dabbing her eyes with a handkerchief as she grasped her son's hand. "I take it your sailing skills are to credit for your survival, Sebastian."

Sebastian smiled wearily. "That and Meryn's excellent swimming. Making it back to the boat through rough seas was nothing short of a miracle."

Lady Trevion laid a hand on Meryn's upper arm. "It sounds like you've had quite the extraordinary experience. I'm sure you're exhausted, my dear. Sebastian, why don't you escort her to her room?"

The garden grew quiet. Such a suggestion was shocking. Even Anaat shifted uncomfortably. Meryn stood—frozen in place. My fists clenched at my side.

Sebastian nodded as if it were an everyday suggestion. "Of course. Come, Meryn. Let's get you upstairs."

With that, he led her away into the castle through the kitchen door. My shoulders slumped in defeat as the servants filed in after them. They surely wouldn't be left alone, but it happened so easily. Even I didn't have the privilege of openly approaching her bedroom door. We had to sneak around like some scandal-ridden affair.

A hand clapped my shoulder. I turned to see Captain Carbor eying me with sympathy. "You look like you could use a drink."

I nodded. Though I'd never consumed strong drink before, I assumed that's what he meant. Meryn disappeared down the hall as Sebastian wrapped his arm once more around her shoulders and I was more than ready. I did need a drink. *Maybe more than one.*

"Come on," said the captain, "it's the end of my shift. Let's head to the barracks."

That night, I drank away my sorrows. The guards were very accommodating and entertaining. They thought it was fun to see someone "deep in their cups for the first time" as they referred to it. The drink spread through me, and I felt myself relax.

They encouraged me to join in their merry songs, but even in my altered state, I knew that would be a dangerous idea. I politely declined and clapped along instead.

When I'd had my fill, Carbor delivered me safely to my room, where I laid down for a while, waiting for the room to stop spinning.

My thoughts continued to jumble as I reeled from the events of this tiresome day. I quietly hummed the new songs I'd learned. My voice still filled the room. It was so rare that I heard my own singing. I wasn't a bad singer. It was unfair that I had to keep a rein on my voice.

Images of dancing and playing together in the music room flashed across my mind. If only Meryn could hear it, perhaps she'd be more inclined to reject Sebastian's touch.

The memory of his arm around her filled me with drunken fury. I wanted to hunt him down and tear him apart for touching her. After all, she was *my* Meryn. Not *his* Meryn. She didn't love him. She loved me.

Did she love me? I sat up in the bed now, nearly tipping off the edge. She certainly liked me. She most *definitely* wanted me. *And why shouldn't she?* I raised my hands toward my face, turning them back and forth. My legs blurred as I struggled to stand. I looked down at the thick muscles growing along my calves. I was, after all, a perfect siren-human specimen. Perhaps the only human-siren specimen.

That old witch lady was probably jealous.
Maybe she wanted me for herself?

I laughed at the thought until my sides hurt. The world tilted as I fell. The cool floor rose to greet me, but I caught myself in time. I braced myself on my hands and knees. The old woman's warning rang in my ears now.

What if she was right? What if Meryn really was in danger? The events of that day were certainly evidence of that. Someone had been determined to hurt Meryn regardless of who else they hurt in the process.

Through my bleariness, the sobering truth reared its ugly head. The moonlight shone bright and silvery across the floorboards of my room. Tomorrow, the moon would be full, and I would have to leave again. If I didn't, *I* would be the one endangering her.

I had come so close to losing her this afternoon. I remembered her hollow, terrified gaze as she walked from the boat. She had looked so worn, so exhausted.

I had to go to her. The hour was late, and she had yet to come to my room. She was sure to be exhausted after the day's events, but I couldn't leave her again without at least warning her. Feeling a little more myself, I rose from the floor, crept out of my bedroom, and half-stumbled my way up to Meryn's room.

When I reached her door, I leaned heavily on the wall next to it as the stairwell swayed behind me. Clenching my eyes shut, I rapped my knuckles on the wooden planks. Though I repeatedly told myself to be quieter, the noise pounded in my ears.

I listened eagerly as soft footsteps approached from the other side. Soft light filled the hall as the door slowly cracked open.

At first, all I saw was a pretty amber eye and a sliver of her face. The eye widened when it landed on me. A frown spread across that beautiful face as she swung the door open.

Her grip was firm as she yanked me into the room. I promptly stumbled across the floor with a laugh.

"Finn, what in the hell is going on? What's wrong with you?"

I found my feet again, trying to stand straighter. A sense of relief spread over me as I looked her over. I could not help but smile as I pulled her tight into my arms. "Nothing, I just wanted to come and check on you."

Meryn crinkled her nose and waved her hand in front of her face. "Ugh. Have you been drinking?"

I shrugged. "I may have spent some time with the guards. They're actually quite a fun bunch when you get to know them."

She extracted herself carefully from my arms, holding onto my shoulders so I did not tip over again. "Well, I'm glad you had fun, but I'm afraid I need to get back to sleep."

Her lips looked so pretty when she talked. They were ripe for the kissing. I missed those lips.

Instinct took over as I slipped my hands around her face, pulling her in for a deep kiss. Meryn made a loud, muffled sound before bracing her hands on my chest and roughly shoving me away. Her face was contorted with anger.

"I don't want to kiss you right now, Finn. You're not yourself. Now, go to bed and I'll talk to you in the morning."

With a grin, I turned around, stumbling over to her bed. I crawled across the sheets, propping myself up on my elbow. "You mean this bed?" I patted the space next to me with a wink.

Fire flashed in Meryn's eyes. She marched over to the bed and grabbed me by the elbow.

"That's enough! Now, get off—"

In a swift move, I wrapped my arm around her waist, yanking her onto the bed. She squirmed underneath me until I promptly pinned her arms above her head.

Her body went still underneath mine, her legs wrapping around my waist. I kissed her neck first, gently nipping and biting at her sensitive collar bone. I felt her body melt into me, her hips rising against mine. Her long fingers laced with my own above her head.

I kissed her lips gently, pressing my forehead to hers. For a few seconds, I just listened to her breathe. I sent thanks to Scalae again as I marveled at Meryn being safe in my arms once more.

Trying to rid my thoughts of what could have been, I continued raining her body with soft kisses. Each time her breath caught I began again. Then, I did the worst thing I could think of.

Instead of kissing my way down her waist, I stopped short, nibbling on her ribs. It was the worst of her ticklish spots. Meryn squirmed and thrashed. Her short, high-pitched giggles were music in my ears.

Finally, I let go of her arms. She immediately moved to pin me to the bed.

Pretending to struggle against her, I allowed her the small victory. Her warm thighs straddled my waist as her long, red locks fell in a curtain around us.

A piece of me broke as I looked at her perched above me, full of joy. The tears I had managed not to shed all day finally fell.

Her soft palm traced my chin as she gave me a knowing look. The terror of what could have been sat between us. I pulled her gently off my hips, tucking her at my side.

My happiness slipped away as I remembered what had brought me to her room in the first place. *The storm.* I tightened my hold around her and kissed her shoulder. "You scared me today. I thought you were..." My throat constricted and I couldn't force myself to continue.

Meryn squeezed my forearm, wrapping it around her chest. "So did I."

"What happened?"

She was silent for a moment. I waited patiently for her to continue, knowing how terrible it must be to relive it again. Her words were a whisper against my skin when she finally spoke. "You probably wouldn't believe me if I told you."

"I would never doubt you. Please tell me?"

"Maybe I should wait until morning—"

"No," I insisted, squeezing her, "please don't wait. The things I've imagined... wondered... all day."

Meryn sighed, nuzzling her face against my ribs for comfort. "All right." She snuggled deeper into my arms and began her tale. "It was just like before when I wrecked Aurin's boat. It was a clear blue sky when we went out. Then, the storm came out of nowhere. And I know this sounds unbelievable, but I could hear a voice mixing with the thunder. It was like singing. It urged the storm on. It felt..." She paused for a moment, as if considering her words.

"It felt like the storm was for me. Like it was aimed at the boat. Whoever was singing wanted me to drown. And then I felt a voice inside me." She hesitated, drawing a shuddering breath. "Sebastian told me to stay in the bottom of the boat, but something was telling me to stand up on the bench instead. I didn't want to, but for some reason... I did it anyway. It was like I wasn't in control anymore."

She wiped tears from her cheeks, and I felt them fall down my chest. A chill crept down my spine as she spoke. I kissed the top of her head again. "You're safe now."

I felt her tense up at my words. It was the same thing I said to her in the grotto before. I shook the idea from my head. *She doesn't remember any of that.*

Finally, she continued. "The boom broke loose and knocked me overboard. I thought I would die, but—and this is really going to sound unbelievable—someone saved me."

I nodded. A flood of disappointment filled me as I remembered the way Sebastian had guided her from the ship. *I should have been there.* "Sebastian." I spat his name.

"No. He was on the boat. This was someone... in the water. A man." She paused for a long time. "He had fins."

My heart nearly stopped beating in my chest. "A merman?"

Meryn nodded. "I know it sounds mad, but I'm telling you. Finn, he had a tail. He told me he was a friend and that he was going to swim me to the boat. And then... he did."

Now it was my turn to be silent. I felt my mind clearing by the second.

A merman saved her. But who? Why?

"What did he look like?" I filled my voice with false wonder and amazement.

"Well, he had dark eyes, a black tail, and... oh! Braids. Black braids."

Renold. It couldn't have been anyone else. He must've been swimming our usual routes at the right time. It was by Scalae's grace he was there.

I breathed a little easier. At least it was someone I knew

I could trust with her. *Not* a siren. I owed him a great debt. Silently, I thanked Scalae for sending him.

"I believe you."

Meryn craned her neck to look at me. "You do?"

I nodded. "I do."

Her eyes grew misty. "Thank you."

"I'll always believe you, Meryn. I love you." I kissed her cheek.

She smiled. "I don't deserve you, Finn. But I'm glad you came to me."

A sting of disappointment pricked me. Not quite the response I was hoping for. Still, closer than we were at the start.

My smile faded a bit. "Another thing I needed to talk to you about... I'll be gone again tomorrow. Until the next day."

Her face fell. "Gone? Again?"

I nodded. "The way I was *that* day... I have a feeling it's going to happen again. And I need to go away. Just for the day."

"But where? Where will you go?"

Pausing, I searched for a way to answer. "Out to sea. Alone."

Sadness twisted her features, but she nodded. "And you promise you'll be back?"

My lips twitched into a grin. "I promise."

We lay together for a little while longer, silently sorting through our thoughts. At last, I rose and left the warmth of her bed to head for my own. Meryn stopped me at her door.

"Thank you for telling me about tomorrow."

I took her hand and gave it a gentle squeeze. "Thank you for trusting me."

She slipped her hand around the back of my neck and pulled me in for a brief kiss. "Goodnight, Finn."

"Good night, my love."

One last kiss goodnight, and I found my way back to my room. That night, I dreamed of my younger days, playing with Renold under the water, and training together. Even in my dreams, I knew he was the best friend a merman could ask for.

Chapter Twenty-Seven

Meryn

To my relief, I was allowed to sleep in the day following my "accident." Not even Anaat dared to disturb me. When I awoke, it was nearing midday. I snuggled deeper into my pillows, debating whether I could go back to sleep.

The warmth of the sun stretched across the sheets as I rolled over. I watched out the window as fair-weather clouds floated through the clear, blue sky. It was going to be a gorgeous day. Hopefully, it would stay that way.

Without Anaat's presence to primp and prod me, I donned one of my regular dresses. It was a plain, powder-blue material, with no stays or swollen layers to make my hips larger. I put my naturally curly tresses in a simple braid. My feet practically skipped through the halls as I smiled triumphantly. Anaat would likely murder me, but at least I'd die comfortable.

I was fortunate enough to make it to the kitchen without interruption. Our cook, a sweet, older woman, heaped mounds of food on my plate. The servants doted on me, offering their sympathies for my experience. I'd known most of them for many years and it was a comfort to have them near without the pressuring presence of my sister and the Trevions.

After taking my time in the kitchen, I strolled through the halls, not in any particular hurry to join anyone else. My heart ached for Finn's soothing voice. Things just weren't the same without him. Our carefree days together were the happiest days of my life.

Why did the Trevions have to come and ruin everything?

The more I thought about Finn, the more my heart both warmed and ached. Where was he at that moment? Was he in pain? The way he was the month prior, on that awful day, was not like him at all. The manic obsession with the piano... the shouting... was he mad? It was a possibility. Although the truth was, I cared deeply for him—mad or not.

After all, I'd been accused of madness myself.

I smiled at the thought of him. It frightened me to think of our imminent departure. It frightened me to think of such an infinite commitment to anyone, yet I couldn't imagine myself happy with anyone else. His proposal kept floating back to the surface of my thoughts.

"We could leave this place."

When he said those words only a few days prior, it scared me. Too many things were happening at once. I only wanted freedom from everything and everyone. I still wanted to be free. But the more time I spent away from Finn, the less I wanted to be free from him. Our plans to run away filled me with an overwhelming yearning. I couldn't imagine a life without him in it.

Was this love?

Finn had said those words to me. *I love you.* The only time I'd ever heard those words from anyone was from Mother, and now Sebastian. I knew Sebastian's words were false. They came from a place of desire and possession, not a place of love.

I didn't understand love in the way Finn said it. Quite frankly, the prospect made me nervous. To say such a thing was surely a promise. It was the ultimate commitment—a sacred vow from one heart to another. I'd only known Finn for two months. Two *beautiful* months...

As I was lost in my pondering, I failed to see Sebastian coming toward me until we met in the middle of the hallway. His face lit up as I approached.

"Good afternoon," he greeted, eyes sweeping me up and down. "You're looking... different."

I lifted my chin just a little. "This is what I normally wear."

Sebastian nodded. "I see."

He didn't seem that impressed. *Good. Let him be absolutely repulsed.*

"Well, if you'll excuse me, I've got things to do," I said as politely as possible as I moved to side-step him.

He wrapped his hand around my upper arm. I snapped my eyes to his and found them solemn.

"You know we're supposed to be spending time together, Meryn."

My cheeks burned. "It is preferred, yes. Required? No. Now, let me go." I shrugged my arm, but his grip tightened as his eyes bore into mine.

"After what happened yesterday, you would spurn me so rudely?" His words were sharp. Not the charming fellow he'd been the last few days.

I narrowed my eyes and fumed. The audacity of his grip on my arm was quickly bringing my temper to a head. "It is you who are being rude right now, *Sebastian*. I'm not yours to command. In case you have so conveniently forgotten."

We stared each other down for a moment before his grip finally released. His lips stretched into a charming smile, though his eyes didn't quite reflect it. "Very well, then. I see you are still recovering from our ordeal. We'll catch up later." Sebastian turned and walked away, leaving me to breathe a sigh of relief.

I spent the rest of the day in the music room, working on a new song. My heart felt unsettled. Too many things laid upon it. The words in the storm... the mysterious merman...

and Finn. For some reason, I had the overwhelming feeling that the three were connected somehow. I couldn't figure out how or why.

I'd never talked to Finn about the old sailor legends of merfolk, and yet he knew what a merman was. Was it another piece of his memory resurfacing? Perhaps he was a sailor? He must've heard stories, at the very least, at some point.

An even stranger thought popped into my head.

What if he was a creature of the sea himself?

My very own merman. I laughed at the thought. He had a very lovely set of strong legs. The thought of them made my heart flutter.

Still, it was a curious notion. And a muse of inspiration. What would make a merman grow legs? The better question would be *why* one would ever want to? Land was boring and isolating—full of rules and horrid things like heavy dresses and greasy suitors. No. It would have to be quite a dramatic thing indeed for someone to ever give up that kind of freedom. Something like...

Love.

My fingers hovered over the piano keys, pausing the new melody I'd been playing for hours. Words finally surfaced to match them.

A son of the sea
Loved a daughter of land
Beneath swirling waves
He longed for her hand
He pined for her smile,
The light in her eyes
The joy in her laugh
And hope in her sighs
He gave up his fins
To be able to stand
For his heart longed to be
With his love on the land

It was the strangest song I'd ever written. Anaat would probably have me locked away. But it made me smile. I was determined to play it for Finn the first chance we got. He'd find it amusing, at the very least. Perhaps we'd get a good laugh out of it.

When I'd finished penning the song, the sun was setting. Time had flown by. And I relished in my victory of not having to spend it with Sebastian. Perhaps having a break from me would change his mind about spending time together.

Unfortunately, I was accosted by Anaat before dinner and forced into another silly dress. This one was red silk that showed ample bosom and nearly tripped me when I walked. I talked her out of curling my hair again and pulled it in a simple, low bun instead. At least I had one small triumph.

The dinner went as usual. Lady Trevion and Anaat chatted among themselves, while Sebastian and I were left to our own devices on the other side of the table. He was unusually quiet, though I caught his regular glances. His eyes never seemed to stray from the dip of my dress. I was tempted to pick up my plate and move to the other end of the table or feign a dizzy spell and shuffle off to bed. But I was hungry, and Anaat was watching.

By the end of the dinner, I was thoroughly annoyed. I was close to stabbing Sebastian in the eye with a fork if he looked at my breasts one more time. It repulsed me. At least when Finn looked at me, I knew he appreciated me for more than just my body.

After we were done, Lady Trevion again suggested that Sebastian escort me back to my room. This time, Anaat seemed keen on the idea. I was absolutely horrified but forced a smile.

"You know, I'm sure you have better things to do, Sebastian, and it's quite far from your room. I'll be fine to walk myself."

Sebastian rose from his seat, making a great show of "helping" me to my feet. "Oh, nonsense! It's not that far."

I looked desperately to Anaat for assistance. She merely beamed.

"You're most considerate, Sebastian."

I wanted to throttle her. Still, I accepted his arm and let

him lead me away from the safety of the dining room. We strolled through the shadowy halls, my heart pounding in my ears.

"I missed you today," Sebastian confessed.

I bit back a stronger retort. "Did you, now?"

He chuckled. "You know, you keep me on my toes, Meryn. I'll give you that."

"What's that supposed to mean?"

"It means you have spirit." Sebastian's arm hugged mine. "Not so easily tamed as other women."

My brows rose. "And tell me, Sebastian, have you 'tamed' many women?"

Sebastian paused. "A few." He then met my stare with a heated expression. "But none like you."

I should have run at that point. Or vomited. I certainly felt like vomiting, but he had me in his clutches.

We reached the archway to my stairwell at last. I avoided eye contact as I bobbed my head. "I've got it from here. Goodnight, Sebastian."

I turned to flee up the stairs, but Sebastian caught me by the arm, yanking me into him. His hand linked around my waist as he backed me into the wall, eyes burning into mine. He leaned into me, pressing his chest to mine as I wriggled beneath him.

"You know, with most women, they can be tamed with flowers and sonnets." His breath brushed my lips. "Do you know how I've dreamed of taming you, Meryn?" He grinned lustily. "Over the piano... and the library desk..." He planted a nipping kiss on my cheek. "The dining room table... and the boat. *Especially the boat...*" Another kiss on the corner of my mouth as I struggled against him. "I want to make that boat rock until you are crying out for more."

I was just starting to growl an angry response when he grabbed the back of my head and crushed his lips to mine. His other hand left my waist to snake up and grope my breast. I fought against him, turning my head to break the kiss.

"Get off of me!" I shouted, finally gathering enough of a hold to shove him away.

Sebastian's face crumpled. "Why?"

I shot daggers from my eyes. "I do *not* want to make love to you, Sebastian!"

His lips curled sardonically. "You don't want to make love? Meryn, I've been waiting an entire year for you. You know how I feel about you."

Steam was practically coming out of my ears. "How you feel and how I feel are two *very* different things. I'm not going to just lie on my back just because you want me to. I'm not a horse you can tame, Sebastian!"

He chuckled cynically and planted his hands on his hips. "So, Lady Meryn Blumley is a lady after all. Is that it?"

I crossed my arms. "You sound surprised?"

The smile faded from his face. "All right then. If you want to be proper about it, then so be it. But I mean to have a taste of you before I put a ring on your finger, Meryn. So, I highly suggest you reconsider this high-minded notion of abstinence, or you could be putting your own prospects in jeopardy."

I stared at him, chest heaving in anger. "You don't know what you're talking about."

"Oh, I don't?" He jabbed a finger toward the ground as his brows furrowed. "I know that I'm your *last chance*, Meryn. I'd rather be your first choice, but if I get to have you either way, I will bear it. And you," the finger pointed at me, "should be grateful I want you at all."

My jaw fell open. "Grateful? *Grateful?* Grateful to be treated like a—a whore?" I glowered as his words rang in my ear. I knew that there was surely gossip about me, but nothing like this.

"You, sir, are a barnacle on the ass of a whale. And I bid you *goodnight*." I turned and stomped up the stairs, muttering curses. I heard swiftly retreating footsteps and felt a smidgen of relief that he hadn't pursued me further.

Upon reaching my room, the moonlight was just starting to spill through the window. Furious at Sebastian's words, I threw a small pillow across the room. The feel of Sebastian's hand on my body remained. Humiliation filled me.

Not bothering with buttons or ribbons, I tried to tear the red dress from my shoulders. The rip of each seam was music to my ears, but I was no match for the ribbons and the stays encasing me like a casket. I would have to wait for Nola to come help me.

Sebastian's kiss still stained my mouth, so I flushed it again and again with water from my nightstand, spewing the drops out the window.

I struggled to calm my breathing, so I set about opening all the windows to let in the breeze. The smell of the sea calmed my rapid breath as I pulled the blanket from my bed tight across my shoulders. The soft fabric still smelled of Finn as I breathed it in.

It would be hard to rest without saying goodnight to Finn, but I hoped to feel his embrace first thing in the morning. In the meantime, I stood, staring out across the silvery horizon, silently praying to Scalae that he was all right, wherever he was.

I needed him to come back to me. His arms were the only arms I craved. Finn was like a soothing ointment for all my troubles.

I sighed as my heart ached. Perhaps I was falling in love with him after all.

Chapter Twenty-Eight

Fivrial

The day was another day of torment, but at least I was away from Meryn and not subjecting her to my primal struggles. I spent it on a beach—far away from the castle. Even farther than the private beach we enjoyed. Not a single soul was nearby.

I spent hours and hours struggling against my instincts. Though I didn't see anyone, I didn't want to take the chance that someone may be near enough to hear me, should I start singing. And I knew that once I started singing, I most likely wouldn't be able to stop. So, I clapped and tapped, trying to focus on anything else but the pull in my throat and the music gradually filling my head.

At last, the sun went down. I disrobed, waiting in the water for the painful transformation to begin. When it hit, my lungs ached as they changed to accommodate the water. Whether on land or in the sea, I was suffocating.

The moment the change was complete, I shot through the water toward the trench. I came closer to Brinn from this direction, but I made sure to keep toward the surface until the last possible moment before diving deeper. To be seen could be a disaster.

I had reservations about going to the trench cave now. Especially after Mrs. Rigby's warning about the dark magic being on me.

Was Wrenna dabbling in something nefarious?

The thought made my stomach churn. Still, I had no choice but to hide away in my usual spot. There was no time to hunt another one.

When I reached the cave, I released my song, and the light danced around me, just as it always did. Hours passed of singing, fighting urges, and feeling the rush of my power. And, of course, the exhaustion and shame that followed. There was always that.

Wrenna came to me as usual, this time staring at me from the mouth of the cave. When I looked up at her, I found her unsmiling. Her eyes were strangely fixated, almost as if she were looking right through me.

"Wrenna? Is everything all right?" I floated upright, keeping my distance.

Her head tilted slightly. An odd smile spread across her cheeks. "Yes, of course. Come with me, Fivrial."

My instincts were screaming. Something was wrong. *Very* wrong. I cautiously swam past her, out of the cave, making sure not to turn my back to her at any time. "Actually, I really should be getting to the surface. The sun will be rising soon."

"Of course it will. But I want you to come with me right now. There's something I want to show you."

A green light caught my attention. I glanced down and saw a glow gathering at the fingertips of her right hand. A voice in the back of my head was telling me to get out of there. *Fast.*

When I met her eyes again, I saw that same green glow blooming from her inky pupils.

"I don't think so, but thank you." I began to back up, a casual smile tilting my lips.

Wrenna's smile faded. Like a shark watching its prey, she advanced toward me. "What's the matter, Fivrial? Aren't I your friend?"

A warning was now screaming through my brain. My tail blazed brightly as I felt the threat arise. Wrenna's eyes fell to the colorful glow of my fins and hardened. It was time to go.

With a powerful flick of my tail, I shot through the water—up and away. Behind me, Wrenna released a primal screech. I heard the swish of her fins as she pursued. I didn't dare look back to see how close she was.

Faster and faster, I swam with every ounce of strength I had in me. It wasn't much after I'd drained myself, but I knew I must keep going. I had to get away. I'd drown the moment the sun came up if I was caught underwater. Wrenna seemed determined to catch me.

The surface wavered above me. I swam parallel to it, pushing myself to go even faster—toward the beach. I could see the pale light overtaking the sky. Sunup was nearing. I still heard Wrenna's furious growling behind me, but it was slowly growing more distant. I hoped it meant she was losing strength.

Finally, I didn't hear her pursuing me anymore. One last, horrifying screech sounded in the distance behind me, and then nothing. I turned my head and saw no sign of her. Cautious relief flooded me.

When I turned back around to continue to the beach, I was startled to nearly run into someone else. I backed up several flicks and then saw it was yet another enemy, though a much lesser threat. Percivan. He wore a smug smirk on his face as he crossed his arms.

I scowled. We were nowhere near Brinn now. He was likely on his way back from a night of siphoning the life force from humans.

"What are you doing here?"

We counter-circled. Percivan arched a brow. "I could ask the same of you, Fivrial. I haven't seen you in a while. Did you finally decide to do some surface singing, or were you hiding in your hole again?"

I rolled my eyes. "I don't have time for this, Percivan.

Your taunting doesn't work anymore." With a shove of my shoulder, I pushed past him.

His mocking voice reached my ears. "You know, I think maybe I finally understand you, Fiv."

"Let it lie, Percivan. I'm done with you," I called over my shoulder, noting the brightening sky.

With a quick flip of his fins, Percivan closed the distance between us and grabbed me by the shoulders from behind. I tried to shove him off, but he held on. His fists squeezed my shoulders painfully. He whispered in my ear.

"That human of yours is delicious."

My heart stopped.

No...

"What did you do to her?" I asked, a thick feeling of dread settling in my bones.

Percivan merely laughed and shoved me away. I whipped around to grab him by the throat, but he was already disappearing into the distance. There was no time to give chase. Above me, the sky was continuously changing.

Gathering up every bit of strength I had, I shot through the water toward the beach.

I had to get there... I had to get to her...

I reached the shallows just as the sun was peeking over the horizon, setting off the painful transformation once again. This time, when I screamed, it was not only from the pain, but pure frustration. *It was taking too long...* The last of the scales were still sloughing off my new legs when I rushed across the beach to grab my clothes.

After dressing in a hurry, I took off through the sand. My weak legs pumped as fast as they could. I had only one thought in my mind.

Meryn.

I needed to find her and be reassured that Percivan was just a lying bastard. I needed to know that she was alive and well and back in my arms. Damn what anyone else thought. I needed her like I needed air in my lungs as I ran across that beach.

At last, I reached the private stretch of beach. I was almost to the castle. I was almost to my love. We'd be together again, and everything would be okay.

Through the dim morning light, I trudged on, nearly tripping over a hunk of seagrass. Just as I was about to continue, something halted me. *Red.*

Instinct screamed at me to *stop.*

My breath caught in my throat as my heart pounded against my chest. I fell to my knees and began pulling away the grasses. A guttural cry escaped me. A familiar strand of red hair glowed in the morning sun. Yards of soaked, blood-red fabric spilled out along the sand. I gathered her limp arms in mine as my mind reeled against what it saw. *No. No. No.*

Meryn.

All the color had fled her beautiful sun-kissed skin, leaving it lifeless and ashy. I gathered her up in my arms and held her to my chest. Her familiar warmth had washed away, carried off by the waves.

"Meryn... no..." My hand shook as I swiped the hair from her face. I could barely see through the tears welling in my eyes. She looked like she was sleeping.

Surely she was sleeping?

"Wake up, Meryn." I shook her shoulder and put my hand to her cheek. No response. Gritting my teeth, I shook her harder. "I said wake up, Meryn!" Still, she did not move. No matter how much I shouted at her, or shook her, or kissed her cold, blue lips, I could not stir her. My voice grew hoarse as I dissolved into screaming sobs, rocking her close to my chest with the cool water lapping at our legs.

Something inside of me broke. The world around me shattered into thousands of pieces. The pain of the transformation paled in comparison to this.

I begged for death as the sobs shook my body. *Let me walk into the sea and let it take me.* I would go wherever she had gone.

All those years spent loving her, watching her grow from a girl to the fiery, wonderful woman she was... our precious few days together... the time spent in her arms... none of it was enough.

I needed more time. More. More of her. I wasn't ready to let her go. Not now. Not like this.

We were supposed to go away together. She was

supposed to be an old woman someday, playing her violin with beautiful, aged hands. And I was supposed to be at her side, accompanying her on the piano.

No... our time had been stolen. Viciously ripped away. I turned my face toward the sky, teeth bared.

"Scalae... Scalae!" My shoulders shook. "Please, have mercy!" I choked on a sob, dipping my head back down to tuck Meryn's under my chin. "Scalae..."

I cupped her face. Her beautiful, beautiful face...

"I love you." Carefully, I tilted her chin, planting another soft kiss on her icy lips.

The morning light cast around us now, creating a false warmth to her frigid figure. I kissed her again.

"I love you. I'm sorry. I'm so sorry," I whispered against her warm mouth.

Warm.

My eyes widened as the realization flooded over me.

"M-Meryn?" I shook her shoulders gently. She did not wake. I pulled close, placing my ear to her breast. Dread overwhelmed me as I struggled to believe. Very faintly, I heard a thumping.

Again, I kissed her. Her lips were a bit warmer than before.

A shock of hope flooded in. "You're alive..."

I could not rouse her, but shallow breaths now continued to pass through her lips. Quickly, I climbed to my feet, gathering her up in my arms. Wasting no time, I took off across the sand again, heading for the hill toward the path home.

My legs were sore, and my back screamed, remnants of the transformation. I pressed on, unwilling to rest for even a moment. She was still far too pale and limp in my arms. Percivan must've drained her completely. It was a miracle breath had reentered her body at all. I silently thanked Scalae as I ran.

At last, I entered the garden gates and burst through the kitchen door, frightening the kitchen staff.

"Help! Go get help!" I shouted as I laid her on the table.

Servants took off in every direction.

The elderly cook was immediately at my side. "What

happened to her?" she cried with wide eyes, bringing a towel to wipe Meryn's face and examine her.

I shook my head. "I don't know. I found her on the beach like this. She needs a healer."

Carbor came running in the door. He was still in his shirtsleeves, sleep hanging in his eyes. "What's happened?"

I repeated what I told the cook, and his eyes grew wide. He turned to another entering guard. "Fetch the doctor. Now!" The guard swiftly disappeared through the door again.

A servant came in with a quilt as Anaat's shouting filled the halls. Soon, she and Lady Trevion appeared, hair unbound and still in their dressing gowns. Anaat rushed to Meryn's side and roamed her hands over her, looking for signs of injury.

"How did this happen?" demanded Lady Trevion, horrified.

"We must get her upstairs and out of this dress or she'll catch her death. Has the doctor been called?" asked Anaat.

Carbor nodded, his face solemn, as he took a step toward the table. "Yes, he's being summoned now."

Before he could touch her, I scooped Meryn up in my arms again and pushed through the crowd of people. I wasn't willing to let another man lay a finger on her. I swiftly carried her through the halls toward her room. Anaat and a very confused Lady Trevion followed.

Anaat ran up alongside us. "Finn, I really think the guards can take it from here—"

"No," I spat before running up the stairs to the next floor.

"Meryn!" Sebastian came running toward us once we reached the top of the stairs. He reached out his arms as if to take her, but I whisked her away from him and glared.

"Stay out of the way."

Lady Trevion gasped behind us. I didn't care. Let the whole damn world be shocked.

Sebastian narrowed his eyes as he followed beside us. "Where are you taking her?"

I ignored him and kept walking. His hand reached out towards her dress. I whirled around with fire in my eyes, shoving him in the thigh with my heel. He stumbled to the ground, eyes wide with shock and indignation.

"Do not touch me or her, or so help me..." I warned through gritted teeth. I glared at where he lay sprawled across the floor. To his credit, he did not move.

Lady Trevion rushed to her son's aid in a flurry of dramatics. Fury was written all over his face, but he didn't dare approach as I turned and continued. Anaat abandoned the Trevions and hurried to my side.

"It's just up—"

"I know the way."

I caught her quiet stare from the corner of my eye. It didn't matter what she thought. Not anymore.

When we reached Meryn's room, a flurry of servants piled in behind us. I placed Meryn gently on the bed, turning her on her side. My hands immediately fumbled with the laces on her back, but a gentle hand laid on mine. I caught Anaat's knowing look.

"It's all right, Finn. We've got it from here." She wasn't angry. As a matter of fact, her eyes were full of pity and what I suspected was regret.

Anaat and the maids expertly removed the dress in far less time than I would have taken.

The heaping pile of material oozed onto the floor, reminding me of a puddle of blood.

My gaze returned to Meryn, who was still as pale as the linens she lay upon. All I wanted to do was get her out of the wet, sandy clothing and crawl into bed with her. *I would warm her myself. Maybe then she would awaken.*

I stalked back and forth as Meryn was undressed and then re-dressed. No one made any attempts to usher me from the room—not even Anaat. That was for the best; my anger was not to be tempted. Not when my heart was raw. All I cared about was her.

"I will wait for the doctor." Anaat watched me pace the room a moment more before disappearing out the door, servants in tow.

Once I was finally alone and allowed to decompress, I stood in the middle of the floor in a daze, my eyes fixated out the window across from me. *Why? Why her? Of all the humans in the world, why did Percivan have to go after the one I loved?*

I perched along her bedside, continually checking her weak pulse. Her breath was weak and strained, but it was there. She barely lived now.

Would she keep on living?

Shame and fury rolled through me.

If I had better control over myself, if I weren't a coward who had to hide out in a cave every full moon, if only I were stronger... I could have protected her. But I wasn't. Even now, I was the product of a dark magic. She deserved better than me and my lies.

Mrs. Rigby was right. I had put Meryn in danger. Now she was paying the price.

My anxiety and rage built to breaking point. I cried out and landed my fist in the small mirror on the wall, shattering it into silver shards. Slits of red formed on my fist. As I stared at my hand, my rage gave way to sorrow. I grasped my hair and slid down to the floor beside her bed. My body racked with sobs.

All my love and grief mingled and spilled from me, as beams of morning light spread across the floor.

Chapter Twenty-Nine

Fivrial

I ended up sleeping on the floor next to Meryn's bed, unwilling to sully it with sand, but also unwilling to pull any servants away from helping her. When I awoke hours later, the sun was waning in the sky. My right hand stung and was covered in deep red stains from the cuts. Someone had covered my shoulders in a blanket.

Everything hurt, but I didn't care.

People streamed into her room. I recognized Bernard as he led several servants in with buckets of steaming water. I sighed and rested my head against the door frame for a moment.

Bernard smiled. His brows drew together in concern. "We're here to take care of you as well, Mr. Fishman."

I nodded, giving them passage into the room to fill the bath. Once the bath was full of steaming water and I was left to my own devices. Meryn's bathroom was larger than mine, but similar. I urgently stripped down, eager to return.

Bernard had brought me an assortment of clothes from my room. My heart ached as I donned the blue shirt and black trousers that Meryn said she liked the best. I longed to hear her voice.

Let her wake up...

There was a small commotion outside of the room as I emerged. Anger filled me. It had better not be Sebastian.

I swung Meryn's door open and stalked down the stairs, ready to tear apart anyone who threatened to disturb her. Instead, there was only Carbor and another guard. As I approached, my lips tipped up briefly. They nodded.

"We are here to assure Lady Meryn's rest and recovery." Carbor's weary eyes studied me.

"Lady Anaat shall be the only one to be allowed passage."

A little tension unwound from my muscles. I would have to deal with Anaat, but at least now Meryn would go undisturbed by the Trevions.

I returned to Meryn's bedside. My feet were heavy as they crossed the floor.

Golden light from the setting sun filled the space. My eyes were immediately drawn to Meryn, nestled under her favorite, colorful patchwork quilt. She slept, her skin still a sickly shade of white. The light caught her unbound curls splayed over the pillow, illuminating the fiery crimson highlights as if they were the halo of a goddess. Even in this heartbreaking state, she still took my breath away.

It wasn't long before Anaat appeared in the doorway. She was still in her nightclothes and dressing gown. She looked worn to the bone. Part of me pitied her. From what I knew of their strained relationship, Meryn didn't warm up to her sister much. And yet, here she was—keeping vigil at her bedside.

"Hello, Finn," Anaat greeted me with a sigh as she settled into her chair. I suddenly realized she must have been coming and going all night.

Is she the one who covered me last night?

As if reconsidering, she began to rise. "Actually, you slept on the floor. Here, you can sit down—"

"No, that's all right. You look exhausted. Please, sit."

Anaat conceded gratefully. She sank back into the chair with a sigh. "Thank you."

I stepped over to the opposite side of the bed and lowered to my knees. Anaat was right there, watching, but I couldn't help it. I slipped my hand around Meryn's, grasping it gently.

Her skin still felt cool, but perhaps not as frigid as before. The blanket gently rose and fell with her chest. There was breath in her lungs. That sight alone brought me overwhelming gratitude.

"The doctor said she is stable, but weak. He just left." Anaat's voice was soft as she spoke. I had slept through the doctor's visit entirely. "He doesn't know why she hasn't woken up yet. There's no telling when she will." The heartbreak in Anaat's voice was clear. "There's no rhyme or reason for why she's like this, either. No injuries or evidence of any kind. I..." She wiped tears from her cheeks. "I don't understand it. Why was she out on the beach? In her evening gown, of all things?"

I felt Anaat's gaze trained on me. She was searching for answers I could not give. I could not tell her that a siren's song lured her there, or that he proceeded to do possibly unspeakable things to her while draining her of her life force. I could not tell her that when I found her, she was dead and that only by the grace of Scalae she lived now. So many secrets I had to keep bottled up. They would call me mad and drag me away if I spoke the truth.

"I'm sorry. I don't know."

Anaat sniffled. "I'll never understand why she loved going to the beach so much. She's always been a bit of a free spirit like her mother was."

My attention snapped back to Anaat. "*Her* mother?"

Anaat met my confused stare. "I suppose she never told you we have different mothers. Mine was Father's first wife. She died when I was little. Father later remarried and along came Meryn."

My eyes darted between Meryn and Anaat. I saw some similarities, but honestly, they truly were different. Anaat had fair hair and blue eyes, with a reserved disposition, while Meryn had red hair, amber eyes, and was full of fire. They were two sisters born of night and day.

"I suppose that could explain some things."

We were quiet for a while, lost in our thoughts. I shifted uncomfortably. This was the most I'd ever spoken to her. Meryn was always so insistent on staying away from her sister.

I didn't have any siblings myself, so I didn't know what it was like to have one, much less one I didn't get along with. My parents died when I was young, so it was me and the formidable Grayler growing up. I envied Meryn. It would seem she didn't know what she had—a sister that loved her, despite all their animosity.

Anaat's voice interrupted my thoughts. "How long?"

I looked up to find her staring at my hand, holding Meryn's. It was a simple question, but it held all the weight of the world. I knew exactly what it meant. With a sigh, I brushed my thumb over the back of Meryn's hand and made my quiet confession. "I've loved her for as long as I can remember, it would seem."

"I've never seen her so happy as she was when she was with you, you know. Before the Trevions came."

I smiled, a bit of sadness seeping in. "I think we were both happy."

Anaat gazed at her sister a while, resting her chin on her palm as tears filled her eyes. "When you came, I wanted to send you away. I could tell by the look in her eyes that she was already attached to you. Our father has *very* strict standards for us." She sniffled and wiped her eyes again. "In our lives, love isn't exactly given a priority. Status and especially pedigree are very important to him. To just about everyone, really. I was afraid of Meryn getting her heart broken by wanting someone she couldn't have. But..." Anaat smiled and bit back a sob, "Meryn's heart is too good to care about things like pedigrees. She's better and kinder than the rest of us ever could be. I only wish I could have seen it sooner. Now, I fear it may be too late."

As Anaat dissolved into a sobbing mess, I watched her with glassy eyes. Meryn's heart *had* been broken, but only because her light was being forcibly snuffed. I had no response to Anaat's confession. I merely sat in silence, letting her pour out her sorrows.

At last, Anaat ebbed into sniffles again and fetched a handkerchief from Meryn's bureau drawer. She returned to her chair and took Meryn's other hand in her own. "I don't know how we could ever repay you for what you've done, Finn. She wouldn't be here right now if it weren't for you."

Guilt flooded me. She would be perfectly well if it weren't for me. It was my fault Percivan targeted her. Me and my lies.

My love was selfish, just as Mrs. Rigby had said. Still, I could express none of this to Anaat, so I merely shook my head. "There is no debt, believe me."

"But we have wronged you, Finn. Pushed you aside to make way for another. I have no control over my father's demands. When he returns, things may be very different. But I can promise you that in the meantime, I will not keep you from her, Trevions or no."

My eyes widened. "Anaat, you know your father will not approve of that."

She laughed. "You let me worry about my father."

I wanted to hug Anaat. She was taking a great risk by making such a promise. I hoped it was one she could keep. "When will your father return?"

"A message has been sent, but it will take several days to reach him. It may be a couple of weeks before he can make it home." She fingered the lace on the edge of the handkerchief. "I'm afraid the Trevions will still be around for a while."

My heart fell a little. I only had a month left before the spell wore off. Even if I never heard 'I love you' from Meryn's lips, I wanted to be near her as much as possible. I wanted to soak up every moment of her presence.

"You know, the servants brought something from the music room..." Anaat rose and crossed to the bureau again. She picked up a page of sheet music and returned to her seat, studying it. "I think Meryn was working on it yesterday."

"A song?"

She nodded and passed it to me. I glanced it over and

handed it back, my cheeks heating. "I'm afraid I can't read it."

Anaat nodded and held up the paper. "I can't sing, but it says:

A son of the sea
Loved a daughter of land
Beneath swirling waves
He longed for her hand
He pined for her smile,
The light in her eyes
The joy in her laugh
And hope in her sighs
He gave up his fins
To be able to stand
For his heart longed to be
With his love on the land

She smiled wistfully. "She's always written the strangest things. It's sweet, I suppose."

I stared at the paper, my breath pausing. How? How could she...

My wide gaze swept to Meryn's sleeping face. *She knew?*

Something broke within me. My face contorted with emotion before I choked on a torrent of sobs. I rested my forehead on the back of Meryn's hand and released my tears. My story... *our* story... there on paper, written in her own hand. The truth laid bare.

A hand laid on my shoulder and I heard the rustle of clothing as Anaat kneeled at my side. "I'm sorry. I know this is hard."

I could barely speak. "I... I..." It was on the tip of my tongue. "The song. It's about... me."

Anaat laid the paper on Meryn's lap and squeezed my shoulder. "She always did have such a poetic interpretation of things. I'm sure she thought of you when she—"

"I'm not speaking figuratively, Anaat." My heart pounded. I couldn't look her in the eye. The truth was surging out of me. I'd lost all resolve. "I haven't been honest. Not with you, not with her, not with anyone."

Her stare burned into me. "Finn, what are you trying to say?"

I paused and took a deep breath. "Anaat, I don't have memory loss." Swallowing hard, I continued, "And I'm not really... human."

"Finn, I think you need some rest—"

"I don't need rest, Anaat. I'm trying to tell you the truth!"

A long silence followed as her eyes remained fixated on me. I was sure she was about to call for the guards and have me dragged away at any moment. Then the unexpected occurred.

"You came from the sea..." Her hand slipped from my shoulder. "Finn... *fins*..." Fear permeated her voice.

Panic rising, I stood and backed away with shaking hands. Anaat rose, her wide eyes sweeping over me. Her jaw hung open.

"You're a... aren't you?"

I held out a placating hand. "Now, Anaat—"

She gasped and clamped her hand over her mouth. "Oh heavens! Oh, my..."

Clenching my eyes shut, I took a stabilizing breath. "Sit down, please."

Slowly, Anaat sank onto the edge of the bed with a small nod. Her fright was clear, but I saw cautious fascination in her eyes. I was frightened, myself. This was not the conversation I was prepared to have with Anaat first.

"I..." My throat bobbed. "Yes, I am a merman." The words sounded so strange to my ears.

Anaat looked like she was going to fall over at any moment, but she clenched her robe and pressed her lips into a line. "A merman," she repeated with a nod. "All right."

"Yes. I am..." I gestured toward the music laying atop Meryn's still form. "The son of the sea she wrote of. I only have legs now because of a very, very powerful spell. And only for a short time, I'm afraid."

She studied my legs with raised brows. "So, you gave up your *fins* for Meryn?"

I nodded and gazed at Meryn's peaceful face. "I did."

"But why? I don't understand why you would do such a

thing. For love? I mean, how could you love someone you didn't even know?"

Her questioning was starting to sound a bit like scolding. "I loved her from the moment I laid eyes on her many years ago when we were young. I can't explain it, but I just felt an undeniable connection. Like I needed to be near her. I needed to watch over her. So many times, I wanted to reveal myself to her just as I was—tail and all. But there are very strict laws we have to abide by."

Anaat nodded as her eyes fell to the floor. "Sort of like my father's."

"Yes, I suppose."

"So, what caused you to finally break such laws?"

My fingers brushed the hair from Meryn's temple as I reminisced about our moments in the Green Grotto. "I finally met her. After her boat sank in the storm."

Anaat grew quiet. I looked to find her with a quivering lip. "You saved her that day, didn't you?"

I nodded and returned my attention to Meryn. "It was the first time I felt her in my arms. The first time she saw me with her own eyes. The first time we... kissed." My smile faded. "But she panicked when she saw my fins. I uttered a spell to make her forget me and then swam her to the beach near the castle."

Anaat sniffled. "Maybe part of her still remembered after all."

"I guess so."

"Finn." Anaat reached out and grasped my forearm. I found her desperate gaze. "Please, if you know what happened to her, you have to tell me."

My brows lowered. "You won't like what you hear, Anaat."

Her eyes hardened. "My sister is lying in a bed, barely clinging to life right now. If you know something, you had better say it." She released my arm with a push.

She was right.

"Anaat, have you ever heard of a siren?"

Her gaze remained fixed. "I have heard tales."

"Well, you're looking at one."

Anaat's eyes widened as she rose from the bed. She

stumbled backward until her back hit the window. "You stay away from me!"

I rolled my eyes and pinched the bridge of my nose. "Really, Anaat? You think I would endanger you *now*?"

She pursed her lips. "You tell me."

Growling in frustration, I planted my hands on my hips. "I do not hurt people. I go out of my way *not* to. I've never sung a note to Meryn."

Her eyes narrowed. "Do you swear it?"

I scoffed. "Of course, I swear it."

Releasing a long breath, Anaat's shoulders relaxed a bit. "Then, what does this have to do with Meryn?"

"It was a siren who hurt her. A very bad one." Shame flooded my features. "He did it to hurt me."

She quickly returned to Meryn's side, grasping her hand. "How? H-how do we make her better? What do we do?"

My heart ached. I didn't know how to answer.

Anaat's fiery eyes snapped to mine. "Finn! What do we do?"

"I-I don't... I don't know. And that's the truth." I pressed my palms to my eyes. "This is all my fault."

Hands gripped my wrists and ripped them back down. Anaat grabbed me by the shirt collar and glared at me. "I don't care whose fault it is, I just want her better!" She shoved me hard. "Think hard, siren. There must be something, *someone* who can help."

I racked my brain, fighting the panic. "I don't... wait." A thought floated to mind. "Mrs. Rigby."

Anaat's brows knitted in confusion. "The old witch woman?"

Nodding, I felt a smidgen of hope. "She's the only other one who knows my secret. She knows about the merfolk."

Anaat tapped her finger on her chin. "If she has any answers, then we must see her."

"We?"

She shot me a dry look. "You think I'm just going to sit around and wallow? Of course, 'we!' Now, stay here with her while I go get dressed." Anaat crossed the room and stopped at the door, whirling back around. "What's your real name, by the way?"

"Fivrial."

"Hmm... Well, *Fivrial*, let's hope Mrs. Rigby can save our Meryn."

With that, she left the room. Releasing a sigh of relief, I sat on the edge of the bed and buried my face in my hands. I couldn't believe what had just happened. My secret was out. And Anaat *believed* me. A weight had lifted off my chest.

I turned to Meryn. She had not moved a muscle during everything that'd just happened. My heart lurched. We had to find a way to help her.

Wrapping my hands around her cheeks, I leaned down, pressing my head gently against hers. My heart ached when again her lips did not return my kiss. I sank my head to her chest, listening to the weak beats of her heart.

"I promise I'll fight for you, Meryn. Just hold on."

Chapter Thirty

Fivrial

It wasn't long before Anaat returned, dressed and ready to go. She was wearing all black, and her hair was a frizzy mess, very uncharacteristic of her high-nosed ways. Not far behind her was Nola, Meryn's beloved maid.

"Are you ready, Fiv-Finn?" Anaat stumbled with the new name, pulling her shawl tighter around her shoulders.

I rose from Meryn's side, noticing Nola's bold stare for the first time. She wasn't entirely pleased with my presence. Averting my eyes, I nodded. "Yes, I'm ready."

Before crossing the room, I turned back and placed a soft kiss on Meryn's forehead. Her long lashes remained still on her alabaster cheeks. For a moment, I lingered. Leaving her side was a true test of strength. But I pulled myself away at last and joined Anaat at the door.

"I'll look after her," Nola assured Anaat before her eyes jumped to me. "I love her as if she were my own." Her message was loud and clear. It wasn't merely Anaat's approval I needed to win.

We made a swift exit out the door and down the winding stairs. Upon stepping into the hallway, we were joined by a young, fair-haired guard I recognized as Hugh. Two more remained behind to guard the entrance to Meryn's tower.

I had to rush to keep up with Anaat's persistent pace through the halls. She was practically running, worry twisting her features. I couldn't blame her.

We were nearly to the kitchen when our path was interrupted. Sebastian saw us coming and jogged to meet us. When he caught sight of me, his eyes hardened, and his jaw tensed. He jabbed a finger in my direction.

"*You.*" His fists clenched, he stormed toward me.

Anaat leaped between us, throwing her hands out. "Sebastian, not now."

Sebastian tried to side-step her, but Anaat was quick to block his path. Hugh was immediately at her side, ready to intervene on our behalf. Sebastian glowered past them, looking as if he were ready to rip me apart. A low warning sound emanated from deep in my throat. The feeling was quite mutual, but we had more pressing matters.

"How dare you keep me from her!" he shouted at me. "Let's settle this like real men. Just you, and me, and our fists. Right here, right now." He began rolling up his sleeves.

My lips curled into a tight smile. "I would ask you kindly to get out of our way, Sebastian."

He attempted to advance, but Hugh held him back with a strong grip. "Stand down!"

"Hiding behind a woman and a guard, are we? Coward," Sebastian spat.

My eyes narrowed as my blood simmered. "You have no idea how much I'd love to see your life force drain away from you right now, but we've got urgent matters to attend to concerning Meryn. So, if you will please put your hatred on hold for a little while and step aside, we would appreciate it."

Sebastian opened his mouth to retort, but Anaat grasped his shirt sleeve and commanded his attention. "I would listen to him if I were you."

"Sebastian."

I whirled around to see a very grim-looking Lady Trevion standing there. Her chin was raised, her hands folded in front of her.

Sebastian immediately took a step back and straightened his vest. "Mother."

"Come here, Sebastian," she coolly instructed.

Sebastian's eyes swept over the rest of us before he cleared his throat and calmly strolled over to his waiting mother. He stood before her, looking like a petulant child.

He opened his mouth to speak, but her hand collided with his cheek. The smack echoed through the hall.

Lady Trevion stuck a finger in her son's face and seethed. "You will behave with dignity and respect those of this household. Now, go to your chambers and cool off."

Sebastian stood there, face flushing in humiliation. Lady Trevion stared him down, daring him to question her. At last, he lifted his chin and walked away.

When he'd disappeared out of sight, Lady Trevion exhaled deeply and threw Anaat an apologetic glance. "My apologies, Lady Anaat." Her eyes flitted to me. "We'll sort this out later with decency, I assure you."

Anaat bobbed her head as she came and grabbed me by the elbow, yanking me toward the kitchen. "Thank you, Lady Trevion. Come, Finn. We must be off."

We swiftly exited the house, grabbing lanterns on our way out. The last glow of golden sunlight was slipping from the sky as we rushed down the path toward town. Our lantern light bobbed on the ground and we ran.

It wasn't a terribly long trek, but my leg muscles were tiring by the time we reached the road. Beside me, Anaat seemed to be fading too. Her steps were resolute, but they slowed as we trudged along.

Above us, the moon cast a white glow upon the road. It dawned on me that it was the last time I'd ever experience new legs again. Come the next full moon, I'd either keep them permanently or regain a tail forever.

I marveled at all the things I would miss about the human world. The warm food, the sounds of the busy townsfolk, the wonderful smells. I quickly banished such things from my mind; the only thing that mattered now was making things right and saving Meryn's life.

At last, we reached Mrs. Rigby's ancient home. A lantern reached out in darkness from the sitting room window. Anaat's urgency was renewed as she ran up the porch steps. I followed her as the door swung open. Mrs. Rigby stood in the dark entryway. Her lips were drawn into a tight frown as her piercing eyes swept over us. Gone was the sweet disposition she had with Meryn.

"Come in," she instructed gruffly, stepping aside.

Hugh took a step back. "I think I'll wait out here."

"Oh, don't be a coward! I'm not going to boil you in a pot and eat you!" snapped Mrs. Rigby.

He turned red and ducked his head. "All right, then."

We filed into the small sitting room as Mrs. Rigby closed the door. She shuffled up behind us and motioned toward the chairs. "Sit down, the lot of you. I've already got tea ready."

Anaat squished her eyebrows together. "How did you know we were coming?"

"I know what I know," Mrs. Rigby called over her shoulder on the way into the kitchen. "Now, please, sit down."

I took the armchair nearest the fireplace, which was now crackling with life. Anaat took the rocking chair while Hugh sat on the small couch. We all perched on the edge of our seats, waiting for Mrs. Rigby.

Anaat tapped her fingers incessantly against the arms of the chair. I watched her eyes scan the strange room as she chewed on her bottom lip. I was sure any moment she was going to fly out of the chair and drag Mrs. Rigby back into the room, kicking and screaming.

Hugh rubbed his wrists, eyes glued toward the front door. He hadn't been a guard for terribly long, but he was local. And just like in Brinn, I supposed word got around fast here when it came to witches. We had Wrenna, they had their Mrs. Rigby. Of course, I'd take Mrs. Rigby any day rather than have another strange encounter with Wrenna.

My gut twisted at the thought of Wrenna—that strange,

ghastly glow in her eyes. She wasn't herself the last time I saw her. Whatever happened, it was far bigger than I ever anticipated. One more thing on the long list of things that were going wrong.

Mrs. Rigby reappeared with her tea tray and quickly doled out our portions. She would hear of no refusals. As she sat down in her chair with her cup, she eyed us all gravely. "This tea tonight is essential, I'm afraid. If you're going to be receptive, you must drink it. No exceptions."

Glancing down at the cup, I hesitated. "What's in it?"

Her hard stare fixated on me. "You, of all people, need to trust me. If you must know, they are herbs—a special blend. Nothing that will harm you."

"Bottoms up," said Anaat with a tight smile before gulping down the tea. Her eyes watered as she erupted in a coughing fit.

Hugh immediately set his cup on the table while I patted Anaat firmly on the back.

"Are you all right?" I asked, throwing a scowl at Mrs. Rigby.

Anaat nodded and waved me away. "Yes," she croaked, "it's just hot."

I rolled my eyes. "I could've told you that."

Gathering my wits, I drank the tea as fast as the temperature would allow. Hugh reclaimed his cup with shaking hands and followed suit. When we finished, we set our cups on the table and turned to Mrs. Rigby in anticipation. I didn't feel anything strange or out of the ordinary happening. No extra limbs appearing or mystical forces swooping through the room.

"So," began Mrs. Rigby, "let's begin by you all telling me how you are feeling right now."

Hugh shrugged. "I'm terribly frightened of you because I think you're going to disembowel me and use my innards for one of your spells." He immediately clamped his hand over his mouth as his eyes grew wide. "Why did that come out of my mouth?"

Mrs. Rigby's mouth twisted in a half-grin. "Truth tea. It seems to be working."

"Truth tea?" cried Anaat, her eyes bulging.

"Yes. I suggest you not attempt to lie, either. It's quite uncomfortable." Mrs. Rigby settled down in her chair and folded her hands across her stomach. "Now, the truth tea makes you both vulnerable to the truth and receptive to it. But *only* the truth, and it only stretches as far as one's knowledge."

When her eyes landed on me, I knew it was in large part directed my way. I'd been too wrapped up in falsehoods to consider her previous warnings.

I nodded. "Then you must know why we've come."

She peered at me, head tilted to one side with a knowing look. "You did not heed my warning, siren. And now Meryn is in danger."

"Siren?" barked Hugh.

I caught Anaat's head whipping between us out of the corner of my eye. "Warning? What warning?"

Taking a deep breath, I launched into an explanation. "Mrs. Rigby sensed what I was the moment she laid eyes on me." I looked at Hugh, who'd gone white as a sheet. "Yes, I am a siren. I sought the help of a sea sorceress to gain legs so I could be with Meryn. But it's only temporary, and I have until the next full moon to hear her tell me she loves me, or else I revert to a siren and never have legs again." Shamefaced, I returned my attention to Anaat. "I didn't tell Meryn what I was. I lied and let her think I had lost my memory instead."

Anaat stared at me coldly. "Why *did* you lie to her?"

"Because I thought she wouldn't love me for what I was. And I wanted her to tell me she loved me genuinely, not because she was trying to work around a spell."

"Well, she'd be in love with a lie! How would that be *genuine*?" She smoothed her shaking palms over her skirt and pursed her lips. "And the warning?"

My throat felt tight. This was a truth I didn't want to admit. Still, out it came. "Mrs. Rigby told me the magic on me was dark, and that if I didn't tell Meryn the truth soon, tragedy was imminent." I felt Mrs. Rigby's stare from across the room.

The fire crackled behind me. Everyone was waiting for me to continue my confession. My heart broke as I remembered Meryn's lifeless form waiting for us in the tower. The words continued to spill out as a deep sense of regret and relief filled me. I was glad to be honest for once, but if only I'd been honest sooner. Tears streamed down my cheeks as I hung my head in shame.

"I didn't listen. I was afraid I'd lose her."

The room was heavy with silence as my words were absorbed. My heart felt like an anchor in my chest. I wanted to flee. I longed to hide from the ugliness. But there was no running anymore. My selfishness had come at a cost.

Anaat sucked in air through clenched teeth and flew from her chair with a roar. Her palm slammed into my cheek. I took the blow in stride, knowing I deserved the sting of pain radiating through me.

"You're not the only one who would lose her, Fivrial! I love my sister more than I've ever shown it. I have feared something bad happening to her every single day of her life, because..." She swallowed hard. "Because my life would be nothing without her in it. And here you come in, loving her, making her the happiest I've ever seen, and yet you couldn't bring yourself to be honest with her? If anyone in the world would have believed you, it's *her*!"

The air around me felt thin. My head spun. I couldn't bring myself to look Anaat in the eye. "I... I..."

"She loves you, Fivrial! Words or not! And she *trusts* you. You have violated that trust. And now, she pays the price." Anaat grabbed hold of my shirt collar and forced me to look into her burning eyes. "If my sister dies, I will filet you myself." With that, she shoved me and plopped back down in her chair.

Her words reeled through my mind. I had no doubt in my mind she'd make good on her threat. I deserved it.

"Now that's settled," Mrs. Rigby continued. She did not seem at all surprised by Anaat's sudden outburst. "Let's talk about why you came."

My stomach turned in knots. "A siren sang to Meryn last night. He drained her of her life force. I found her dead on the beach this morning." Anaat gasped in horror. I dropped my gaze to the floor and continued, remembering the feel of her cold body in my arms. "I called out to Scalae and breath re-entered her." Tears slid down my cheeks. "But she won't wake up."

"She has the breath of Scalae sustaining her, but her life force must be rejuvenated soon. Otherwise, she will sleep forever." Mrs. Rigby's words were clear and certain. I had no reason to doubt she spoke the truth.

"Life force?" blurted Anaat. "H-how do we 'rejuvenate' her 'life force?'"

Mrs. Rigby's gaze shifted to me. "There are two ways: collect it from the vessel in which it now resides, or through a long and arduous task. Either way, time is of the essence."

My heart raced as I leaped to my feet. "What about my life force? She can have it. Just tell me how."

The old woman shook her head. "I'm afraid you've got no real human life force within you. You've never partaken in the way of sirens."

"She can have mine!" Anaat's words pierced the air around us as she rose from her chair.

Mrs. Rigby fanned her hands in the air. "Calm down, calm down! Neither one of you need to die to save her. The task is dangerous, but nothing quite so dramatic. By the Goddess..." she muttered, rolling her eyes.

Anaat and I looked at each other with deep sighs. We would've truly laid down our lives for Meryn without a second thought. I would've spilled every drop of my blood if that's what it took. I would've *easily* spilled every drop of Percivan's, but without a tail, hunting him down would be impossible. Even then, he'd have a clear advantage.

"What do we do?" I implored.

Mrs. Rigby rose with strain etched on her withered face. "You must go to the Temple of Scalae."

"The temple?" said Anaat. "Why? What's at the temple?"

"Sacred waters, blessed by Scalae herself." The witch's ominous words wrapped around us. I watched Hugh's eyes grow large once more. "Here, be a dear and follow me to the kitchen, Finn."

Just like that, the moment was broken.

"Fivrial," I corrected as I fell in-step behind her.

Mrs. Rigby waved her hand in dismissal. "Whatever.

You're taller than I am, and I don't feel like getting out my ladder."

As we entered the cozy kitchen, strange smells again hit my nose. "What is that smell?" I blurted out, sniffing the air.

"Herbs and spices. Used for cooking and... other purposes. Now, on that top shelf there—please grab that brown sack." I reached around the shelf, dust falling across my face. My eyes began to water, but Mrs. Rigby continued instructing me. "No, not the large one, the smaller. Yes, that's the one."

I procured the correct bag, pulling down a bundle of smooth, brown material with a thick string cinched around the top. Mrs. Rigby nodded her thanks as I handed it to her.

I watched in wonder as she grabbed a metal spoon and an even smaller empty sack.

"What's that?" I asked, watching with great interest as she spooned the blend of fragrant herbs into the small sack.

"This will be your payment to the priestesses," Mrs. Rigby explained.

My brows knitted. "Payment? What is it?"

"It's a tea that calms the nerves. The priestesses are often sent women with troubled minds, whose families cannot, or will not, care for them. They do the best they can, but sometimes a little help is needed. I've been aiding them for many, many years."

The light in which I saw Mrs. Rigby shifted a little. She could be harsh, but she had a heart. Perhaps that's why Meryn admired her so much. The truth tea drew my thoughts from my lips. "I think that's very kind of you to do that."

Mrs. Rigby nodded. "Thank you, Fivrial." She cinched the small bag and held it out to me. As I took it, her hand enclosed mine, and she stared. "Now, listen carefully: when you go to this temple, you must enter alone. They do not let just anyone in. You will be questioned thoroughly by the high priestess before they give you a vial of the waters. And she doesn't need a tea to draw the truth out of you. Don't underestimate them just because they are women in a sacred place. It can be very dangerous there."

I looked down at the bag in my hand. "Will this be

enough to satisfy them?"

She hesitated, following my eyes. "There will be... tasks."

Swallowing hard, I nodded. "I'll do whatever it takes."

"I believe that you will. It's not going to be easy, but you will do your best."

Meeting her eyes, I found them to be sincere. She'd drank the truth tea with the rest of us, but somehow, I got the sense that she didn't need it. "Thank you for helping us. I'm sorry I didn't listen to you."

Mrs. Rigby patted my upper arm and sighed. "Love can make fools of anyone, I suppose. I do believe that beneath all the pretense, you are sincere. That will carry you through this." She wiped a tear from her withered cheek, stepping past me. "Come, time is short."

I followed close behind. "How short?"

We rejoined Anaat and Hugh, who were waiting anxiously. Mrs. Rigby reclaimed her place in her chair. "You have five days, at best."

"Five Days? That's not much time," fussed Anaat, wringing her fingers. "The temple is a two days' ride."

"One by sea," corrected Hugh.

Anaat growled in frustration. "Yes, if you want to be dashed upon the rocks! No, it has to be by land. Should we fail..." She gripped her forehead.

"Fivrial will be the one to go," announced Mrs. Rigby. "Someone may escort him, but he will be the only one that can enter the temple."

"What?" Anaat's eyes widened. "But he's-he's a *man*. I thought they didn't let men in the temple?"

Mrs. Rigby pointed a knobby finger at me. "They'll let *him*."

Anaat's jaw fell open, but no retort came. At last, she closed it and nodded. "Very well. I suppose I should stay with Meryn, anyway. But Fivrial, you must leave right away."

I gripped the bag. "Of course."

Anaat whirled around to the young guard. "Hugh? Do you know the way?"

Hugh's eyes widened. "I don't, but Penton does."

"Good, then he shall escort Fivrial." She tightened her shawl around her shoulders and stormed toward the door. "Come, we haven't a moment to lose. Hugh, you must help prepare for the journey. I want them gone within the hour—"

"Wait!" called Mrs. Rigby, once again rising from her chair. She shuffled over to a small table next to the rocking chair and opened the drawer beneath. For a moment, she dug around, muttering to herself, before pulling out a necklace. She hurried over to me and looped it around my neck. The fine silver chain settled around across my chest. In the center was a large white pearl.

"What's this for?" I asked, holding the smooth pearl between my fingertips.

She grasped my shoulder. "Good luck. Keep it on you at all times."

With a nod, I smiled briefly in gratitude. "Thank you."

Mrs. Rigby patted me on the back. "Now, off with you. I will come visit Meryn in the morning."

With that, we grabbed our lanterns and fled the house into the moonlight.

Chapter Thirty-One

Meryn

The full moon bathed the forest in an ethereal glow as the carriage pulled away, leaving Finn and me on the doorstep of the ivy-covered stone cottage. Cool night air had me pulling my red fur cape tighter over my bare shoulders. When I caught Finn's smiling eyes, a flood of warmth filled me. I would never get tired of those beautiful, clear blue pools. He looked like a god in his tailored white suit. His ginger locks spilled in waves over his shoulders.

"Are you cold?" he asked me again, rubbing his hands over my cape.

I grinned. "Extremely."

"Well, then." The space between us closed as Finn dipped his head down and brushed his lips against mine. "Let's get you inside, Mrs. Fishman."

Without warning, he moved his arms behind me,

sweeping me off my feet. My gold dress spilled out of the cape as his warmth enveloped me anew. We laughed as he fumbled with the doorknob beneath my massive skirts. At last, it opened. He carried me effortlessly across the threshold of our new home.

A fire was already laid for us in the small fireplace. All around the room, candlelight set the room aglow. Spread along the hearth were warm blankets. Someone had set out wine and fruit on the small dining table. It was a cozy space, and it was all our own. Between Finn's hard work and my father at last relinquishing my dowry, we were finally set up for a lifetime of simple bliss.

Scarcely had the floor met my feet before Finn was lifting my chin with warm fingers. I sighed against his soft touch as he caressed my cheek. "You've just made me the happiest man alive, Meryn." His thumb brushed my lower lip as his gaze flicked downward. He smiled softly. "I don't think I could express just how happy I'm feeling right now."

I slipped my hand into his hair and his eyes slid shut peacefully. He loved it when I played with his hair.

"How about you give it a go?"

Finn's eyes flickered open and then darkened with desire. His fingers trailed from my chin, skimming the skin of my throat until they rested at the clasp of my cloak. With unmatched skill, he unhooked the clasp, letting it fall in a heap on the floor.

My dress sleeves were short, only hugging my upper arms. Finn's fingertips brushed my exposed collarbone and traveled downward, trailing the slope of my breasts. All the while, his eyes were burning into mine as his face grew more flushed. When his gaze dropped, he bit his lower lip.

With heartbreaking tenderness, Finn unlaced my dress, letting it slide to the floor. Next came the underskirts and my stays. He helped me step out of the mountain of fabric with a smile. This time, I wore nothing underneath. His heavy eyes drank me in as his hands skimmed over the curve of my hips.

With a flirty grin, I unbuttoned his jacket, followed by his vest. While I unbuttoned his shirt, I pulled him close for a sultry kiss. Finn hummed approvingly, wrapping his hands around my waist. I worked my way down through the buttons until he promptly shrugged it off, exposing his glorious upper body. I let my hands travel down his torso, each finger running along the planes of his muscles.

My fingers dipped to the waistband of his trousers, where I slipped the buttons from their holes, peeling away the fabric. I teased, moving closer and then further away from his awaiting desire.

Finn kicked off his boots and allowed me to slide his trousers off, running my hand over the curve of his firm bottom. He inhaled sharply when my touch moved around to the front.

"Meryn..." he groaned in a whisper.

I wrapped one hand around his neck, deepening our kiss while I continued to pleasure him with the other. I stroked up and down, listening to every catch of his breath.

I loved the feel of him.

When I pulled back to look at him, his expression melted into bliss, spurring me on. I wanted to make him feel as good as he'd made me feel. Burning satisfaction filled me as I watched him shudder under my touch.

Finn devoured me with his kiss, his tongue massaging over mine. His groans of pleasure were increasing. Finally, he grabbed my wrist and whipped my hand away. He gripped me firmly behind my thighs, carrying me to the waiting bed. He laid me down on the fur blanket, pressing into me.

The moment he laid on top of me, I froze. The tender skin of my thighs did not meet with warm flesh, but something cold. Hard. *Scales.*

My eyes popped open. They met Finn's wide, frightened stare. *His eyes had changed.* No longer merely blue, but faded into shades of lavender and gold. They were beautiful, but shocking. My mouth dropped open as my gaze slowly fell. Gone were strong legs. A long, thick turquoise tail rested in their place. Broad green fins flopped against the foot of the bed.

My heart raced. I felt Finn's pounding against my chest. We lay there in shock for a moment before a scream tore from my throat.

Finn shook his head in a panic as he braced his hands on either side of my face. "Meryn! Please, no!"

Just as I was trying to scramble out from beneath him, the front door burst open. A wall of water came crashing in, smashing the windows around us. The warmth of the fire extinguished as the flood rose rapidly.

I clung to Finn as the bed began to float. Freezing cold water licked my feet. The house was filling quickly.

Finn remained on top of me, one arm wrapped around my waist as the other propped up his upper body. His head whipped around in terror as we rose toward the ceiling.

"What's happening?" I screamed.

He grasped my chin and forced me to look at him. "Hold onto me and don't let go."

With tears blurring my vision, I nodded, wrapping my arms around his neck. He was still warm as he held me close. Terror filled me as I clung to him with all my strength.

"When the room fills, I'm going to swim you out."

"Don't let go of me," I begged, shivering.

"Never." His lips pressed into my neck as he squeezed me. "I love you."

I clenched my eyes shut. "I love you, Finn."

Finn's back was nearly touching the ceiling beam. "I need you to take a deep breath, okay?" I nodded, noticing the fear in his eyes for the first time. "One... two... three."

I filled my lungs with as much air as they could hold and wrapped my legs around Finn's waist. The world shifted as he maneuvered his tail into the deep, cold water.

The shock hit me, and I had to fight to keep from attempting to breathe. For a moment, we were sinking, and then there was a powerful swish through the water. Finn flicked his strong tail, and we shot through the house and out the door.

I dared to open my eyes. The entire world was full of water. Leaves on the trees wavered in the current. The sky was a glistening surface far above us, the white disc of the moon distorted by the waves. As we swam upward, I looked down to see our happy little home submerged at the bottom of the new sea. The cheery glow in the windows was long extinguished.

When I looked at Finn, I saw his fierce determination. He swam us quickly toward the surface. His chest rose and fell as if he were breathing fresh air. I'd never seen him so wild and beautiful. In that moment, all fear of him leaked away. He was a magnificent creature that I loved—a son of the sea.

His eyes met mine. Unspoken words exchanged in a long gaze as we cut straight up through the waves. The water slipped over my skin like cold silk. Each current caressed my hair, sending chills down my spine. We were flying.

My lungs were starting to ache with the urge to inhale. My brows drew together as I struggled. I tightened my grip on Finn's neck and anxiously looked up at the surface. Still too far to go. There was no way I would make it.

Finn furiously flicked his tail, taking us faster and faster. I felt his muscles contracting rapidly as his lower body rolled with each beat of his fins.

"Just hold on," he said, voice cutting through the water.

I shook my head. Shadows danced in my vision. There wasn't enough time. I was on the verge of drowning.

Just as I felt darkness enclosing me, lips captured mine, forcing an inhale. Water entered my mouth, down into my lungs. It was painful at first. The horrid burning sensation of sea water filled my chest. Then, something strange happened. The ache in my lungs disappeared.

I opened my eyes and found Finn staring back at me. We were still well below the surface. The urge to breathe had disappeared, as the cool water flowed in and out with the rise and fall of my chest. We stared at each other in shock as Finn brought us to a stop.

Somehow, someway, I was alive. I still had legs, but I felt... different, *more alive.*

I brushed my fingers over his cheeks, trailing them out into his beautiful tresses. His eyes slid shut under my touch. He was still my beautiful Finn—tail and all. *My husband.*

Smiling, Finn pulled me in for another kiss, his hand snaking up into my floating hair. I reciprocated with joyous fervor. With lazy flicks of his fins, we rotated in the water, like a slow dance.

We'd danced at our reception, but this was magical in a way I couldn't describe. Thrums of energy pulsed between us like a current. I'd never felt so connected to him. It was as if I were seeing him for the first time. *The real him.*

When we parted, Finn unhooked my arms from his neck and took my hand in his. I lowered my legs from his waist and let myself float freely in the water. I was completely naked, but I didn't mind. With a wistful smile, Finn swam, pulling me alongside him.

We soared over the forests below, now teeming with ocean life. Everything was bathed in a beautiful, wavering, silver light. Finn's tail blazed with a breathtaking, colorful glow. When his eyes met mine, they, too, were illuminated. My laughter bubbled through the water in pleasant surprise.

"I want to show you something," said Finn as he banked to the right. He slipped his arm around my waist again. "Hold on tight."

With a mighty flick, we shot off in a new direction at breakneck speed. Finn whooped in excitement, and I laughed as I clung to him.

I loved this new side of him.

Soon, we were soaring over Arcadia, with the long stretch of sandy beaches far below us. The deep basin of the Aslean Sea overtook the forested landscape, and the waters grew warmer. Finn dipped us downward, and we came closer to the seafloor. Colorful corals and anemones filled my vision. Above the reef, shadows loomed above us, startling me.

A pair of enormous sharks floated just above us. I watched as the rows of teeth searched for prey among the coral. Sensing my fear, Finn squeezed my hand tight.

"It's all right. They know me."

I chuckled nervously. "I'll take your word for it."

After swimming for a while, we came to a deep, black scar in the ground. It stretched far into the distance. Finn descended.

In the back of my mind, my instincts flared. *Don't,* the voice seemed to say. I knew it was the same voice that saved me in the storm.

I shook my head, pulling away from Finn for the first

time. "Finn, I don't want to go down there."

He stopped, glancing between me and the rift.

"Why? What's wrong?"

A pit formed in my stomach. "I don't know. I just think we need to turn back."

I watched him nod, a look of confusion and concern spreading across his face. "Okay, we'll go—"

A deafening roar filled my ears. I clamped my hands on either side of my head as I screamed in pain.

Massive black tentacles spilled from the trench. Glowing red eyes emerged next. The moonlight drifted through the water, glinting off of a circular mouth full of razor-sharp teeth. A gargantuan, bulbous body climbed from the ledge.

I'd seen this before. In a dream long ago. Memories filled my mind. I was in the art studio, looking at old paintings in a book. I'd drawn this monster so many times in my childhood sketches.

Fear had me frozen. "No..."

"Hold on!" Finn shouted as he grasped my hand, tearing through the water.

The creature roared again and unfurled its long tentacles, shooting them toward us like spears. Finn swam as fast as he could, but I knew we would never be fast enough.

We darted through the water, dodging the creature's long tentacles.

Suddenly, a piercing pain rippled across my leg. A shackle wrapped around my ankle, ripping me back the other direction.

My grip broke from Finn's. His eyes were full of panic as he turned around. He swam toward me as fast as he could, his hand stretched toward me as the creature pulled me down rapidly.

I screamed for Finn.

"Meryn!" He desperately reached for me.

Down, down, down, I went. The icy water chilled me to the bone. My hair whipped upward through the current as the light from the moon faded and darkness fell around me.

Chapter Thirty-Two

Fivrial

I shot up in my seat, gasping for air. My heart pounded wildly in my ears. I could still see her in my mind's eye—slipping away from me in the clutches of the dark leviathan. Her screams echoed in my memory.

It felt so real.

In my spirit, I still felt her. I knew it was much more than a dream. Meryn was fighting for survival. Merpeople told legends of Scalae connecting people through dreams. Fear crept through me as I considered what it might mean.

Penton stirred in the seat across from me, his eyes slitting open. "Is everything all right?"

My hand was still over my rapidly beating chest. "Yes. Yes, I think so. Just a dream. Just a bad dream." My thoughts were fractured as reality slowly seeped in again. Taking a deep breath, I closed my eyes and tried to focus.

With a yawn, Penton sat up, his gray cloak slipping from

his shoulders. Predawn light was spilling into the carriage window. We'd ridden most of the night until Penton was falling asleep and the horses needed rest. They gruffed outside now, near the smoldering remnants of the fire.

"I suppose we'd better be going soon, anyway. I'll ready the horses if you want to throw dirt on that fire. A cold breakfast will have to do," he grumbled, shooting me an annoyed glare.

I'd insisted on sleeping in the safety of the carriage that night after we heard a large animal stalking through the woods near our camp. It was the first time I'd ever been that far inland, and I'd heard legends from other merfolk about what horrid dangers lie in wait there. I didn't fancy the thought of being eaten alive in my sleep.

We exited the carriage into the cool morning air. My muscles were stiff. The previous day was a long, exhausting drive. I couldn't ride a horse, so Penton was kind enough to drive a carriage. I felt guilty and useless.

As I kicked up dirt with the side of my boot, I couldn't get the images of Meryn out of my mind. The dream was so incredibly vivid—more so than any dream I'd ever experienced. Our wedding night... the flooding house... swimming her through a new world... it was a mixture of joy and terror. The end left me shaken to the core.

I hadn't been able to save her.

I tried to shake the disturbing images from my mind as we climbed back to our respective positions and took off through the forest again. It was less than a day's journey until we reached the temple. The sooner, the better. Time was of the essence.

I checked and rechecked to be sure that I had the sack from Mrs. Rigby in my pocket. Meryn was lying in bed back at the castle, slowly slipping away, and there was no time for foolish errors.

Before we'd left, I had gone up to see her one last time. Everyone else had left the room to give me a moment alone with her. Her hands were chilled as I wrapped them in my own. Once more, I prayed to Scalae, vowing that I would do everything in my power to make things right, if the goddess would just save her.

Forcing myself from her side was the hardest thing I'd ever had to do.

The sun rose through the trees as we took off along the coast.

The horses expertly navigated the rocks, but I could not force myself to look out the window and see the fall below. Before long, warm colors burst into the sky as sunbeams cut through the upper canopy in glittering shafts of light.

We entered a small stretch of forest now and I finally dared to watch from the carriage window. The greens and browns were rich and magical. The scent of the sea had faded, replaced by the smell of the earth. I let the breeze in, once more overwhelmed by this whole new world. Despite the desperate circumstances, it still filled me with awe.

It was a long day. We only stopped briefly for needed breaks before pressing onward. At last, the trees grew sparser again. The smell of saltwater greeted me once more.

When I looked ahead through the window, a massive stone structure towered over us from the top of the hill. Much like Meryn's castle, it too loomed over the sea.

Tall white pillars surrounded the building, forming an outer courtyard. The vaulted roof was a massive, carved slab of marble. The sun glinted off the stone, catching the shimmering minerals within.

Far more impressive—and much more intimidating—than the castle.

In front of the temple were several large plots of gardens with white-robed women working them. When we drove past, we received numerous stares of curiosity. Some left their tasks to whisper among their companions. I avoided eye contact and nervously bounced my leg, anxious to complete my own task and get back to Meryn.

When the carriage came to a stop, I took a deep breath before opening the door and stepping out into the sunshine. I heard immediate chatter among the women as they left their work one by one to congregate nearby. Warmth rose in my cheeks. I was not used to being the subject of so much attention.

I stepped up to the group, nervously clearing my throat. I produced the sack of tea from my pocket. "I'm here to speak to the High Priestess. I've been sent by Mrs. Rigby."

A middle-aged, dark-haired woman stepped out from among them. Her brows drew together. "A man comes seeking the high priestess?"

I nodded.

Scarcely had I responded when she turned on her heel. "Wait here." I watched as she stalked across the garden and up the stairs to the outer courtyard. A large set of weathered white doors opened into what I assumed must be the temple.

It was a long, awkward wait among the other women. None of them made a move to talk to me, but it was clear that I was the subject of their quiet conversations. Their eyes swept me up and down as if I were a curious new specimen.

At last, the dark-haired woman returned. She stood on the steps before the great doors, motioning with a jerk of her chin. "Galia will see you now. Follow me." She turned, not bothering to wait for us, and started toward the temple again.

I followed her swift pace, glancing back at Penton, who nodded. He was under strict orders to wait outside for me. We'd be leaving quickly once I got what I came for. I hadn't told him what that was, but he knew it was for Lady Meryn's benefit. It seemed that was good enough for him.

When we entered the temple doors, I was surprised to find it bright. Enormous, opulent, gilded mirrors hung on the white walls. Each mirror caught the light from open the open breezeways and cast it around the room.

In the center of the interior courtyard, a clear pool recessed into the floor, surrounded by steps on all sides. A stone effigy of a mermaid with long, flowing tresses and upraised hands stood in the center. Water spilled from a large clamshell in her palms.

I peered into the water as we passed. It looked ordinary. Was this the mystical pool Mrs. Rigby spoke of? I didn't feel anything abnormal. It wasn't like Wrenna's pool. No glowing creatures swam around.

"Are you coming?"

My attention snapped back to the woman, who was

standing halfway up the steps, waiting for me to continue. I hadn't realized I'd slowed to a complete stop. Blushing furiously, I nodded and quickly rejoined her.

Up more steps and across a broad expanse of white marble floor, we came to another, smaller door. The woman knocked softly, but the sound echoed through the room.

After several moments, another female voice responded. "Enter."

The woman assisting me turned the gilded knob, and we entered a smaller, shadowed chamber. A single, enormous shaft of light spilled in from the ceiling. I looked up to see a window inset into the stone, featuring a beautiful square of the clear, blue sky. The light shone onto a massive, gilded emblem carved into the marble floor. I recognized it instantly. It was the symbol of Scalae. A mermaid with her tail curled before her, her hair surrounded by stars.

"This is the man here to see you, High Priestess." The woman bowed her head reverently.

I found myself doing the same, bowing my head toward the floor. Silently, I prayed to Scalae that I wouldn't offend her high priestess.

"Thank you, Rain," a calm voice said from beyond the light. "You may go."

Rain turned without further acknowledgment and left the room, softly shutting the door behind her.

I turned back to the shadows. The longer I looked, the clearer the shapes became. A broad throne on a dais sat directly across from me. In it was a tall figure. She made no move to rise from her seat.

"Come here, siren." Her voice was clear and gentle as the tide. There was, however, a strange authority to it. I found myself obeying immediately.

I crossed under the warm light, the soles of my boots tapping across the hard floor. Each step echoed throughout the room. When I reached the opposite edge of the light, I came to a stop. It was then that she became clear.

I faced a tall, thin, pale woman with a shaved head. She had fair eyebrows over piercing green eyes. Her thin lips settled into an expressionless line across her cheeks. The strange look made her appear ageless. I could neither judge her too old nor too young. Her white robes were pristine, flowing to the tips of her bare feet as she sat on the golden cushions.

"You know what I am?" I asked, keeping my voice low. Even I felt the overwhelming reverence.

Galia nodded. "I do. We commune with the mer frequently. I can sense it in you."

I was confused. I'd never even heard of the temple of Scalae *above* the sea, only the one below it in Brinn.

Her stare penetrated through me. It seemed to strip away all the layers and walls of who I was. "Tell me your name."

"Fivrial."

Galia tilted her head. "Tell me your truths, Fivrial."

The truth came pouring out immediately as she held my gaze. Every detail, down to the pain of my transformations. It felt like ages that I stood there, telling my story. Even my private times with Meryn were spoken of. It was as if a tidal wave had been unleashed and I was powerless to stop it.

The high priestess sat and listened without interruption. When I was finished, I felt drained and raw. I wanted to collapse to the ground and bury my head in my hands. My eyes fell from hers.

"You've been through a great ordeal. As has your lover," Galia responded at last. "You come seeking a cure that is nearly impossible."

My heart raced. "Impossible? What do you mean? I thought—"

Galia held up a hand to silence me. "I said *nearly* impossible."

A puff of air escaped me. "Well, I'll do whatever it takes. Here," I pulled the sack of tea from my pocket and held it out to her. "Please take this as payment."

She accepted the sack and uncinched it, breathing in the contents. Pulling the strings on the bag, she tucked it into her robe. "This will grant you access to the chamber."

My brows drew together. "Chamber?"

"Yes," she nodded, "the Chamber of Talgren."

A feeling of dread washed over me as she averted her gaze from mine for the first time. "And what is that, exactly?"

"It is where the blessed waters lie."

So not in the inner courtyard, after all.

"And how may I enter, High Priestess?" I kept my tone respectful, though my patience waned.

Galia nodded to my feet. "You're standing on it."

I turned and swept my eyes across the floor. It was then that I noticed the outer edge of the symbol was slightly recessed.

I took a step backward, into the shadows before Galia's throne.

My throat bobbed. "What exactly is down there?"

She shifted in her seat, looking uncomfortable. "Things far worse than sirens."

That did little to reassure me. The room suddenly felt darker. I turned away from the symbol and walked toward the shadowed corner of the room, running my hand over my beard. Light footsteps followed me.

"You do not have to do this, Fivrial. It is your choice."

I shook my head. "There is no choice. If I'm to save her, I must do whatever it takes."

Galia stepped around to face me. "There is great fear in you. It will not help you down there."

Her brows were drawn tight together. I sensed she was trying to warn me away, but my mind was made up. As was my heart.

I straightened my shoulders and met her stare. "There is no greater fear than losing the one you love."

Galia studied me for a moment, lips pressed into a tight line. At last, she nodded and turned, crossing to the opposite corner behind her throne. A large black cabinet with a single door stood waiting. On the front was the symbol of Scalae, etched in gold. I watched with curiosity as she reached into a hidden pocket within her robes, producing a golden key.

"Come here, Fivrial," she instructed.

I wasted no time in joining her. As she unlocked the cabinet, the interior was red as blood. A silver sword, intricately carved, was mounted in the center. Beside it hung an angular shield, bearing the symbol of the goddess.

She picked up a strap of metal plates and handed it to me. "Put this belt around your waist."

It was surprisingly heavy as it settled around me. I wrapped it around me, fumbling with the fastening mechanism.

Galia rolled her eyes and took over, securing it in place. She reached into her robes again, this time handing me a silver vial in the shape of a teardrop, about the size of my palm. It was heavy as I studied the leaves carved into the sides.

"What's this?"

"That is what you will collect the water in. It clips to your belt here..." Galia showed me a prong on the side of the belt that perfectly hugged the body of the vessel. "And this," she unmounted the shield and held it up for me, "is your defense. Put your arm through that strap and grip the other one."

I did as instructed. Again, I was surprised at the weight of it. When the sword was in my hands, I tried to put on an air of confidence. I had no experience fighting as a human.

"Why do I need these things?" I dared to ask.

Galia's eyes swept across the sunlit floor. "Talgren takes many forms. *Any* form. He guards the waters with great power. And he is not alone down there." Her shoulders rose and fell. Her eyes never left the symbol on the floor.

Galia, the High Priestess, was *afraid*.

"Has anyone ever been successful?"

She nodded. "A few. Very, very few." Her eyes slid to mine. "Only those that are worthy live to see the sunlight again."

My muscles tensed. *Worthy*. That was something I questioned thoroughly.

Is there any worth left in me?

After everything I had done...lying to the woman I loved, putting her in danger with my own selfishness... how could I possibly be worthy of anything?

This was a suicide mission. Still, there was no other choice. If I had to die trying, then die I would. Perhaps I would be with Meryn again in the afterlife.

"Tell me what to do, and I'll do it."

Galia walked me back over to the throne, where she pressed underneath the armrest. The top surface of the armrest popped open, revealing a golden lever, set deep within the side of the throne.

"This lever will open the chamber, revealing a set of stairs. You will descend into the chamber and follow the light to its source…"

As she gave a long list of instructions and warnings, I felt my nerves stand on end. This was going to be bigger than I anticipated. Darker. The heaviness of the task ahead weighed on me.

Thoughts of Meryn lying lifeless in that bed filled my mind.

I would do this. I would do this for her.

"Are you ready?" Galia asked, at last.

I nodded. "I am."

She reached for the lever and paused, placing a firm hand on my shoulder.

I met her sad eyes. A sad thought wandered across my mind. *How many times had she sent a warrior to his death?*

Her lips tipped up in a brief smile. "Scalae be with you, siren."

The gesture touched my nervous heart, but I couldn't bring myself to smile back. "Thank you."

With that, she pulled the lever. There was a low rumbling beneath our feet, followed by the scraping of stone as the circular emblem began to sink and slide away. I stared into the pit before me. Stone stairs wound downward, the light of the sun illuminating the endless spiral.

With a deep breath, I straightened my shoulders and took the first step.

For Meryn.

Chapter Thirty-Three

Fivrial

Further and further, I went in a never-ending spiral. The sunlight reached to the floor of the shaft, and for that I was grateful. I gripped my sword in front of me the entire way, unsure of what I'd meet. The stairs went down so far, I was sure that I was below ocean level by the time I reached the bottom.

Once I reached the last step, I craned my neck up to see the white dot of light up above. It seemed so far away. I did not feel the warmth as I did at the top. A chill settled over me, seeping into my bones.

When I stepped from the light, it took a few moments for my eyes to adjust to the shadows. It was a sizable cave, with walls of black rock. The smell of must and damp reached my nose. Ahead, in the darkness, were several passages to choose from.

I racked my brain, trying to walk through the

instructions Galia had given me. The first: go toward the light. Initially, this seemed to be an impossible task. They all looked dark. But when I stepped closer, I finally noticed a very dim, garish light emanating down one of them.

That was to be my path.

Taking a deep breath, I steeled myself, stepping into the passageway. The light reflected off the glistening rock, coming from around a curve ahead. I picked up the pace, anxious to get out of the darkness.

Just as I was nearly to the curve, the ground gave out beneath me and I plunged into an abyss. I hit the rocky floor with a hard smack, knocking the wind out of me. My sword clattered across the ground. In a blind panic, I felt around for it until my hand brushed the cold metal.

The moment I took it in hand, torchlight lit up all around me. I gasped, climbing to my feet. It was another chamber, with passages leading out like the spokes of a wheel. Torches were posted on the narrow space in between each one. When I looked up, the rock had re-sealed itself. I was closed in.

I whirled around, sword upraised. Every passage looked the same. In my disorientation, I quickly forgot which direction I was facing. The low ceiling above me pressed in, feeding my panic.

The weight of the armor and the weapons grounded me. I was not defenseless, and this was simply another test. I forced myself to focus.

Choosing the path directly ahead, I stalked forward. Again, there was a garish glow—ever so slight—reflecting off the curve of the rock ahead. With greater confidence that I'd made the correct choice, I forged ahead.

Without warning, I plunged again. A shockwave of pain hit as I landed on the hard rock. I groaned and reached for my sword, thankful again it had fallen nearby. Pain sliced my arm where the edge of the shield ripped into it.

When I looked up, I couldn't believe my eyes. Another chamber—identical to the last, down to the placement of the torches. Climbing to my feet, I sucked in air. The ceiling was once again sealed shut above me. This time, I did not turn around. I had to keep my sense of direction somehow.

Last time, I'd chosen the path directly ahead. Now, I had another choice to make. They all looked completely identical. The one just to the right drew my attention for some reason. It was just as good as the others. With a deep breath, I forged ahead.

Again, I fell. Another identical chamber. I screamed in frustration. I charged ahead down another passage, only to plunge again into yet another tomb.

Over and over again, no matter which path I chose, I suffered the same fate.

At last, I was beaten, and my knees bloodied. Lying there on the ground, I felt utterly defeated.

Why is this happening?

I couldn't move forward if the chamber was determined to keep me prisoner. Nor could I even begin to wrap my head around how this was occurring.

This really would be my tomb.

I climbed to my knees and leaned my forehead against the cross of my sword. There was no way I could give up. Even if it took an eternity of trying, it was either die or succeed. Raising my bleary eyes, I was again drawn to the center passage straight ahead. There *had* to be a way.

With great effort, I pulled myself to standing. My chest heaved as I slowly made my way into the passage. This time, I hugged the wall and took one careful step at a time.

I drew minutely closer to the curve, holding my breath and listening for any sign that the rock was about to give way below me. Closer... and closer... then I heard it: the soft crumbling. Leaping with all my strength, I sailed through the air just as the rock gave way. With a hard smack, I landed on firm ground, my feet dangling over the gaping hole.

I scrambled away from it and rose. A smile lit my face, having conquered the trap at last.

Moving along the passageway, I rounded the curve and came to a stop, eyes wide. Crystals as tall and wide as trees stretched from floor to ceiling. Every glittering color filled the space. Each reflected the light, like walking into an enormous jewel box. Soft glow emanated from them, catching the prisms in a magical display. A winding passage lay ahead.

The air was stifling the moment I stepped into the chamber. I wanted to roll up my shirtsleeves and trousers as sweat dampened my skin, but time was not on my side. Ignoring this new discomfort, I cautiously moved ahead.

The path was a long one that moved slightly uphill. I wasn't entirely sure how long it would be until I reached the water. All I knew was that once I got there, it would be extremely hard to resist the temptation to drink it myself. My tongue was soon parched.

A clicking sound from the left caught my attention. I paused and listened for it again. Nothing. All was calm. The moment I took a step, I heard it again, this time from my right. I stopped to investigate.

This time, a shadow darted out of the corner of my eye. No sooner had one appeared than another zipped by on my left. More and more clicking noises rose, like the patter of rainfall.

Finally, I saw it. A gangly creature with shining black fur and knife-like talons hung from a crystal above. Its bulbous body was short, with a small round head that bore glowing red eyes. Its mouth dripped large drops of saliva from its razor-sharp teeth.

More and more popped out from behind crystal structures, their talons clicking on the hard surface. Drool dripped from their open mouths onto the path as their eyes fixated on me. One dropped from the ceiling, blocking my way ahead. It crawled on all fours toward me, snapping its hungry jaws.

I backed away, sword raised. The creature growled, the low tones reverberating in my chest. There was a thud behind me. Pivoting to the side, I found another one had dropped not far below, blocking my escape.

They crawled toward me from either direction, ready to devour me.

Suddenly, the first one lunged at me. I raised my shield, and it bounced off. I barely had time to react as it leaped again. With a swing of my sword, I caught its arm with a sickening crack. The creature skittered away, howling.

There was no time to relish the victory as the other

leaped on me. Its sharp talons sliced into my shoulders. My scream filled the walls of the cave. Whipping around as fast as I could, I sent it sprawling to the ground.

Before it could advance again, I drove my sword into the center of its body, twisting it. When I pulled the long blade from its body, the creature was still. More and more creatures dropped onto the path.

I knew I could not hold off so many—at least not for long. I beat each off with my sword, dodging talons and deflecting their sharp teeth with my shield. Blood splattered along the walls, soaking my shirt and catching in my hair. I was tiring quickly.

Before long, they surrounded me. The beasts merely climbed over their dead companions and closed in.

Though vastly outnumbered, I refused to panic. There had to be a way out of this. Some way forward.

Taking a deep breath, I centered myself. There was only one other weapon I had that might work. Only one small sliver of hope.

I opened my mouth... and sang. I had no way of knowing if it would work on these creatures.

It was a song written by Meryn that she'd sang to me the first day we were in the music room together. It was still etched in my memory, as vivid as the day I'd heard it. Though I had no tail, the music burst forth in echoing waves all the same.

The creatures wailed, holding their clawed hands over the sides of their heads. A great chorus of pained cries filled the chamber. One by one, they fell to the floor in utter agony.

I sang, loud and strong, as I cautiously made my way up the path again, leaping over them. They made no move to follow, some growing silent on the floor. It was the opposite reaction I'd come to know. Certainly, none of them desired to be near me, yet their lives were being drained all the same.

At last, their cries faded into the distance as I reached the end of the path. A long, rocky passageway lay before me. The air was once again dark and cool. Once I entered the safety of the passageway, I finally allowed myself to stop singing.

Not far into the passage, a loud slam behind me brought out a startled cry. I whipped around and found the entrance to the crystal chamber was now sealed by a large stone block. Ambient light shone from behind.

Upon turning, a more shocking sight greeted me. There, lining each side of the hallway, were countless floor-to-ceiling windows with gilded frames. Beyond them was a garish, blue-gray fog that gave off a soft glow.

I cautiously walked ahead.

My eyes adjusted to the light again. At first, there was nothing. And then... something.

A figure appeared in the fog, repeating in each of the windows. I gripped my sword, ready to fight whatever horrid creature came smashing through. But then I nearly dropped my sword altogether.

The fog lifted just enough to reveal the clear details of the figure. I couldn't believe my eyes.

"Meryn?"

Not just one, but over a dozen, each standing on the other side of the glass with tears in their eyes. The mirror image reflected many times over.

My hand outstretched, I approached one in shock. She met my gaze and reached out to touch the glass. From my peripheral, the others did the same.

"Help me, Finn," Meryn pleaded. Her voice echoed all around me. Tears streamed down her cheeks. "You have to help me. Please!"

Her skin glowed. She was alive and healthy. Her red hair fanned around her, beautiful as ever. But her eyes were so very sad. I pressed my hand to the glass, desperate to feel even a small bit of her warmth. I felt only the cool surface beneath my palm.

"I'm trying. I promise."

She pounded on the glass, face twisted in anguish. "You must go back, Finn. Don't go any further. Please!"

I wanted to argue, to tell her I could not go back to a world where she wasn't with me. Just as I opened my mouth to explain, an arm grabbed her from behind, pulling her away from the mirror.

Her screams filled the cavern. I called her name, pounding on the glass. A man's face appeared over her shoulder as his arm banded across her chest. My jaw fell open. *Percivan.*

He stood on two legs, dressed in all black. A menacing smile stretched across his cheeks. Meryn struggled against him, but he held a silver dagger to her delicate throat.

"Hello, Fivrial," he greeted in a sinister tone. "So happy to see you again."

"Go back, Finn! Get out of here!" Meryn begged.

Percivan tightened his grip, squeezing her throat as she struggled to breathe. He sneered. "I would take her suggestion if I were you."

As he spoke, the slab blocking the crystal chamber rose again, opening the way. Panicking, I glanced back and forth between the horrible scene being played out before me and the way back.

"Let her go!" I shouted, banging on the glass.

Percivan sneered. "You would like that, wouldn't you? Maybe I will if you turn around."

The more I stared at the scene, the more something felt off. I stepped back and looked around me. The windows all showed the same thing: Meryn and Percivan. All of them mimicked each other in perfect time. My head cleared as I squeezed my eyes shut to the horror.

"This isn't real."

Meryn sobbed. "Finn, please, look at me."

I turned away and re-oriented toward my destination. My grip on the sword was shaking. My heart raced, but the fear was unsubstantiated. The illusions around me were just that—illusions.

It wasn't really my Meryn. The blade at her throat was not real. Percivan was not there.

I took a step and Percivan growled, "I wouldn't do that if I were you!"

Glancing in one of the windows, I saw him edge the knife over her throat, drawing a trickle of blood. Meryn cried out in pain. I ripped my gaze to the floor. "You're not real."

"Finn! Please! Turn around!" Meryn cried desperately.

Pressing onward, I forced my feet to move. I wanted to drop my sword and shield and slam my hands over my ears to drown out the sound of her cries.

A thump reached my ears. Percivan shoved Meryn up against the glass, gripping her by the hair. His knife was still at her throat.

"I'll do it, Fivrial! I'll bleed her dry if you take another step!"

"It's not real... it's not real..." I whispered to myself over and over as I picked up my pace.

"Finn, don't you love me?" Meryn whimpered as her tears smeared the glass. "Why are you doing this to me?"

It cracked my heart in two. I wanted to stop. I yearned to smash through the glass and rescue her. The only reason I was down there at all was to save her. But logic told me to keep walking. The only way to truly save her was to complete my mission.

Galia warned me of distractions—warned me to keep going no matter what I saw. This must be what she had spoken of.

I had no idea just how hard it would be.

I took off in a run, training my eyes ahead. The gallery stretched forever. There had to be an end. Percivan shouted louder and louder, getting rougher with Meryn as she cried out for me and begged for her life. It was pure torture.

At last, when I finally saw the end of the passageway, Percivan whipped his knife across her throat and there was a gushing spray of blood against the glass. I cried out in horror, but still charged ahead. Finally, I reached the end.

I stopped. I didn't want to see. The image of blood shooting against the glass was burned into my mind. But still, I turned around for one last look.

Upon turning my head, I gasped. All the windows were gone, and there was nothing but solid black rock on either wall, stretching into the shadows. No Meryn, no Percivan, no blood. It was gone. I was left raw and dazed.

My bloodied shoulders rose and fell as I sucked in air and tried to calm myself. None of it was real. Meryn was still lying in her bed, back in Arcadia, waiting for me to get through this. I'd conquered my fears and the temptation to give into them.

With a shuddered breath, I turned around to enter the next phase.

The ceiling gradually grew higher until it soared above me. I was on a wandering path between tall rock formations in a large chamber. Blue light reflected above them, hitting the ceiling and catching the sparkling stones embedded within. The source of the light was coming from somewhere ahead. I could only hope the path would take me there.

Onward I trod, sword still gripped in my blood and sweat-covered hand. My arms were growing weary from holding the heavy objects. Still, I knew I must continue.

Finally, the rock formations on either side of the path receded, and I found myself standing in a vast, open chamber filled with a blue-white glow.

I lowered my sword and shield in awe.

Ahead, beyond a small hill, was the source of the glow. A thrum of tingling power washed over me the closer I came to the beautiful light. I knew in my spirit that this was what I'd come for. After everything I'd just been through, my reward was in front of me.

Meryn's salvation.

Just as I reached the base of the hill, a low growl echoed through the chamber. Stopping short, I raised my sword and shield again. Something else was in there with me.

My eyes grew wide as a massive red figure rose beyond the hill, soaring toward the ceiling as it stood.

My thoughts raced as panic threatened to overwhelm me. *Was it a man? A creature?* Its head nearly reached the roof of the cave.

Shining, red skin... inky black robes... yellow eyes... angular features... I tried to make out the obscure form towering over me. It was the most frightening sight I'd ever beheld.

Talgren.

In his left hand was a black staff with a glowing blue crystal atop that mingled with the light that still lay beyond the rise of the hill. His piercing eyes trained on me under hairless brows. When he spoke, his voice boomed like thunder.

"State your purpose."

Gathering my wits, I tried to calm my shaking limbs and speak with confidence. "I come seeking the waters of Scalae."

Talgren tilted his head. "And you think yourself worthy?"

I gulped. "I believe I am."

Drawing a deep breath, Talgren pounded his staff on the ground in a sound that sent pain shooting through my ears. "You must prove your worth, siren."

My brows raised. "Prove? Haven't I already done so?"

Ignoring my question, Talgren lifted his staff and pounded it again as he opened his mouth and uttered booming words I could not understand. Again and again, he pounded the staff in a deafening display. I backed away, scanning the area for an escape. When I turned, I found the rock formations had sealed themselves to form a solid wall behind me. I was trapped.

When I looked back toward the hill, another sight arrested me. There, rising from the glow, was another, smaller figure. A man with wavy red locks and piercing blue eyes. In his hands were a sword and shield, identical to mine.

I was staring at myself.

His unfeeling eyes trained on me as he descended the hill. Every step brought my nightmare closer. This wasn't possible.

My back hit the rock as I swallowed past the dry lump in my throat. "I-I don't understand!" I shouted at Talgren. "I've proven myself!"

Talgren merely watched as my double approached me with a raised sword. I put up my shield and tried to still the racing of my heart enough to think. This wasn't me. It was merely another trick.

The man's eyes widened in fierce determination as he reached me. The sword came crashing down against my shield. Real or not, he was going to kill me if I didn't do something.

With a mighty shove, I pushed him away and regained my position. We circled each other. As we did, he spoke in my voice.

"I see you, coward. You think you can defeat me?"

I squared my jaw and raised my sword. "You're not real."

His lips curled into a sardonic grin. "Meryn's real enough. After I'm finished with you, perhaps I'll go sing for her."

Rage flooded me. With a cry, I lunged at him and swung the sword. He deflected at the last moment with his shield. Laughing, my double continued to block my blows with amazing agility.

"You'll have to do better than that, Fivrial. You're such a failure at everything you do."

The truth cut quicker than a blade. It was true. I *was* a failure. I failed at being a siren. I failed at bringing Meryn to love me enough. I failed to do the honest thing. And now I was failing to save her.

My despondent thoughts caused me to let my guard down for a moment. It was just long enough for my double to bring the tip of his sword around and slice my upper left arm. I cried out in pain and staggered back, nearly dropping my sword. Blood bloomed on my sleeve.

Smiling in satisfaction, the other Fivrial banged his now-bloodied sword on the front of his shield in a menacing display. "What's the matter, Fivrial? Can't take a scratch? You're such a minnow."

Glowering, I regained my footing and lunged at him again. He dodged my blade and spun around, catching me in the upper back with his blade.

I screamed as the sharp edge bit through the skin of my shoulder blade. Falling to my knees, I dropped my sword, sending it clattering across the rock.

A boot came sailing into my gut, knocking the wind out of me. I crumpled to the ground with my knees bent, sucking in air. My double circled me, sneering. "You're so pathetic. Look at you, curled up like a weakling."

Another kick to my back had me screaming in agony again. Stars leaped into my vision. He bent down and roughly grabbed me by the hair before spitting words in my face. "I'm going to get that water, and after I do? I'm going to ravage her while you rot."

Something snapped within me. Realization hit. This was the end of the road. Real or not, Meryn's life was at stake and I couldn't lie down and take it.

With a growl, I reached up and slammed the top edge of my shield into the side of his face. He sprawled to the ground with a cry.

As I rose and towered over him, fear filled his eyes. Blood poured from a gash on his cheek. I kicked his hand, sending his sword clattering across the ground out of reach. He scrambled back and held up his shield. With a swift kick, I caught it under the rim and lift it before whipping my sword down and slicing the forearm holding it underneath. He cried out as his grip loosened and the shield slipped down his bloody arm to the ground. I shoved it away with my boot and advanced.

"You," I ground out as I lifted his chin with the point of my sword, "are the coward now."

His throat bobbed as he ceased his retreat. Sucking in air through clenched teeth, he met my eyes with resignation.

"Do it, Fivrial."

My lips curled into a sneer as I pressed the point of the sword into the soft flesh of his throat ever so slightly, bringing drips of blood. I wanted to empty every drop on the floor. It would finally put an end to this pretender and clear my path.

"Just do it, Fivrial," he challenged. "Run me through. End my life and claim your victory. It's what you want, isn't it? To end me?"

Something gave me pause. Why was he so determined to die? The look in his eyes was almost begging for me to spill his blood. The look in *my* eyes.

"Do it!" He held his hands out to his sides, offering no resistance. "Put an end to me. You know I'm a failure, Fivrial. There's no point in waiting. Don't be weak."

That word again... *failure.* Slowly, it dawned on me. I wasn't staring at some separate entity that looked like me. I was staring at *myself.*

All of my doubts, my fears, my self-hatred—it was at the point of my sword, begging to be vanquished. Begging for blood to be spilled. But all of it was a part of me. It was part of the complex notes that made *Fivrial*.

The sword fell from my hands. My double looked at me with wide eyes. "What are you doing?"

I fell to my knees before him. "No more... No more..." Without another word, I pulled him into my arms and crushed him to my chest. Tears filled my eyes. "I forgive you."

For a moment, he sat there, stunned. Then arms wrapped around me. A deep sigh escaped him. Our battle had ended in the most unexpected way. An overwhelming sense of peace passed between us.

Light flooded beyond my closed lids. When I opened my eyes, the other Fivrial was a blaze of white. And then... he was gone. The light sank into my skin, flooding me with warmth. A tingling rushed through my veins. When it subsided, every ounce of pain was gone.

I ran my hands over myself. No cuts, no blood. I was as clean and whole as I had been the moment I took the first step into the chamber. Quickly, I climbed to my feet and looked around. There was no sign of my double.

After recovering my sword, I turned back to Talgren, who stood patiently beyond the hill. He spoke, his voice reverberating through every pore. "You have proven yourself worthy, Fivrial."

It was then that I fully understood. It was never Talgren I had to prove it to, or even Meryn... but myself. All my worth had been hinged on my failures and successes, and I lost myself in the process. Grayler's words came flooding back to my mind, "Figure out who you are, and don't flee from it."

Had I really run so far? It didn't matter how worthy I was to anyone else, I had to be worthy of myself.

I sighed. A new sense of peace settled in. And a new sense of determination. I *was* going to save Meryn. And we would be okay. *I* would be okay.

With confidence, I strolled up the path to the top of the hill. A small glowing pool awaited in a crater inset in the rock. The crystal blue water radiated magic. Its light spilled around me, wrapping me in peace.

I glanced up at Talgren, who nodded. After setting my sword on the ground, I unclipped the vial and uncorked the lid. I kneeled, carefully submerging the vial in the powerful waters, letting it fill. Warmth crept up my arm as I did. My whole body felt relaxed and rejuvenated with each passing moment. A smile spread across my face.

It wasn't just joy emanating from the waters; it was hope.

When the bottle was filled and secured on my belt once more, I grabbed my sword and stood. Talgren waved his massive hand and the wall to my right crumbled away, revealing an arched opening into a sunlit chamber. I saw the base of the spiral staircase waiting for me.

"You may take your leave. Scalae be with you," said Talgren, eyes trained on me.

I bowed reverently. "My thanks." Wasting no more time, I quickly descended the hill and crossed the chamber to the exit.

I'm coming, Meryn.

Chapter Thirty-Four

Fivrial

The journey back to the castle was rushed. Once I made it back into the temple, I returned Galia's armor in a hurry before fleeing outside to the carriage. Penton explained that I'd been in the temple for nearly a full day.

Time was running short.

We pushed the horses hard, barely stopping. I couldn't sleep, couldn't eat, couldn't *rest*.

Penton responded to my urgency, not once questioning our pace.

At last, we pulled up to the castle as the sun was disappearing below the horizon. I leaped out of the carriage before it came to a complete stop, rushing up the front steps and through the doors.

No one dared stand in my way as I ran through the halls. I passed Sebastian but didn't bother throwing so much as a scowl his way. He was entirely unimportant now.

When I reached the base of the tower stairs, the guards stepped aside to grant me access without question. Taking the stairs two at a time, I reached the top and burst into the bedroom. There, I found Anaat sitting at Meryn's bedside, holding her hand. Nola stood behind Anaat, grasping her shoulder.

When Anaat looked at me, her eyes were red and puffy. Her face crumpled with emotion. "It might not be enough."

Rushing to Meryn's bedside, I found a heartbreaking sight. She was a few breaths away from entering the underworld. Her skin was pale—all traces of color gone from her cheeks, and her lips had become blue as her lungs struggled to fill with shallow, wheezy breaths. The sight was like a punch to the gut.

"I have the water. Prop her up," I instructed, pulling the vial from my pocket. Anaat and Nola slipped their arms under Meryn's neck and shoulders, elevating her off the pillow. I uncorked the lid and grasped her chin.

"Meryn, if you can hear me, I need you to swallow this." I prayed she understood.

There was no response beyond the continued labored breathing. Sending out a silent plea to Scalae, I pressed the edge of the vial to her lips. Careful not to spill a single, precious drop, I tipped the blue waters into her mouth.

Despite my efforts, some dribbled down the sides of her mouth. Fight back panic, I poured even smaller amounts. It took several tries, but finally she began to swallow.

At last, the vial was empty. I tossed it aside, and we carefully laid her back down. Then... we waited.

Hours seemed to pass as I watched for a change. I smoothed the hair from her face, crushing her hand in mine. "Come on, Meryn..." I quietly urged.

Night fell around us. No one bothered to light the fire. No lantern's glow would push away the darkness in the room. Anaat cried softly as Nola stood stoic behind her mistress.

I closed my eyes again.

Surely, it will work. It must work.

Slowly, the pink returned to her lips. Her breathing steadied slightly. We watched the improvement with hopeful eyes.

The moments passed by. We waited... and waited... until an hour had gone by. Still, her eyes remained closed. Her features were still far too pale. She breathed, but not the deep, restful breath of one simply sleeping.

Anaat wiped her weary eyes. "When will she wake up?"

I shook my head. "I don't know. Galia didn't say how long it would take."

"Galia?"

"The high priestess at the temple. I don't think she expected me to be successful. And I was so anxious to get back afterward that I didn't stop to ask any more questions." I exhaled sharply. "I'm sorry."

Anaat reached across the bed and grasped my forearm. "You got the water, Fivrial. You've done what you can. Thank you."

I threw her an appreciative glance. Anaat's grip loosened and suddenly she slumped over the bed with a hiss. Immediately, I stood to assist. "Anaat?"

Nola was already at her side. Anaat sat up and leaned into her, her eyes heavy. "Sorry, I haven't slept in days. My head is killing me."

I caught Nola's concerned eyes and sighed. "Anaat, you need to rest."

Anaat shook her head as she pinched the bridge of her nose. "Absolutely not. I'm not going to leave Meryn's side. If she should wake—"

"Then I will be here," I assured. "You're doing her no good by wearing yourself to the bone. You both look like you could use rest."

"He's right, dear," chimed in Nola. "She's improved now, and she won't be alone. Let's get you off to bed."

After staring at her sister with furrowed brows, Anaat finally nodded. "All right, then." Her eyes snapped to mine. "But you send for me the *moment* anything changes, do you hear?"

I nodded. "You have my word."

Tension visibly fled Anaat's shoulders as she dragged herself to her feet. Nola looped an arm around her back and squeezed her. "Come, dear. You'll have a nice warm bath, too..."

The two women exited the room, leaving me alone with Meryn at last. I looked at her still form lying under her favorite quilt and my heart pinched. How long would she be like this? How long until she smiled again? I brushed her cheek with my knuckles. It was still far too cool.

Anaat wasn't the only one with a blazing headache. I clenched my eyes shut as the pain ebbed and flowed.

We'd been through hell. Now, all there was to do was wait. I wasn't about to leave my love's side, however. When she woke up... *if* she woke up... I would be there.

I watched her in debate for a moment. Then I peeled back the blankets, slipped my arms underneath her shoulders and knees, and moved her over a little. After tucking her back in, I removed my boots and crawled onto the bed.

I snuggled up next to her on top of the covers and wrapped my arm around her waist. So many nights, we'd slept in this position—feeling the rise and fall of our chests. If anything should happen, I was going to be right there with her.

She wouldn't be alone.

My eyelids were growing heavy as I gazed at her beautiful profile. She was still breathtaking, even in the state she was in. A tear rolled down my temple as I drew a shuddered breath. "Keep fighting, Meryn. I'm right here." I pressed my lips to her shoulder. "I love you."

I don't know how long I slept, but my sleep was fraught with nightmares. Beasts chased me in the dark. Percivans appeared from nowhere, with knives at Meryn's throat. I watched her blood spill to the floor again. The images swirled around in my mind like a great tempest.

When I finally woke, it was to a crash of thunder. I bolted up in the bed with a gasp. I turned to Meryn, my hand resting on her chest. Her heart was still beating and her breathing steady. A sigh of relief escaped me.

My relief was short-lived.

The thunder rolled again, and this time, my ears attuned to something else echoing across the sea. My blood turned to ice. "No!"

I flew from the bed to the window as the room lit up with flashes of green and purple lightning. The sound filled my ears; *chanting*. This was no ordinary storm, and it would not just be those on the sea who felt its wrath.

As the lightning filled the sky, I saw a horrifying sight on the watery horizon. The silhouette of tentacles—massive and curling out of the sea. A great beast rose from the waves.

A beacon of green light appeared at the top of the bulbous body, shining across the sea, heading straight for Arcadia. The choppy waves rose high, splashing into the air. The entire sea looked as if it were being shaken up inside a glass.

My heart pounded in my chest. I knew exactly what I was looking at. And it was impossible. She was dead, and yet here she was, resurrected before my eyes...

Rowen, the goliath witch of the deep.

Something caught my eye below, an even more gut-wrenching sight—humans, hundreds of them, trudging in a daze toward the beaches. They stood along the shoreline, facing across the waves into the garish light.

I fumbled with the window lock until it swung open. "No! Stop! Go back!" I shouted at the top of my lungs. Not one head turned. Their ears were closed off to anything but the siren song.

In horror, I saw servants from the castle file out down the hill to join the crowds. Among them, the Trevions... Nola... and Anaat.

My stomach churned. Everything was going wrong. Somehow, I was unaffected, but equally helpless to do anything. There was no way for me to stop the beast.

I turned back to Meryn. She was still sleeping, undisturbed. Probably the only human left in their bed. I could just lie back down next to her. I could plug my ears until the horror had passed and every life force on that beach was drained. The merfolk would exhaust themselves trying to take Rowen down. Grayler would lead a mighty effort... but would it be enough?

The more I stood there, the more I knew I must act. I could not sit by and let this happen. My days of hiding in a cave were over. This was bigger than me, bigger than Meryn. Somehow, I had to put a stop to this.

Stalking over to the bed, I leaned over her, pausing to take in every single one of her delicate features for the last time. Gulping down my surge of emotions, I kissed her soft lips and touched my forehead to hers as I grasped her cheek.

"I love you, Meryn. Thank you for everything. I'm sorry."

With that, I tore myself away and fled the room before I could second-guess myself. The image of her face was burned into my mind as I rushed down the stairs and the empty halls. Every moment we'd spent in those very spaces... every smile, every laugh, every note we'd played together... it all surged through me like a sweet wave. Even our tears and arguments—it was all there. Our time together was whole and full of life. She had made me whole—as a man, as a mer, as a *person*. Even if I died now, it would be without the regret of a life unlived.

When I burst through the kitchen exit and took off down the outer stairs, I saw a dark figure with puffs of gray hair running and limping across the hilly field toward the castle. My eyes widened as I ran to meet her.

"Mrs. Rigby? How—"

She shoved a round green vial into my hands as she panted. "No time! Get to the water and drink this." She stopped for a moment. Her hands rested on my shoulders. "Fivrial, once you do, it can never be reversed."

I clenched the cold vial in my palm. The death of my life with Meryn was contained within it. Everything would change once it passed my lips.

Colorful lightning flashed above us. Mrs. Rigby's eyes were briefly illuminated. It was then that I saw the brilliant colors swirling around in the gray. My brows rose in shock.

"You... you're a siren, aren't you?"

Her eyes darted toward the beaches. "It was long ago. I'm afraid I'm too old to survive another transformation now." She grasped my arm. "But you're not. You have to reclaim that which you stole, Fivrial."

"Grayler's trident? But it's just another weapon—one of many."

She shoved her finger in my face. "It was the trident of Scalae, you fool!"

My head spun as my jaw fell open. Again, I looked across the waters at the light. The *green* light.

Realization struck me. *How could I be so foolish?*

"Wrenna..."

"Go, Fivrial! Run as fast as your legs will carry. I will look after Meryn, but you must not waste any more time."

Shaking off my shock, I nodded. "Thank you, Mrs. Rigby. And goodbye."

I took off down the grassy hill toward the path to the pier. Pumping my legs as fast as they would go, I dodged people still walking mindlessly toward the beach. Their eyes were unblinking, fixated on the green light. It sent eerie shivers down my spine. Even when I bumped into them, there was no acknowledgment. They were lining up to attend their own slaughter.

When I finally reached the pier, I found it empty. I went to the nearest dock, ran to the end, and quickly stripped out of my clothing. The only thing I kept was the pearl necklace Mrs. Rigby had given me for luck before I left for the temple. I needed all the good fortune I could get.

I cast one last, long look back at the castle, at Meryn's tower. I bid her another silent goodbye before yanking the stopper from the top of the bottle and downing the bitter contents. I tossed the bottle amongst my clothes, bracing my palms on the edge of the wood. The angry waters greeted me as I slipped into the depths.

Almost immediately, the transformation started. I struggled, sputtering against the battering waves as the agony took hold. It was exceedingly painful—much more than the other times. But it was mercifully quick. Skin and muscle split open as leg bones snapped together for the last time. My scales shot out and locked together. Sharp pain in my lungs signaled the change was complete.

The moment I was no longer human, I dove beneath the highest waves. Faster and faster, I swam. The water was murkier than normal, full of turmoil.

I flipped my fins as fast as they would go, passing frightened mermaids. Mothers would flee toward the coast with their children and the elderly. They would hide among the rocks and grottos or attempt to swim up one of the few rivers that fed into the Aslean Sea. Their faces were full of terror as I rushed by. My heart twisted at the sight.

It felt like ages before I finally saw the trench. My tail and eyes blazed brightly as I dove into the crack. The water around me flashed green and purple from the lightning above the surface.

The entire sea was alive with power. *Her* power. A crackling tingle washed over me with every flip of my tail.

Finally, I reached the bottom of the trench, darting into the passageway that led to Wrenna's cave. When I got there, I found it in disarray. The mirror had been smashed and broken objects littered the ground. Wasting no time, I lifted larger pieces of wreckage and sifted through the rubble for any sign of the golden weapon. Nothing.

I searched and searched but found nothing. Only ruins. I grasped my hair and uttered a curse.

Think, Fivrial, think!

My eyes were drawn to the blue glow of the brine pool. It sat as usual—small creatures darting about. A thought popped into my head. Could it be possible? It wasn't safe, surely. But there was no other place left.

Swallowing my doubts, I approached the pool. I took a deep breath and plunged my hand into it. I could not see it once it dipped below the surface. In a panic, I retracted my hand again. Everything appeared to be intact. With determination, I stuck my hand back in and felt around the shallow bottom. My eyes widened when my fingers brushed something hard. I wrapped my hand around it and lifted the heavy object.

Out of the water, I pulled Grayler's weapon. The trident of Scalae glowed in the dim light of the cavern. I floated there for a moment, taking it in with reverence.

A boom of thunder brought me back to reality. Chanting reached my ears, even down at the bottom of the sea. There was no time to waste.

Trident in hand, I fled the trench. The beast was to the north. I swam as fast as my fins could carry me. On the way, I passed sparse numbers of bloodied mermen swimming back toward the coast. They stared at me with wide eyes, but none dared to stop me. Except for one.

"Fivrial?"

A hand grabbed my arm, bringing me to a halt. I turned to see Renold, blood seeping into the water from gashes on his upper arm and forehead. His brows lifted before he threw his good arm around my neck. "It *is* you!"

I extracted myself and clapped a hand on his shoulder. "Renold, there's no time. What's happening at the front?"

His eyes fell. "We're losing. Many dead. Grayler's trying to rally them, but even able-bodied mer are fleeing. Scalae has abandoned us."

My grip tightened on the trident as I pressed my lips into a line. "Not yet, she hasn't."

Without another word, I shot off through the water, leaving Renold calling my name. Weaving through the kelp forests, around large, fleeing sea life, and over the steep towers of Brinn—I swam as I'd never swam before.

Before long, I saw the great black shadows. Colorful flashes caught my eye as lightning glinted off scales. Mermen with spears and tridents of their own were dodging the tentacles as they swooped through the water. Mer were being crushed alive and pulled from beneath the waves. Their screams filled the water around me, only to be stopped short when tentacles crushed them into silence.

Their weapons were mere needles against the thick, black hide. The sight was sickening.

I'd never get close enough that way. It was a miracle Renold was still alive. Off to the wings, I saw more troops in formation, ready to advance under Grayler's orders. He floated nearby, shining silver trident in hand. My eyes flitted to the one in my hand. Overwhelming guilt seized me.

I swam, keeping far from the reach of the tentacles until I reached Grayler. He didn't see me at first, but when his eyes finally caught mine, they widened. "Fivrial?"

Shame flooded me as I held out the trident. "I've done wrong by you, Grayler. This is all my fault. I've come to make it right again, but I fear it may be too late."

Grayler stared at me, not even acknowledging the trident. His presence alone was overwhelming, more than the witch decimating our people at that very moment. I wanted to hide, but my days of hiding had come to an end. And so I met his stare head-on.

At last, he spoke. "You will wield it." My brows furrowed as he continued. "It's always been meant to be in your hands, Fivrial. For this moment."

"But Grayler—"

"There is no time," he snapped. "Now, go."

Squaring my shoulders, I nodded. There would be no goodbyes, no affection. Only a directive to be obeyed.

One at which I must not fail.

Chapter Thirty-Five

Meryn

The darkness subsided with the presence of a soft glow. Cold gave way to gradual warmth. My vision cleared as the light grew brighter.

I sat up with a deep gasp. Whipping my head around, I was safe in my own bed, rather than in my clutches of a sea monster... but I was not alone in the room.

A figure stood at the foot of my bed. A woman—bathed in a golden glimmer that illuminated her pearl robes. A crown of stars and shells rested atop her scarlet curls. Her golden eyes smiled down at me.

My heart pounded in my chest. I was dreaming. I squeezed my eyes shut, trying to make the image go away. The moment I did, my ears attuned to a horrific sound: chanting in the distance.

"Meryn." The soft, female voice spoke. It was a *familiar* voice.

I opened my eyes and found her still standing there, watching me. Slipping from the blankets, I crawled across the bed and stood. Cautiously, I reached out and touched her cheek. My fingertips connected with real, warm flesh.

Tears filled my eyes. "Mother?"

She smiled and cupped my hand with hers. "It's me."

Overwhelmed, I threw my arms around her neck and sobbed. Mother gathered me into a tight embrace. As she did, I felt a rising current of energy seep into my skin. My head buzzed and tingled.

My eyes opened, and I stood back with a gasp. Even after breaking the connection with her, the feeling grew stronger. I grasped my arms and swept my eyes over my body, only to find that I was now *glowing*. Golden ribbons of light danced around me.

"What's happening?"

Mother grasped my hands and brought my attention back to her. "Don't be afraid, Meryn. There's much to tell, but time is short."

I shook my head. "I don't understand. I thought you were dead?"

"No, dear. I'm not, but—"

The chanting outside drew our attention as it increased in volume. Strange lightning flashed. Mother's face crumpled with concern. "There's much to explain, but we don't have the time. People are in danger." Her earnest gaze found mine again. "*Fivrial* is in danger."

I stared at her in confusion, my anxiety rising. "I don't understand any of this. What is going on? Who is Fivrial?"

Mother grasped both sides of my head, eyes boring into mine. "I need you to listen to me very carefully, Meryn. I need you to *remember*."

My eyes grew wide, and I grasped at her wrists, but her hands remained clamped firmly on either side of my head. "Wait! I don't know if I want to—"

"Meryn," she urged. "*Be brave*."

The words left her lips as a command. The pressure swelled inside my mind. An ache grew from deep in my head, radiating outward. It grew and grew until I was crying out. But with it came images. I clenched my eyes shut, but still the images danced across my mind.

Stars... the moon... the surface of the sea... diving below that surface... a new world... Finn. Only... not Finn. He was as he was in my dream—colorful eyes, sparkling tail, and fins. Finn was a merman.

I felt my body relax now, welcoming the images in like a long-lost friend.

The first storm... my boat... chanting... darkness... a grotto... Finn... Fivrial. A kiss...

More knowledge, lost to me, rushed through my mind, implanting themselves in my memory. The knowledge spread through every bone. It swam through my veins.

Power filled me. Knowledge of things past and present. With it came strength, compassion. Every creature under the sea flashed before my eyes. From the smallest plankton to the goliath witch wreaking havoc at that very moment.

They were not merely a part of something... they were a part of me, and I of them.

The images flooded through like a tidal wave until I was filled to bursting. It was as if my mind were deep in slumber, only to be awakened to the brightest sunlight. The sunlight was now inside of me—coursing through my veins, escaping from my fingertips. And the *warmth.* I was so very, very warm. I was lightning and sun and sea—all dancing with each other.

When I opened my eyes, the pain was gone. So was the fear.

I knew what I must do.

My mother released her hold. She stood before me with a proud smile. She was radiant as the sky, but I was the sun. My glow now filled the room, nearly overtaking hers.

I walked to the window, my newfound strength surging through me. When I looked out, I focused on the great beast in the distance. It was nothing to see beyond the storm, to pierce the waters and the clouds. Dozens of tentacles rained destruction and death. A green light pierced the night, drawing souls to the beach.

Wrenna... Rowen. The names floated to my mind naturally. Near them, I saw a solitary merman. *My merman.*

My eyes narrowed. He was in danger.

The window before me opened wide. I turned back to my mother who was just joining me. She took my hand. "I will bear you down there, but you must make your own way from there. Remember, the sea is under your power. Use it wisely."

My fingers crackled with lightning, instincts already taking over. I nodded.

"I will not fail."

Taking my hand, my mother squeezed it. "I know you won't."

Without further word, we soared through the open window like birds, our skirts fluttering in the breeze. Below I saw the horrific sight of the townspeople trudging mindlessly toward the beach, where they all gathered, staring across the sea. It was a sickening sight. And it angered me. They were innocents lined up for the slaughter.

We floated down over the shallow water. Our feet touched the surface as if it were firm ground, and we did not sink. The moment I came into contact with the sea, I felt a thrum of energy. I felt *connected.* And I knew exactly what to do.

Focusing across the sea, toward the green light, my intention snapped in place. The sea was at my beck and call. We were one. And together, we would stop this threat.

I took my first steps toward Rowen.

Chapter Thirty-Six

Fivrial

The underside of the witch loomed ahead. Like a massive squid, the tentacles splayed out in every direction. I would never get anywhere near her that way. After taking a moment to think, I swam out some distance and surfaced. A shocking sight greeted me.

A round lower body sat above the tentacles, but growing from the top of that was a small, slender waist. The upper body of a mermaid... *Wrenna*. The green light was shooting from her eyes across the sea. Her mouth was expressionless as she rained death upon those around her. This was not the old Wrenna I knew. Or perhaps I never knew the real Wrenna.

Somehow, I had to get within throwing distance. I had combat training like the rest of the mermen. Something I never thought would be put to use in a million years. My life had been spent spurning such things, but now I was grateful for all those years of Grayler pushing me.

"Wrenna!" I called, my voice rising and falling with the waves.

Immediately, the green light swept over the water and shone directly on me. I squinted and averted my eyes. The chanting continued, even as her calm voice cut through the chaos. "There you are. I've been waiting for you, Fivrial."

Her response chilled me. Was I playing into her game?

"Wrenna, you have to stop this!"

The light dimmed enough that I could make out the features of her face. Her lips were wrenched into a frown. "You always did think far too much of humans. Far too much of *her*."

All this time... I slowly put the pieces together.

The chanting... the storms... Meryn's accidents...

The mystery cleared. Still, I needed to hear it from her lips. "Why are you doing this?"

"I gave you everything, Fivrial. I even gave you a choice, and you chose her. You chose *them*. Weak humans who plunder our seas." The vitriol in her tone was chilling. "I could've given you so much more if you just looked at me."

Her words brought me to a shocking realization, something I couldn't believe I didn't see before.

Wrenna was in love with me.

Every bone in my body filled with dread. I gaped at her. She'd gone mad... over love? No. It was more than that. I felt the power thrumming through my chest. She didn't get this way alone.

"You're not alone, are you?"

Wrenna's lips twitched into a manic grin. "I am one with the spirit of Rowen. She has been quite accommodating." As she said that, she waved her fingers, a green light dancing among them.

A sickening feeling filled my stomach. She was possessed. It was worse than I ever imagined. I clutched the trident tighter.

Her eyes fell to the weapon. Amusement lit her face. "What do you have there? A toy?"

I arched a brow. "Something like that."

"Really, Fivrial?" She tilted her head. "You think that

will defeat me?"

"Well, we'll find out now, won't we?"

I ducked beneath the waves. The light swung around, trying to follow me below the surface, but I dove deep. Swimming along the seafloor, I gave the tentacles a wide berth. Swimming in a broad circle, I sensed Wrenna's monstrous body shifting in the water. I pushed myself to go faster.

A tentacle came crashing down in front of me. I dodged to my right at the last moment, evading the giant suckers. The sand kicked up, turning the water murky.

At first, I panicked as I struggled to see, but I quickly realized I could also use it to my advantage—to evade detection.

Around and around, I swam. Darting in and out of range, back-tracking, doing anything I could to throw her off my trail. I did my best to calm myself and dim my glow.

Focus. Swim.

At last, I ended up before Wrenna once more. Her glowing eyes were still sweeping around, searching for me, when I rose from the waves. I raised my trident above and reared back, homing in my enhanced vision, aiming the triple tines at her chest. It would be a deadly blow if it met its mark.

Something clamped around my body, stealing my breath. A massive black tentacle lifted me out of the water. The pain was so great that my grip loosened, the trident slipping from my hand and into the roiling sea.

Wrenna's eyes pierced mine as she swung me up to meet her face-to-face. The bright beacon dimmed to a green glow, her lips drawn into a tight frown.

"A valiant effort, Fivrial. I think you will find, however, that I do not give up so easily."

I braced my palms on the slick tentacle and tried to wriggle free, but my strength was waning. "Let me go, Wrenna," I croaked.

She caressed the side of my face, her frown softening. "Let you go? Why would I want to do that?"

Dizziness started to creep in. I drew a ragged breath and clenched my eyes shut. "You have to let me go, Wrenna.

I'm... I'm not yours to have."

The grip tightened around me and I cried out in pain.

"Oh, and I suppose you belong to *her?*" Her tone was biting. "Well, let me let you in on a little secret—you were never going to be hers, anyway."

My eyes popped open, and I met her cruel stare. "What? What are you saying?"

Wrenna's lips curled back into a tight grin. "Were you really so stupid to think three little words would give you legs forever? You think magic runs on *love?* Come now, Fivrial. Don't be a fool. I needed the trident. And after I made use of it..." She sneered down at me, a great burst of laughter emanating from her chest. "I could make use of you."

I wanted to throw up. That whole time, all my efforts to win Meryn were in vain? To think I was never meant to have a life with her filled me with an ire I didn't know I had. I glowered and spoke through clenched teeth. "Why would I want you if you deceived me?"

Wrenna chuckled. "And why would she want you knowing you did the same? Don't act like you're an innocent, Fivrial. We're not so different."

"You're killing our people, Wrenna. You're..." I gasped as I strained against her tightening grip, "...killing me."

The grip loosened a bit, and I took a deep breath as the pain lessened. My head started to clear. I forced myself to meet her eyes again and found them less harsh. Perhaps a measure of compassion was left in her.

I knew I had to appeal to it somehow. "Please," I begged. "Just let it go, Wrenna. If it's me you want, then take me. But don't let others suffer for it."

She searched my eyes for a moment, her brows softening. Then they hardened again. "I will have you, Fivrial. But I will not be an outcast any longer. I will not be hunted down like a monster." Her lips tugged into a manic smile. "My power grows stronger by the moment. I will be even more powerful than Scalae herself once I drain the humans of life. I will be *untouchable.* And then? You and I will rule the seas. Together."

Her words shook me to the core. Wrenna had gone

completely mad with power. There was no convincing her. I was to be captive to a monster for the rest of my days if something didn't change.

"Listen, I—"

Wrenna cried out in agony. The tentacle unfurled and I plunged through the air, hitting the water with a painful smack. Stars filled my vision as I sank beneath the waves.

It took a moment, but I regained my bearings and swam further from Wrenna's reach before surfacing again. What I saw had my jaw hanging open.

There, impaled in the middle of her tentacle, was the mast of a large sailboat. Blood ran from the wound like rain, reddening the water. Wrenna screeched in pain, her other tentacles beating the water furiously. Then, her eyes suddenly grew wide and fixated across the sea.

A bright glow bloomed, overtaking the green light. Slowly, I turned. My heart all but stopped beating.

There, walking across the surface of the water, was the figure of a woman clothed in white. Golden light swirled, dancing around her in ribbons. Her eyes were beautiful beacons, cutting through the darkness. Flowing red curls intertwined with shimmering strands.

I was staring at the impossible... *my Meryn*.

In her wake were dozens of unmanned boats, following her outstretched hands. The waters at her bare feet calmed as she walked, as if a path were being laid before her. I couldn't believe my eyes, but felt it in my chest. The thrum of pure energy pulsed as she drew near. She was alive. *More than alive.*

When Meryn was at my side, she came to a stop. My gaze was glued to her radiant face as she towered over me. I got the overwhelming sense that she was untouchable. Unsure of what to do, I just floated in the now-calm waters surrounding her and watched the shocking display.

"Scalae..." said Wrenna in a trembling voice.

When Meryn spoke, her voice was wrapped in a rush of whispers that swept across the surface of the water and converged in the sky. "I believe you speak of my mother."

"M-mother?"

A small smile appeared on Meryn's lips. "I am Meryn,

daughter of Scalae, goddess of all seas. And you..." Meryn twitched a finger and a giant wave of water rose from her right-hand side and paused midair. Another large sailboat sailed to the top of it and stopped. "...have displeased us greatly."

I stared at Meryn in disbelief. My mind raced. The whole time we were together—the pull of her music... her love of the sea... the wildness about her... her draw to all things magical...

Meryn was a demigoddess.

To think of the magnitude of power that lay within her, just under the surface, brought on wave after wave of awe. To see her now in all her revealed glory held me captive. I couldn't flee. I couldn't think straight. All I knew was that she didn't need my help anymore.

"You think you can best me, do you?" I turned to Wrenna and found her scowling. "Well, I think you'll find that you're not the only one with great power on this sea tonight. Perhaps it's time for a new goddess to arise?"

The chanting grew louder and louder until it was nearly deafening. I clapped my hands over my ears to block it out. Wrenna's light shot out from her eyes in blinding flashes that repeated over and over in a disorienting display. My stomach churned. Everything looked as if it were moving in a strange, slow motion.

A low growl split the air as Wrenna came closer. A tentacle ripped the boat from her wound. Another hoisted the craft into the air.

It was sailing through the sky, straight at us. The wall of water Meryn had been holding back shot forward, colliding with Wrenna's boat mid-air. Wood and other shrapnel came flying at us, but a wavering, golden shield of light erected around us. The objects bounced off and fell into the water, leaving us unscathed.

When the light dimmed, debris surrounded us. Towering waves rose around us on either side, boats atop them. Through the flashes of lightning, I saw the shadows of enormous whales, sharks, and squid suspended in place. They stood at attention, ready to attack at a mere flick of Meryn's finger.

Wrenna's tentacles flared upward as her eyes narrowed. "You're nothing but the child of a crumbling artifact. Your tricks do not impress me." She let out a primal scream and came flying across the surface of the sea, front tentacles outstretched. Blades appeared all around the rims of the suckers. They shot out at us like arrows.

My first instinct was to swim in front of Meryn, but I couldn't leap high enough out of the water to block her body. The moment I tried, a fountain of water rose to surround me, pushing me behind her. Again, the golden shield flared around us and the blades bounced off harmlessly.

The towers of water crashed into Wrenna over and over, bringing her advance to a halt. Boats smashed against her, stabbing into her tentacles, piercing her large body. Her furious, shrill screams filled the night.

Suspended in a column of water, I was now equal to Meryn's height. I reached through the surface into the open air. My fingertips brushed her hair. A powerful shock of energy shot through me the moment I did. Immediately, I retracted my hand back into the water.

Her calm voice filled my mind. "You cannot touch me right now, but I will keep you safe."

I felt a burst of warmth spread through me, like an embrace. It felt like... her. Though it clashed against my protective instincts, I remained in place.

When the crashing waters cleared, Wrenna's small upper body lay hunched over. There was blood everywhere. The sea was littered with wood and sails. Sharks stirred the water where they fed on severed portions of tentacles.

"Is she dead?" I asked tentatively.

Meryn shook her head. "Not yet."

The chanting died down to nothing. Lightning and thunder ceased, and the raindrops grew scattered until they stopped.

The surface of the water below Meryn's feet rose upward in a large swell, taking us with it. She walked forward, bringing us closer and closer to Wrenna until we were standing before her. I watched nervously as Meryn reached down, grabbed Wrenna under the chin, and lifted her upright.

Blood coated Wrenna's teeth. She coughed as her eyes slid open. Her chest labored to rise and fall with each wheezing breath.

"Wrenna, it is time for you to abandon this form and step from the darkness," said Meryn, with no hint of animosity in her voice.

Wrenna's reply was strained. "They abandoned *me*. Scalae..." She grimaced in pain. "...abandoned... me..."

"Scalae has not abandoned you. It's not too late," insisted Meryn. "I will help you."

"I don't need you," Wrenna seethed. Her eyes shifted to me and her brows twisted with pain. "I don't need either of you!"

A glint of gold in her eyes caught my attention. I heard the steady dripping of water behind us. My tail blazed brightly with fear as I flicked it as hard as I could, diving from the fount of water toward Meryn. I banded my arms around her and dropped to our right, barely missing the tines of the trident as it went shooting by.

Meryn and I fell into the swell of water, which immediately whooshed downward to become level with the rest of the sea once more. We tumbled around in the rolling current before golden light burst from her skin and brought us to a stop.

My head swam at the rush of power coming from her. Meryn pushed me away and swam to the surface. The sensation passed, and I shook my head to clear my thoughts before I followed her upward.

When we broke the surface, the night air was finally still. Meryn tread water nearby, her eyes and hair still aglow. I followed her gaze to Wrenna.

Wrenna was slumped forward once more, the trident impaled clean through her chest and out the other side. Her tentacle had slipped from the handle and lazed on the surface of the water, among the broken ships and blooms of blood.

It was a sickening sight. Though I was glad the threat had passed, I had to look away. Wrenna was once my friend, and it broke my heart to see that this was her end. The fact that she would have taken my life and Meryn's in one fell swoop was gut-wrenching.

I lifted my head and my gaze instantly linked with Meryn's. A mixture of sadness and gratitude shone in her eyes. There was so much to say. I didn't know where to start.

We rose from the water with a lifting of her palm. Her feet skimmed the surface while my lower body was encased in another fountain. Her eyes tore from mine as she spoke. "Come with me."

Meryn took off at a quick pace along the water, bringing me along with a subtle wave of her hand. Debris parted for us, giving a clear path forward. We didn't walk straight back to the crowded beach, however. I knew exactly where we were going.

Our beach.

Chapter Thirty-Seven

Fivrial

It was a long, silent walk. I didn't have to flip my fins once as the fountain moved alongside her at a steady pace. My thoughts whirled through a myriad of emotions along the way.

When we finally reached the beach, we stopped in the shallows. Meryn lowered me into the water, where I sat on a large boulder that rested just beneath the water's surface. As if stepping down a flight of stairs, Meryn stepped down from the top of the water until she was standing on the sandy bottom. We were level once more.

She would barely look at me. I wanted her to look at me, but the shame was overwhelming. Perhaps it was best she didn't.

A light from above caught my attention. At first, I thought it was the moon coming through the parting clouds, but when I took a second look, my breath ceased. The light was golden and wavering. And *descending*. Among it was the figure of a woman.

As she got lower, her features became clearer. Long, wavy red hair that reached her hips, a shining crown rested on her head...

Scalae.

I could feel it in my chest. Her power. I immediately braced my palms on the rock on either side of my tail and bowed low. I heard splashing in the water and peeked up to see Meryn step back up to the surface to embrace her mother.

When Scalae spoke, it resonated in my veins. "Well done, Meryn."

I sensed her draw near until the two of them were standing over me. I couldn't contain my shaking. I'd been taught my whole life to respect and fear the power of Scalae. And I had betrayed the trust of her child.

Scalae spoke again. "And you, Fivrial, have my gratitude."

In shock, I dared to raise my head. "Thank you, Great Lady Scalae."

The light drew nearer, and I felt a soft hand on my shoulder. "Rise, Fivrial."

With great hesitation, I sat up and found Scalae bending down, smiling at me. Her smile was like the brightest sun, filling me with peace. I took a deep breath as the tension fled my muscles.

After righting herself, Scalae took Meryn's hand. "I have revealed my true nature to my daughter tonight. And her own. She is still coming into her full power and is much changed, as you may have guessed."

My eyes darted between them. They bore a great resemblance to each other. Meryn stared at her feet as her lips twitched up in a smile.

"Forgive my boldness," I began, "but I was under the impression that her mother had died at sea?"

Scalae's gaze fell. "I could only sustain my mortal form for a number of years. Even now, I only have a few more moments. My family was unaware of what I was. I tried to tell Meryn's father many times, but each time he thought me mad, and I had to wipe his memory of the conversation."

I nodded and stared at the water. "The Spell of Forgetfulness."

"Yes. I believe you are familiar with that."

I felt a pinch in my chest. "I am."

Scalae smiled brightly again. "You have saved and sustained my daughter, my only flesh and blood. I wish to grant you a gift. You have only to name it and it's yours."

A gift? I looked at my fins. It would be so easy to ask. It would be so easy to have legs and live happily ever after as a human.

When I looked at Meryn, however, I found her unsmiling, her stare distant. At that moment, I realized that things would never be the same between us. My deception was laid bare, and I had sullied the sunshine we once shared. It was time for me to accept responsibility for my actions. No more harm.

"If it's all right, I would like... to not hurt people. My voice—it harms. Take my song. Take my voice altogether, if you must." I fought a surge of emotion. "I don't want to be a siren anymore."

Scalae's brows knitted. Her face was thoughtful. "You have wrestled for far too long with this, Fivrial. I will help you."

With a lifting of her finger, I found myself rising from the rock, out of the water until I was nearly above the level of their heads. My tail hung dripping below me.

"What's-what's happening?"

Scalae lifted her palm level with her lips and blew a strong puff of air. A cloud of golden, glittering dust shot into my face. I inhaled and immediately started coughing as light burst from my mouth, originating from deep inside my throat. Warmth radiated up and down it like a wave.

As the light disappeared, I began to sink into the water again. Finally, I came to rest on top of the boulder. All was calm. I felt... normal. My brows furrowed as I looked to Scalae. "What happened?"

She smiled. "Try to sing."

Immediately, I tensed up, my eyes flitting to Meryn. "Is it safe?"

Scalae nodded. "More than safe."

After a moment of hesitation, I opened my mouth and vocalized a simple tune. My voice came out clear and strong as ever. I stopped and blinked at Scalae, who looked quite pleased. "I don't understand? I can still sing."

"And you're still a siren, only not... quite. Your voice will no longer take life force. It will grant healing instead."

My eyes widened. "*Healing?*"

"Healing of the sick and injured. I think perhaps it's a fitting task, don't you think, Meryn?"

I found her still gazing at the surface of the water. She glanced at her mother with a brief smile and nodded. Scalae wrapped her arm around Meryn's shoulders and squeezed.

"Now, I must be off."

Meryn's eyes widened in panic. "So soon?"

Scalae turned to her and grasped her cheeks. "I'll come to visit you again, my dear. Now that you've come of age, between my power and yours, I can visit more often. And I'll be watching over you until then."

Tears filling her eyes, Meryn nodded and buried her face in her mother's shoulder as the two embraced. Scalae stroked her hair, kissing the top of her head. "I know. I'll miss you, too."

After a few more moments of embracing, they finally parted. Meryn wiped her eyes and smiled. "Goodbye, Mother."

Scalae grasped her hand. "Goodbye, Meryn." Her eyes flitted to me. "I believe you two need to have a conversation. Take care, now." Without further word, she stepped away across the surface and ascended quickly into the sky. We stood together until she was out of sight.

When Scalae was gone, Meryn sighed and turned to me at last. She returned to my side and stepped back down into the water.

The air was heavy between us. I wanted to dive in and swim a bit deeper—hide my tail beneath the waves. I was full of shame. But there was no going back now.

No more hiding.

Meryn spoke first, her voice cracked with emotion. "I remember you now, you know." My gaze snapped to hers. I found her golden eyes filled with tears as she continued. "I remember the storm, the boat, the kiss... Fivrial." She broke eye contact. "You didn't have to do it. Make me forget you."

Her words only served to justify the overwhelming guilt. "I know."

She swept her eyes over the beach and shook her head. "Why did you do it in the first place?"

"Because humans aren't supposed to see us—"

"Not that, Finn," she sighed and placed a palm on her forehead, "*Fivrial.* Why did you save me?"

I stared at her. "Because I loved you."

She laughed cynically. "How can you love someone you don't even know?" Her hurt-filled eyes found mine. "Do I even know you now?"

My heart pounded in my ears. This was not going well.

"You know me better than anyone has ever known me, Meryn."

Meryn's face twisted with an onslaught of tears. "I let you in. I let you in, and you weren't even real. I gave myself to you. I—" she took a stabilizing breath.

Once again, my eyes fell to my tail, which now glowed as my own tears hit the water. "I wanted to get to know you. And I wanted you to know me. In a way that you wouldn't be afraid of me."

Her fists crashed through the water, shooting it high into the air. "It wouldn't have mattered, Fivrial! Yes, I was scared when I saw your tail, but you never gave me a chance. You never let me love you as you were." She cursed and buried her face in her palms. "You should have trusted me."

Everything was falling apart before my eyes. *We* were falling apart. And I didn't know how to salvage it.

"I'm so sorry, Meryn. I have no excuse."

Meryn sniffled and hugged her arms. "What are we going to do? Where do we go from here?"

I stared at her. The only thing I wanted to do was fall at her feet and beg her forgiveness. But there was nothing left to say that could make it better. "I don't know."

At last, she looked me in the eye again. "I don't know how to go on without you, Finn Fishman."

My heart crumbled as my lips quivered. "Then don't."

We stood, gazes locked, chests heaving in the night air. A current was flowing between us, drawing us in. The light in Meryn's eyes dimmed. She took a step toward me and my heart leaped. But then she stopped.

"Time. I need time."

"Meryn, I..."

She turned and trudged toward the shore, ignoring my outstretched hand. I watched her go until she was out of sight, never once turning around to look at me again.

I broke down, weeping into the waters around me.

My entire world had just walked away.

Chapter Thirty-Eight

Meryn

It was the hardest thing in the world—to walk away from him on that beach. Part of me wanted to throw myself in his arms, merman or not.

My heart was bruised. More than bruised. *Shredded*.

By the time I made it back to the beach by the pier, I'd cried myself sore. A massive crowd of townspeople were standing around in their nightclothes, chatting and scratching their heads. They were all confused, many pointing to the empty boat docks and the masses of debris floating in the sea. Some were crying hysterically, their livelihoods destroyed.

I did my best to contain my newfound power—to tame the glow. Any time I brushed up against someone, however, they immediately leaped away, staring at me strangely.

"Meryn!"

I barely heard my name before two arms wrapped

around my neck, pulling me into a tight embrace. Anaat only hugged me for a moment before she let go, practically falling. She swooned into Nola's arms. I reached out to grab her, only to pull away.

Anaat quickly regained her senses. She stood, clinging to Nola. "Meryn, what's happened to you?"

I looked down to see that I was glowing again. It seemed I had less control as my nerves increased. A few people were staring and whispering among themselves. I had to get out of there fast.

"We need to get home. Now," I urged as I took off running through the crowd. They parted for me, gawking.

Anaat and Nola hurried after, keeping up as best they could with my lightning pace. When we reached the outer edges of the crowd, we found Lady Trevion and Sebastian making their way back as well.

Sebastian sighed in relief when he saw me, reaching his arms out, as if I would run into them. "Oh! Thank heavens you're all right! I've been—hey!"

I deftly evaded him and rushed onward. Without another word, the two of them joined our procession. We swiftly passed other servants trudging back to the castle.

I had to get indoors. I had to get out of sight.

The moment we were in the safety of the castle, I exhaled sharply and let my light radiate. It filled the kitchen as I came to a stop at last.

Lady Trevion shrieked behind me. I whirled around to see them standing in shock. Sebastian cursed as he caught his fainting mother. Anaat was wide-eyed but approached me slowly. Nola turned to shoo away the other servants and guards trying to come in.

My eyes met Anaat's as warm tears welled, spilling down my cheeks and over my quivering jaw. "Anaat..."

Shaking off her astonishment, Anaat waved her hand toward the hall door. "Come, we'll talk in my room."

Nodding, I gratefully exited the kitchen and we rushed through the halls to Anaat's room on the second floor. It was a large white room with a balcony overlooking the sea. Over the horizon, the first hints of sunrise were beginning to split the sky. Anaat made quick work of drawing the drapes and sealing us safely inside.

I crawled onto her bed, hugging my knees to my chest. The shock of everything came crashing down on me.

"Meryn." Anaat's voice drew my attention. She pulled up a red armchair and sat at the foot of the bed, facing me. Her eyes swept over me and my light. Swallowing her clear astonishment, she spoke calmly. "Tell me what's going on?"

How do I even begin to explain? How does one break news like this?

Anaat was frightened. The thought of frightening her more was unbearable. But there she sat, despite my change, waiting patiently with me.

Words slipped numbly from my lips. "My mother is Scalae."

Anaat's stare widened. "But *your* mother, she-she—"

"Died. Her mortal body, yes. But she's not dead, Anaat. She's... a goddess." My limbs shook. "And I'm... this." The whole bed rumbled as tears dripped faster down my cheeks. They glowed brightly as they splashed against my damp nightgown.

"Calm down, Meryn," soothed Anaat. "It doesn't matter what you are. You're my sister and you're safe, and that's what matters. Everything is okay now. I'm right here with you."

I took deep, slow breaths, slowly calming myself. Anaat tentatively laid a hand on my sandy foot. I could tell she was uncomfortable but tolerated it as I reined in my power the best I could. With a small smile, she squeezed my toe like we did as kids.

"Now, I want you to start from the beginning, and tell me what happened tonight."

"You won't like what you hear, Anaat."

She arched a brow. "I almost lost you, Meryn. Nothing else could shake me worse than that."

Pausing, I stared at her. If only she knew what I was about to tell her. With great trepidation, I entered into the tale. Everything that occurred the previous night, from the moment Mother awakened me, receiving my powers and memories, the battle... and Fivrial. Worst of all, him. I spoke of the memories with him I'd lost, the truth of his time with us, and the ramifications.

When all was said, Anaat was raw with emotion, but in a quiet sort of way. Tears waited in her eyes, jaw slackened, but she made no sound. I'd overwhelmed her. Flooded with guilt, I sighed. "I'm sorry. I know this is all a lot to take in."

Anaat nodded. "It is, it is... but Meryn, you've borne it all. And you're still here. I suppose we have Finn to thank for that. But our people wouldn't be alive right now if it weren't for you. And..." She sniffled. "I haven't made things easy on you, have I?"

My brows squished together. "Easy? What do you mean?"

She sighed, squeezing her eyes shut. "This whole time you were growing up, I've been trying to force you into a mold that clearly did not fit you. I was harsh with you; didn't stand up for you when I should have." Anaat stared at her feet. "You needed a sister to be there, on your side, and I failed you in that respect. The truth is, I thought that by keeping you grounded that I was keeping you safe." Her eyes met mine. "But really, I needed to help you fly."

I wanted to throw my arms around her, but instead I just sat there, staring. What she'd just said to me lifted an enormous weight from my shoulders. More than she could ever know. The validation alone brought a lump to my throat.

"It hasn't been easy for either of us," I confessed. "In a way, we're like oil and water, I suppose. Neither of us had any idea I was... what I am."

Anaat raked her hand over her face. "Oh, stars. All the servants and half of our town must know something is going on. The Trevions, most definitely. And when Father hears of it..."

I gripped the hem of my nightgown, the grit of sand biting my fingers. "Do you think Sebastian has fled the house in terror?"

Anaat burst out laughing. "Well, it would be quite convenient if he had fled the house. I'll probably send them away."

My eyes widened. "Really?"

She stared at me incredulously. "Meryn. Do you have

any idea what Fivrial did to save your life? Do you honestly think that Sebastian Trevion holds a candle to him? No, Sebastian is far below your standards now—*and* mine.

I pursed my lips. "And the standard is lying to me? Not trusting me to give him a chance?"

Anaat steepled her hands under her chin. "He *loves* you. Yes, he made a mistake, but don't doubt for a second that his love is genuine. Under every pretense, every spell, everything—there is genuine feeling there. Between the *both* of you."

We sat, staring at each other for a moment. I knew that she believed what she was saying. But was it the truth? Did he really love me when everything else was stripped away? I couldn't face it. Not yet.

"So, you're not going to push me to marry Sebastian anymore?" I asked with a hopeful nod.

Anaat shook her head. "I will not."

"What about Father?"

She took a deep breath and averted her gaze. "Let me deal with Father. It's high time someone stood up to him."

My heart brightened just a bit. "Thank you, Anaat."

Anaat nodded and rose from her chair to peek out the window curtain at the lightening sky. "And as for *you*, you need to make a decision."

My shoulders tensed. I knew what she meant. "Anaat, I don't think there's any way things could possibly work now. I mean, he's a... and I'm a..."

A grin tugged her lips. "Meryn, you love each other. You will figure it out."

"Anaat, I don't know."

"You would be stupid to throw him away," she snapped, grin disappearing. I blinked at her as she released the curtain and scowled at me. "You know what I went through, Meryn—what a loveless marriage looks like. What a *cruel* man looks like. It's not every day that people find their soul's mate. You have, and yet here you are, acting as if he's expendable."

I frowned at her. "He hurt me, Anaat."

"Then fight through it! Argue with him, tell him he ripped your heart out. Let him beg your forgiveness if you must, but do *not* give up on him. You'd be giving up on one half of yourself."

Growling in frustration, I pounded my fists on the bed, shooting out flashes of light. "Time, Anaat! I just want some time!"

She grunted. "Time? How much time? Life is short, Meryn. Too short to waste on anger. You never know when the ones you love may leave this world. Like Mother." There was an edge of bitterness to her words.

"Anaat, I—"

"Don't say you're sorry, either. Just... do the right thing and listen to your heart. Fivrial loves you, Meryn. Regardless of what's happened, you do not have to doubt that. He went through hell to save you. He offered to drain every drop of his own blood, if that's what it took. Don't muck this up."

I stared at her. "Why are you so adamant about this?"

Anaat came and sat on the edge of the bed. "Because I love *you*. And I want what's best for you. And I truly believe that includes him."

My brows crinkled. "I love you too, Anaat."

That was the first time we'd ever sincerely uttered those words to each other. It was the first time I'd ever *felt* as if she loved me. We had wasted too many years being at odds. I'd forgotten what it was like to have a real sister that cared.

"Now," said Anaat with a sigh. "Let's get bathed and get the sand off my bed, shall we?"

It was two days before I ventured outside of Anaat's room. I couldn't bear to go up to my own. Being up in the tower, I just felt too... exposed.

I made my way to the art room. The moment I walked in, I knew I'd made a mistake. There were paintings everywhere. Paintings of *him*. Him smiling and laughing. All the paintings from the day he was unsettled—playing the piano with manic passion.

Approaching each cautiously, as if they would bite, I allowed my gaze to linger on his face. His firm brow... the slope of his nose, how it flowed into his pursed lips... it was so intense. So incredibly beautiful. Even his hands, painted from other angles, were magnificent. His long fingers were graceful, yet strong. It was as if they were created to play that very instrument.

When I skimmed my fingers over the worktable, I paused. A memory arrested me. Encased in each other's arms in a fit of passion... his lips on my skin... never wanting it to end...

I drew a shuddered breath and snatched my hand away. Too many reminders. Turning quickly, I exited the room, heading for the safety of more public parts of the house.

As I walked through the halls, I heard my name.

"Meryn?"

When I looked up, I found Sebastian reaching the top of the stairs. He approached me cautiously, without his usual charming smile. It was far too late to pretend I hadn't seen him. I waited passively for him to reach me.

"I thought you'd gone?" I noted, trying to contain my disappointment.

Sebastian nodded. "We're about to leave, actually."

"I see."

He gestured toward the music room. "Is it possible for us to speak for a moment?"

Folding my arms across my chest, I arched a brow. "You may speak to me right here."

Shrinking under my coldness, Sebastian nodded again. "I suppose you have every right not to trust me now."

"You are a womanizing cad. Of course, I don't trust you."

Sebastian stared at the floor. "I owe you an apology, Meryn. And I'm not just saying that because you're obviously—" his eyes swept over my now-glowing form before averting again uncomfortably "—different. I disrespected you, and for that, I am sorry."

My eyes narrowed. "All right. You've made your apology. Now—"

"But I wasn't lying when I said I loved you." His gaze finally met mine. I simply stared back, speechless. He continued. "I'm not going to force you into anything. I won't let my father make any more conspiratorial arrangements with yours, either. But just know that if you ever find it in your heart to forgive me, and find even a shred of affection for me, I'd be most honored to have you as my wife, Meryn."

When I glanced down, I noticed his hands were shaking as they wrung themselves. This was an honest-to-goodness proposal. My jaw fell open momentarily before I snapped it shut again and squared my shoulders.

"My answer is no, Sebastian."

Hurt flashed over his features before they hardened. He lifted his chin slightly. "And why not? Is it that—that man?" The bite in his tone only set off my agitation, causing my glow to brighten. Sebastian took a step back, paling a bit.

"His name is *Finn*. And no, it's not because of him. I wouldn't marry you. I do not love you."

Sebastian eyed me with disdain. "Then you must be incapable of it."

I laughed at his ego. "All right, I think it's time you left."

Drawing a deep breath to soothe his wounded pride, Sebastian pursed his lips. "Gladly. Farewell, Lady Blumley," he said coldly before turning on his heel and stalking away. I watched him go with a satisfied smirk.

The rest of the day was a restless one. And the days following. I couldn't settle anywhere. Everywhere I turned, there were reminders of Fivrial. He'd affected every corner of the castle for me in one way or another. Memories and the phantom sound of my name on his lips bombarded me.

As time went on, I grew increasingly agitated.

What was wrong with me?

I prided myself on my independence. Yet, there I was, incapable of keeping my own mind in order.

Nights were the worst. I slept little. Anaat was growing agitated with me for keeping her awake with my tossing and turning. I couldn't help it. Every time I closed my eyes it was either a nightmare awaiting or Fivrial, waiting to make love to me. More often than not, I retreated to the music room with a bottle of wine on those late nights. I played my violin in somber tunes to match my mood. It was cathartic, but not curative.

One night, I found myself in Fivrial's old bedroom. I'd

avoided that part of the house for the most part. It was there that the strongest memories were. The room wasn't the same without him, but I felt the embers of his presence all the same. My soft glow filled the room, even as I crawled onto the bed and tucked myself under the covers. My palm rested on the cold pillow next to me, willing him to appear.

Perhaps it was the wine, but I wanted nothing more than to feel his arms around my waist again. I longed to feel him tucking me to his chest as we drifted off to sleep together. His warmth was the only cure for my ailment. His kiss would be the only thing to heal the sickness in my heart.

I fell asleep with my tears staining the pillow.

Father arrived home the next day. I was immediately scooped up in his arms when he found out that I was alive, and quickly released again when my light flared. The look on his face was somewhere between fear and astonishment. It took a lot of explaining and re-explaining.

He asked about Mother repeatedly, and I told him everything I knew. It broke his heart to know she was out there somewhere and not with him. I'd never seen my father cry before, but tears flowed freely.

"You still love her, don't you?" I asked one such evening when I found him standing in his study near the bay windows, staring out across the sea. It seemed he gazed across those waters nonstop those days.

Father ran a hand through his disheveled hair and nodded. "I do. Time heals many things. Some things... it does not."

"You know she will be coming back to visit me? Now that I'm... well..."

The corner of his lips tugged into a smile as his eyes swept the glow-filled room. "You know, I never would've guessed. My little Meryn has been so full of light this entire time."

I eyed the empty bottle of wine on his desk. Father rarely imbibed, but I couldn't blame him after everything that had happened. I took a seat in one of the chairs across from him and slumped back, staring at the ceiling. "I'm not so little anymore, I'm afraid."

"No, I don't suppose you are." Father sat on the edge of his desk with a deep sigh. "I don't always do the best thing, Meryn. Sometimes, I think I do, but it turns out to be the wrong thing."

I looked at him with an arched brow. "I'm not sure I follow."

Father nodded. "I thought I was doing the right thing by pushing you to marry. I thought that if you were married to a good man from a good family, you would somehow be settled and take your place in society as a proper young lady. I worried there was something..." His brows flinched. "...*wrong* with how I raised you. I was so lost after your mother passed. And I couldn't—didn't know how to face that."

The words stung. He thought I was defective somehow, just as I'd always suspected. I shifted uncomfortably in my chair, unsure I wanted this conversation to go any further.

Father looked at me wearily. "But I was the wrong one, Meryn. I didn't see you for what you were. There's nothing wrong with you. There never has been. And I'm sorry for keeping you at arm's length because I believed there was."

Surprised by his words, all I could do was nod, swallowing back a lump of emotion. I rose from my chair as Father approached. We shifted awkwardly for a moment as his warm arms wrapped around me. He hadn't embraced me since I was a child. I stiffened at first, but soon melted into his arms. I hadn't known how badly I'd needed that hug.

"I want you to be happy, Meryn. That's all I ask. Whatever and wherever that may be. With *whomever*. Find your happiness, and don't let it go for all the world."

I pulled away, wiping my eyes. Father grasped my shoulder, looking at me earnestly. "And just know that you have my blessing."

"Father, I don't—"

"Meryn." He lifted my chin. "You have my full, unhindered blessing. Follow your heart."

My heart. It was leading me to a place I wasn't sure I

was ready to go. There was only one way to find out.

Chapter Thirty-Nine

Meryn

I waited until well after the others were in bed. It was a warm night, with clear weather. The half-moon and the stars shone like diamonds on a blanket of black as I slipped from the castle. Once I was far enough away from town, I sighed, releasing my light. It would guide my way better than any lantern.

When I reached the private beach, my eyes scanned the water. I was disappointed to find no signs of anyone. After taking off my shoes and robe, I started to make my way to the water, but then paused. Looking around once more to ensure I was truly alone, I reached down and grasped the sides of my nightgown, slipping it off. I stepped out of my undergarments, tossing them onto the pile before unbraiding my hair with a sigh. I was completely naked, out in the open. It was both nerve-racking and freeing.

With a smile, I took off across the beach and crashed

against the surface of the water. I skidded to a stop as water sprayed around me. The cool water lapped at my lower legs, but I willed myself not to sink. Laughing, I ran and skipped, dancing as if I had my violin. I wish I had brought it.

Twirling and whirling, I moved to the melody filling my mind as I navigated the waves. The wind flowed through my hair, slipping over my skin, dancing with me. I took one giant leap and landed on the tiptoes of my left foot. With minimal effort, I balanced there. Smiling in disbelief, I jumped to the toes of my other foot. And then... I lifted it.

My eyes widened. There I was—floating in midair. I stared at the space below me. Slowly, I lowered my feet to the water's surface, quickly pulling them back up again. Still, I remained suspended. I lifted my arms and held them out to my sides, willing myself to rise. Little by little, I lifted. As I did, I lowered my feet again. They no longer touched the water.

I was *flying*.

"Meryn?"

At the sound of my name, I plunged into the deep water with a splash. The coolness encased me as I tried to gain my bearings and kick toward the surface. When my head broke into the night air, I took a deep breath. Hands wrapped under my arms, giving me something to hold onto.

Blazing jewels stared back at me. Fivrial's brows lowered in concern. "Are you all right?"

I nodded as I calmed myself. "I think so."

A small smile appeared as he released my arms. "Sorry if I distracted you. I didn't think you'd be here."

"I didn't think you'd be here either," I confessed. "I thought I was alone." My cheeks colored when I realized I was completely nude when I was above the water. I whipped my head around. "Are you alone?"

"Yes. I come here at night, but I'm always..." His face fell. "What are you doing here? It's late."

"I couldn't sleep." *Without him.*

"Me neither."

Our eyes met. I saw the flash of longing staring back at me. He ripped his gaze away. "I'm sorry. I'll leave."

A sense of panic overcame me. I reached out and

grasped his upper arm. "Don't."

Fivrial stopped his retreat, looking at my hand on his arm.

"Why not?"

I could hear the hurt in his voice. It pained me; it mirrored my own.

"Because I can't bear it." His brows flinched, but I continued. "No matter where I go, how much I try to distract myself, how hard I try to shut you out, I can't. You're in my sleep. You're in my music. You're in the air, Fivrial. You've utterly invaded my soul. And you know what I've come to realize?" Fivrial finally raised his eyes to meet mine. "That there is no separating *you* from *me*."

"Meryn, I can't be anything more than what I am. Not anymore." He looked down at his glowing tail with a sigh.

I pulled myself up to him, chest to chest, and cupped his cheek. When he returned his gaze to me, I smiled. "Good, because I love you just the way you are."

Fivrial's arms slipped around my waist as he searched my eyes. "You love me?"

"I do."

Tears rolled down his cheeks. I wiped them away, raining kisses on each cheek. When my lips connected with his, it was like finding my way home.

Sweetness and salt...

Fivrial's hand slipped up my back into my hair while lazy flicks of his powerful tail kept us afloat. I was happy to let him take over so I could keep my power tamed. As we sought each other, I found myself more and more lost to the world around us.

Eventually, his hands slid down to my legs and lifted, bringing them to wrap around his waist. I felt the smooth scales against my inner thighs, stirring a curiosity. As we kissed, I trailed my hand down his back, feeling the broad transition between flesh and scale. Fivrial hummed under my touch.

Breaking the kiss, I brought my forehead to rest against his. My chest heaved. I bit my lip, unsure of how to ask the question.

"Will it... work like this?"

He nodded, his eyes smoldering. "Oh, it will. Believe me, it will."

Our lips collided again. Fivrial slid me a little lower against his pelvis. A bulge in his scales pressed directly against my most sensitive area. He moved his hands over my bottom, rubbing me against him as he moved. I whimpered behind his kiss.

Fivrial chuckled against my lips. "That's just a little tease until we get to the shallows."

"Shallows?" I asked numbly. When I looked around, I found we were significantly closer to shore.

He shrugged. "You're not the only one with water tricks." With that, he flicked his fins hard, his back aimed toward the beach. I clung to his shoulders as each movement rippled through his tail, rubbing against me.

"Fi... Fivrial..." I moaned breathlessly.

His heavy gaze trained on me. "Do you like that?"

I nodded, unable to form the words.

He kissed my neck and laughed into my skin. "Just wait until I get you on that beach."

It wasn't long before I felt sand against my feet. Fivrial flipped me around. I crawled backward against the soft sand, his eyes burning into mine as he followed, using his powerful arms.

When he had me where he wanted me, he yanked my ankle gently, bringing my body to a stop beneath him. We were only half on the beach, the water lapping over my legs and his beautiful, blazing tail.

My eyes traveled over his strong upper body, down to that bulge in the front of his tail that hovered just above me. Out of curiosity, I slid my hand down his torso and rubbed the heel of my palm over it. The scales were softer there— more flexible.

Fivrial released a ragged groan as his eyes slid shut. Smiling in satisfaction, I did it again. This time I moved slower, adding pressure to my touch. A sharp gasp escaped his lips as he nearly fell apart under my touch.

"It's... sensitive... right now..." he explained through heaving breaths.

I pulled him down for a deep kiss, gently pleasuring

him. He grew warmer under my touch as the bulge throbbed. Heat scorched through me with each pulse. His hips moved against my hand.

At last, he reached down and snatched my hand away. He pulled it to a spot near the bottom of the bulge, guiding my fingertips under a pocket-like patch of scales, where they brushed against a familiar, hardened member. With a little tug, it emerged. I looked down with wide eyes. He was larger than I remembered.

Fivrial leaned down, planting nips and kisses around my lips. "Don't worry. I'll be gentle," he purred in my ear.

Warm shivers chased up my spine. I caught his chin in my fingertips and stared at him through heavy lids. "Not too gentle. I've missed you."

He devoured my lips again, pressing himself on top of me. With great care, he guided himself inside my slick entrance. I grasped his shoulders and drew a sharp breath as he filled me.

Fivrial paused. "Are you—"

"Yes, don't stop!" I begged.

He continued his slow, torturous movements until we fully connected.

I brushed my fingers over his flushed cheeks. He grasped them and brought them to his lips, kissing them before bringing them around behind his neck.

"You might want to hold on."

"Why?" I asked, already suspecting the answer.

He leaned down to where his hot breath grazed my ear. "Because this will be intense."

I barely had time to process his warning before the first thrust came. I gasped for air and clutched his head to my chest, a position he didn't seem to mind.

Glowing across the dark beach, my light immediately sprang forth. Fivrial groaned in response. The glow of his fins joined mine. Now it was my turn to be concerned.

"Are you all right?"

He responded with another thrust and feverish kisses across my neck and shoulders. Again and again, he moved, his tail blazing brighter.

We dissolved into a moaning frenzy, releasing every bit

of pent-up passion we'd been saving for each other. I was overwhelmed by the feel of him inside me, on me, the heat of his lips on my skin, the smoothness of his surprisingly warm scales between my thighs. Our lights danced and mixed in a beautiful flurry as the water rushed over us. Sand in my hair, waves at my feet... a marrying of land and sea.

"You feel so good..." he moaned as he pumped into me and dragged his lips across my breast.

My inner tension was building. "Fivrial..."

"I love the sound of my name on your lips. Say it again," he commanded roughly.

"Fivrial."

He picked up his pace. I dug my fingers deeper into his shoulders. My body began to feel loose and tight at the same time.

The golden light grew brighter. Fivrial seemed to feed off of it, growing more fiery with each passing moment.

"Come on... that's it..." he growled.

I moaned, holding on to him for dear life. He wasn't kidding when he said he would be intense. It was nearly too much for me to take. This new him was wild.

Just when I thought I couldn't take anymore, I reached my release. My cries filled the night, lost in the roar of the waves around us. My whole body locked up with the intensity as Fivrial pounded into me faster and harder.

Moments later, he moaned loudly. His body slowed to a stop as he spilled inside me.

We were a heap of panting and light. Sweat dripped from our exposed upper bodies as we lay connected. Fivrial lifted his head from my chest, propping his elbows on either side of my head. With a smile, he gazed down at me. His eyes were bright and swirling with colors.

I snaked my hand up along his jaw, brushing the hair from his face. "You are so beautiful."

He dipped his head down and kissed me softly. "I love you, Meryn."

"I love you too."

We lay there for a while longer, trading kisses and basking in the feel of each other. At last, we made our way back into the water where we floated on our backs, watching the stars.

"How are we going to make this work?" asked Fivrial, brushing his knuckles down my forearm.

I shrugged. "I don't know. Just like this, I suppose."

"What about in the cold months? Or when the weather is bad?"

My heart fell. "I hadn't thought of that. But... I guess I would wait for you. Until it was warm again."

A hand slipped around mine. "You would wait all that time?"

"Of course, I would. You're my soul's mate, Fivrial."

He brought my hand to his lips. "I wish we didn't ever have to be apart again. I miss sleeping next to you."

I sighed. "I know. If only there were a way." Tucking my legs down, I straightened in the water and faced him. "I would gladly be your wife."

Fivrial faced me with raised brows. "You would?"

"I would."

Gathering me up in his arms, he kissed me sweetly. "There's so much I wish I could show you. There's a whole world down there."

A sad smile lit my face. "I wish I could see it."

His fingertips lifted my chin and his eyes met mine. "We *will* make this work. Somehow."

Somehow, we had to. Even if it meant waiting. My heart could never give him up again.

We spent more time together at our beach until the sky began to lighten. It was then that I finally forced myself to kiss him farewell and exit the water. I pulled my clothes on over my wet skin and set off for home.

My heart ached as I cast one last longing gaze toward Fivrial. He swam parallel to the shore for a bit before finally disappearing beneath the surface.

Sadness was already tugging at me. I had to go back to a cold and lonely bed. Now that everything was out in the open and we had reconciled, I longed for him even more.

By the time I made it to the castle, tears were stinging my eyes. I bypassed Anaat's room and went straight for my old room in the tower. After cleaning up and changing nightgowns, I pulled out my sketchbook from its hiding place and sat on the bed. Despite the sleep tugging at my eyes, I couldn't get him out of my mind. I flipped through the book, lingering on every single image of him. My skills didn't do him justice. Still, I brushed my fingertips over his face and sighed.

"Oh, Finn..." I sobbed, pulling the book to my chest as I laid my cheek on it.

A bright light filled the room. I gasped, squeezing my eyes shut. When the light subsided, I opened my eyes and stared in confusion.

"Mother? You're back already?"

Mother smiled and sat on the end of my bed. She laid a hand on my forearm and gave a gentle squeeze. "I am. I've got a little unfinished business, as it turns out."

My brows crinkled. "I don't understand."

She chuckled. "I've got to tie up some loose ends." Her eyes traveled to my bedroom door and her smile faded a bit. "I think it's time I had a conversation with your father. Explain some things."

I thought about Father and his confessions. "I think he'd appreciate that."

Mother's attention returned to me. "May I see your book?"

For a moment, I froze. I had only shown them to Fivrial. She was looking at me patiently. With a sigh, I realized there was no point in hiding them anymore. I was done with secrets. I handed her the sketchbook, letting her peruse my drawings.

Her brows lifted the more she flipped through the pages. "These are very good, Meryn. You've captured him well."

I smiled as my cheeks colored. "Thank you. I had a good subject."

After closing the book, Mother looked at me poignantly. "You must miss him now, being separated by the elements."

"I do. We've decided that we'll find a way to make things

work, though." I tried to say it with confidence, but my voice shook. "I love him. And that's all that matters."

She reached out and hooked my hair behind my ear, just as she used to do when I was a child. "Oh, sweetie."

The way she said that told me that she saw through my bravery, through my confidence. The truth was, I was scared to death. Scared that it would be too much. I was scared that he would get impatient and decide that I wasn't worth waiting for.

As if these thoughts were being spoken aloud, Mother shook her head. "You shouldn't worry. The bond between you is nigh unbreakable. However, I think I may be able to help."

My eyes met hers. "Help? How?"

Mother grinned. "As I said, unfinished business. Now, it will require a bit of sacrifice and time, but—"

"Yes!" I cried, throwing my arms around her neck. "Whatever it is, yes."

Chapter Forty

Fivrial

I did not see Meryn for three days after our encounter. Every time I swam to our beach, she wasn't there. Worry pricked me.

Things were very different around Brinn. Percivan was killed in the counterassault on Wrenna. Probably best that way, considering I would've done it myself. Grayler wanted to groom me to become Siren General someday, so he announced that he would step up my training. I was now revered among the merfolk for my heroic actions and my encounters with Scalae.

I shied away from the attention. All I wanted was time with Meryn.

The trident now rested in my den, mounted on the wall. It belonged to Meryn, not me. I was keeping it safe for her until I could give it to her myself. To think that she was the daughter of Scalae was still awe-inspiring. To think that she wanted me was nigh-unbelievable. I only hoped that her absence wasn't a sign that she'd changed her mind.

A few days later, I lazed on my nest, staring at the ceiling. I'd already made the trip to the beach and once again found it empty. Perhaps she'd be there in the evening. The next day, I'd have to start my training again. It would take all my daylight hours and likely leave me exhausted by nightfall. Grayler insisted on a full schedule.

My fingers brushed over the pearl on the necklace Mrs. Rigby had given me. I thought of the times I'd met her, and how I missed the fact that she was a siren. Perhaps that's why Meryn was drawn to her. As a daughter of Scalae, all things from the sea were surely of natural interest.

I only hoped that still included me.

"Hey."

I looked over to see Renold in the entrance, arms crossed as usual. I threw him a brief smile.

"Hey."

"Are you just going to lie there all day, Fiv?"

Rolling my eyes, I turned to look at him. "Why? Do you have any better ideas?"

Renold shrugged. "Maybe."

"Like what?"

"As in, maybe I have someone I want you to meet?"

He was smirking in the usual way he did when he was up to something. I blew bubbles from my mouth and shook my head. "Renold, I've told you— I'm not interested in meeting any 'maids."

My words trailed off as I saw a flash of red and gold swim by the other hole. My ears caught the faint sound of singing. I knew that tune anywhere. Brows furrowing, I shot up, swimming across the room. "What was that?"

Renold clapped me on the shoulder. "Why don't you go find out?"

"This better not be a scheme of yours," I warned.

He raised his palms, a smirk still pasted on his face. "No scheme."

Shaking my head, I darted out of the hole, whipping my head right and left. All I saw was the normal flow of merfolk about their daily business. Then, out of the corner of my eye,

I saw it again: a flash of gold to my left.

With a flick of my fins, I took off, following the glow along a large rock formation. Every time I rounded a curve, I saw the edge of a gold fin again, disappearing ahead of me. Faster and faster, I swam, winding through rocks and coral, in and out of caves, chasing the golden fins. Female laughter reached my ears.

At last, I shot far above, looking for signs of the mermaid. I finally spotted her.

Her golden fins floated near the sandy bottom, head turning back and forth. Her beautiful, long red hair flowed in the current.

I dove as fast as I could. She looked up just as I reached her. Amber and gold, married together in large, beautiful eyes. I wrapped my arms around her as we hit the bottom. Her sweet laughter filled my ears as we rolled in the sand. Our tails whirled together, creating a cloud of sand and dust. When we stopped tumbling, she lay on top of me, arms still tucked into my chest.

She was here. *My Meryn.*

Briny tears leaped to my eyes. "How are you here?"

She smiled. "You're not the only one my mother gives gifts to."

My eyes traveled over her in disbelief. She was radiant fire and gold. "Meryn, you're... you're... beautiful."

I brought my hand up to cradle the back of her head, pulling her in for a deep kiss. Over and over, we sought each other's lips. When our kiss parted at last, she pulled back, running her fingers over my beard. "I'm sorry I had to be away. I had to say some goodbyes."

"Goodbyes?"

Meryn nodded. "I'm here to stay... if you'll have me."

I held her tight to my chest. "You're my life-bound mate, my wife, my everything. From this moment on, do you hear?"

"As long as you're mine."

We kissed again. She caressed my cheek. Her light grew across the dark of the sea, dancing and bending with my own.

"I love you, Fivrial. Take me home."

The End.

ABOUT THE AUTHOR

Heather Carter is a neurodivergent writer composing stories since childhood, with a particular passion for all things fantasy romance. Of Songs and Saltwater marks her debut into the world of indie publishing. Currently, she lives in the St. Louis area with her family and an extremely spoiled cat. When not writing, she enjoys creating music and drinking copious amounts of coffee.

Of Songs and Saltwater

ACKNOWLEDGEMENTS

This novel was a labor of love with many helping hands.

First and foremost, I would like to thank my husband, Matthew, for being so supportive of me during the many hyperfocused hours I spent hunched over my old laptop at the kitchen table, tapping away the story swimming in my head. Thank you for being patient on those days I worked from dawn until late night, when I subsisted on coffee and hugs.

I would like to send a big shout out to my alpha and beta readers, who had eyes on this project during its infancy: Janna Rice, Kaila Mielke, Amber Turner, Morgaan Peace, Liahona West, Sarah Marlow-Flake, Miriam Benarroch-Altman, Brittany Hair, Kari Robinson, Laura Vanden, Ashley Mespelt, Cherron McDonald, Coy Haddock, Yuy Ren, Alexandra McPartland, and Katherine Schober. You all brought me confidence and tough love when I needed it most.

I would also like to thank Frina Art for the beautiful book cover that brought Meryn and Fivrial to life.

A SNEAK PEEK OF THE THIRD VEIL

Chapter One

Echoing words replayed in my head.

"Do not trust the three-headed dragon. Run with the moon. The phoenix will show you what you seek."

The events of the previous night still haunted me as my boots tapped along the cobblestone in the brisk, late October air. I brushed an errant dark curl from my face and shivered in the only coat I owned. Serena, the most lavished courtesan at our house of night, had passed it down to me. It was too thin for chilly, English winters. I was cold, tired, and pale. Dark circles hung under my eyes, as I had not slept well, for fear the creatures would return.

No one, not even Daisy herself recalled the words she'd spoken so clearly to me, nor the strange and terrifying slip of reality when the tall, faceless shadow figures made their appearance. One moment, Daisy had been ill in bed, and the next, she'd grabbed my arm, pointed at the figures, and uttered those chilling, nonsensical words. I was still panicking after they left, after the light and warmth rushed back into the room, but I was the only one to remember.

After getting very odd looks, I had dropped the subject, thoughts of the madhouse repeating over and over in the back of my mind. Daisy was the one who saw things—ghosts and ghouls haunting our home and place of employment. We all knew it, but we didn't talk about it. No one else ever saw anything... until last night. Until *I* saw.

I tried not to think about it as I walked past the church, tall, white, and ever pious. For polite society, it was the Lord's Day, but the last time I had attended the sole church in Baden, our small, sleepy town, the upturned noses and horrified whispers were enough to shame me out the back door for good. My ilk was too sullied for pristine pews, even if I was only a servant and not a prostitute. Everyone knew— to be associated with The Silk House, the infamous brothel of Swift Street, was to have a cold, black stain that could never wash away.

The closest I got to things of heaven was listening to Charlie Foster sing hymns with his clear, strong voice as he pitched hay into the horse stalls. I spent most of my days off with him at his small farm just outside of town, where he lived with his widowed father. With no care to what people thought, they had never darkened the doors of a church as long as they'd lived in our community.

I'd been listening to Charlie since we were children. He grew from a wiry little boy with dark eyes too large for his olive face into a man cut from the cloth of something divine. Tall, broad shoulders, hair black as night, and a smile that could outshine the sun. If not for his lack of fortune, he would've had a trail of high-society females always trotting after him, waving their delicate little handkerchiefs. As it was, I had little stake in such things. At twenty-four, I was as good as confirmed as a spinster.

Watching him now from his barn door, I drank in every sweet note that emanated from his full lips. After the constant bombardment of debauchery, and especially the horror of the previous night, his song was like a healing balm to my bruised soul.

Charlie Foster was my church.

He did not notice me until I opened my mouth and sang with him, my higher harmony melting with his rich tones. Without ceasing, Charlie glanced in my direction and continued his work with a smile in his eyes. I picked up a bucket of oats and began feeding the horses as we sang in perfect harmony together, our song rising through the barn roof and into the heavens.

After most of the work was done, we climbed up into the loft, lazing in the hay, as was our custom, eating the sweets I'd swiped from Meg's massive stash.

I mulled over the scary experience from the previous night, trying to think of how to broach the subject. At least half a dozen times, I opened my mouth to confess, but then I saw his content, carefree smile, and closed it. He knew my darkness and every fear, and I could trust him with my life. But this day was a good day with Charlie. I couldn't bring myself to taint it with talk of monsters. Not yet. I decided to savor his smile a little longer.

"You know, I think we're doing a service to Meg," said Charlie, biting off a piece of honey taffy. "Too much candy can't be a good thing for her."

"Yes, I'm sure if she ever found out, she'd thank me. Maybe even give me a raise." I threw him a wink and sank my teeth into one of the lemon cookies.

Charlie snorted. "You mean start paying you an actual wage instead of injuries?"

His words stung a bit, but they were honest, as always. I winced as I pulled my sleeve a little lower over my wrapped, aching wrist. I hated Meg. She'd injured my wrist over a minor infraction the day prior. One of many injuries I'd borne because of her wrath over the years. She ran an impossibly tight ship for a bawd. And no shred of compassion for her only child.

Someday, I'd be free of her. She was all the blood family I had left in the world, but my heart held no love for her. It held more love for people like Daisy, a fellow servant who'd practically raised me.

I picked through the hay at my side. "That'll never happen. I guess I really can't complain about a place to live, though."

Charlie's brows drew together. "I can't stand to see your own mother treat you like that."

"One could hardly consider Meg a mother, but... it beats the workhouse. For now."

He sighed and rolled his eyes. "Or the streets. You know they fished some girl out of the river in Stralsburg last week? Blue and black and all bloated—"

I jammed an elbow into his rib and scolded him as he howled in pain.

"That's disgusting! Ugh!"

Chuckling, Charlie managed a hoarse reply. "That's right. I forgot about your delicate sensibilities. Proper Queen Victoria, you are."

"Oh, I'm *delicate*, am I?" A handful of hay launched at his face, sticking to the taffy he was about to consume. "How many 'delicate' females would shovel stalls and climb rickety barn ladders to gossip with you? With the rats and spiders up here?" A shudder of disgust hunched my shoulders.

Selecting another taffy, Charlie carefully unwrapped it, keeping a wary eye on me. A twisted grin etched his face as he took a bite and tucked a hand behind his head.

"I don't know. I've had a few girls enjoy the hay with me."

First, I smiled. Then, I giggled. Before I could compose myself, a full-out fit of laughter seized me. Rolling, I laughed until I was red in the face.

"What? What's so funny?" he asked, sitting up with wounded pride.

Catching my breath and my wits, I wiped my streaming eyes and tried not to laugh again. He was pouting like a child.

"Are you talking about Tina? That two-bit ninny from Adler, who checked herself into the nunnery afterward?"

His eyes narrowed, sending me into another fit of giggles, remembering the way she'd chased and thrown herself at him relentlessly, only to take a different kind of veil after she finally got her chance.

"Or perhaps Adelaide?" I continued with a sly grin. "She was the one who was obsessed with your singing, right? The blonde?"

This broke the pout, and he snorted. "Oh, her! God, I had nearly forgotten about her wretched singing voice. It sounded like a dying rabbit."

I shoved his arm. "Charlie Foster! What a cruel thing to say!"

He quirked a brow and crossed his arms. "Oh?"

I tried to remain serious. "Yes... she surely couldn't have sounded any worse than a dying cow."

"Yes, well, it's the hay, you know." He winked with a wicked grin.

"Oh, of course," I said gruffly with an exaggerated wink.

We stared at each other for the space of five seconds before I imitated a dying cow. Dissolving into fits of laughter, we threw hay at each other and made animal noises, laughing even harder when the horses below whinnied in response.

When at last our sides ached and tears streamed from our eyes, we lay in the straw, catching our breath. This was what I needed. Charlie always knew how to make me laugh, even on the worst days.

I tossed another piece of candy at Charlie with a smile. He returned the smile, even as something more somber clouded his expression.

"Yes, all good fun, but... I was actually thinking about you."

The quiet, even words instantly killed my contented joy. The air stilled. I froze, feeling his too-serious eyes on me. Charlie was rarely serious.

A heavy feeling formed as I rolled away from him, tucking an arm under my head and hugging my stomach with the other. Why did he have to bring it up? Why couldn't this just be a carefree day?

"You know we agreed not to talk about it."

Charlie sighed and tossed his candy. "Yeah, I know."

Sitting up, I fought the urge to raise my voice. "Then, why bring it up? It's done and in the past. Forget it already."

His eyes met mine, full of longing. "I've tried. I can't."

Warmth flooded my cheeks and rushed downward as my heart hammered against my ribs at the surfacing of a memory. Our bodies entwined on a cold, rainy evening... his heat mingling with my tears of grief. A surge of unbridled passion that had come out of nowhere during the lowest moment of my life.

It was right after...

I stood, fighting my darkening mind. Shaking, I stepped over to the open-air window overlooking the rolling pastures. Dark, gray clouds blotted out the sun, whipping the biting autumn wind into my face. Chills chased down my spine. Blacks and browns had replaced the green landscape, with some rebellious colorful orange and yellow leaves hanging on until the very last moment. I tried to focus on those colors. Anything to keep me from slipping.

"I'd be lying if I said I didn't think about it too," I confessed distantly. "You were... the only good thing about that day. But I was not... well. You know that. That day, it—"
A lump rose in my throat, cutting off my words.

I couldn't pull my coat tight enough around my shoulders. Nothing could prevent the violent shudder that ran through me. The memory of my father's unseeing eyes and the blood gathering around his twisted body at the bottom of the cellar stairs flashed through my mind's eye unbidden, sending a wave of nausea through me that I forced down with a hard swallow.

The familiar rush hit before I could stop it, and it became difficult to breathe. Tingling numbness spread, no matter how hard I tried to fight it. My heart pounded in my ears, and my veins coursed with a rising fire. The room tilted as I gripped the ledge of the window.

No, not now...

"Charlie..."

Seeing me sway, Charlie grabbed the blanket we'd been laying on and wrapped it tightly around my shoulders before banding his muscular arms around me. Hyperventilating, I let my eyes close as my head dropped back against his shoulder. He lowered me to the ground until I was sitting against him. Beads of sweat formed on my brow.

Keeping deep pressure through his arms, he began the routine.

"You're okay... just focus on my voice... breathe... and breathe... and breathe..."

His voice sounded muddled, as if it were underwater. The sounds of screaming and crying flooded my mind like a dark echo, replaying that awful day. The smells, the scenes, the fear... The barn faded away like smoke.

I was back in the dormitory, the last person rising in the early afternoon after working through the night. A quick pain shot through my head as if something impaled clean through. Dropping to my knees, I cried out and clutched it. As the minutes ticked by, the pain never returned. Carefully, I inspected my hands for blood, and even checked in the small mirror near my bed for signs of injury. Nothing. A relief, but my nerves remained on edge as I dressed quickly in the cavernous room. Meg would whip me if I were even a moment late.

A scream ripped through the house—one that shook the walls and the bones of all within. I knew at once that something terrible awaited below. Tearing down the back stairs, I descended each level with lightning speed, following the sounds of the horrified cries. Even before I reached the top of the musty cellar stairs, I knew in my heart what I'd find.

Marge tried to block me from going down there, pleading with me to turn around, not to look. I shoved her aside with inhuman strength and flew down the stairs, where blood and death greeted me. My father, gone forever. My own scream filled my ears until they felt as if they would burst.

www.ingramcontent.com/pod-product-compliance
Lightning Source LLC
Chambersburg PA
CBHW060352260626
47160CB00006B/2289